A SOLAR SYSTEM'S WORTH OF ADVENTURE

awaits you in this original collection that explores the entire Sol System, from the planets and their moons to the Asteroid Belt to the interstellar visitiors that periodically pass through our section of space. So fasten your safety harness, rev up those rocket engines, and get ready for the trip of a lifetime with such memorable stories as:

"Ghost's of Neptune"—As they landed at the science base on Neptune, Celeste thought the biggest problem she'd have to confront would be her ex-husband. Little did she dream what awaited her beyond the hangar doors. . . .

"Moments"—It should have been an open and shut case, murder on the Moon to Europa run. There was no doubt who the victims and their killer were—or was there . . .?

"Ringflow"—The Saturn mission had been his dream for as long as he could remember. Now he was here and it was everything he'd imagined and more—much, much more. . . .

SOL'S CHILDREN

SOL'S CHILDREN

edited by Jean Rabe and Martin H. Greenberg

DAW BOOKS, INC.

DONALD A. WOLLHEIM, FOUNDER

375 Hudson Street, New York, NY 10014

ELIZABETH R. WOLLHEIM
SHEILA E. GILBERT
PUBLISHERS

www.dawbooks.com

ACKNOWLEDGMENTS

Introduction © 2002 by Jean Rabe.
Old-Boy Network © 2002 by Timothy Zahn.
Mirrors © 2002 by Brian A. Hopkins.
In Finnegan's Wake © 2002 by Jack C. Haldemann II.
Ghosts of Neptune © 2002 by John Helfers.
Moments © 2002 by Kristine Kathryn Rusch.
'Roid © 2002 by Jeff Crook.
The Demons of Jupiter's Moons © 2002 by Mike Resnick and Mark M. Stafford.
Ringflow © 2002 by Tom Dupree.
Martian Knights © 2002 by Stephen D. Sullivan.
Omega Time © 2002 by Russell Davis.
Son of a Belter Earl © 2002 by Roland Green.
An Acceptable Risk © 2002 by Ed Gibson.
Patience © 2002 by Donald J. Bingle.
A Coin for Charon © 2002 by Janet Pack.
The Grand Tour © 2002 by Brian M. Thomsen.
Least of My Brethren © 2002 by Michael A. Stackpole.

CONTENTS

INTRODUCTION
  by Jean Rabe   9
OLD-BOY NETWORK
  by Timothy Zahn   11
MIRRORS
  by Brian A. Hopkins   35
IN FINNEGAN'S WAKE
  by Jack C. Haldeman II   56
GHOSTS OF NEPTUNE
  by John Helfers   78
MOMENTS
  by Kristine Kathryn Rusch   125
'ROID
  by Jeff Crook   143
THE DEMONS OF JUPITER'S MOONS
  by Mike Resnick and Mark M. Stafford   160
RINGFLOW
  by Tom Dupree   170
MARTIAN KNIGHTS
  by Stephen D. Sullivan   180
OMEGA TIME
  by Russell Davis   209
SON OF A BELTER EARL
  by Roland Green   216
AN ACCEPTABLE RISK
  by Ed Gibson   236
PATIENCE
  by Donald J. Bingle   249
A COIN FOR CHARON
  by Janet Pack   263

THE GRAND TOUR
  by Brian M. Thomsen   280
LEAST OF MY BRETHREN
  by Michael A. Stackpole   294

INTRODUCTION

by Jean Rabe

STEPPING beyond Earth's boundaries in search of new life and adventure—and discovering in the process things we cannot put a name to—that's the heart of great science fiction yarns. And that, and more, is what you will find in this collection of tales by the genre's greatest voices.

Seventeen authors were asked to weave stories set within the physical boundaries of our solar system, visiting the planets and asteroids that are Sol's children. And each of them delivered the proverbial tenfold.

Timothy Zahn and Stephen Sullivan went to Mars; Don Bingle started with the Moon; Ed Gibson journeyed to mist-shrouded Venus; Brian A. Hopkins, Mike Resnick, and Mark M. Stafford played with Jupiter's moons. Kristine Kathryn Rusch wove her tale on a space station; Tom Dupree chose Saturn; Jack C. Haldeman II, Russell Davis, and Brian Thomsen selected the entire solar system as their backdrop. John Helfers tackled Neptune and Jeff Crook grabbed one big asteroid while Roland Green went after several. My good friend Janet Pack searched for her story on Pluto, and Michael Stackpole . . . well, let's just say he did some soul-searching.

So find a comfortable easy chair, sit back, put your

feet up, and dig into this book. You'll be indulging yourself in some truly excellent science fiction. It's your turn
to step beyond Earth's boundaries. Mystery, adventure,
and a sense of wonder await.

OLD-BOY NETWORK

by Timothy Zahn

Timothy Zahn has been writing professionally since 1980, making an actual living at it since sometime in late 1984. He is the author of more than sixty short stories and nineteen novels, including five Star Wars *novels. His latest book is* Angelmass, *published in September 2001. He lives on the southern Oregon coast with his wife, their teenage son, and about seven of those pesky computer things.*

THE sunlight was glowing softly through Rey's eyelids when he woke up that last morning. For a few minutes he just lay there, luxuriating under the warm weight of the blankets and comforter, happy to be alive.

She had smiled at him again.

He smiled to himself at the thought. The left side of his mouth didn't join in the smile, of course, but for once he almost didn't even care. At first the half-paralyzed face had bothered him terribly, even more than having been made a cripple. But today, none of it seemed to matter. Because it hadn't seemed to matter to her. And if it didn't matter to her, it certainly shouldn't matter to him.

She had smiled at him. For the fifth time in the past four weeks—he'd been keeping count—she had smiled at him.

He yawned deeply. "Curtains: open," he called.

From across the room came a soft hum as the filmy curtains were pulled aside. He pried open his eyelids—rather literally in the case of his left eyelid, which had a tendency to glue itself shut overnight—and looked outside.

The sun was high up over the stark Martian landscape. He'd slept in unusually late this morning. But that was all right. Unless and until Mr. Quillan called for him, his time was his own. And if that call held off, and if he was lucky, he might see *her* again.

His chair was waiting beside his bed where he'd left it. Throwing back the blankets, he maneuvered himself to the edge of the bed and got himself into it. "Chair: bathroom," he ordered. Obediently, the chair rolled across the room and through the wide door of his bathroom. He took care of the usual morning business; and then it was time for a quick shower. The breakfast he'd ordered last night should be waiting by the time he was done.

Idly, he wondered what the meal would consist of. Mr. Quillan had been talking with the other men and women on the Network quite a lot lately, and that much Tab-Rasa sometimes played funny games with his memory in general. Still, surprises could be pleasant, too. By the time Rey was dressed and back in his chair, the tantalizing aroma of Belgian waffles was wafting through the bathroom door. He rather hoped he'd asked for bacon with it, but it turned out he'd ordered a side of sausage instead. No problem. He liked sausage, too. He would just order bacon tomorrow. Maneuvering his chair up to the table, wondering what *she* liked for breakfast, he began to eat.

*   *   *

"So this is Mars," Hendrik Thorwald commented, gently swirling his coffee cup as he gazed out the floor-to-ceiling windows at the landscape and the cluster of domes that made up Makaris City. "Not nearly as claustrophobic as the Ganymede Domes."

"That's because here you can at least walk around

outside without a full vacuum suit," Archer Quillan pointed out, sipping at his own spiced coffee as he watched the circling motion of the other's cup.

It was almost as if Thorwald thought he was holding a brandy snifter. A simple nervous habit? Or did it imply that the man drank too much? Neither added up to much of a recommendation in Quillan's book. But in this case, Quillan's book didn't matter. Thorwald's net worth had reached the magic trillion-dollar mark, and McCade wanted him in, and that was that. His wealth had made him an Old Boy, as McCade sardonically called them, and he would be offered a spot in the Old-Boy Network.

"Of course, you need an air supply and parka," Thorwald said. "Still, it's not as cold as the travel books made it sound."

"Hardly worse than a typical Swedish winter, I imagine," Quillan said politely.

"Hardly at all." Turning away from the window, Thorwald resettled himself in his chair to face Quillan again. "But you didn't ask me all the way to Mars to compare weather. We've had our breakfast; we've had our coffee. Let's talk business."

"Indeed," Quillan agreed. Straight and direct, with neither belligerence nor apology. Much better.

"Actually, it's not so much business as it is an invitation. You've reached the magic trillion-dollar mark, and the thirty or so of us already in that rather exclusive club would like to congratulate you on your achievement."

Thorwald inclined his head slightly. "Thank you."

"But as you'll soon realize, if you haven't already, making a trillion dollars is only the first step," Quillan continued. "The challenge now is to hold onto it. Currently, you're Target Number One for every con man, minor competitor, and ambitious young Turk in Northern Europe, all of whom hope to pry some of that money away from you."

"Joined by every governmental taxing agency from Earth to the Jovian Moons and back again," Thorwald added sourly.

"Absolutely," Quillan said. "And with all of them nipping at your heels, I would venture to guess that your biggest headache these days is that of secure communications."

"Hardly an insightful guess," Thorwald pointed out. "That's *everyone's* biggest headache. Even the best encryption methods I can get my hands on can't keep up with the government snoops and industrial spies."

"Indeed," Quillan said. "And of course, there's also that awkward time lag whenever you're transmitting across the solar system. It would be nice to eliminate that, wouldn't it?"

The gentle swirling of the coffee cup came to a halt. "I seem to remember from school that that's a basic limitation of the universe," he said, his eyes searching Quillan's face.

"That's what they taught in my school, too," Quillan said. "Tell me, Hendrik: what would you give to have an absolutely secure information and transmission channel? I mean *absolutely* secure?"

Thorwald snorted gently. "Half my fortune. Cash."

Quillan smiled. "Then you're looking at a real bargain," he said. "All it will cost you is a mere eight hundred million dollars. Paid to the right people, of course."

Carefully, Thorwald set his cup on the polished crystal coffee table. "Tell me more."

"I'll do better," Quillan said, getting to his feet. "I'll show you."

*   *   *

"Downstairs?" the broad-shouldered man repeated, his thick forehead wrinkling. "You were just downstairs yesterday."

"Because downstairs is where the piano is," Rey said, the frozen left half of his mouth slurring the words slightly. Grond was one of Rey's caretakers, which meant he was on call whenever Rey needed something his chair or automated suite couldn't handle. He was also, Rey had long ago decided, something of a private watchdog.

"Yeah, but so what?" Grond grunted. "You've got a perfectly good keyboard in your room."

"That's a keyboard," Rey explained patiently. "The piano downstairs is a baby grand. There's a big difference in how it sounds."

The wrinkles deepened. Obviously, that was something Grond had never noticed. Possibly music itself was something Grond had never noticed. "Mr. Quillan isn't going to like you going downstairs all the time."

"He's never said I couldn't," Rey countered. "Just that he didn't want me talking to anyone."

"Yeah, but every day?" Grond objected. "You're up and down those stairs like a yo-yo."

"Would you rather get a couple of guys and move the piano upstairs?" Rey suggested helpfully.

Grond exhaled disgustedly. "Fine. Whatever you want."

"Thank you," Rey said. "Chair: library."

He felt his heart starting to pound as the chair passed the second floor landing and began climbing down the wide staircase. Down here, on the mansion's first floor, was where *she* worked. *Let her be working in the library today,* he pleaded silently with the universe. *Please. Let her be in the library.*

There were three women in traditional black-and-white maid's outfits working on the brass and wrought iron when Rey reached the bottom of the stairs. None of them was *her*. As usual, none of the maids even looked up as the chair rolled along the hallway toward the library. It was as if Rey didn't even exist. Maybe they all had orders to treat him that way. Or maybe they just didn't like him. No one here really liked him. Except *her*.

There were two other maids dusting the old-style books lining the shelves as he rolled through the library door. Again, *she* wasn't among them. Rey's heartbeat slowed back to a quiet ache as he made his way across to the baby grand piano, trying hard not to let the disappointment drag him down. All right, so two days in a row had been too much to expect. He would see her again. Maybe tomorrow.

"You got half an hour," Grond warned, crossing the room ahead of him and moving the piano bench out of the way. "Then it's back upstairs."

Rey nodded, not trusting himself to speak. He settled his chair in place in front of the keyboard and punched in Beethoven's Moonlight Sonata on the music desk. Tentatively, he began to play. He wasn't very good at it. In fact, he rather hated playing the baby grand. There was no way to play it quietly, and every mistake and hesitation seemed to echo accusingly back across the room at him. Grond's glowering presence a few steps away didn't help either. But he had to pretend he was enjoying himself. This piano was his best excuse for coming downstairs, and he didn't dare let Grond know the truth.

He had finished playing what he could of the Beethoven and had shifted to some easier Stephen Foster when a movement across the room caught the corner of his eye. He turned his head to look—and felt his heart leap like an excited child. It was *her*. His breath felt suddenly on fire in his chest as he watched her walk alongside the shelves, a brass-polishing kit in her hand. So far she hadn't looked in his direction; but her path was bringing her ever closer to the piano. Eventually, he knew, she would have to notice him. And when that happened, would she smile again?

He kept playing, his suddenly stiff fingers feeling as wooden as xylophone keys. She was coming closer and closer. . . .

And then, just before it seemed impossible that she could avoid seeing him, she looked over at the piano. Her large brown eyes met his—and she smiled. It was like the first drink of water splashing down the throat of a weary desert traveler. This was no ordinary smile, not just the kind a proper servant would politely offer one of the master's other employees. This was a real, genuine smile. The kind of smile a person saved for a good friend.

He had no illusions as to what she could see in him, not in this wheelchair and all. But between Mr. Quillan, the unsmiling caretakers, and the rest of the oblivious household staff, he longed for someone who he could just talk to. Someone who could care for him solely for who he was. Someone who could be his friend. Maybe, just maybe, she could be that friend.

"Susan?" someone called from the doorway.

Her eyes and smile lingered on Rey's face for another second, lighting his heart and soul. Then, almost reluctantly, he thought, she turned back toward the door. "Yes?" she called.

Susan. So now he had a name to go with the face and the smile. *Susan.*

"You haven't finished out here yet," a woman's voice said, an undertone of disapproval to it. "Come do this first."

"Yes, ma'am," Susan said. "I'm coming."

Her eyes flicked back to Rey, and she smiled again. Not the same wide smile as the first, but a smaller, private one. The kind of smile shared by friends who are both in on the same private secret. The kind of smile that promised she would be back later. She turned and walked across the room. Rey watched her go, the image of that smile dancing in front of his eyes. He was sure of it now. She would be his friend.

There was a heavy tap on Rey's shoulder. "You going to play, or what?" Grond rumbled.

With a mild surprise, Rey realized his fingers had come to a halt. "Of course I'm going to play," he said, shifting back to the Beethoven with new vigor. Susan would be back, just as soon as she'd finished out there. She would be back, and she would smile at him again. Beneath his fingers the piano was singing now—and then, from his chair, came a soft trilling sound.

He could have cried. No, he begged the universe. *No. Not now. Not when she'll be coming back any minute.* But the universe didn't care. With a tired sigh, he let his fingers come to a halt again on the keys. "Chair: Mr. Quillan's office," he ordered sadly. The master had called, and it was time to go to work.

* * *

"The basic neurological theories are obscure, but there for the taking," Quillan said as he gestured Thorwald to a chair in his private, ultra-secure third-floor office. "The genius of our associate in Ghana was in pulling it all together. And, of course, having the will to act on it."

"Telepathy." Thorwald shook his head, as if not sure he approved of the word. "Frankly, I wouldn't have believed it."

Quillan smiled. "Frankly, you still don't," he said. "That's why you're here. McCade thought you'd find the demonstration more effective if you were a few million kilometers away from him at the time."

Across the room, the door chimed. Quillan keyed the remote, and the panel slid open to reveal Rey in his chair. "Come in, Rey," he invited. "Hendrik, this is Rey, my personal terminal of the Old-Boy Network. Seventeen years old, in case you're wondering. The younger they are when we get them, the better they react to the procedure."

"A cripple?" Thorwald said, frowning.

"An unavoidable side effect of the process," Quillan explained as Rey rolled into the room, the door sealing shut behind him. "It turns out the human brain hasn't got enough spare neurological capacity to handle telepathy. Some creative clearing and retasking is needed."

He stood up as Rey rolled to a stop beside the desk. "You basically need two clear areas to work with," he said, circling around behind the boy. "The first is the section that operates the legs. No big loss; a programmed wheelchair can let him get around just fine." He touched Rey's left cheek. "The other is the lower left side of the face. Smile for Hendrik, Rey."

The skin around Thorwald's eyes and lips crinkled

with revulsion as Rey gave him that broken half-smile of his. "I see," he said.

"Disgusting, isn't it?" Quillan agreed. "All completely reversible." It wasn't, of course, and he and all the rest of the Old Boys knew it. Sometimes he toyed with the idea of telling Rey the truth, just to see what the boy's reaction would be. So far he'd resisted that temptation. Maybe someday when he was particularly bored he'd give it a shot.

"Have any reversals actually been performed?" Thorwald asked.

"At another eight hundred million a shot?" Quillan said pointedly. "Besides, in the fifteen years the Network has been running, all the telepaths have worn out well before the ten years they signed on for. Easier and cheaper at that point just to replace them."

Thorwald sent an almost furtive look at Rey. "Should we be talking this way?"

"Not a problem." Quillan patted Rey's shoulder. "Rey is an excellent telepath. I'm sure he'll go the distance."

"Besides," he added, gesturing to the flesh-colored band around Rey's neck as he sat back down again, "standard procedure is to give our telepaths a dose of TabRasa-33 after every session. Memory scrambler; wipes out all short-term memories for the preceding twenty to thirty minutes. I could tell him I'm going to kill him tomorrow and he wouldn't remember a thing about it an hour from now. Well, let's get started."

Reaching into his desk, Quillan pulled out a stack of photos and a small picture stand. "Pictures of each of the others' terminals," he explained, showing Thorwald the stack as he set up the stand in front of Rey. "All Rey has to do is visualize the face, and the other telepath will pick up on the signal."

"And then?" Thorwald asked.

"Then we're in," Quillan said, selecting the photo of McCade's current telepath and putting it on the stand. "Go ahead, Rey."

For a moment Rey gazed at the photo, as if trying to

memorize it. Then, that familiar but still creepy look
settled over his face. His eyes seemed to glaze over, his
half-functional mouth went a little slack, and he let out
a huffing sigh.

"He's in contact," Quillan murmured. "Now it's just
a matter of the other telepath sending for McCade."

"By phone?"

Quillan shook his head. "Single-tone, single-duration
signal button on the wheelchair," he said. "You never,
ever want to have anything near your telepath that can
record or transmit."

"Including other people?" Thorwald asked.

"Especially other people," Quillan agreed grimly.
"Except for his caretakers, no one in this house is allowed to talk to Rey or even get within three meters
of him."

"Why don't you just lock him up?" Thorwald asked.

"Counterproductive," Quillan said. "You let your telepath get too bored or in too much of a rut and he burns
out faster. It's cheaper in the long run to let them roam
around a little. You just have to make sure there's no
way to pass information back and forth. He's not allowed any writing instruments, obviously."

Abruptly, Rey seemed to straighten up. "Hello?" he
said.

"McCade?" Quillan asked.

There was a brief pause. "Yes," Rey said. "Quillan,
I presume?"

"Correct," Quillan said. "I have an acquaintance of
yours here with me. Would you care to say hello?"

"Hello, Hendrik," Rey said. "I trust Archer is treating
you well?"

"Quite well, thank you," Thorwald said. His eyes,
Quillan noted, had the suspicious look of a small child
watching his first magician. "What's new at the ranch?"

"Well, we've got six new lambs," Rey said. "Looks
like we may get another twenty before the season runs
its course. Has Archer invited you to drive up Ascraeus
Mons yet?"

"He has, and I've turned him down," Thorwald said.

"Barbaric place, this. The next time we meet, I think we'll do it at *my* house."

"Now, be honest, Hendrik," Rey said. "Is it Mars you find barbaric, or Archer's lack of a proper wine cellar? When you visit him, Archer, you'll have to talk him out of a bottle of the '67 Bordeaux Sanjai. I understand he bought up the entire year's vintage, except for a few bottles that went to some New York hotel by mistake. Which one was it again, Hendrik?"

"The Ritz-Aberdon," Thorwald said, shaking his head. "I don't believe this."

"Neither did I, at first," Rey said. "But as you see, it does work."

"So it would appear," Thorwald said. "So aside from allowing me to safely tell rude jokes about the President, Secretary-General, and Chairman of the Financial Reserve, what exactly is this good for?"

Rey made an odd snorting noise. "Shall we give him the standard example, Archer?" he invited.

"Certainly," Quillan said, smiling. "At the moment, Hendrik, Mars is nine light-minutes from Earth. That means that information traveling by radio or laser takes nine minutes to get from there to here. Jonathan, what's the Unified European Market doing at the moment?"

"Odd that you should ask," Rey said. "As it happens, Bavarian General Transport hit a peak price of eighty-nine point three exactly four minutes ago. Two minutes later, the profit-hunters moved in, and it's been on its way down ever since. Eighteen points so far, with no signs of a turnaround. I believe, Hendrik, that you have some minor investments in BGT?"

It was as if someone had touched a match to Thorwald's lower lip. His whole body jerked, his eyes lighting up as the true reality of the situation suddenly caught up with him. "God," he bit out, twisting his wrist up to look at his watch. "But—"

"Exactly," Quillan said, reaching to his desk computer and punching up his InstaTrade connection. "The news of that eighty-nine high won't hit the Martian Repeater Lists for another five minutes, and the downturn won't start for seven. Would you care to place a sell order? Effective, say, six minutes from now?''

"God," Thorwald muttered again, swiveling the computer around and starting to punch in his personal codes. "The possibilities—"

"Are endless," Quillan agreed. "Stock manipulation, advance warnings of news events that could affect your holdings or your businesses, tips to share back and forth without all those ambitious young Turks listening in. The sky's the limit."

"Or rather, the sky is no longer the limit," Rey put in dryly. "You can do conference calls, too, by setting out two or more photos for your telepath. *That* one can have uses all its own. As we all found out in that Estevez matter a few months back."

"Indeed," Quillan said. "The Securities Enforcement people got suspicious of Sergei Bondonavich and planted a spy on him. When Mr. Estevez suddenly disappeared— down an abandoned salt mine near Berchtesgaden, I believe—the rest of his group descended on Sergei like middle management attacking the company Christmas buffet. He spun them a complete frosted sugar cookie, then hotfooted it onto the Network with a conference call and clued the rest of us in on the story he told. By the time their associates came knocking on our own doors ten minutes later, we were able to corroborate every detail."

"All without a single indication that there'd been any communication between us," Rey added. "As far as I know, they still haven't even located Estevez's body."

"All right, I'm convinced," Thorwald said. "What's the catch?"

"There isn't any," Rey assured him. "Each of us in the Old-Boy Network has basically arrived. Each of us is powerful enough to be largely immune to attacks from the others, even if one of us was foolish enough to try. No, at this point our main focus is to bite off the heads of the smaller fish nipping at our tail fins."

"And to deal with the self-appointed guardians of all

that is right and good," Quillan said contemptuously. "The solar system is our private pond now, to borrow Jonathan's fish metaphor. Why not swim together?"

"I presume Archer's already quoted you the price," Rey said. "The only other requirement is that you share secrets and information with the others in fair value for what you receive. And, of course, that you maintain complete airtight security on the whole operation. If you'd like, we'll give you a week to think about it."

"No need," Thorwald said, straightening up from the computer. "I'm in."

"Excellent," Rey said. "Then enjoy the rest of your stay, and call me when you get back to Earth. I'll have things set up, and we'll go from there. Oh, and do try to get up Ascraeus Mons at least once. No trip to Mars is complete without it."

"I'll think about it," Thorwald said. "Good-bye, Jonathan."

He looked at Quillan. "Is that right? Do I say good-bye?"

"You can," Quillan said. "Rey, break contact. How was it?"

He watched as Rey gave the little shudder he always did as he cleared the connection. "Pretty clear," the boy said, rubbing at his lips. "The other . . . he didn't seem completely on track today."

"What does that mean?" Thorwald asked, frowning.

"The contact wasn't as sharp as it should have been," Quillan explained. "At least, in Rey's estimation."

"What could cause that?"

"The other telepath might have been distracted," Quillan looked at the clock. "Or tired—it is only four A.M. at McCade's ranch. Any misfires, Rey?"

"No," Rey said hesitantly. "I don't think so."

"Misfires?" Thorwald asked.

"As Rey listens to what I'm saying, the other telepath hears it through his ears and brain," Quillan explained. "Rather like hearing an echo, I expect. The other telepath then repeats the message back to McCade, and it's Rey's turn to hear the echo as he speaks."

"That's why there was that pause before the other end answers," Thorwald said, nodding. "McCade had to get the message relayed, and then answer."

"Correct," Quillan said. "Misfires are when the other telepath doesn't repeat the message exactly the way it was sent. Usually it's only a dropped word here or there, and usually it's just carelessness or a case of someone using sentences too long or complicated for the telepath to handle."

"But if it's not?"

"Then it could be the first sign of a burned-out telepath," Quillan said bluntly. "At which point, that particular Old Boy is advised that it may soon be time to upgrade his equipment." He patted Rey on the shoulder. "Fortunately for McCade's wallet, it sounds like his mouthpiece is holding up just fine." He shifted his hand, squeezing the collar around Rey's neck in the proper place. "That'll be all, Rey."

"Yes, sir," Rey murmured, his eyes starting to glaze over as the TabRasa trickled into his bloodstream.

"Go take a nap," Quillan added. "Chair: Rey's bedroom."

The chair turned and rolled across the room.

"Trouble?" Thorwald asked as the door opened and passed the chair and its dozing passenger out of the office.

"I don't know," Quillan said slowly. "It occurs to me that there's another possibility for that sub-par connection just now. That it may not be *McCade's* telepath who's tired or distracted." Quillan got up from his chair. "Help yourself to my cigars, or anything else you want. I'll be back soon."

*   *   *

Rey woke abruptly, with the disorientation that always came after a dose of TabRasa. After three years he was used to it, but it was never entirely comfortable. Still, there were worse things in life. Much worse things. He could certainly put up with it for the remaining seven

years of his contract. And when he had finished, Mr.
Quillan would give him back his legs and his face, and
he would get the bonus money he'd been promised. And
his parents and siblings would finally be able to get off
that dirt-scrabble Central American farm and have the
kind of financial security that had never been more than
an impossible dream for anyone in his village. For a
minute he let himself enjoy that thought. Then, bidding
his family a silent good-bye, he began searching for the
edge where memory ended and this most recent gap
began.

Yes; the library. The piano. Beethoven.

Susan.

He let her image hover in front of his closed eyes,
tracing every line and curve in his memory. Making sure
that, no matter how much TabRasa Mr. Quillan gave
him, he would never, ever forget that face. That face, or
that smile. That smile that had promised she would be
back. . . . With a start he opened his eyes and looked
over at his clock, then grabbed for the arm of his chair.
Less than an hour had gone by since the library, which
meant she was probably still cleaning somewhere in the
house. If he could figure out where, he could at least
explain to her that he hadn't just casually run out on her.

He wasn't supposed to talk to anyone except his caretakers, he knew. But surely Mr. Quillan would understand this one time. Surely he would.

*   *   *

"That's her," Grond said, nodding across the solarium
at one of the three maids polishing the brasswork around
the flower pots. "Name's Susan Baker; came on about
three months ago. A little standoffish, the housekeeper
says, but she has no complaints about her work."

"What about her attention to Rey?"

"Probably the last month or so," Grond said. "That's
when he started acting strange. Making excuses all the
time to go downstairs."

Quillan nodded, studying the girl. About eighteen

years old, thin, dark hair, plain mousy face. Not at all attractive, to his way of thinking. "But she's never talked to him?"

"No, sir." Grond was positive. "At least, not on my watch. Hasn't even gotten within four meters. All she's done is smile."

Mentally, Quillan shook his head. Such a lot of fuss and bother over so very little. If it was, indeed, a lot of fuss and bother. "Go get her," he ordered, stepping to one of the chairs beside the curved windows and sitting down.

A minute later she was standing in front of him. "Yes, sir?" she asked tentatively.

For a moment Quillan just gazed up at her. Sometimes letting an underling squirm under a direct glare could squeeze out a glimpse of a guilty conscience. But she just stood there, looking puzzled. "I understand you've been trying to meet my nephew," he said.

She frowned a bit harder. "Your nephew, sir?"

"The boy in the wheelchair," Quillan amplified. "Recovering from a serious accident. Weren't you told when you arrived here that if you saw him you weren't to speak to him?"

"Yes, sir, I was," she said. "But I haven't spoken to him."

"You've smiled at him," Quillan said, making the words an accusation.

Again, nothing but more puzzlement. "I smile at everyone," she protested, her face looking more mouselike than ever. "I was just trying to be friendly."

"I don't want you to be friendly," Quillan said firmly. "Not to him. The psychological aspects of the accident have been far more severe than even the physical damage. He needs time to work it all through."

"I understand, sir," she said. "But . . ."

"But?" Quillan echoed, making the word a challenge.

"Wouldn't it be better for him to mix with other people?" she asked, the words coming out in a rush. "To see that he can be accepted just like he is?"

Quillan raised his eyebrows. "Are you telling me that

my thousand-dollar-an-hour psychologists don't know what they're talking about?" he asked pointedly.

She actually winced. "No, sir," she said in a low voice.

"Good," Quillan said. "I would hate to think I'd been wasting all that money when an unschooled cleaning woman had better advice to give. You're to stay away from him. You're not to talk to him, or look at him. You're especially not to smile at him. Is that clear?"

"Yes, sir," she said, bobbing her head.

"Good," Quillan said. "Then get back to work."

"Yes, sir," she said again. In that peculiar gait people have when they're trying not to look like they're hurrying, she hurried away.

Grond stepped to his side. "Sir?"

"I don't know," Quillan said thoughtfully. "She seems such a pathetic specimen to be distracting our terminal."

Abruptly, he came to a decision. "Give her a month's severance and get her out of the house," he said, standing up. "Right now. Tell her we'll collect her things from her room and send them on to her at the Ares Hiltonia—set up a room there for her. You pack her bags yourself, and make sure to look everything over carefully while you do."

"Yes, sir," Grond said. "What exactly am I looking for?"

"Anything that might suggest she's more than the waste of skin she appears," Quillan said. "A camera, perhaps. Nothing electronic gets into this house that I don't know about, but it's possible to make a purely mechanical camera."

"If there's anything there, I'll find it," Grond promised. "You want her *just* out of the house?"

Quillan rubbed his lower lip as he gazed across at the girl's back. Grond was right. She was almost certainly harmless; but on the other hand, Rey was a multimillion-dollar investment. There was no point in taking the risk. "You just give her that month's severance," he said. "I'll call Bondonavich and have him get whoever handled Estevez to take care of her more permanently."

Grond's lumpy forehead wrinkled. "You're going to have *Rey* send the order for her to disappear?"

"TabRasa is a wonderful invention," Quillan reminded him. "You just get her out of my house."

"Yes, sir."

Hunching his shoulders once, Grond headed across the solarium. Giving the girl one last look, Quillan headed for the door. No, Rey wouldn't like it. Not at all. But by the time he realized what was going on, the call would be in progress and there would be nothing he could do about it. And the boy would certainly get over it. TabRasa was indeed a wonderful invention.

*   *   *

She wasn't in the library. She wasn't in the main hallway, either, or the kitchen, or the dining room. Where could she be? Sitting in the middle of the hallway, Rey looked around him at the various directions he could go, his heart pounding uncomfortably. He wasn't even supposed to be down here alone, never mind giving himself a tour of the house this way. So far the only servants he'd seen were all at a distance, and as usual none of them had given him a second glance. But sooner or later, if he kept at this, he was bound to bump squarely into someone.

And then what? Would he compound his disobedience by asking where Susan was? At this point he didn't really know what he would do. All he knew was that he needed to find her. Turning the chair around, he headed down the main hallway. Somewhere back here, he had heard, was a stairway that led down to the servants' quarters.

He had just rounded a corner off the main hallway when an older man emerged from the theater room. "Rey!" he said with surprise. "What are you doing here?"

Rey froze. *Someone was talking to him!* And not just someone, but a man he'd never seen before in his life. Some guest of Mr. Quillan's?

But whether or not Rey knew who he was, it was clear

he knew who Rey was. "You're not supposed to be down here alone," the man growled, striding toward him. "Where's your caretaker?"

"I—I don't know," Rey managed. "He's not—"

"Get yourself upstairs," the man snapped. "Right now."

"Yes, sir," Rey said automatically. "Chair—"

He stopped short as a face suddenly seemed to appear before his eyes, pushing aside his mental picture of Susan. "Yes, I'll get him," he murmured in response to the silent call, pressing the signal button underneath his chair's armrest.

"What is it, a call?" the man asked, glancing around. "Come on, we'd better get you to his office."

"He says it's very important," Rey murmured. "Vitally important."

"What's vitally important?" Mr. Quillan's voice came from somewhere behind him.

The man looked up over Rey's shoulder. "He's got a call from someone," he said. "I thought you said he's not supposed to be down here alone."

"He's not," Mr. Quillan said grimly, coming around the chair into Rey's line of sight and glaring down at him. "Rey, what are you doing here?"

"Vitally important," Rey repeated. "Must talk to you. Now."

"Damn," Mr. Quillan muttered. He glanced around, gestured toward the door across from the theater room. "Chair: Conference Room One. It's secure enough," he added to the other man as the chair started rolling, "and faster than getting him upstairs to the office. This just better be *damn* urgent."

A minute later they were in the conference room. Mr. Quillan checked the monitors built into the table, then dropped into one of the chairs. "All right, we're secure," he said. "This is Quillan. Who is this?"

As if it were being carried down a long hollow tube, Rey heard a man's voice in the distance. *This is McCade.*

"This is McCade," he repeated.

We've got a problem.

"We've got a problem," Rey echoed.

Or rather, you do. I've just learned Enforcement has planted a spy on you—

"Or rather, you do," Rey said. "I've just learned Enforcement has planted a spy on you—"

Named Susan Baker.

"Named Susan Ba—" Abruptly, Rey faltered, her face springing into sharp new focus in front of his eyes. Susan Baker? *Susan?*

"What?" Mr. Quillan snapped, bounding up out of his chair. "Susan *what?*"

"Baker," Rey stammered. "I—Mr. Quillan—"

But the other wasn't even listening. "Grond!" he shouted into his remote as he sprinted toward the door. "Stop her! Don't let her get out of the house!"

He slammed the door open and was gone. *What's happening?* the voice echoed through Rey's mind.

Rey didn't answer. Swiveling his chair around, he started toward the door. A hand grabbed at his shoulder. "No, you don't," the other man bit out. "Where do you think you're—?"

The last word came out in a strangled gasp as Rey slammed his elbow with all the strength he could manage into the man's abdomen. Maneuvering the chair around the table and potted trees, he rolled out the door. They were all there, down by the bend in the hallway: Quillan, Grond, and Susan. Grond had a grip on Susan's arm, holding it bent behind her back. Her face—that wonderful, kind face—was twisted almost beyond recognition with pain and fear.

"Stop!" Rey shouted. Or at least, he tried to shout. Instead, the words came out as barely a squeak. Susan's eyes flicked to Rey's face, a wordless plea there . . .

And with a sudden blaze of anger, Rey sent the chair rolling toward the trio at full speed. Words weren't going to stop Grond now, he knew. From somewhere in the distance he could hear the warbling of some kind of alarm—

And then, to his astonishment, five men charged into view around the corner of the hallway. Grond barely had time to snap a warning before three of them leaped at him, wrenching Susan's arm out of his grip and wrestling him to the floor. One of the others pushed warningly at Quillan's chest, while the last hurriedly pulled Susan away from the confusion. "You all right?" Rey heard him ask.

"I'm fine," she breathed, looking over at Rey again. "There's Rey," she added.

"Right," the man said briskly, beckoning Rey toward him. "Rey? Come on over."

Rey let the chair coast to a halt where he was, staring at them in confusion. Did Susan know these people? What were they doing here? Who were they?

"It's all right, Rey," Susan called, smiling weakly as she rubbed her arm. "Don't worry. These are the good guys."

Quillan snorted loudly. "And they'd better enjoy themselves while they can," he said. "You've leaned way over the mark with this one, Winslow. *Way* over. By this time tomorrow you'll be on suspension, pending charges of gross misconduct."

"No, I don't think so," the man beside Susan—Winslow— said calmly. A dozen more men appeared around the corner, all of them dressed in police uniforms, and strode purposefully past Rey. Glancing over his shoulder, he saw them start checking the rooms. "Come on, Rey, join the party," Winslow added. "It's all over. Really."

Hesitantly, Rey nudged the chair forward.

"Let's run through the formalities, shall we?" Winslow said, turning his attention back to Quillan. "Archer Quillan, you're under arrest for stock manipulation, illegal business practices—" He paused dramatically. "*And* obstruction of justice and accessory after the fact in the murder of Securities Enforcement agent Juan Estevez."

Quillan snorted again. "And you'll be awaiting a full psychiatric examination on top of it," he said scornfully. "You couldn't make charges like that stick to the floor."

Winslow smiled. "You might be surprised," he said. "You see, we finally have a witness to all this sludge-water manipulation you and your trillionaire buddies

have been indulging in. Someone who can quote your
words exactly. Yours, *and* Jonathan McCade's, *and*
Sergei Bondonavich's. Everything you've said on your
cozy little Old-Boy Network for the past month, in fact."

"You are insane," Quillan insisted, looking at Susan
and then Rey. "There's not a thing either of them can
tell you. I've made sure of that."

"Who said I was talking about either of them?" Winslow countered, shifting his eyes toward the corner.
"Julia?" he called, raising his voice. "It's safe—come on
in." He looked back at Quillan. "We knew we couldn't
get anything from the inside," he said. "Between Tab-
Rasa and electronic countermeasures, you had all those
bases covered.

"And so we arranged for you to deliver the information *outside* the house. To us."

"You're bluffing," Quillan said flatly. "Nothing has
left this house."

"Ah, but it has," Winslow said. "We figured that with
all this paranoid secrecy, you'd probably have Rey
locked away someplace where he would be starved for
human contact. So we provided him with a friendly face.
A face that, hopefully, he would always have hovering
at the edges of his mind."

"A pathetic face," Quillan said contemptuously, looking at Susan.

"In your opinion," Winslow said. "But obviously not
in Rey's. Tell me, Quillan; have you ever heard of a
carbon copy?"

' Quillan frowned. "A what?"

"A carbon copy," Winslow repeated. "That's an out-
of-date term for a duplicate you make of a communication to send elsewhere. That's basically what we were
getting."

Quillan was looking at the man as if he were crazy.
"What in the System are you talking about?" he demanded. "There aren't any copies."

"That's where you're wrong." Winslow gestured at
Susan. "Meet Enforcement Agent Trainee Susan Con-
verse."

And then, from around the corner, rolled another wheelchair. A wheelchair just like Rey's. A wheelchair holding a young woman.

A woman with a very familiar face . . .

Quillan inhaled sharply. "And," Winslow added quietly, "meet Susan's identical twin sister Julia. As you can see, your associate in Ghana was willing to cut himself a deal."

*   *   *

"We'll want you to stay on Mars another couple of weeks," Susan said, setting a mug of hot tea on the table in front of Rey as she slid into the seat across from him. "Just in case we need you to add to your deposition."

"So what Mr. Quillan said was true?" Rey asked, looking down at his tea, afraid to look directly at her. Her, or her sister. "When they took him away? That you were just using me?"

"They needed to be stopped, Rey," she said gently. "They didn't believe any of the rules applied to them anymore. Juan Estevez was just one example of the sort of thing they were getting away with every day. Quillan would have killed you, too, once you were of no more use to him. Just as he killed the telepath he had before you."

She reached across the table and touched his hand. "But that said, no, we weren't just using you. Any more than we were just using Julia. Or me."

"You and Julia volunteered," Rey said bitterly. "I didn't have any choice in the matter."

"How could we have asked you?" Susan pointed out. "Quillan had you totally isolated."

"From everybody except Julia," Rey countered, his voice coming out harsher than he'd expected. "You ever think of that? *She* could have asked me."

"Winslow suggested that," Julia's slightly slurred voice said softly from Rey's left. "But I was afraid to."

The sheer surprise of the comment got Rey's gaze up out of his tea. She'd been *afraid* to? "Why?"

To his surprise, he saw tears gathering at the corners of her eyes. "Because there was no proof I could give you," she said softly. "I was afraid you'd think I was just trying to stir you up against Quillan. I thought you'd never want to see me or talk to me . . ."

She looked away. "There's no reversal, Rey. We're going to be like this for the rest of our lives. We're never going to fit in anymore, not with anyone. I was afraid if you started hating me . . ."

Rey looked at Susan. There were no smiles there now, on that face whose every line he'd memorized. Nothing but love and heartache and sadness as she gazed at her sister. He looked back at Julia. Then, hesitantly, he reached over and took her hand. "It's okay," he said. "Really. I've never hated anyone in my life. I'm sure not going to start with you."

She looked back at him, blinking away the tears. Then, almost as if afraid to believe it, she gave him a tentative smile.

A half smile, with the left part of her lips frozen in place. A nervous, almost frightened smile.

Rey smiled back. With the enormity of the sacrifice she'd made now crashing in on her, what Julia really needed was someone who could understand her. Someone who could care for her solely for who she was. Someone who could be her friend. He would be that friend.

MIRRORS

by Brian A. Hopkins

Brian A. Hopkins is the author of Something Haunts Us All *(1995),* Cold at Heart *(1997),* Flesh Wounds *(1999),* The Licking Valley Coon Hunters Club *(2000),* Wrinkles at Twilight *(2000),* These I Know By Heart *(2001), and* Salt Water Tears *(2001). He is the recipient of two Bram Stoker Awards and has been a finalist for both the Nebula and the Ted Sturgeon Memorial Award. Brian lives in Oklahoma with his wife and two children. You can learn more about him by visiting his Web page at http://bahwolf.com.*

THE observatory at Io is almost ready.

The platform with its complex array of mirrors and lenses has been finished for some time now. It glitters against the backdrop of Jupiter, a splash of blinding white diamond amid the swirling colors, ringed by the blue torus that houses the labs, living quarters, and control modules, trailing long black cables that siphon power from the electrical storm of Io's plasma tube. In another few months, the sixty-four-thousand-square-kilometer silver dish jutting up from Io's seething volcanoes and sulfur beds will be polished. Even from here, looking down from the lounge of the *Bonaventure*, I can see hundreds of small droids swarming its surface, honing each microscopic irregularity. When they're done, when the eye that Ling Mei Chow designed is finally

focused on the rim of the universe, some say we'll see
all the way out beyond the Hubble Limit, all the way to
the birth of the universe, to that microsecond of creation
known as the Big Bang.

I don't profess to know how it all works. I don't know
how it's possible to peer into space that's expanding
faster than the visible light it sheds. I only know that
mankind hopes to soon look upon the face of God. But
the face they'll see, drifting out there somewhere between Jupiter and Hubble's impenetrable wall, won't be
God's. It'll be a man's face, looking back toward the
friends and the lovers he had known, completely unremarkable unless the mirrors and lenses are brought to
bear on the eyes, and there, in those lackluster brown
depths, might be seen the anguish of guilt and the grim
certainty of fate.

                    *   *   *

It was Ling Mei who met the *Bonaventure*'s shuttle
when it docked. We stood just inside the air lock for a
long and awkward moment, studying what fifteen years
had done, looking for the subtle clues that might inform
either of us what ground we were on with the other,
before she finally pushed my jumpbag aside and pressed
her face against my chest.

"It's good to see you, Kev."

"You, too," I said, pressing her slender body close.
Even now, millions of miles from home, her hair smelled
the same as always. It would always remind me of
Hawaii, of the flowers we'd hunted in the volcanic nooks
of Mauna Kea.

She held me at arm's length, her dark eyes as unreada-
ble as ever. "I think you've put on a little weight," she
chided.

I smiled. I was a good thirty pounds lighter, and she
knew it. There'd been a lot of lean years, a lot of times
when work had been more important than eating, more
important than . . . well, anything. I knew that Ling Mei
would certainly agree. Work kept the memories at bay,

filled the voids in life—the empty places once filled with
friends and lovers. Sometimes, out on the edge, taking
risks and high on adrenaline, it was easy to forget.

"How is he?" I asked.

Her eyes dropped. "He's still asking for you."

"How's his arm?"

"They had to take it. He lost a lung, too." She ran
her hand along her left side. "A lot of other tissue. Some
ribs. His spleen."

"They can replace all that, can't they?" I swallowed.
"I mean, none of this is permanent . . . right?"

She nodded, met my eyes again. "Not here, though.
Back on Mars. In a hospital on Luna or Earth. Maybe
even at LaGrange." She touched my cheek. "But he
won't leave until this mess is fixed, which is why he
called for you."

A facial muscle began to twitch beneath her fingertips,
so I caught her hand and held it to keep her from noticing. "Take me to him," I said, starting her down the
long curve of the corridor. Walking, she would be less
inclined to see the dismay in my eyes.

I thought they'd called me because . . . because of
who we'd been to one another all those years ago. Because when you really need an old friend, none of the
bullshit that has come between you really matters anymore. I thought disaster was a catalyst for burning back
the layers of pettiness and anger, until all that was left
was a core of who we'd been to each other . . . before
the problems. Before the breakup. Before I'd left to start
Kevin Farber Enterprises, leaving Farber & Muldoon
Mining to Andy.

But they hadn't called me because I was Kev.

They'd called because I was Kevin Farber and had
mined every known mineral in the solar system.

"What do you think of all this?" Ling Mei asked.

"The observatory?"

"Yes. Hard to imagine it'll be finished soon, isn't it?"

"I'm surprised the funding's still flowing in. Everyone
seems focused on Europa right now."

She shrugged. "Don't think they haven't tried pulling

my funding. We've been cut to the bare bones in recent years. Damn the excavation at Europa anyway. What are a few invertebrate life-forms frozen in the ice going to do for us? Can we talk to them?"

"Well, they do prove that life on Earth wasn't a singular accident. If there's life on Europa—"

"Exactly!" she exclaimed. "If there's life on Europa, then there's life elsewhere. Io will prove that. With the resolving power we'll bring on-line, we'll be able not just to count the planets around distant suns by observing data anomalies, but actually look down through the clouds of those planets and count the number of hairs on the heads of their smallest life-forms. Forget Europa. This is where the action will be in five years."

Assuming I could fix whatever mess Andy Muldoon had got into, I thought.

She'd passed several side corridors, but now took one on our left. A sign indicated that the infirmary was ahead. A couple of turns and through several doors, past a nurse who frowned at Ling Mei and beat a hasty retreat, and then we were standing beside Andy's bed. My old friend looked up from a sheet-shrouded form that seemed smaller by half, smiled past the bandages that covered the left side of his face, and held out a weak hand. I took it.

"I knew you'd come," he whispered.

*   *   *

When I first met Andy, we were kids living under the domes on Mars. I was eleven; he was a year or so younger. I had just spent several hours arranging otherwise worthless red stones into a massive castle, complete with parapets and bastions, an arched gate, and a domed central keep. Each corner of the castle featured a tower overlooking the scorching red sands. Igneous shapes stood atop the towers like gargoyle sentinels, the porous pockets in the rock forming unblinking eyes and howling mouths.

"What are you doing?" asked a boy I'd never seen before.

I shrugged, embarrassed to have been caught off guard. Though the boy had crossed a hundred feet of open ground to walk up beside me, I hadn't seen or heard him coming. My obsession with fitting every stone just right had completely occupied me.

"Just building a castle," I told him.

"What are you going to do with it?"

The truth was that I still played with dolls, a pastime for which my father belittled me at every opportunity. He thought it amusing that such a "big boy" (I was tall for my age) still played with "baby toys." He'd come home from working in the labs, covered in dirt, exhausted, and he'd find me in my room or out in the backyard playing. They weren't dolls in the sense that little girls played with dolls; rather they were "action figures." Bill Blast, Galactic Ranger. Ernest Wallinger, Captain of United Star Command's *Vector One*. There were aliens: the beguiling Cycatrix of Venus, the little green Gruntbugly from Arcturus, and the massive and six-limbed MongoCelluloid, whose home planet no man had yet been able to find. I had planned to bring them all out tomorrow to inhabit my castle, to battle along its parapets and from the peaks of its towers, to storm its gates like medieval knights, but with lasers and sonic shields, vaporizing mines and atomic grenades. The castle might have been discovered on some forgotten moon by a team of explorers who had accidentally awoken the monsters within, or it might be the hiding place of the outcast Emperor Yog, chased throughout the universe for the stolen secret to immortality . . .

But I was embarrassed to tell Andy all that. He might laugh at me for playing with dolls, the way my father did. He might tell the other kids when school started in a few weeks, kids who were already taking on responsibilities and working with their own parents to help colonize Mars. They wouldn't understand that my father didn't want anything to do with me, that he'd only brought me

along because having a family was part of the requirement for getting here. I'd be the laughingstock of Mars
Colony 7.

So I lied.

"Nothing," I told him. "I just thought I'd build all
these towers and stuff, and then . . ." What made sense?
". . . And then bombard it with rocks."

"Stellar!" Andy said. "Can I bomb it with you?"

What could I say? "Sure."

He began to gather fist-sized stones, the missiles that
would bring down several hours of meticulous construction. "My name's Andy. Andy Muldoon. My dad works
in the mine."

"Kevin Farber," I replied. "Mine's in hydroponics."

"Gotta have veggies," Andy laughed. He tossed me a
rock. "You want the first shot?"

I shook my head, feeling sick. "Nah. You go ahead."

So he lobbed the first rock. It caught the northeast
tower a solid blow about halfway up, there where I'd
skillfully crafted a large window. It was the tower's
weakest point. The rock plowed through the wall there
and sprayed rock chips and crimson dust from the back
side as it burst through. The tower crumbled in on itself,
spilling down into the castle proper and out across the
hot sand.

And so it began with Andy, that everything I would
ever build he would unwittingly tear down. It was as
true for Farber and Muldoon Mining as it was for that
castle on Mars. It was just as true for my love of Ling
Mei Chow.

In being my friend, Andy would undo me. From the
very first day we met.

*   *   *

The mining supervisor's name was Craig. First or last,
I couldn't say. It was stitched on the breast of his jumpsuit, and it was all he said when I shook his hand. I met
him in the shade of the nearly three-hundred-kilometer-
diameter mirror, near the central girder anchoring it

deep in the bedrock of Io, coincidentally where the main
shaft of the argentite mine had its entrance. My descent
from the torus had required armed guards. "Are you
afraid they'll attack the labs?" I'd asked.

"They've never been seen on the surface, but we're
not taking any chances," the guard had told me.

Craig keyed his mike. "I'll show you the way down."
The glow of distant volcanoes reflected in his faceplate
obscured his features, but his voice was not a friendly one.
"Give me a minute."

I stood looking out across the landscape, spellbound
by the chaos that surrounded us. Craig ignored me, following the guide rope toward the entrance to the mine.
It was necessary to use the rope to keep your feet on
the ground. Reluctantly, I followed him, but my eyes
were on the scenery.

Volcanoes raged across Io's surface. Though the ground
here was stable, elsewhere it was riddled with massive
surface and subsurface lava flows. From space, Io was a
mottled yellow, orange, red, and black, her shading pri-
marily based on the colors that sulfur takes on at various
temperatures, as if she'd been photographed with a special heat sensitive film. Andy's first step in establishing
his mine would have been to understand these colors. It
would be crucial to know the layout of the lava flows
and calderas and lakes, to avoid the lava plumes and
fountains. A misstep here could mean instant death, a
plunge into silicate lava at temperatures as hot as 3,100
degrees Fahrenheit. Contrast this with Io's average surface temperature of -240, and the moon becomes something of an enigma for anyone not versed in geophysics.
The white stuff that crunched beneath my boots as I
reluctantly followed Craig toward the drop shaft of the
mine was sulfur dioxide frost, a frozen form of the gases
fueling the plasma torus Io left in her wake as she
looped around Jupiter.

Andy would have to understand the tidal effects of
Jupiter, too. A mass that large would alternately heat
and cool a rock the size of Io as it followed its elliptical
orbit. Io's surface would alternately rise and fall by as

much as 100 meters—a difficult proposition for any mining operation. We'd perfected floating shafts for just
such contingencies, though, back when we were teen-
agers working for Andy's dad.

Io's atmosphere had remained something of a mystery
until the first survey crews arrived to take core samples.
Io is surrounded by a cloud of sodium, potassium, and
oxygen. The sodium was inexplicable, as none had been
detected on the moon's surface. But the first core samples yielded heavy subsurface deposits of sodium chlo-
ride. It was the first indicator that there was more to Io
than met the eye. Later surveys revealed enormous
pockets of silver sulfide—argentite. It was the largest
source of argentite discovered in the solar system. But
for the cost of mining and transportation, the argentite
might have been viewed as an enormous source of
wealth. Ling Mei saw it as the raw material for a giant
mirror. And, of course, she had Andy to mine it for her.

My gaze followed where geysers on Io's horizon
ejected gas and yellow sulfuric dust hundreds of kilometers into space. Some of these settled back under Io's
minute gravity into elegant umbrella-shaped plumes
sixty to four hundred kilometers high. Other streams had
achieved escape velocity and arced out to form a yellow
trail encircling Jupiter, a cloudy brume in which approximately two trillion watts of power is generated, following
magnetic field lines down to Jupiter's surface where it
flashes as lightning in the atmosphere. Ling Mei had
tapped this power to remove the sulfuric acid from the
silver sulfide, leaving behind pure silver for her mirror.
The tube was as dangerous as it was beneficial, though.
Its radiation was deadly. It was unsafe to spend many
hours outside the shielded walls of the observatory—
one more reason for the miners that Andy had created.

Looking up, I could see that there were pockets of
gas trapped on the underside of the mirror, trickling
around the edges to form hazy rivers whose destination
was the stars.

I pointed. "You think she'd have thought about that
interfering with the mirror?"

Craig squinted against the sunlight reflecting off the windows of the torus. "You're asking the wrong person, buddy. Maybe she didn't realize there'd be outgassing from the mine. And none of us ever thought we'd have trouble closing the damn thing when we were done. Andy's toys were supposed to shut off when he was done with them. You ask me, Andy's mind hasn't been on the job."

"You're probably right about that," I said, realizing only afterward that I hadn't keyed my mike. But I was thinking that the gas on the underside of the mirror was more than would be bleeding from the mine. There were bound to be thousands of surface vents located beneath the observatory.

Craig wasn't paying any attention to me, though. We'd reached the drop shaft, and he was punching a keypad for access. When the number was in and a light on the panel flashed green, he set his hand on the handle and canted his head expectantly.

I indicated the hellish landscape. "I thought there were mountains?"

"Over the horizon," he replied. "You going to sight-see all day or do you want to go down?"

*　　*　　*

The air 13,800 feet up on Mauna Kea is so thin that Ling Mei and I would nearly pass out making love. That first time, I lay there with her long brown legs wrapped around my waist, too weak to even roll off her, having experienced the most incredibly draining orgasm of my life. She lay gasping for air for a long minute until finding the voice to tell me to get the hell off of her. We lay there, side by side, then, for hours watching the stars revolve around Polaris, our view only partially obscured by the bulk of one of the Keck observatories.

When she could move, Ling Mei reached out and touched my face, a gesture that had bothered me at first, but I had slowly become accustomed to it. It was her way of getting my attention, of connecting with the focus of her gaze. It was a trust issue with me; my father had once had a habit of touching the red welts he'd just left on my cheek. This was before Mars, before he'd become so busy that I rarely saw him, before I'd started spending all my time with Andy and his dad. But the connection remained in my mind: touch my face and it hurts.

"When the shafts are finished, you'll leave?" asked Ling Mei when she had my attention.

She was referring to the shafts Andy and I were drilling for the new observatory. The two Kecks in tandem had a resolving power equivalent to a single eighty-five-meter mirror, one of the largest on Earth at the time, but it was hardly enough power for Ling Mei and her astronomers. A new telescope was going in, but first they needed deep pilings to anchor it in the lava rock of Mauna Kea.

"We've already got a job lined up off world, Ling Mei." I rolled onto my side and stared at her, admiring the way our portable heater set her bare skin aglow. I couldn't imagine leaving her forever. "You could go with us."

She shook her head, her hair glistening with stars. I caught the smell of lilies, whether from her or from some hidden cranny in the rocks, I couldn't say.

"I don't want to leave you," I confessed.

"But you will," she countered. "You and Andy. Inseparable."

"This isn't about Andy."

"Well, it's certainly not about me. You could stay."

"I have to go where my business takes me."

"And *my* business keeps me here . . . with my telescope. One day I'll build a larger, more powerful one, maybe out there somewhere." She waved a delicate hand at the star-swathed sky. "Someplace that's not subject to the weather and ice up here." Just the night before, a track on one of the Kecks had been jammed with ice. It had taken four hours to free it, four hours in which the astronomers who'd rented time fumed at Ling Mei. "But I need a much larger mirror than has ever been built before, something in which I can look back to the dawn of time."

"Sounds like a time machine, not a telescope."

"A telescope *is* a time machine, Kev. When you look at the sun, you're seeing light that left the sun about eight minutes ago. The Keck can collect light that has traveled about twenty-five thousand years from the center of our galaxy—several thousand million years from the Big Bang. With a larger telescope, I hope to one day witness that epoch when the first stars and galaxies emerged from the primordial gloom."

"I thought there was a limit on what you could see. The Hubble Limit?"

She nodded. "The Hubble Constant defines the rate at which the universe and all its objects are moving apart. At some point in the distance cosmologists theorize that space-time is expanding faster than the speed of light. It's a wall beyond which we'll never be able to look with conventional methods."

"Ne plus ultra."

"What?"

"No farther," I explained. "It's what's written at the Pillars of Hercules, the classical symbol for that which lies at the edge of the known."

She rolled over and trailed her fingers across my chest. "That's where you'll always find me, then. Just the other side of those pillars. Pushing the edge out a bit farther."

"And when you can't go any farther?"

"Then I'll know everything there is to know, Kev. I'll have looked on God . . . whatever *she* is."

We laughed then and made love again as ice formed in a ring around our little circle of heat. When the sun reddened the horizon, we dressed and headed down to Waimea to join Andy for breakfast.

Andy was sullen and withdrawn, irritated that I had been up on the mountain all night when there was work to be done today. Ling Mei took it upon herself to cheer him up. She sat on his lap and nibbled at his ear. It was all in fun. We laughed about threesomes and Ling Mei sandwiches. We were crude and naughty. I didn't see the undercurrents. I didn't see Andy's fear that I might actually abandon our business to remain in Hawaii with Ling Mei. I didn't see Ling Mei's realization that the only way to have me forever was to get rid of Andy. I didn't see how their two strategies would bring them together, that I would actually become the odd man out. It built slowly. Ling Mei would mention Andy more and more on those long nights on the mountain. Andy would ask about Ling Mei more and more during the days.

I was blind.

When I walked in on them in the shower together, having returned early after being stood up by a new client, I was staggered. Both their plans to drive me from the other worked. How was I to know, however, that they would wind up staying together?

*   *   *

The elevator dropped for a full two minutes. Knowing its rate of descent (I had, after all, installed hundreds of them), I knew we'd descended more than a thousand meters. When we hit bottom, I used the handrails to bring my feet back down to the ground. Craig opened a storage compartment, removed a zero-recoil shotgun, and offered it to me.

"No thanks."

"Three men died in here," he said.

"I know. You carry the gun if it makes you feel any better."

He laughed. "I'm not going with you. You're on your own from here. I'll send the elevator back down for you, but I'll be topside."

He jacked a round into the gun, pointed it at the door, and set his back to the wall of the elevator with his hip braced under the rail. "Open the door whenever you're ready, partner."

In the pocket on my right thigh was the transmitter Ling Mei had given me. I took it out, switched it on, and showed it to Craig.

"Uh-huh. You think those five dead men didn't have those?" he asked.

"You saying they don't work?"

"I'm saying that I'm not taking any chances," he said, echoing the sentiment of the guards who'd brought me to the surface.

I put the transmitter back in my pocket, but left it switched on. I hit the elevator button and the doors hissed back. The light of the elevator revealed ten meters of dark corridor. The walls were dark porous rock, streaked with yellow sulfuric dust. More dust swirled up from the floor, disturbed by the doors and the pressure differential. The mine possessed its own atmosphere.

"Lights?" I asked.

"Motion sensor activated," he replied. "You move into the corridor, they'll come on. Fifty meters in, you'll come to our main staging area. The computers there will give you the layout of the mine shafts and anything else you want to know. Plenty of equipment there for whatever it is you think you're going to do." His voice was heavy with sarcasm.

"I won't be long. Just want to get a feel for the place."

He shrugged. "Makes no difference to me. The *Bonaventure* leaves tomorrow . . . I plan to be on her. Far as I'm concerned, this job's over. You sure you don't want this gun?"

"Did it help the others?"

"No."

"Then I'll pass." I stepped from the elevator to the rocky floor of the cavern, using the rail just outside to steady myself. Lights for thirty meters came on. The elevator doors closed behind me, and I heard the motor cycling Craig back up to the surface without so much as good-bye.

There's a silence to a mine that's ethereal. A calming that comes from the weight of all that rock surrounding you. The weight of a grave. The disarming quiet of arrested time. I put one foot in front of the other, started the long walk to the staging area and beyond. Somewhere up ahead . . . Andy's monsters would be waiting.

                    *   *   *

I stared out the viewport at Io and the backdrop of
Jupiter below, trying not to notice the reflection of Ling
Mei as she studied my own reflection in the glass.

"What will you do?" she finally asked.

"I don't know. I have to see them first. Are you certain they have to be destroyed?"

"Destroyed. Removed. It doesn't matter. The law says
we can't leave them on the surface if they're not indige-
nous to Io. You know what happened to Calisto."

The nightmare on Calisto had involved self-replicating
robots, though, not biological entities. Andy's genetic
faux pas might be a lot harder to fix. The law said humans were the only entities allowed a permanent footing
on another planet or moon, though. You couldn't leave
robots running amok on Calisto any more than you
could raise ostriches on the Moon . . . or leave Andy's
miners in Io's mine.

"It's not like there's another life-form down there to
worry about," I said.

"Doesn't matter. Europa has shown them how easy it
is to overlook the possibilities. Perhaps there's an eco-
system yet to be discovered on Io—or yet to be developed. Andy's miners could upset the balance." She
touched my shoulder. "We planned for all of this."

"The gland Andy talked about?"

"Yes. The gland is receptive to a unique frequency. It
releases an enzyme into their system. Their cells are subject to massive failure when subjected to the enzyme."

"A meltdown."

"It's quick and relatively painless."

"Doesn't sound like it."

"You're anthropomorphizing them, Kev."

"No. I'm acknowledging a responsibility to something
the two of you created. You can't just create life when
money gets tight and then shut it off when the job's
done. They mined the argentite from which you ex-
tracted the silver for your mirror and now you're done
with them.

"But I don't think they're done with you."

We were quiet for some time then, each lost in our own thoughts, each uncertain how to proceed with the other, until finally I asked her, "What do you hope to see in your mirror, Ling Mei?"

"I hope to answer my questions on the origin, scale, and ultimate fate of the universe. The nature of its contents. The prevalence of other worlds. The potential for kindred consciousness. These are the things that all astronomers look for, Kev."

"You once told me that your telescopes were windows into the past."

"They are."

"Perhaps," I speculated, "the past is best left buried. Perhaps there are no perfect mirrors and what looks back at you is never what you wanted to find."

*   *   *

The wide, smooth-walled caverns had clearly been formed with standard drilling equipment, the sort of machines Andy and I had designed and perfected for work in this sort of substrata. But there were many side passages that had been carved by something else. Something smaller and with what at first appeared to be a haphazard sense of direction. Clearly, Andy's miners had taken to following the argentite veins, removing as little extraneous material as necessary. It was precision mining as I'd never seen it practiced before. It was beautiful in its simplicity, but incredibly dangerous. With the tidal shifting of all these passages, only the shored-up corridors made by the big equipment could be relied upon. The smaller side passages could collapse and close without warning, as subject to change as natural gaps in the rock.

I waited in the staging area, a large cavern crowded with shrouded equipment, crated supplies, and computers in dust-proof enclosures. Everything was covered with sulfur dust. I noticed that the pale blue of my suit had taken on green-yellow highlights as dust accumulated in the folds and joints. The edges of my faceplate were tinged sepia. The fingers of my gloves were permanently brown.

I waited, knowing the miners would come to me.

They came first as shadows: spindly, multilegged, insectlike shapes that flitted and rippled across the cavern, elongated by the spotlights, made more terrifying by the irregular surface of the walls. My hands were shaking and my knees had gone weak. I needed somewhere to sit. Why was I here? Because Andy had asked me? Or because even after all these years I couldn't disappoint Ling Mei Chow? The Io observatory was her life's work. And I couldn't deny that a part of me still loved her.

The miners stood three meters high. Their carapaces were the color of the sulfur that they ingested to survive. What better life-form to engineer for Io than one which fed on sulfur, breathed the sulfur dioxide gas of the caverns? Cells can be engineered to burn sulfur compounds. The energy derived from this oxidation can then be directed toward the splitting of carbon dioxide into separate carbon and oxygen atoms. This is the opposite of oxidation: reduction. Using a process called carbon fixation, the organism would then link the carbon atoms to form carbohydrates and other materials that go into building cell walls and organelles. The organism would liberate oxygen as a byproduct.

Their six legs were long, triple-jointed, and black as iron. They'd have to be dense and powerful, designed for digging through rock. Forward of the legs, where the head of the animal joined the body, were two double-jointed gripping limbs equipped with three-clawed hands. They were an intentionally crude design, capable of working with man-made tools, but more suited to digging. The head was eyeless. Instead of sight, they relied on a steady subsonic hum and directed shrieks emitted by a melon-shaped growth. The same organ probably received the echoes from this signal, giving the miner a three-dimensional map of its environment, accurate with or without light. In the vacuum on the moon's surface, they'd be unable to communicate, but the mines were flooded with sulfur dioxide gas and, though constantly venting, under pressure from the volcanic activity beneath the surface.

As the first one approached me, I saw that its thorax was damaged. There was a ragged, half-healed incision, rimmed with black necrotic tissue. As a second miner approached, I saw the same wound repeated, and it dawned on me why Andy's transmitter was useless.

The miners had located the glands and removed them from their bodies.

I showed them empty hands, praying they would understand the gesture. Six of them surrounded me. Andy had confessed to creating an even dozen of them. They'd lost half their number before figuring out the glands.

I turned slowly, studying them all, hoping for some sign of leadership from one of them. There was nothing. Except for slight variations in coloring, in the pattern of sulfur dust spread across their carapaces, each was indecipherable from the next.

I keyed my mike for broadcast mode.

"Can you understand me?"

One of the miners extended a claw to the nearest wall and scratched a long jagged checkmark: ✔

"I mean you no harm."

No response. The gauges in my suit registered the overlapping vibrations of their sonic probes. They were studying me. Waiting for a threatening move. I had no doubt that if I made one, they'd cave in my chest the way they had done Andy's. They'd killed three men already. What was one more to them? Claws that had mined the heart of Io would make short work of flesh.

"Do you understand that your job here is finished?"

Another checkmark.

"And that you can't stay?"

An ✗ carved so deep that chips of rock crumbled away from the jagged edges.

I pointed toward the surface. "They want to shut you off."

✗

"You understand it'll only be a matter of time before

some military presence is brought in. Men have died. Resistance can only end in your destruction."

No response.

"If I could arrange a compromise by which you could remain here unmolested, would you be willing to continue working the mine?"

A moment's hesitation. I could only guess at the discussion Dopplering back and forth among the six of them. Could I be trusted? Did they want to trade their lives for servitude? And perhaps they were even smart enough to understand the questions I was asking myself. The argentite had been mined for its silver content. What little remained was hardly worth continuing the operation. That left sulfur compounds, and none were valuable enough to warrant mining and transporting off the moon. What remained on Io that was worth their lives? I was hoping I'd already stumbled upon the answer to that.

The nearest miner reached out with a forelimb and hooked a claw in the seal where my helmet joined my suit. The gesture was obvious. With a simple twist, the suit could be ruptured and I would die trying to breathe sulfur dioxide. But what did it mean by the gesture? Why threaten me now?

With its other claw, the miner scratched a long line in the wall, then two other lines at its end to form an arrow. They stepped back, leaving me an exit in the direction of the arrow.

So . . . they had reasons of their own for meeting with me.

"You want to show me something?"

✔

*   *   *

There were two shafts, smooth enough to have been drilled by the heavy equipment, but smaller, which made it obvious that the miners themselves had tunneled them. Within each shaft sat one of Andy's drone vehicles, the wheels replaced with crude skids. To the rear of each

vehicle was welded enough propellent to put the damn
thing into orbit, complete with a hastily rigged ignition
system. I tried to peer around the vehicles, to look down
the length of the shaft, but the machinery obstructed
the view.

"I don't understand," I told them.

One of them set a claw against the wall, scratched a
flat disk and a torus. Beneath that, it drew an elliptical
shape: Io. Then it drew the tunnel . . . then a line from
one to the other.

"They're missiles."

✔

I swallowed. If one of those vehicles was to punch
through Ling Mei's observatory . . . "What are your
demands?" I asked.

It cocked its head.

"What do you want?"

The miner's claw gouged a deep circle around the
shape of Io.

*   *   *

Craig was waiting for me on the surface. "Chow has
been calling for you."

Was she worried for her observatory or worried about
me? I found myself wanting to believe in the latter.

Craig must have seen some of this on my face. He
shook his head.

"Andy Muldoon died an hour ago."

*   *   *

Before boarding the *Bonaventure,* I built Andy a sleek
black coffin. I set his face behind a panel of clear plexi-
steel, so that he would forever look out on the stars we'd
dreamed of as boys. I kissed his forehead before sealing
him in, loving him as much as I'd hated him all those
years for having destroyed what we were to one another.
I wanted to see the boy who'd befriended me on Mars,
the boy whose family had become a refuge from my own

troubled relationship with my father. But all I could find
in his face were the hard lines of a man who'd spent
most of his life in one mine or another. Life with Ling
Mei Chow had left nothing soft in him, nothing of the
boy I had known.

Craig helped me jettison Andy with what I hoped was
enough velocity to escape the pull of Jupiter. Ling Mei
stood by and watched, her eyes sad, but dry. She was
already thinking about tomorrow. Such had always been
her way. I doubt she understood how much either of us
had loved her. I could only wish, in hindsight, that Andy
and I had loved each other more.

I had explained the situation below to Ling Mei.

"I won't allow my observatory to be blackmailed!"
she had fumed.

"They want to live, Ling Mei, just as we all do. What
you don't understand is that you need them."

"What? Why do I need them? The mirror's finished.
I don't need the mine."

"How much do you think you'll see through a yellow haze?"

"We'll seal the mine. Andy had all this worked out."

"Andy wasn't thinking clearly. The mine is just a small
part of the venting going on below your observatory.
You've got a sixty-four-thousand-square-kilometer dish
out there, Ling Mei. That's sixty-four thousand square
kilometers of Io sitting beneath it, sixty-four thousand
square kilometers of shifting surface and volcanic activity and lava vents. There's only one way you can keep
all of that sealed and directed away from your dish.

"You need one hell of a permanent mining crew, one
that's not subject to the radiation of Io's plasma tube,
one that can live and breathe sulfur dioxide, one that
will make Io a home. It's in their own best interests to
seal their underground environment. Without an atmosphere, they're blind."

"But the law . . ."

"The law does not apply to a permanent maintenance
facility, which you obviously need. You might have some
trouble getting approval, but I know you, Ling Mei.

You'll get it. You won't let a little political squabbling stop you from seeing your dream fulfilled."

"But they've killed . . ."

"An unfortunate accident, Ling Mei. You'll make sure that it's seen that way."

"I suppose it could be arranged."

"And you'll need more of them."

"What?"

"It's sixty-four thousand square kilometers, Ling Mei. It's going to take an army of those things. They'll shape Io for you, make it compatible with your observatory."

"But Andy engineered them to be sterile."

"Just leave that to them. They understand enough to remove your shutoff gland. They'll take care of this problem, too. All I'm suggesting is that you allow it to happen. It's in your best interests."

She stepped forward, touched my face with tentative fingers. I didn't pull back; it was as if her touch didn't even register.

I shook my head. "No."

"You didn't even let me ask."

"Didn't need to."

*   *   *

As the *Bonaventure* slipped out of orbit around Jupiter, the glare of Ling Mei's unblinking eyes played along the ship's flank, briefly blinding me there in the lounge. I took a moment to rub the spots from my own eyes. When I was done, the view had shifted, and what lay before me was nothing but an open sea of stars.

Let others look into the past in search of universal origins and answers.

I will look ahead, where the only thing shining back at me is the mirror of my soul.

Tomorrow beckons.

IN FINNEGAN'S WAKE

by Jack C. Haldeman II

*Jack C. Haldeman II (1941–2002) was the author of
seven novels and more than one hundred and fifty
shorter works. His last major writing project was the
novel* Ghost Dance, *a collaboration with Jack Dann,
the sequel to their novel* High Steel. *His other novels
include* There Is No Darkness, *written with brother
Joe Haldeman;* The Fall of Winter; *and* Bill, the Galactic Hero on the Planet of Zombie Vampires,
coauthored with Harry Harrison.

*He studied biology and environmental engineering,
and received a bachelor of science degree in life science
from Johns Hopkins University in Baltimore, Mary-
land. Jack worked at the University of Florida as Coor-
dinator of Computer Applications for the Institute of
Food and Agricultural Sciences.*

THERE was no way that Spacer John was going to
make it. Nine planets in nine days. And the way his
luck had been running, he'd need a miracle just to break
out of Mercury's orbit.

Things looked grim indeed.

He sipped his drink slowly. It was the specialty of the
house, a fuming concoction called Molten Lava. It had
a kick, if you liked burning sensations. All the drinks in
the Hot Spot either fumed, sputtered, bubbled, or

boiled. It was just another theme bar in just another orbiting spaceport.

This particular spaceport, however, which hung in the perpetual shadow on Mercury, was special. It was the official starting point for the Finnegan Prize. Ten million credits for the first person to hit all nine planets in nine days.

People had been trying for decades to take the old geezer's prize, but only Spider, rest his soul, had come close. A slight miscalculation had pancaked his ship into Naiad, the innermost moon of Neptune. Nine years later it was still glowing like a miniature star. Spider's Delphi power plant had started some sort of a chain reaction on the moon's surface. Most scientists estimated it would burn itself out in a thousand years or so. Others predicted it would reach critical mass and Neptune would have a new set of rings.

Either way, it came out the same. John's old friend was dead. And the Finnegan still hadn't been won.

Spacer John had a plan to win the Finnegan. What he didn't have was a clue.

A clue that is, about how to score a ship powerful enough to take him to Pluto in nine days. He'd arrived at the Hot Spot piloting a two-week unlimited mileage rental from Earth, figuring something would come to him. So far nothing had. The sponsors were friendly enough to him, but when it came down to scoring a ride, they backed off quickly.

He was pretty much tapped out. To tell the truth, if all of his creditors and ex-wives got together and pooled their various claims on his sorry assets, he'd be wiped out ten times over. Only some fancy financial footwork kept his head above water and his unicard green. Not gold, not platinum, but green. The lowest shade, if the truth be told. Not good for much except renting clunkers like the one that he'd piloted here.

Spacer John was a born pilot. It was all he'd ever wanted to be. He'd grown up on Mars in the Schiaparelli Dome in the shadow of the largest spaceport on the planet. As a child, he watched the rockets take off to far and distant places. More than anything he wanted to leave, to sit at the controls of a real spacecraft. Instead, he made a nuisance of himself by driving anything he could get his hands on, and driving it fast.

When he was seventeen, he plowed the family dune-skipper into a canyon wall while racing a neighbor. It was his third accident that year. Two weeks later a friend of his father's offered him a job with his mining company in the asteroid belt. He left happily and his parents were not all that upset to see him go.

Life out in the Belt was loose and rugged. That suited John just fine. The rules and regulations that had surrounded him on Mars were practically nonexistent out there. All that counted was moving the minerals and moving them quickly.

As he'd hoped, John was able to get close to the pilots. He spent all his spare time with them, soaking up everything. They took him under their wing, a kind of mascot at first. As a favor to the kid, they let him take the controls of a tug when he was eighteen. By the time he was twenty, he was a pilot, and a damn good one.

Money drove everything in the Belt, and time was money. John was very fast. That counted for a lot.

He quickly moved from the tugs to the skimmers, fast one-seater vehicles used to ship critical parts from one place to another. Skimmer pilots always tried to outdo each other. John was the best. The fastest in a very fast crowd.

He left the Belt when United Transport hired him as a courier pilot. John mostly ran the inner planets, sometimes carrying nothing but hard copy between corporate offices on Earth and Mars. On weekends he raced.

First it was hobby racing. You could almost always find a race somewhere on any given weekend. The sport was extremely popular, and there were local circuits everywhere. John bought a secondhand skimmer and had it converted to racing specs. He drove that skimmer with a passion. John had a knack of knowing just how far to push. He'd go right to the edge, but not beyond. He won a lot of races and had a lot of fans.

United Transport eventually realized that John would be more valuable to them as a public relations tool than as a courier. They started sponsoring him, and he quickly moved up from the small races to the big time.

The professionals raced in a regular series of events run every four to six weeks. John did well from the very beginning. He was Rookie of the Year right out of the box, and maintained that high standard from then on. He won a lot of races, lost some, but always handled his equipment well. Above all, though, he kept his eye on the Finnegan. Three times he tried it, but he never really came close.

The rest of his racing career was going great. United Transport was happy with him, and he'd built a loyal following of fans. Other pilots respected him. Life was good.

Then Ganymede happened.

Mechanical failure? Pilot error? It was never officially determined.

United Transport dropped him. When you lose a ship that cost that much, the owners only remember who was at the controls.

He was a freelance pilot now, catching whatever work he could. He raced when he was able to, which was not often.

Another Molten Lava slid out of the rotator in front of him. "I didn't order this," he said.

The holo bartender shimmered and smiled in front of him. "No problemo, John," said the bartender, who, thanks to the way John had programmed his unicard, looked exactly like every other bartender that he ever saw in places like this. "Compliments of the lady in booth three."

John swiveled his barstool and scanned the crowded bar. A young woman half his age caught his eye and waved. He walked over to her, conveniently forgetting the telling fact that he had met each of his ex-wives in bars exactly like this one.

"Thanks for the drink," he said, settling down across from her. "Spacer John."

"I know who you are, John," she said. "I'm Spider's daughter."

John nearly spilled his drink. "No," he said. "No way. You can't be little Andrea."

"I'm not so little anymore." She was a grown woman, middle twenties, red hair, green eyes.

"That's pretty obvious. You must have been about seven when I last saw you."

"Thirteen," she said with a sad smile. "I remember you and Dad sitting in the kitchen at our old place in Marsdome Three, planning strategy for the Finnegan, kidding each other. It was a happy visit."

John smiled. "Yes, I remember."

"He always thought you would beat him."

"Spider was a better pilot."

"Yes, but you were luckier. He always said luck would win out."

"And *I* always thought—"

Someone spilled a drink on his shoulder. It foamed and bubbled, but stopped just short of burning through his jacket. John looked up and groaned. It was Will Perry—not his favorite person.

"Spacer John." Perry was tall and solidly built, with the massive upper body of a professional fireball player. "I thought you were dead. Heard you were odd man out in a romantic triangle gone south. Something involving firearms was the word going around."

"No such luck." John slid across the seat away from the man, wiping his shoulder with a napkin. "Andrea, this is Will Perry."

Perry nodded vaguely in Andrea's direction and leaned over to continue talking to John. "Got me a great sponsor for the Finnegan. TruTech Mining. Company owns half of the processing plants in the Belt. Money's no object with them. They set me up in a Mark IV chassis with a Dynoblast converter."

He took a hit from his drink. Foam bubbled in his mustache. "Who's footing *your* bills, John?"

"I'm currently weighing several offers."

Perry snorted. "No sponsor? That's a kick." He stood up "Just as well, though. Save your money. The Finnegan's as good as mine."

"A Dynoblast," said John, shaking his head as Perry walked away. "Damn."

"It couldn't happen to a bigger jerk," said Andrea.

"Pardon? You know him?"

"I've never met him in person, but Dad spoke about him. He couldn't stand the guy. He cheats."

"What?"

"He used an oversized mass driver in the Eight Ball Run. Switched the plates back before inspection."

"You're kidding me!" Will had made his reputation winning that Eight Ball.

"Rumor has it that he's scammed the beacons for the Finnegan."

"That can't be done," said John. The beacons, which sent out the time and date signals used in the Finnegan, were in tight orbits around each planet. They had extremely low power transmitters. You had to be practically sitting on one to pick up the signal. Accuracy on the approaches was one of the main points of the Finnegan. "It's impossible to scam the beacons."

Andrea just laughed. "The word in the pits is that he can pick up a signal over a thousand clicks from the beacon."

"What pits?" asked John.

"I've been working as a mechanic since Dad died. Local stuff around Mars. Mechanics like to talk, especially gossip, and I'm a good listener. I'm also a pretty good mechanic."

"I don't doubt that," said John. "You've clearly got the genes."

"And you clearly need a mechanic."

"What I need is a ship and a sponsor." John sighed and looked around the bar. There were lots of familiar faces. The top pilots were gathered. Although the Finnegan could be won at any time, the relative positions of the planets made a big difference. This was a particularly favorable arrangement. They weren't lined up like dominoes, but it wasn't going to get any better for a good many years.

"You're here," said Andrea, "So you must have a ship. Unless you came in a shuttle, that is."

They both grinned at that. Pilots hated shuttles. They hated *anything* they weren't flying themselves, but the shuttles were the worst—plodding tin cans.

"I've got a rental Westfield. Eight years old."

"Not too bad."

"I started out with a twelve-year-old Fairfax I rented from Spaceways when I left Earth. It was all I could afford. Piece of junk died on me. I had to be tractored into MarsPort 2. After the tow, I discovered Spaceways would give me a free upgrade if I had trouble. Some new customer satisfaction thing. I hadn't expected that, but I wasn't going to argue. That's how I ended up with the Westfield."

"It's an okay ship if you're taking the family out for the weekend, but it's hardly built for speed."

"I wasn't intending to try the run in a Westfield."

"You got anything better? You see any sponsors breaking down doors to sign you up? After Ganymede, I don't expect you're on the top of anybody's list."

The Mars to Ganymede Harrison Memorial was run every five years, commemorating a medical flight by the legendary Chuck Harrison more than seventy-five years ago that had saved an entire research team on Jupiter's moon. It was a solo run. It had been his last run with a sponsor.

"That wasn't my fault. The shields—"

"I know all about it. I've been keeping my eye on you."

"That's flattering, but—"

"You do pretty good as an independent. You do the best you can with the equipment you've got. You're consistent, too, usually finishing in the top ten, sometimes in the top five. I like that in a partner."

"I finished third in the Phobos to Europa dash last year."

"That's up with the big boys."

"I *am* one of the big boys."

"With a consistent sponsor you are. Without one, you'll always be struggling. We need a big win."

"Wait a minute!"

"What?"

"What's this *we* stuff? And did you say *partner?*"

"For a fast pilot, you're slow on the uptake."

"What exactly do you mean by partner?"

Andrea stood up. "Let's take a look at the Westfield."

It was impossible to just walk out of the bar, as crowded as it was with pilots. They stopped every few steps to exchange greetings with people they knew. John was pleased to see that Fast Eddie was giving the Finnegan another try. Fast Eddie had been an old geezer when John was just starting out and he hadn't gotten any younger. But he was a sharp pilot and one of the nicest guys on the circuit.

The Hawk, however, was a royal pain. He was also blocking their way out the door.

"And here's a pilot some of you might remember," droned the Hawk, who insisted on wearing an old-fashioned livecam. "Spacer John. No, we haven't seen a whole lot of this man lately. Sponsor trouble is the word out on the street. John, do you have anything to say to my audience?"

"No."

"Well, you sure haven't shown us much since Ganymede either."

"Give the guy a break, Hawk," snapped Andrea. "He was third in the Phobos to Europa dash last year."

The Hawk turned so the livecam was pointed at Andrea. He paused a moment while the face recognition software scanned the woman and whispered in his ear.

"And here we have the daughter of the late Spider Murphy. Spider was killed attempting the Finnegan nine years ago. Tell me, Andrea, what does it feel like to be the daughter of a famous dead guy?"

John shoved the Hawk out of the way, and they headed for the docking level.

The Westfield was dwarfed by the other ships docked

around it. Its cheerful yellow paint job was no match for the splashy holographic corporate logos on the sides of the racers.

Andrea didn't waste any time when they got to the cramped control room. "I want to check something," she said. "Crank up the auxiliary power. And let me have a look at the rental contract."

"Wait a minute," said John, passing her the contract. "What's this all about?"

"We're going to win the Finnegan," she said.

"You can't be serious."

"I want this as much as you do. You just don't understand it yet. With you, this is all about the race, the prestige, the challenge, the money. My story's simpler. I want to win this one for my dad. Warm up the auxiliaries, will you?"

John flicked two switches and something started humming deep in the ship. "Why us?"

"You're a damn good pilot. I've spent my life learning how to tweak the most out of these machines. We'll make a great team." She folded up the rental contract and passed it back to John. "Move over," she said.

Confused, John turned over the pilot's seat to the woman. "But we can't do this in a Westfield," he said. "Not enough power."

"I never said we would." She reached for the stick and rotated it slightly. The smooth humming of the auxiliaries was replaced by a harsh grinding noise.

"What the hell are you doing?"

"Rotating the ship ten degrees."

"You can't do that! We're docked. The tractor is holding us solid."

"I know," she grinned. Two sharp reports rang out, echoing against the metal walls. The auxiliaries whined free for a couple of seconds and then shut down with an uneven clanking noise.

"I can't believe it. You've trashed the ship."

"Burned gyros, unless I miss my guess. I suppose we'll have to drop by our friendly local Spaceways office. It's upgrade time."

John could not believe it, but with Andrea doing the talking they managed to upgrade to a class III Needlenose. The clerk was most apologetic. Gyros hardly ever failed. And two at the same time? While docked? The man was so chagrined he gave them a two-class upgrade instead of the advertised one-class.

Spacer John was a happy camper. The Needlenose was the workhorse of the courier trade and he knew it like the back of his hand. He could make this baby sing.

Andrea put on her tool vest and disappeared for a couple of hours. "I think you'll like these numbers," she said when she returned.

"Give me the big picture first," said John.

"Well, obviously I had to locate and bypass all the so-called safety features Spaceway puts on its rental units—governors, rev limiters, and so forth. That brought it back to spec. Next I worked on the plasma drive and the fusion components. The default settings for these are for longevity, and frankly I don't care a whole lot about what happens to this bucket after it's lasted the nine days we need. I stepped things up a tad. Well, a bit more than a tad, to be honest."

"I'm impressed."

"Don't be. That just takes us to where the other pilots are."

"So the edge is my skill?"

Andrea laughed. "I'm definitely counting on your skill. That and a little help from my friends."

"How's that?"

"A couple months ago a friend of mine cracked a beta version of the next generation Maxwell software. It's highly classified government stuff, state of the art. I plugged the revised Needlenose specs into it and flashed the mainframe. Check it out for yourself."

John palmed the display to life, choosing the raw numbers option rather than the simplified icon representation. He stared at it for a few seconds, sorting through the streaming numbers.

"Damn," he said softly. "Now I'm *really* impressed."

The Maxwell software was many things, among them a command level shell. Properly installed, it provided a universal interface and control system to any ship. Pilots would be lost without the Maxwell, forced to train for months every time they shifted to a new ride. Below the top level displays the Maxwell held every piece of information on the ship and its drive system, including tolerances and maximum stress points. John nodded, taking it all in, getting a feel for the Needlenose's potential. Hell of a ship, all tweaked up this way.

John pulled his preference disk out of the pouch on his hip and slid it into the reader below the display. He selected race mode and felt the chair shift position to his favorite driving configuration.

All pilots had a personal preference disk, or PPD. It meshed with the Maxwell and carried all kinds of information: how many Gs he could take and for how long, how deep he was willing to dive into a gravity well, how far he would push the equipment under a variety of conditions. He had programmed several modes to select from, including economy, courier, "hurry-up" courier, and race mode.

"How's your G-load tolerance?" he asked, fingers dancing over the touch-screen.

"I can take anything you can," she said. "My G-suit is charged and ready to go."

John touched in a rough itinerary, Mercury to Pluto. Race mode at the extreme setting. He updated the beacon positions by flashing Central.

"This is by far the best I've seen," he said. "But we're still short."

"How short?"

"This predicted scenario comes out to a hair over eleven days. Not good enough."

"What did you dial in for the beacon approaches?"

"The standard. Come to a screaming near-halt, pick up the signal and then blasting away."

"What if we do a full-bore flyby?"

"You're kidding."

"Work out the numbers."

"Let's see. Impossible to do on the Mars or Earth beacons. Too much traffic to account for." John was muttering to himself. "The rest are doable, though, except, of course, for Pluto. Pluto's dance with Charon gives the beacon a funny spin. Saturn will be dicey. The beacon's inside the innermost ring. That's going to be a fun ride."

"So what do you come up with?"

"Give me a second." His fingers were a blur. "Ten days, two hours."

"So we shave the two hours."

"How?"

"You're the pilot. Pick your spot."

John nodded. His heart skipped. This could happen.

"How sure are you of the Maxwell beta?"

"It tests out solid. Looks good on paper."

"On paper?"

"It's a beta. It's never actually been run, of course."

"Of course."

"So what do we do?" she asked.

"We leave in the morning. Get a good night's sleep. You'll need it."

There was vast amusement about John's and Andrea's rental being entered in the Finnegan, but there were no rules against it. There were few rules at all. You could run anything you wanted. You could even change ships if you desired. All that mattered was the log that collected the time/date stamps. Anything under ten days, zero minutes would take the prize.

Spaceways, however, would probably have had serious objections about this particular use of one of its rentals— had it known in time. Fortunately, it didn't. The same clerk that had given them the upgrade was far too busy to realize what was happening. He was dealing with a crowd of angry mechanics with complicated problems. All the mechanics were Andrea's friends.

When the clerk found out, it was too late to stop them. The corporate office, upon hearing from the clerk, took an unexpected slant. Since they clearly couldn't do anything about it, they'd play it to the hilt for publicity purposes. If he wrecked the ship, they'd sue him, or his estate, as the case would probably be. On the remote chance he could actually win this thing, they'd treat him like a hero. No amount of money could buy press like that.

Meanwhile Andrea and John had their hands full. Immediately upon receiving the transmitted time/date stamp from Mercury, they threw up full shields and blasted into the sun's gravity well using a trajectory calculated to take full advantage of the slingshot effect to propel them toward Venus.

It was a rough, rough ride. Probably the worst they would have to face. The shields covered the viewports and in the flickering, shifting darkness the control room seemed smaller than ever. The phase-shift converter, which displayed a large portion of the G-forces, was maxing out. If it went, that would be the whole ball of wax. Andrea couldn't leave her gel-packed chair for repairs as long as they were in the dive.

"I'm reading seven Gs inside the suit," said John. His voice was ragged with the pressure and the plummeting. "Occasional peaks up to eight point two. How you doing?"

"A walk in the park," she lied.

"We're really picking up speed, though."

"Tell me about it," she gasped.

At a preprogrammed point on the far side of the sun the engines stepped up to 110 percent. It gave them a real kick.

"Ten Gs. Eleven. This is it."

Andrea was having difficulty breathing. Pain burned across her chest.

"Twelve!"

Her peripheral vision was starting to flicker and blur. She was on the edge of blacking out.

Then, suddenly, it receded.

"We made it," gasped John. "We're free."

"I'm not sure. What kind of Gs are we reading?"

"On the hull or on us?"

"On us. The rest of the ship will hold together or not."

"Seven Gs."

"Too high. We can't take that for nine days. Can you

tweak the phase-shift converter using the Maxwell? We need to get the relative numbers down."

"Okay, I'll give it a try." John was busy at the screen for a few minutes. "I can get it down, but only for a few minutes. It doesn't want to hold calibration. Something's out of whack."

"So take it down. I'll go work on it."

Andrea could tell when John made the adjustment. The force dropped to about three Gs. She felt light as a feather. Relatively speaking.

"I should be able to hold this for about ten minutes," John said. "Nothing past that, though."

"That's plenty of time," she said, hoping that was true.

Andrea unstrapped herself from the gel-chair, moving slowly and carefully toward the rear of the ship. Along the way she picked up the tools she thought she might need.

Since almost everything aboard the ship was considered by Spaceways to be non-user-repairable, she had several plates and grids to remove before she got to the phase-shift converter. A quick visual inspection showed nothing of note. She would have loved a loose wire or something, but no such luck. She clipped a meter to various patch points and studied the readings.

"Four more minutes," shouted John. "I can't get it to hold."

The calibration system itself checked out okay. There had to be something else wrong, something else in the system.

"Two minutes. I'm sorry. We're losing it."

Something else. Hurry. Something related. With the end of her probe, Andrea tapped a rheostat. It rocked back and forth in its socket. Of course! That was it. The rheostat wasn't supplying clean voltage to the calibration system. She tightened it down and adjusted the settings.

"Yikes," yelled John. "Whatever you did worked. Everything is stable."

Andrea closed things down and returned to her chair.

"Good job," John said. "I've isolated the cabin and shunted a large part of the forces to the hull. At this rate of acceleration, we should only be pulling relative three Gs in our chairs."

"I can handle that."

"With the occasional peak, of course."

"Of course," she said, and closed her eyes.

After all their concern, the first flyby went smoothly. Venus was a mottled sulfurous ball off to the left when the chime announced that they had acquired the time/date stamp. The swing around the planet was a little tight, but nothing like what they had been through.

The main thing was that John had accurately calculated the beacon's position. If they had been too far away, they wouldn't have picked up the signal and it would all be over. If they had to turn back and catch a missed beacon, they'd never make it.

They slept in shifts. John punched in his calculations over and over again, frowning a lot. "Take a look at this," he said finally. "Let me know what you think."

"Just explain it to me." It hurt to lean over far enough to see his display.

"Okay. Earth is too crowded for a full-bore flyby. I propose we hit the retros hard right inside the Moon to slow us down just enough to get a fix on current conditions, get a quick read, and hit the throttle."

"It's a plan."

"We'll still be going pretty fast, though, considering the clutter."

"Nobody said this was going to be easy."

John nodded and smiled. It wasn't easy, and there were only a handful of people who could even attempt it. He was walking the edge, and it felt great.

They didn't really have a separate retro system. It was just a matter of rotating the ship 180 degrees. This time the gyros held.

The retro burn was crushing, and he almost blacked out. He'd called it a little too close. John took about ten seconds to scope out the situation and another three seconds to punch in the coordinates. The ship swung back around, and he slammed down hard on the throttle.

The chime of the time/date stamp was simultaneously

accompanied by a buzzer and a flashing red light over John's display.

"What's all that?" asked Andrea as they dove down into Earth's gravity well.

"The light was a proximity alarm," John said, fighting the controls. "I got just a little too close to the beacon. We almost bought ourselves an expensive hood ornament."

"And the buzzer?"

"Speeding ticket."

Andrea chuckled.

"No problem," said John. "If we win, I'll just take the fine out of petty cash. If we don't make it, it's just one more creditor trying to get blood out of a very dry turnip."

When they left Earth, John took his turn at sleep.

Mars presented much the same logistic problems as Earth. Things were pretty crowded in orbit. John was getting worried about their times, and proposed a different solution.

"We both know Mars, and I'm proposing that we come in hot with the proximity alarms at full range. If I can get our speed right, I ought to be able to dodge anything that's in our way. If we don't do it that way, we're going to lose a half hour we can't afford. Maybe more."

"So what's too slow, and what's too fast?"

"That I'm going to have to figure out, mostly by calculation, partly by feel."

*   *   *

Andrea woke up as the ship rotated for the braking burn to slow them down. It only lasted a few seconds, and John swung it back around again.

"Got it figured out?" she asked.

"I think so."

"You *think* so? What do you—"

"Here we go. Cinch yourself in real tight. This is going to get hairy."

Red lights and warning beeps were going off every-where. John hit the controls hard left and then back again. An indistinct blur sped by them on the right. Something big came rushing toward them and John dipped under it at the last minute. Then it was a rush of jerky movements and shadows slipping by, a frantic slalom that seemed to last forever. Then, suddenly, the welcome time/date chimes and John, nearly simultane-ously, hit the go fast button. The alarms quit ringing. A few beats later, the buzzer rang.

"Another ticket?" asked Andrea.

"I'm afraid so," said John. "My mother always told me I drove too fast."

Later, John relaxed as Mars receded. He stared out the window.

"You know," he said, "I never felt much one way or the other about Earth, but Mars always feels like home. I guess that's wrong of me."

"I feel the same way, but I never spent much time on Earth."

"I have, and I always come away with mixed feelings. There is so much beauty there and so much history—our history, going back to the first amoeba. But on the other hand, most of it is crowded and dirty. There's too much—I don't know—gone, ruined. It's sad."

"We've built a good life on Mars."

"Yes, but there's hardly anything human that's over a hundred years old. It's not like on Earth, where you can turn a corner and see a cathedral that took six hundred years to build."

"On the other hand, on Mars you won't get mugged while you're looking at that six hundred-year-old cathedral."

"Point taken."

Jupiter was in a good position to avoid most of the asteroids, but John wasn't too worried. He knew his way through the Belt.

"How do we stand against the others?" John asked.

Andrea popped up the screen in front of her. Half the screen was data and the other half was live planet-to-planet coverage. The Hawk was doing the narration, so she cut the sound way down.

"Six of us left about the same time. Brandy either took a bad line around the sun or had trouble. Either way, his exit shot him out on a bad line. He lost too much time right at the start. He's out of it."

"*Brothers-in-Arms* had a gyro problem that took too long to fix. They've given up. Nelson took a far too conservative swing around Venus. He can't possibly make up the time, though he's still going."

"How about our friend Will?"

"Mister Scumball Perry is, unfortunately, doing fine, as is Fast Eddie. They left a few minutes before we did, and that's about where they are now. How do the projections look?"

"It's close. I'll have a better feel after Saturn."

Andrea did several sweeps of the engine area before they approached Jupiter. There was always preventive maintenance to do, along with general troubleshooting and testing. She replaced a couple of circuit boards that looked iffy and switched out a breaker box.

* * *

Jupiter, for all its mass, was not a hard shot at all. Basically the same full-speed flyby of the beacon and a slingshot out in the right direction.

John was beginning to make this look easy. Andrea knew full well that wasn't the case. It was only his skill that made it look easy. Actually, it was hard as hell.

At this point there wasn't any choice about Saturn. The approach to the beacon had to be full speed, regardless of the fact that it was inconveniently located. John had set up a course that would come up under the rings, flash past the beacon, and exit over the rings on the other side.

It sounded beautiful. And dangerous.

It proved to be both. The underside of the rings was a spectacular view and although the time/date acquisition went okay, the slingshot was rough. They took quite a pounding and the exit wasn't as clean as John wanted. He was pretty hard on himself. Andrea left him alone.

The Gs had been hard and erratic, so she went back to check the phase-shift converter. She went over it top to bottom twice and couldn't find anything. When she returned, John was smiling.

"Found it," he said. "A tiny glitch in the beta software for the Maxwell, nothing that would amount to anything in normal operations, but it made a big difference under the stresses we're putting this baby through."

He looked inordinately proud of himself. Andrea gave him a hug. "Good show," she said. He blushed, and Andrea busied herself elsewhere to give him time to recover.

Actually, Andrea welcomed any busywork or distractions on this particular leg. Neptune was ahead, and its moon Naiad, where her father had died. She'd never been to this place.

"Look at this," John called out. "We're close enough to track Perry and Fast Eddie."

Andrea went over and looked at the screen.

"That's Perry in front and Fast Eddie right behind. This one's going to be close."

"So what should we do?"

"Get ready for a wild ride. We're going to pull out all the stops."

The remaining hours were busy, and Andrea was grateful. Eventually the time came to pack herself inside the gel-chair.

Neptune hung before them, and as impressive as it was, both of them were looking at Naiad, which was still glowing from Spider's wreck.

"He was a good man," said John softly.

Andrea nodded. "You were his best friend."

John sighed. "He must have been a great daddy. He raised one hell of a kid, you know."

Andrea kept staring at the burning moon, tears in her eyes.

"You ready for the last dive?"

Andrea brushed away the tears. "You bet I am," she said, pulling the webbing tight. "Give it all we've got."

John picked it up a notch.

"Look up there. We're so close you don't even need the screen. You can see them out the front port. That's Perry, a little ahead of Fast Eddie."

"It looks like they're both going to do a full power flyby past the beacon."

"That's all there is, Andrea. If anyone blinks from here on in, they lose. Look, they picked up the beacon. They're only something like thirty seconds ahead of us. They're headed for their slingshot. Wait! No, damn it, no!"

"What's happening?"

"Perry just cut in front of Fast Eddie. His wash will screw him up."

"Oh," cried Andrea. "Look!"

Fast Eddie's ship was rocking back and forth. Then it started tumbling out of control.

"Damn it, damn it, damn it."

The time/date signal rang out and John kicked the engine hard. Fast Eddie's ship was a shower of sparks arcing across Neptune as it disintegrated.

"I'm overriding the slingshot program. Going in manually, hard and hot. I'm going to catch that son of a bitch."

It was one rough ride. Steady ten to twelve Gs with peaks of fifteen. John couldn't imagine what forces were pulling at the hull. Everything hurt, and things started going in and out of focus. The ship was bolting and rocking. Every piece of metal in the control room seemed to be shrieking. John blocked all that out and concentrated on only one thing: taking a better, faster line through and coming out ahead of Perry.

He succeeded.

"What a rush," gasped Andrea. "Did we make it?"

"We did."

Perry hung slightly behind them. He had more power, but they had picked up more energy in the slingshot maneuver.

"Can you take these Gs for a few more hours? If I cut back, we're going to lose."

"I can handle it," she said, and knew she would, even though it was so hard to breathe and everything hurt so bad.

They were quiet from then on. It hurt too much to talk. Perry hung just where he was, not gaining, but not losing ground, either.

Eventually Pluto and its moon Charon appeared on the screen.

"Decision time," said John.

"What's to decide?"

"For one thing, I could give Perry a taste of his own medicine by swinging a little to the side and catching him in my wash."

"You couldn't do that, John, and you know that."

"Yeah, I couldn't live with myself. But it made a nice fantasy for a couple of hours. You know we'll have to go in hot to win. If we slow down to pinpoint the beacon, we'll lose. Perry just needs to get close and that would give him enough time to do it."

"John—"

"Wait. I've got something else to say. When I took manual control of that slingshot, it was a dangerous move and I didn't consult with you. It's your life, too, and I shouldn't have done it."

"There wasn't time to discuss it, John. I trust you."

"Help me out here. Pluto and Charon have unpredictable dynamics. I know where things *should* be, but that doesn't mean they *will* be there. If we go in hot, there are four different things that can happen, and only one of them is good. We could hit Pluto. We could hit Charon. We could be too far from the beacon to pick up its signal. Or, as unlikely as it seems, we could be on target."

"You forgot the hood ornament option."

"Right. That's one out of five."

"Let's go for it. Like I said, I trust you."

There were no more adjustments to make. Everything

was dialed in. Pluto was so incredibly small they couldn't see it until a split second before they were there.

They held their breath. One beat. Two beats. Three.

The time/date chime rang as Pluto and Charon, indistinct blurs, rushed by.

John cut the engines, turned the ship and started slowing down. The great weights on their chests eased up. Perry roared past a few seconds later without even slowing.

"What does the slip say?"

"Nine days, twenty-three hours and seventeen minutes. You did it, John. Dad always said you would."

"No, *we* did it," John said. "Partners all the way."

"How do you feel, John?"

"Aside from the fact that I feel like every bone in my body's been broken twice, I feel fine. You?"

"Ditto, partner. Ditto."

They hung in the darkness of space for a while before starting back, each lost in their thoughts of the past and future.

GHOSTS OF NEPTUNE

by John Helfers

John Helfers is a writer and editor currently living in Green Bay, Wisconsin. A graduate of the University of Wisconsin–Green Bay, his fiction appears in more than twenty anthologies, including First to Fight, Once Upon a Crime, Merlin, *and* Historical Hauntings, *among others. His first edited anthology,* Black Cats and Broken Mirrors, *was published by DAW Books in 1998 and has been followed by several more, the most recent being* Knight Fantastic *and* Villains Victorious. *Future projects include editing even more anthologies as well as a novel or two in progress.*

POSEIDON Base, Neptune, 4.13.2103
0325 Greenwich Mean Time

They're all gone now. I'm the only one left.

Xenobiologist Alan Carpenter stood with his back against the freezing hallway wall, trying to slow his panicked breathing. He scanned the corridor with quick, jerky movements, like prey that knew an enemy was near. The halogen spotlights mounted on his exposure suit turned darkness into daylight, at least for fifty meters. The audio pickups on his exposure suit were set to maximum, able to detect the slightest noise at two hundred meters. But only silence and blackness greeted him in both directions.

He stared down at the portable industrial welder in his gloved hands, its nozzle jury-rigged to spray a five-foot tongue of flame. It might as well have been a bouquet of flowers for all the good it was going to do him.

What? His head jerked up, eyes squinting in the darkness. *Was that a footstep? Maybe someone else . . .* His mind eliminated the idea as soon as it had come. *Di Ponzi, Leighton, Arundel, Jackson . . . They're all gone, taken by . . . whatever's out there. And whatever's out there is coming for me next.*

Alan shook his head, feeling beads of sweat run down his forehead. *Neptune was supposed to be dead, an ice cube. How were we supposed to fucking know?*

I've got to get to the reactor, start the meltdown. The base must be destroyed. No one else can come here, he thought. *Hopefully, our last message got through.* Gripping the welder so tightly that his fingers grew numb, he crept down the hallway, trying not to make a sound.

Funny, the thing I've waited all my life for happens. And here I'm going to destroy it. He managed to catch his hysterical laugh before it exploded inside his helmet. *That way lies madness,* he thought. *You've got a job to do, so get going. Be quiet and . . .*

A noise reverberated through the deserted corridor. Alan stopped, cocking his head to listen. The sound echoed again. The eerie whisper of something approaching.

Nonononononono. He knew what that sound was. A sob constricted his throat, the fear locking the rest of his body rigid. Not daring to breathe, he turned his head, dreading looking back beyond the plastic rim of his suit.

The hallway was empty.

Alan trembled with relief. He reached up to wipe his face, but his hand clunked against his faceplate. His breathing sounded artificial and harsh in his ears. With one final glance at the hall behind him, he resumed his journey deeper into the bowels of the station.

Four years of labor to build this place, he thought. *It cost one hundred billion dollars and the lives of seven men. And I'm going to end it all with the push of one button.*

He came to a T-intersection, and looked down each passageway, his suit-mounted lights causing shadows to dance along the ice-rimed walls. Nothing. He was alone. With only the ghosts and the dead for company.

Stop it, stop thinking about them, they're gone. Which way, which way? He brought up the internal map of the base and plotted out the quickest route to the power room. He was so engrossed in his planning that, even with his senses stretched razor-sharp, he didn't hear another whisper behind him in the hallway. The next one, however, made his head snap up.

He spun, spotlights searching for any sign of movement, welder ready.

Again the emptiness mocked his efforts.

Goddamnit, I know I heard something. He stood there tensed to run, but waited. The noise sounded again, a rasping this time that echoed in the corridor. It came again, and again, the shushing sound of something brushing over rock or ice. An indecipherable whispering accompanied the movement noises, a sibilant chorus of faint voices calling to him, beckoning him . . .

The sounds seemed to be getting closer. *But there's nothing there. The hallway is empty, I've got no readings at all. Mind's playing tricks on me. . . .*

An ice fragment broke from above Alan's head and shattered on the floor, making him jump. Another piece fell, and then another. The sounds paused for a moment, then continued. He stared at the walls and ceiling in horror.

Time to go, time to go now! Alan turned and ran with clumsy strides, the heads-up display still showing the route to the power room. The noises were louder now, on all sides of him, and any second he expected the ice sheets to come crashing down as they erupted from the walls and came for him. Panic lent him speed, and as he came to another intersection, he crashed off the wall and rebounded down the left corridor, sobbing, gulping great drafts of recycled air into his lungs as he struggled to reach the double doors at the end. Every impact of his boots on the floor sounded as loud as an explosion to him, but he didn't care, he just needed to win this last race—

—And then he was staggering almost into the doors that led into the reactor room, his suit cushioning the sudden impact. Dropping the welder, he scrabbled for the key card in his zippered breast pocket, yanking the plastic slab out and shoving it into the lock slot. The sec computer scanned the electromagnetic card with agonizing slowness.

Where? Where are they? Alan noticed that the noise had stopped. He glanced up, looking at the ceiling, then the walls to either side. Nothing. No shushing, no whispers, no rustling in the walls around him.

He turned, shining his suit lights down the corridor one last time, in case they had left the cover of the walls and were coming at him in plain sight. Behind him, he heard the pneumatic doors hiss open and, still keeping an eye on the empty corridor, he pulled the card out of the slot and backed through the doorway.

With a shaking hand he inserted it into the matching slot on this side and listened to the doors hiss shut again, thinking it was one of the most beautiful sounds he had ever heard. He leaned his head against the ceramplast doors and tried to slow his racing heart.

Perhaps it was the stress of the past week, running, surviving, and all the while living with the constant feeling of being hunted that alerted him. Perhaps it was the fight-or-flight awareness of an animal who knows, somehow just knows, danger is nearby.

He didn't hear anything in the reactor room. No glimpse of movement caught his eye. All the same, the sensation that he was not alone came over Alan with a horrible certainty.

They were herding me here, like a cow to the slaughterhouse. He straightened, and in the brief moment before he fainted from overwhelming shock, he heard a sibilant, breathy noise that he could have sworn sounded like laughter.

*　　*　　*

U.P.N. Science Vessel Epona, *8.11.2103*
0812 G.M.T.

"Stabilized planetary orbit achieved."

The computer's modulated announcement stabbed through Celeste Wolfrum's concentration, but she kept her arms locked, holding the weight bar steady. Only the slightest tremor betrayed her tired muscles.

One more rep. Just one more, then you're done. The bar was set to a gravity weight of sixty-five kilograms. One hundred forty-three pounds. Her personal best.

She inhaled and lowered the bar to her chest, held it there a brief second, then exhaled, imagining it floating up on the thin column of air streaming from her mouth. The bar rose, rose, rose, until her sleek, muscled arms were straight again.

"Hold bar at zero Gs," she commanded, then released the smooth metal and sat up, leaving the weight bar suspended in midair, supported by its own antigravity field. Because space was always at a premium in starships, technology had been used to make the exercise room of the United Planetary Nations vessel *Epona* as compact as possible.

Celeste grabbed a towel and walked over to the small window set into the wall, wiping away sweat while looking down at the brilliant blue planet below.

Actually, from what Clayton said, it's more like a glob of molten rock inside an iceball surrounded by a huge blue gas cloud, she thought. *Still, it is beautiful.*

Neptune's atmosphere was mostly composed of hydrogen and helium, with traces of water vapor and methane. It was the methane that made the gas giant glow a lustrous blue. The huge cloud surrounded a thick mantle of frozen methane, ammonia, and more water, which encased a molten rock core. Neptune's core gave off

more than twice the heat it received from the sun, keeping
the frozen chemicals on its surface in constant motion and
causing gigantic continents of solidified methane to roil
and shift. This energy exchange also caused Neptune's
notorious winds, the strongest ever recorded in the solar
system, at times reaching speeds of more than two thousand kilometers per hour. Celeste put her hand on the
porthole and imagined that she could hear the wind
scouring the planet's surface, whipping up the solidified
elements into a chemical storm of cosmic proportions.

Great vacation spot I've chosen this year, she thought,
and smiled.

The doors on the other end of the room hissed, and
a balding, stocky man stepped inside, his features bright-
ening when he spotted her.

"Ah, Celeste, I thought I'd find you here," said Clayton Forrester, the expedition's lead scientist. "We've
matched orbit with Pangea II, and will be departing for
planetside in eight hours."

"Thanks, Clay. I've still got a few more tests to run
on the geothermic surveying equipment, but that won't
take long. Other than that, I'm all set."

"Yes, except I don't think you've gotten more than
five hours' sleep a night." The shorter man's face radiated concern. "You know, Celeste, the closer we get to
Neptune, the more time you spend in here."

"Have to keep bone mass up, you know that," Celeste
said, patting her face dry with the towel.

"I know ship regs state one hour of exercise every
twenty-four. You've been quadrupling that lately. You're
not still worried about seeing Alan again, are you?"

Nothing like being obvious, Celeste thought. Clayton
and her ex had been on good terms until the divorce.
While that had been more than five years ago, Clayton
had a long memory for people who tried to screw over
his friends. She hid her reaction by turning back to the
window, staring at Neptune's azure atmosphere. "I wish
you didn't read people as well as you do planetary
strata."

"Look, everything you both went through, that was

all over and done with a long time ago," Clay said. "I'm sure he's let it go. Now it's time for you to do the same."

Easy for you to say, she thought. *You didn't have to give up the assignment of a lifetime for a man who left you anyway.* She forced a game smile on her face and turned back to him. "You're right, Clay. We're both professionals. I'm sure Alan's left all that behind."

"That's the spirit. And if we get there, and he doesn't behave, well, screw 'im," the short, bespectacled geologist said. "We'll send him topside to collect methane samples with a portwelder. Celeste, you're the best damn ex-bee I've ever seen. Poseidon may have gotten that prick first, but we got you, and I thank my lucky stars for that every single day."

Celeste smiled again and shook her head. "Clay, you're incorrigible."

"Part of my natural charm," he replied. "We're going to have a final procedure briefing at oh-nine-hundred. I'll see you there."

"Clay?"

The other scientist stopped at the exercise room doors. "Yes?"

"Do you think they're all right down there? I mean, we've been in range for hours and haven't even received their broadcast beacon yet."

Clayton shook his head. "On a planet with a skewed magnetic field, heavy chemical atmosphere, pea-soup cloud cover, and what is probably a decaying radioactive core, you're surprised a radio transmission can't get through? Don't worry, kiddo, they knew the odds were strong that they'd be cut off from just about all contact when they went in two years ago."

She nodded. "True. At least we know their landing was successful."

"They had everything they would possibly need to survive, even on this ice-blue hellhole, just like we will. I'm sure we'll find them all snug and bored out of their minds, waiting for us to get down there to relieve them."

"Right. I'll see you at the meeting," Celeste said. *And boy, do I look forward to kicking my sanctimonious ex*

*off the planet. I would've handled the divorce just fine, if
only Alan hadn't stolen Poseidon from me. I should've
made it to Neptune before that asshole. I should've been
there first. Well, I'm here now, and I'm not backing down
again for anyone.*

Celeste hit the steamshower for a quick clean, pausing
when she was finished to look at herself in the mirror.
Not bad for a thirty-five-year-old, she thought. *Gee, Alan,
too bad you'll never get to touch what you lost.* She ran
a hand through her short dark brown ringlets, slipped
into her undergarments, then pulled on a dark blue
jumpsuit, the color of the science division of the U.P.N.'s
Exploration Corps.

Then she headed down the narrow corridor, to the
briefing room. The rest of the science crew was already
there, waiting for the meeting to start. No one was talking, but there was an undercurrent of subdued excitement in the room. Celeste felt it, too, wanting nothing
more than to get off this space taxi and get down to
business on Neptune.

She nodded to familiar faces. Maggie Tempett, the
team astronomer and the only other female member,
nodded back. Maggie had mistaken Celeste's increased
activity in the exercise room as a romantic possibility,
since that was where she spent a fair amount of time as
well. It was a notion the slim xenobiologist had disa-
bused the other woman of as soon as possible. The tall,
leggy redhead had laughed off the attempt, and the two
had become good friends, often teaming up to protect
each other's back against the men when they grew too
much to handle alone.

Jackson Mattingly tipped her a wink and a smile from
his place near the door. Unlike the rest of the team,
who had doubled up in either physical or theoretical
sciences, the muscular black man had only one primary
scientific skill, communications. His other talents had
been gained during the seven years he served as a combat medic in the North America Republican Army. He
was the only other person to use the exercise room as
much as Celeste did, and she often found him simfight-

ing. He had offered to teach her a few moves, but she had demurred, not feeling comfortable with the idea. *But maybe once we're settled in the base,* she thought. It would be an interesting way to pass the downtime.

Across the table, Rydell Martingale was whiling away the minutes by calculating something that was no doubt esoterically complicated. Martingale was their engineer, and, while clichéd to say it, he related to machines and their concepts and quirks much better than he related to people. He was also very handsome, with his constant flipping of an unruly sable-black forelock back from his model's face distracting both Celeste and Maggie more than once. Not being one to pass up an opportunity, Maggie had made a play for him early on in the team's formation, but he had evinced no interest in her, leaving her to speculate endlessly why not.

The other two Celeste didn't know quite as well, since both had been added to their team only three months ago. Anthony Carver, the thin, quiet meteorologist, and Julian Armitage, the distant, superior nuclear technician. Both had come highly recommended, but Celeste knew that looking good on paper and performing in the real world were two different things.

The doors opened and Clayton walked in, absently tossing a ceramplas datastick in one hand. "Ah, everyone's right on time. Even Mister Martingale, I see." The remark caused the young engineer to look up, a sheepish expression on his face. Everyone smiled or chuckled, as Rydell's tendency to miss meetings altogether was well known.

Clayton strode to the head of the table, displacing Armitage with a tip of his head, and inserted the datastick into the holotable slot. A three-dimensional model of Neptune flickered into life, with a small green dot in orbit high above the illusionary planet's surface, floating in geosynchronous orbit with a larger red dot blinking on the planet's surface.

"By this time tomorrow, we'll be at Poseidon Base, settling in for a year of experiments. The dropship will be leaving the *Epona* at fifteen-thirty hours. Flight time will be approximately one hour fifteen minutes, longer than expected, but it seems a storm has whipped up in the area, and we'll have to skirt around it to arrive at the base."

"Turbulence," Armitage muttered. "Great."

"Once there," Clayton continued, "we'll take approximately two days to get briefed on the status of the ongoing experiments, then the planetside crew will transfer back to the dropship to head out, and we'll take over. I want the entire switchover to go smooth as silk. So everyone should check their equipment lists one more time, all right?"

A chorus of groans came from the rest of the survey team, and Celeste shook her head. *Good thing I'm almost done with my list,* she thought. *Maybe I'll be able to get a couple hours sleep before beamlaunch.*

"Questions?" Clayton asked.

"Have we established contact with Poseidon yet?" This came from Jackson.

"No voice channel yet, but we've locked onto their signal beacon. Too much atmospheric disturbance here, even for tight-beam transmissions. That ion-methane storm so close to the base isn't helping either. We all know Neptune's a difficult beast, but our touchdown schedule goes as planned. Anything else? All right, then, I'll see you all in three hours in the landing bay." He gave them an impish grin as he walked out of the room.

"Bleeding slave driver, Forrester is," Armitage said, frowning.

"That's why he's the best," Celeste replied. "Clayton doesn't miss a thing, and he makes sure no one else does either. Given a choice, I wouldn't work for anyone else."

"Hear, hear," Jackson agreed. "Besides, I'd think you scientists wouldn't care what you have to do to get out here and explore a new world."

"That's exactly why I'm here, Carver," the meteorologist, said, his soft voice containing a trace of southern drawl. "Even if U.P.N. hadn't offered triple our usual salary for this assignment, I'd still have volunteered. Hell, I'd have paid them for the opportunity. Not often you get to study a gas giant like this from the inside out."

"Now I've got to recheck my scopes. Damn that For-rester," Maggie said with mock annoyance, as she and the others filed out of the room.

Only Rydell was left behind, so engrossed in his calculations that he didn't notice the rest of the group had left.

* * *

Just under three hours later, Celeste stood with the team supervising the last crates of equipment being loading onto the dropship *Rhiannon*.

The *Rhiannon* was a squat cargo hauler, with protruding stubby wings for maneuvering in a planetary atmosphere. It was built to weather the vacuum of space as easily as the violent skies of Neptune. Her pilot, Jim Gorman, was pacing around the ship, handling the preflight checklist himself. Even though Celeste barely knew him, the sight of him examining the ship made her feel a little less nervous about what might be a bumpy journey planetside.

Along with the normal solid plasma fuel rocket engines, the dropship had a large, bulbous protrusion rising from its rear fuselage. This was the gravity tether engine, a field projector that enabled the ship to utilize a planet's own gravity field for flight and propulsion. Even though Neptune's gravity was a bit stronger than Earth's, the winds could blow so hard that they might disrupt the ship's flight, making it impossible to control. The tether engine would act as an anchor, connecting the ship to the planet so it wouldn't get blown into the ground.

Once they were close enough, the pilot would ride the incredible wind streams and use the directional rockets to steer toward the base, where an automatic tractor beam would lock on and pull the ship into the docking bay. To protect its hull from debris whipped up by the constant winds, the ship generated a repulsor field, protecting it against any supersonic particle they might encounter during the journey.

Everyone was dressed in bulky pressure suits, to ensure that they would stay conscious in free fall, since the *Epona*'s tractor beam would launch the dropship with a force approaching five Gs, to conserve the *Rhiannon*'s fuel for the flight back.

Celeste watched Clayton bound around the dock like a space-suited rabbit, everywhere at once, making sure everything was running according to schedule. After one final conversation with the flight crew chief, he turned to his team.

"Everyone on," he said.

The seven members of the science crew clomped on board. Clayton came after, followed by the pilot, who closed the pressure door behind them. They wound their way through the fully-loaded cargo bay to the passenger section, where two long benches were mounted against the walls. There were five point harnesses and pulldown safety cages waiting to envelope them.

High-tech spiderwebs, Celeste thought, as she strapped herself in. The others did the same, with Clayton purposely sitting across from Celeste. Their eyes met, and he winked.

Gorman walked down the narrow aisle, checking to make sure that everyone was locked into place. "We'll be launch-ready in a few minutes. Everyone sit tight and keep your eyes on the lights here. Just to remind you, green means go." Pointing to a lightboard near the door, he headed for the cockpit.

The overhead lights dimmed, and the subdued chatter trailed off to silence. Celeste's attention wandered, although her eyes kept glancing toward the cockpit's closed door. *If Alan could do this three years ago, I can do it now. No problem.*

There was a slight sensation of movement. The dropship shuddered, and a loud mechanical noise vibrated through the passenger area. *That would be the bay doors.* She imagined the dead blackness of space yawning below them, with the bright blue coldness of Neptune waiting far below.

The lights above the door winked on. Blue glowed first to signify the drop was imminent, then three sets of yellow, then green.

Celeste's world compressed to an indistinguishable howl as the *Rhiannon* was propelled away from the *Epona* at thirty-five hundred kilometers per hour. The straps tightened around her body, and she felt the pressure suit inflate to force her blood to keep circulating. She experienced a sensation of overwhelming light-headedness, and her eyes rolled back in her head for a moment. To her right, she heard a long, blurred smear of sound. *Someone's moaning,* she thought. *Frightened or sick or both.* Then all other noises were lost in a roar that could be felt in every bone in Celeste's body as the ship's rockets fired.

The walls and floor of the passenger cabin began vibrating as the *Rhiannon* entered Neptune's upper atmosphere, skipping along the gas cloud until it slid though the roiling pockets of hydrogen and helium. A muffled crackling meant small frozen particles were encountering the repulsor field, impacting the energy shield with the force of a bullet.

The buffeting grew worse the lower they went, until the passengers were wrenched and jolted by the sudden slams and drops of the *Rhiannon*. The turbulence was making Celeste nauseous, but she leaned back, closed her eyes, and concentrated on not throwing up. She had no idea how much time had passed when the intercom clicked on.

It was Gorman. "No doubt you're feeling every bit of these eight-hundred-kilometer-an-hour winds. Don't worry. We're halfway through the flight, and right on time for our landing. Temperature planetside is a balmy negative 210 degrees Celsius, with little variation expected for the next hundred thousand years or so. Just sit back and enjoy the roller coaster, and I'll let you know when we're on final approach."

Despite the pounding she was taking, Celeste felt a twinge of excitement. *Everything I went through the past five years—the training, the studies—has been worth it. Just wish I could see outside,* she thought, although she knew that would be impossible, as there wasn't enough ambient light for vision.

Minutes passed, and the pressure began lifting from her chest. Celeste opened her eyes and studied the other team members. Maggie, Jackson, and Rydell looked fine. Armitage and Carver looked a bit green—newbies. But Carver had retained just enough spirit to nod at her and offer a shaky thumbs-up.

It wasn't much longer before the buffeting lessened, and Celeste figured they were nearing the planet's surface. The ship slewed back and forth as Gorman maneuvered the ungainly craft closer to Poseidon Base.

"Final approach. We've locked into the base's signal beacon and are coming around. E.T.A. is approximately six minutes."

Because of the gargantuan storm systems that ravaged the planet, Poseidon Base was protected by a shield similar to the one that enveloped the *Rhiannon*. The ship would be brought in on autopilot by the base's tractor beam, and the shield frequencies harmonized so the ship could pass safely through the barrier. Celeste's stomach rumbled, although she couldn't tell if it was nerves, nausea, or a mixture of both.

The sandpaper sound of the airborne particles impacting the *Rhiannon*'s shields suddenly ceased altogether, and the ship stopped pitching and yawing. Now the descent was smooth and calm.

We're in. We're inside Poseidon, Celeste thought. Just like that, her discomfort disappeared, replaced by a cresting tide of anticipation and confidence.

With one last faint bump, the *Rhiannon* docked. A few seconds later the cockpit door slid open and Gorman stepped out to enthusiastic applause. Now that his business was completed, his professional demeanor seemed to loosen up, and he was grinning like a nullball captain who had just scored the winning goal.

"No no, just throw U-creds, please. Now let's get off

this crate and see your digs." He hit the release button, and the safety cages lifted. Gorman walked past them and disappeared into the cargo bay.

Celeste stood, feeling her spine pop as she reached for the ceiling. Beside her, Jackson rolled his neck, the vertebrae audibly cracking.

A call from the back made heads turn. "Professor Forrester, could you come here?"

Clayton headed aft. Celeste craned her neck to try and see what was going on, but Armitage was blocking her view.

"Space travel and I don't get along very well," Armitage was telling her. He still looked a bit green.

Celeste thought she spotted Maggie and Rydell exchanging a covert grin at his comment. *Everyone remembers their first few jumps,* she thought, shutting out Armitage's continued diatribe about the problems he experienced.

Clayton appeared among them again, his face a mask of concern. "Folks, you'll need to get into sealed suits. It seems there's been a leak in the hangar, and there's minimal air pressure here. Shouldn't be anything to worry about, but we aren't going to take any chances."

With a minimum of poking and contortions, the team got into their heavy exposure suits, which contained built-in comm systems, as well as breathing and heating units.

"Hey, prof, why aren't the other scientists here to greet us?" Armitage called as he wrestled with his helmet.

"Jim wasn't able to contact anyone inside," Clayton said. "It's probably nothing, maybe the comm relay for the hangar is shorted out. You know how touchy electronics are in an atmosphere that varies this much. Also, we're a little earlier than expected. I'm sure they'll be waiting for us inside."

Clayton bent closer to Celeste, pretending to close a Velcro pocket. "Stay next to me when we go in," he whispered.

"Why, what's up?"

"I've got a feeling something isn't right here. Just stick close by, all right?" He straightened up and put on his helmet, then turned to the others. "All right, if everyone's ready. Jim's at the outer door now."

One by one they filed toward the rear of the ship. Clayton, nodded, and Jim hit the manual door release.

* * *

The scientists tromped down the gangplank into a dark, icy hole. Except for the lights on their suits, the hangar was pitch-black. The spotlights pierced the darkness to their full range and still could not find a wall.

"Some welcoming committee," Celeste heard Armitage grumble across the comm. "You'd think they'd be glad to see us."

"Everyone relax," Clayton said. "I'm sure there's a logical explanation for all this. Jim, the hangar door should be this way."

With the pilot and Clay in the lead, the team made its way across the hangar floor. Neptune's gravity was just a fifth more than Earth's, so the trip was relatively easy, despite everyone feeling a few dozen kilos heavier. The subzero temperature inside the huge building made the material of the exposure suits stiffen and crinkle with each step.

"Clay, my suit sensors are reading the hangar temp at minus eighty-nine degrees Celsius. Is it supposed to be this cold out here?" Carver asked.

"Not to my knowledge. Jim, the shield was still up, correct?"

"Absolutely. I would have known immediately if it hadn't been. The funny thing was, the tractor beam wasn't operational. I had to guide us in manually. Here's the doors."

Their lights now illuminated a frost-rimed metal door. Gorman tapped on it, causing thick chunks of frozen condensation to fall away. He hit the door keypad on the side. The red light flashed, then remained red, instead of turning green as expected.

"Door's stuck," Gorman said.

"Rydell, see what the problem is," Clay said. The engineer slipped up and tried the button, with the same result.

" 'S okay." Rydell extended a fiber-optic cable out of his glove and threaded it into a data port below the keypad. After a few seconds, he turned to Clayton. "Sec-subroutine's on auto-override, with no way to break the code in a hurry. The strange thing is, I'm not finding a matching pad on the other side. It's as if someone destroyed the inside controls."

A shiver raced down Celeste's spine. "Can you open it?" she head herself asking.

"Naturally, just give me a minute." The lanky engineer shifted in his suit, and everyone was quiet, either looking around or at each other while waiting for him to work his scientific magic.

Celeste opted to look around, trying to pierce the darkness. She imagined she could feel the cold creeping through her suit, stealing away the warmth, robbing her of the feeling in her hands and legs— *Stop it!* she chastised herself, shaking her head. Just to be sure, she wiggled her fingers and toes inside the suit.

Just then there was a click, and the light turned green. "All yours," Rydell said.

Standing where she was, Celeste noticed that Jackson was off to one side, apart from the others, where he would have an unrestricted view of the corridor. Just as she was about to ask him why, the door hissed open.

The inside corridor was just as black as the hangar, or it would have been if they could have seen past the pile of food and equipment crates blocking the hallway and reaching to the ceiling.

"What . . ." Gorman said, vocalizing the thought that had been on all their minds.

Rydell was already moving forward, inserting himself into the narrow space between the crates and the wall.

"Ry . . ." Clayton warned.

"Don't worry, I'm not going far—there it is. Just like I told you, the inside pad's been destroyed. Looks like acid of some kind." There was a crunch. "Yup, I just stepped on the broken beaker. My suit's not reading any kind of breathable atmosphere here, Clay. Temperature's better, only four degrees Celsius in here."

"Maybe an underground rupture below the shield depressurized the base before anyone could seal it. After all, the repulsor isn't airtight," Clayton said.

"And no one would be able to get to a pressure door in time? Not bloody likely," Julian said. "Besides, that doesn't begin to explain the disabled door or the barricade of boxes. Something's definitely wrong here. Maybe we ought to leave, let an UPNEC investigation crew handle this."

"Maybe they were trying to keep someone from getting out," Celeste mused aloud. "Maybe one of the crew members lost it, tried to sabotage the hangar or the tractor beam."

"Lost it? Is that the clinical term? I thought you called yourself a biologist," the Englishman said.

"And that's what I am, not a psychologist," Celeste replied. "I have no idea what happened here, but I think we should take a look around."

"Enough! While you two are wasting time, there could be injured people in there." Clayton's voice cut through their argument. "We need to get inside, get the systems back on-line, and figure out just what the hell is going on here. Rydell, Jackson, Gorman, let's start clearing these boxes. The rest of you keep your eyes open for anything unusual."

"You mean anything more unusual than what we've just seen?" Carver drawled. There was a moment's silence, then a few uneasy chuckles.

The three men set to work clearing a path to the other side. Working together, they were done in a few minutes. The rest of the group gathered around the cleared opening.

"Well, they had plenty of food," Gorman said, leaning against a box of vacuum-sealed thermorations.

"Where's the crew? You'd think with twenty people here someone would come to meet us," Maggie said.

"Twenty-four," Jackson corrected. He tipped his head

toward the inky opening. "I can't raise anyone on the base frequencies. We need to take a look around."

Clayton nodded. "Yes, let's check it out. Everyone stay together, and at the first sign of trouble, we all head back to the ship. No dissension on that. Does everyone understand?"

There were muttered agreements all around. Jackson led the way, then Gorman, then Clayton. Rydell went next, then Celeste, Maggie, Julian, and Carver.

The hallway stretched on into the distance, the suit lights bobbing and weaving, casting formless shadows on the ice-coated walls.

"I wonder if someone purged the atmosphere on purpose?" Carver said as they walked. "Maybe someone thought they had to depressurize the entire base."

"But to what end? I agree with Celeste. I think someone went off the deep end. But who got the space-crazies is what I want to know—and why. Let's head to Main Operations, hopefully there's something there that will tell us what happened here," Jackson said, still in the lead.

The team wound their way through the halls for several long minutes, until they came to the doors of the operations room. Again, the portal was blocked by heavy boxes, but these had been thrown up against the double doors as if in great haste, dozens of crates piled up in a senseless jumble.

Jackson shook his head. "Why would they seal off the ops room like this?"

No one volunteered any suggestions.

Carver cleared his throat. "You know I'm starting to agree with Julian. Maybe we should bug out of here, let NARA or the Pentagon investigate."

"I want to find out what happened here," Clayton replied. "But . . . anyone who wants to go back to the ship is more than welcome to. You can sit tight there while the rest of us poke around."

No one moved.

"As I thought, safety in numbers," Clayton said. "In

that case, Julian, Tony, Celeste, you're up now. Let's get this cleared and get those doors open."

Celeste and the men set to work, pushing and hauling boxes. While she struggled with the crates, her mind roiled. *Did something happen to Alan? Is he . . . his body . . . here somewhere? Where is everybody?*

When the doorway was clear, they spotted the keypad, also glowing a sullen red. Rydell came forward again and worked his wonders. "Everyone stand back," he said, activating the door.

And something tumbled out.

Celeste caught the impression of two limbs reaching out for something, anything, to hold onto. Then the form hit the floor, disintegrating, in a frosty white cloud.

Maggie, Carver, and Rydell jumped back a step, then order was restored. But for a few seconds, no one moved, everyone's eyes locked onto what was left of a human being.

"Well, I think this answers the question of what happened to the crew," Julian's voice finally broke the silence. "More than likely they ended up just like this frosty bloke here."

"Shut up," Jackson said as he stepped into the room beyond.

The command center was frozen in time. A thick coating of frost lay everywhere, carpeting the floor with a layer of slippery white that crunched underfoot. Frozen water vapor clung to the equipment consoles, the chairs, the walls—and to the bodies.

Seven people were sitting at various stations around the room. An eighth occupied the captain's chair in the middle. The corpses looked calm, at peace, their arms folded or on the armrests of their seats. Their eyes were closed, their skin chalk-white, hair dusted with snowy particles.

"What in the name of God happened here?" Gorman said, his voice just above a whisper.

"That's what we're going to find out," Clayton said, his authoritative voice snapping everyone out of their shocked stares. "Julian and Rydell, I want you to head down to the reactor and see if it's still operational. Let me know what you find when you get there. The most important thing is to get this room up and running, scan the base for life—or anything else that might be around.

"Jackson, Celeste, I know you've both had medical training. Get to the medlab and see if there's any evidence that this may have been some kind of epidemic."

"Shouldn't we at least try to contact the ship? The *Rhiannon*'s got a tight-beam laseradio, and it might be able to get through to the *Epona*," Gorman said.

"It's worth a try," Clayton admitted. "But I don't have a lot of hope for even tight-beam transmissions to get off-planet until this storm passes, which, as I understand, won't be for another day or two. Still, you and I will head back and try it. Maggie, Tony, you going to be all right here handling the bodies and figuring out who they are?"

"Oh, yeah, Clay, surrounded by dead folks, we'll be just fine," Maggie said.

"Maggie, I need everyone at their peak here. Something killed everyone here, and I want to find out what it was," Clayton said.

"Clay, we'll be fine," Tony said.

Clayton gave final instructions: "Nobody let anybody else out of their sight, and everybody keep your group channels on."

*   *   *

Although Celeste never would have admitted it, she felt more secure with Jackson at her back than with anyone else. But even so, the mystery of the base gnawed at her. *Why lock themselves inside the command center? To keep some disease from spreading? And where's Alan? Is he dead, too? Is he . . .*

". . . you have any idea what's going on?" Jackson's voice broke through her thoughts.

"Right now, your guess is as good as mine," she replied, smiling in spite of the tension.

"According to my map, the lab's just around the next corner," Celeste said.

Their comms crackled to life. "Clayton?"

"Yes, Julian, what did you find?"

"Something very peculiar down here. We've reached the power plant without incident. At the door we found an industrial welder, modified into a crude flamethrower. Somebody was afraid enough to make it into a weapon."

Celeste and Jackson exchanged glances, then looked up and down the black hallway.

The comm continued to crackle. "Spare me the theatrics, Armitage. What else did you find?"

"In the reactor room, I think there was some sort of confrontation. Boot prints in the frost leading up to the door. They go in, then it looks like some kind of scuffle. There's some strange tracks here." A pause. "Wait, this gets better. According to the readouts, the reactor is on, and producing at full power. But no other systems in the base are activated—light, life-support, tractor beam, nothing. It's all been shut down, well, everything except the shield generator, which is working just fine."

"Good thing, too," Jackson muttered. Since the density of Neptune was just under half of Earth's, the entire base floated on an antigravity field that pushed off the core's own gravitational field. If that system failed, the base would quickly sink into the ocean of frozen hydrogen that comprised Neptune's crust.

"So it's all right to power up?" Clayton asked.

"Just give the word, and I'll have the juice flowing in no time."

"Wait a minute, Armitage," Jackson broke in. "If most of the energy from the reactor isn't going to power the base, where is it going?"

"Well, that's just it, I'm not sure," he replied. "Hey, I was just chuffed to the max to find the reactor online. Otherwise we'd be living in our suits for the next few days."

"Will activating the power to the base cause any problems?" Clayton asked.

"The backup systems are probably frozen, so we'll

have to make sure they're not drawing any power, or they might explode—which would be double plus ungood. Probably take me about an hour to check, then we should be all right," Julian said.

"What about that drain?" Jackson asked again.

"When I run the diagnostics, I should find out where the bloody draw is. I'll let you know," Julian replied. "If nothing comes up, I'll hit the base power and stand by if there's a spike. Whatever would be using power from here would have to be huge to use everything this unit produces."

"Anyone else have anything yet?" Clayton was talking to all of them.

"Tony here. We're almost finished with the, uh, staff. I noticed that the pad on this side has also been disabled. Looks like they locked themselves in here."

"Celeste, how about you and Jackson?"

"Jackson and I have almost reached the medlab," Celeste turned back to Jackson, then pointed ahead.

The pair walked the rest of the way down the corridor, the surrounding silence oppressive. A few more steps and they were in front of the laboratory doors. Celeste licked her dry lips and nodded. Tensing, Jackson hit the control.

The doors hissed open. Their suit lights revealed a scene of utter destruction. Cabinets were overturned, medical equipment smashed, the remains of chemicals in brilliant crystalline sprays decorated the walls. What looked like a pair of legs stuck out from a refrigerator that was lying on its side.

"Whoa," Jackson said. "Someone had a serious rage problem here. Hey, Celeste . . ."

Celeste was frozen in her tracks, eyes locked onto something she couldn't put a name to. "What—what is—" she whispered, too softly for Jackson to hear.

Humanoid in shape, the being stood a bit over two meters tall and was abnormally thin, with what looked like the curves of a rib cage featured on its high, shallow chest. There was something strange about its shape, almost as if it had been stretched on a rack. Its skin was bone white, except for a smear of bright color on one arm. There was no visible hair anywhere on its body, and it wore no garment, the space between its legs a sexless nub. Its arms and legs were almost sticks, with bulbous, rounded joints at the elbows and knees. Its hands and feet were elongated, a parody of human, the fingers and toes ending in sharp talons.

Its face was cadaverous, white and elongated as well, with a nose that began small at the bridge and flared into two-centimeter-wide nostrils. Small holes with bony protrusions curled out on each side of its head. Its protuberant eyes were closed, but the veined lids seemed to flutter slightly as it stood there.

It's . . . alive? Celeste was dimly aware of her mouth making some kind of noise as she tried to get Jackson's attention, her eyes never leaving the alien. She shifted her weight to take a step backward, trying to put a bit of distance between her and it, all the while thinking, *There's something familiar about it, I don't know how or why I know that, but I know I recognize something about it.*

". . . *Celeste* . . ." She thought she heard someone call her name, but she couldn't tell where the voice had come from. The lipless slit of the creature's mouth hadn't moved.

Out of the corner of her eye, she saw the flare of Jackson's light as he turned toward her. She tried to speak, to warn him about what he would see, then his light hit the corner of the room.

"Holy sh—" was all he had time to say.

Then the alien's eyes opened.

Celeste had the impression of large faceted golden-green eyes widening in awareness. Then, before she could think or react, the creature blurred into motion, its spindly arms on her shoulders, its nightmare face speeding toward hers. Its lipless mouth opened, and she saw a solid serrated ridge of what she assumed was teeth of some kind. The alien's head shot forward, those teeth quivering to sink into her face . . .

. . . only to rebound as its head struck the transparent

plexiglass of Celeste's helmet. The impact staggered her, and she would have fallen if the creature hadn't been holding onto her. As it was, her head bounced off the back of her helmet. She couldn't think, couldn't move, her mind was numbed by the speed and ferocity of the attack. A sound between a grunt and a scream rose in her throat, but all she could do was stare at the monstrosity, its face and that gaping hole of a mouth coming at her again.

Celeste saw a crazy strobe of light, and she was rocked again, only this time to the side. Jackson came in from her left and slammed into the alien, knocking the thing to one side. Jackson's arms were wrapped around it, and he planted his feet, trying to pull it off her.

The creature's arm shot out like a piston, and Jackson sailed through the air to land against the far wall. Its other arm latched onto Celeste again.

Celeste had regained her senses. Her suit lights bobbed and flickered as she grabbed the alien's arm with both hands. The suit was made of a Tyvek-Kevlar weave and was practically impervious to cuts or piercing, so she suspected the creature wouldn't be able to put a hole in it, no matter how hard it tried. Still, she needed to get away from it. Getting her feet under her, she wrenched the alien's arm away from her shoulder.

It was like trying to tear an iron bar out of a prison window. The limb was as rigid and immobile as solid titanium, the clawed hand holding her in an unbreakable death grip.

A scream-sob escaped Celeste's throat as she watched that implacable, inhuman face swivel back toward her, its arm again reaching up to grip her, that maw drawing nearer. This time it seemed solely intent on her helmet.

"*. . . help me . . .*"

The clawed hands fumbled across her helmet, scrabbling across her visor as if seeking a way in. *Holy shit, it's trying to get inside,* she thought.

A bright sapphire blue ray of light shot across Celeste's vision and impacted the alien in the head. Although the light beam had no mass, the ugly burn it made staggered the creature and made it step back.

"Celeste, get the hell out of the way!" she heard a voice shout over her comm. Her arms and legs couldn't obey fast enough. She fell backward, landing heavily on her rump, then scrambling on her hands and feet, risking one glance over her shoulder.

The alien, the top of its head blackened and raw from what looked like a laser burn (*where did that come from?*) had recovered already, and was heading her way, those hellish arms once more reaching out, long fingers crooked into grasping claws.

She came up against one of the overturned cabinets, which jarred her to a painful stop. The alien continued its advance. Celeste pulled her legs up to her chest and waited. And when the thing took one more step, she kicked out with all her might, aiming for what she hoped was a kneecap. The blow landed with no appreciable effect, not even staggering the creature. It loomed over her, that gaping mouth opening and closing. Celeste threw up an arm, prepared to fight to the last. The thing reached down, and through the adrenaline and fear she again saw the bright splash of color on the creature's upper arm as its hand touched the faceplate of her helmet. She got a good look at it this time, and her mouth dropped open in shock. *Is that what I think it is? Oh, my God . . .*

Suddenly the alien was bathed in more harsh white light. Distracted, it turned to evaluate this new threat—just in time to see an iron bar slamming into its head. This time the alien was knocked off its feet, falling against the wall. It twitched once, then slumped, unmoving, a sizable dent in its stretched skull.

Jackson sprang over an upended examination table and ran to Celeste. "You all right?"

She nodded, trying to swallow the asteroid-sized lump in her throat.

"Stay here, I'm going to finish that thing," the big man said. He started to rise, only to be stayed by her grabbing his arm.

"Wait. Let me get up," she said.

"Don't. You could be hurt and not know it."

"I'm fine, just a little knocked about," she said. "I have to show you something."

With Jackson's help, Celeste got to her feet, wobbling a bit, but managing to stay upright. The door cycled open, and Clayton, Maggie, Gorman, and Tony all charged in, each of them trying to ask what was going on—they'd obviously heard the scuffle over the comm.

"Where'd you guys come from?" Celeste asked.

"What do you mean? It sounded like you both were getting killed in here," Clayton said, the blood draining from his face as he stared at the white-skinned thing on the floor. "I told Armitage and Rydell to keep working on the enviro-systems, get them running as soon as possible. They heard everything as well."

"An alien," Maggie stated. "It's an honest-to-God alien." She, along with everyone else, couldn't take her eyes off the creature.

"No kidding," Jackson said. He turned to Celeste. "What did you want to show me?"

Celeste tugged him toward the creature.

"Keep back!" Clayton warned.

She shrugged. "I think Jackson knocked it into next week. Obviously we'll restrain it, but you have to see this first." Reaching down, she was about to touch the creature.

"I'm warning you, Celeste, if this thing even twitches, I'm giving it a stainless-steel lobotomy," Jackson said.

Steeling herself, Celeste touched the alien's sloping shoulder, moving so her suit lights shone on its chalk-white skin.

Gorman asked first. "What is that?"

Maggie answered him. "Isn't it—a tattoo?"

"Uh-huh," Celeste said. "It's an old Earther cartoon character, called Marvin the Martian, if I remember right."

"My God, you don't mean . . ." Clayton began.

"Yes," Celeste replied. "This is—or was—Alan."

*   *   *

"Let me get this straight," Julian said. "You think that something turned Alan into—whatever that thing is now, and the rest of the crew—"

"I don't know what happened to the rest of the crew," Celeste replied. "All I can say is that that thing in medlab was once my ex-husband, Alan Carpenter. I don't have any idea how he got that way."

It was an hour later, and the entire team was sitting in the empty command center. Although Julian and Rydell had restored power to the base, it would be some time before the air processors and environmental systems restored the temperature and atmosphere. When power was returned to the medlab, they had found that one of the stasis restraint tables was still operational, and they wasted no time placing the alien . . . Alan . . . on it.

"Jesus, what have we stumbled into here? Base scans show no one else is alive in here except us."

"What do you mean—us? What about that thing in the lab?"

"I mean Alan—or whatever he is now—does not read on the base sensors," Rydell said. "I mean, what the hell was that?"

"Well, that's just one of the things we should try to— no, we need to find out," Celeste said. "Clay, did you manage to get a message off to the *Epona?*"

Clayton looked at Gorman, who nodded. "Yeah, we made contact and informed them of the situation. They told us to investigate further, as long as there is no danger to our team. Since the base is deserted, I don't see a problem with that. They also advised us to try and locate the missing personnel. And they want the unknown life-form restrained and brought back for further study. They're already converting one of the quarantine rooms into an examination chamber."

"What? I'm not going anywhere in a ship with that thing. And just how in the hell are we supposed to find

anyone when we already know they're not on the base?
Go outside and yell for them? Look, the obvious thing
is to get the hell out of here and call in the UPNEC
investigation team," Julian said. "I don't know about the
rest of you, but I certainly didn't come here to end up
like . . . these . . ."

"Bodies? You'd better watch your mouth," Tony
Carver said. "Two of those people I carried out of here
were friends of mine."

"I understand that, but do you want to end up like
Alan? There's no reason for us to stay here any longer
than we have to," Armitage said.

"No reason? No reason! Over a dozen people are
missing, and probably dead! The one survivor that we've
found has been turned into I don't know what! And all
you're interested in is saving your own skin!" Celeste
said, rising from her chair. "Besides, we're the only ones
around for a few billion miles who can look into this.
At the very least, we owe it to them to find out what
happened!"

"Whoa, a little hot under the collar about the ex, eh,
Celeste?" Armitage smirked, but sat back down. "I'm
just giving my opinion on the matter, that's all."

"I think we'd be better served if you shoved your
opinion up your—"

"Celeste, Julian, that's enough!" Clayton snapped.
"You two are like children, I swear. Now be quiet and
focus on the task at hand." He let out a deep breath.
"Celeste, we're not going anywhere until we have a few
answers. Now, the first thing I want is a search of the
entire base, from the kitchens to the living quarters and
everything in between. We still have people missing, and
I want them found. Julian, since you've shown so much
concern for the lost crew, you and Tony can look for
them."

"Celeste, you and Jack get back to the medlab, try
and figure out what happened to Alan. I know, I know,"
Clayton said, holding up his hands to forestall her pro-
test. "You're not a doctor. But you are our resident
xenobiologist, and that makes you the most qualified to

head up the examination. Jackson, your medical training might help as well. Maggie, Rydell, why don't you two go to the kitchen and see if there's any food left? I know no one really feels like it right now, but we could all use something, especially after what we've been through. I'm going to finish off-loading some of the equipment from the *Rhiannon*. Some of the surveying equipment may prove useful if we have to scan outside the base. Any questions?"

"Yeah, when can we take off these damn suits? I'm starting to feel like a foil-wrapped baked potato," Jackson said.

"Actually," Rydell activated his collapsible helmet visor. "It's still a bit cold, but the oxygen content is leveling off nicely. Wear a couple of layers of clothes and you should be fine."

"Before we leap to that conclusion, what if what turned Alan into that whatever-it-is is an airborne virus or toxin?" Julian asked.

"If it was, it was destroyed when the air was purged from the base. I don't care if it was alien or not, nothing survives in a vacuum."

"Then how was that thing still alive in the medlab?" Tony asked.

"There was still a nominal, although unbreathable atmosphere in here when we arrived. Not that I'd care to take a guess *what* that thing breathes. Besides, the medlab was sealed off from the rest of the building, so you should run a scan of that room for foreign life-forms—I mean, besides the one you already have there, of course. Anyway, I've been running filter tests for anything down to fractions of a micron since I started the vent systems, and . . ." The engineer checked his suitcomp again. ". . . they picked up nothing. If it was a virus or anything like that, it's gone now."

With sighs of relief the team undid their own helmets and tasted air that, while still recycled, hadn't come from a breath unit.

"All right, everyone, you've got your assignments. Gorman, you're with me," Clayton said, using his sleeve to wipe the sweat off his forehead. "Stay in touch, and I don't need to tell you what to do if you see anything unusual."

"Yeah, soil yourself, then regroup," Maggie said. "After the medlab, I really don't think anything will surprise me anymore."

* * *

8.11.2103
1629 GMT

"My God, this is amazing," Celeste said to herself as she scanned the data she had managed to pull after three hours of struggling with the machine. The computer systems had been destroyed, but Clayton had ordered the drives collected and sent to the *Rhiannon* for further study. Jack was finishing that up now.

Just in case they were at risk of any kind of contamination, Celeste and Jack had changed into sterile surgery suits before going back into the medlab. In order to move about more freely, they had put Alan into a stasis dome and restrained him, sealing him off from all contact. Their examination was being performed by the machines that were still operational in the lab.

"What kind of mutation or viral infection could have done this?" she mused. With a start, Celeste realized that the words she had just spoken had been transcribed into the recorder she was using to compile her notes of the exam. *Brilliant work you just did there.* Sighing, she commanded the recorder to delete the last sentence, then began again.

"Subject is suffering from a virus or contagion of unknown origin. Symptoms include— Jesus, where to begin?" she said. "Physiology of subject has been altered on a cellular level, creating an altogether new, or never before discovered life-form." *But how did this happen? And where did it come from?*

Flexing her fingers, Celeste walked over to her suit

and pulled out the insulated liners from her gloves, slipping them over her chilled fingers.

Glancing at Jackson's suit hanging next to hers, Celeste saw an odd black patch on the left glove. She picked up the sleeve and took a closer look. The tip of the index finger had a charred, blackened hole in it, as if it had been burned by something from the inside.

Like a blue flash of light, she thought.

"Celeste . . ." a voice echoed in her head, almost sounding like it originated there, instead of from somewhere in the room.

"Jackson?" she asked, dropping the sleeve and turning around.

Save for her and the Alan/alien, the room was empty.

"Please . . . help me . . ."

Celeste looked around, trying to figure out where the voice was coming from. She checked both the suit comms, but neither was activated. She went over to the stasis dome and looked down at Alan, trying to remember if he had moved in any way since she had left him.

"Touch . . ." That same feathery voice tickled her mind again. Celeste leaned over the table, trying to listen, her hand reaching out almost of its own volition toward the table controls—"

"How's it going in here?" This voice was different and came from behind her, making her yelp and spin around. Jackson stood inside the door, a small packet in his hands. "Whoa, sorry, didn't mean to startle you."

"No, that's all right, no need to apologize," Celeste said. "This whole situation has got me on edge. What about you? Aren't you nervous walking about these corridors by yourself?"

"My nerves were removed in army basic training a long time ago," Jackson said with a grin. "Although, I must admit, I move through these corridors much faster than I normally would. Here, I brought some food. The choices aren't very appetizing. It looks like most of the food on base was ruined. Only the vacuum-sealed crap is left. You can have a tube of reconstituted green stuff or reconstituted brown stuff.''

"Lima curd surprise or tofu bean surprise, what a decision. Well, as long as there's Tabasco, I don't mind," Celeste said, realizing just how hungry she was. "I picked up a table over there, why don't we take five and dig in?"

"Best suggestion I've heard since we got here." Jackson walked to the small alcove and sat. "How's our friend doing?"

"As well as can be expected, I guess. I just got the body scan software on-line while you were gone. Whatever's been done to him, it's incredible. If I'm interpreting the scans correctly, his elbows and knee joints have been reconfigured into a ball-and-socket configuration. Holding his arm at a ninety-degree angle from his body, he can rotate his forearm at the elbow up to two hundred and seventy degrees in either direction. It's the same with his knees."

"Um, how would he stand up then, if his leg joints don't lock like ours?"

"That's just it," Celeste said, wolfing down a squirt of food. "I'm not sure about this, but I think he's supposed to move around on all fours, kind of like a quadruped, each leg moving almost independently of the others. And that's just the beginning. I haven't even gotten to the reconstruction around the face yet, or the modifications to the torso. There are some organs in there that I can't . . . identify, for lack of a better word."

"Damn, this thing will make your career, won't it?" Jackson asked.

"Well, I suppose so, I mean, if it's proved conclusively that an alien organism or bioagent was what . . . transformed him," she said.

"I don't know of many Earth diseases that make you grow a half-meter taller, fuse your teeth together, and turn you bone-white," Jackson replied.

Celeste was silent, not responding to his jest. She toyed with her meal instead, the food tube forgotten as she looked back at the stasis table.

"You're wondering if anything of Alan is left inside there, aren't you?" Jackson asked.

Startled, she looked up. "Wherever did you get that idea?"

"Hey, I'm in communications, remember?" Jackson said. "What you do is just as important as what you say. Also, if I found someone I cared about like that, it would probably be on my mind as well."

"Yeah, well . . . I guess you've probably heard that there was trouble between Alan and me."

Jackson had the grace to look away. "I . . . heard a few things through the grapevine."

Celeste smiled. "Anyway, it was pretty messy. But this is the last thing I expected to find here. And the last thing I'd wish on anyone, even a slimy ex-husband."

"Amen to that," Jackson said, sliding a bite of food out of a tube. "You'd think after a century they could get this stuff to taste like something recognizable."

Celeste set her tube on the table. "Yeah, I guess. By the way, I never got the chance to thank you for saving my life."

"Well, I couldn't let the only eligible female member of the team be an alien's snack," Jackson replied. "Seriously, I'm sure you would have done the same for me."

"Still, it was impressive, you sailing over the table and whomping it over the head like that. Good thing that table leg was nearby."

"Yeah, just luck I guess," Jackson replied.

"That laser must come in pretty handy at times," Celeste said, her eyes fixed on him.

Jackson looked up in surprise, the tube of concentrate squirting out between his fingers. "Damn, damn, damn. Nice work, Professor, but it shouldn't have been that hard. Hell, I'm surprised I kept it secret this long."

"You are cybered, aren't you?" Celeste said. "I looked at the table where the leg came off. The sheared screws looked fresh, like it had just happened an hour ago."

"Well, you know what they say. 'You can take the man out of the army, but you can't take the army out of the man.' Let's just say in my case that statement is even more true," Jackson said, leaning back in his chair.

"But if you're still cybered, what are you doing with us? From what I heard, the military doesn't let cyber-ops out of their sight—" Celeste's words trailed off as the implication of what she just said hit her.

"Before you get all worked up, let me explain. I've been your team's communication's op for three years, and I've done everything by the book, whatever Clay asked of me, no questions, no problems. You see, I really respect what you all do. When they asked me to join your team, at first I viewed it as being put out to pasture." Jackson ran a hand across his close-cropped hair and glanced behind Celeste at the table. "Now that I've seen that, I'm thinking my pasture's a long ways off."

"So, let me get this straight. The military assigned you to us?"

Jackson nodded.

"Why? We're a planetary survey team. We map and study dead worlds, lifeless balls of rock and ice."

"You've studied dead worlds and moons," Jackson agreed. "At least, from what I can see, you have until now."

"What are you—" Celeste followed his gaze to Alan, still lying motionless under the stasis field. "You mean the military knew there might be something here?"

"Whoa, not so fast. This is on a need-to-know basis and . . ." Jackson looked again at the Alan/alien's chalk-skinned body. "You know what, fuck it, at this point, you need to know."

Her raised eyebrows encouraged him to continue.

"Back in '89, and this is 1989, understand, the NASA space probe *Voyager II* flew by Neptune, sent back a whole shitload of info. One of the tidbits we got was the fact that Neptune's core puts out twice as much heat as it receives from the Sun. That's the part that made it onto the Web pages. But what they didn't say was that the heat being released from Neptune's core was far too steady and regular to be unstable magma emissions. In other words . . ."

"It was being artificially produced."

"And the lady wins a Turbo-Mutt doll. There was something here, and NARA wanted to find out what. In '47 we sent up the *Prometheus* probe from Mars, specifically designed to orbit Neptune and locate the power source. It circled this blue marble for eighteen years, while we analyzed every scrap of information it sent back."

"And?"

"In the end, we couldn't locate where the power emissions were coming from. The entire surface, such as it is, radiated energy of some kind. We weren't sure if the damn variable magnetic poles were screwing up our readings or what. Some scientists even speculated that maybe the magnetic fields were containing the energy emissions, channeling them, and thus producing the readings we were getting. Then in '62, O'Herlihan invented his practical grav/anti-grav platform. Naturally, the army wanted to go to Neptune, see just what the hell was giving off those readings, but that damn Indian subcontinent war broke out. By the time we had finished arbitrating peace between the Greater India Nation and the People's Theocracy of China, you scientists had beaten us to it, saying that exploring our solar system was top priority, needing to go beyond the bases on Mars and Io, farther than anyone had before. Very libertarian of you. So they built Poseidon Base. And the military immediately began planning for this day."

"Wonderful," Celeste muttered.

"Heck, you guys were supposed to be the first team here," Jackson said, shaking his head. "But . . . unexpected delays meant we couldn't launch when we wanted to."

"What delays?" Celeste asked.

"Well . . . specifically." Jackson pointed at her. "You weren't available."

"You've got to be kidding," Celeste said.

"Not about this, it's just too damn big to joke about," Jackson said. "I had worked with your team for more than a year by then, including Alan. I knew how you guys worked together. I wanted the whole team to go, but when Alan pulled his mindjob on you, he got assigned to the team that was going here first. Good thing, too, because as soon as he was gone, you started coming out of it."

"They didn't know . . ."

"How could we let the first team come out here with an unknown power source and not warn them? That's what you're thinking. Answer's simple. We made sure their geologist was ill, and couldn't go. So they likely wouldn't know about the source, and they'd have no one here who would be testing the planet's surface. They'd just come here, do their tour, collect their samples, run their tests, and leave, no problem."

"But there was a problem," Celeste's eyes were daggers.

"We didn't count on anything like this happening. Nobody had a clue we were sending these men and women to their deaths. Do you have any idea what it would take for anything to survive on this planet for a night, let alone months or years? Something we couldn't even fathom. Neptune was empty, an ice cube. For what it's worth now, I am sorry about what happened here. We do owe it to them to find out what caused this."

Celeste said nothing for several moments. Then she inhaled sharply. "Why? Why do you want to find out? For NARA's weapons research division? You boys need to find something even more efficient to kill people with?" Celeste pushed her chair away from the table and crossed her arms, her whole body shaking. "Goddamn it, there isn't anything the military won't contaminate with their presence, is there?"

"Celeste, listen, this mission goes back farther than you realize. . . ."

"What I'm realizing is that eight people are dead, probably the rest of them as well, and perhaps there could have been something done to stop it."

Jackson's voice was calm. "I'm telling you, I've been in the planning stages of this mission for the past seven years, and we had no idea that anything like this would happen. I know it doesn't mean much now, but I give you my word that NARA did not send the first team out here to get killed. The tests they were doing were laying the groundwork for our mission."

"*Our* mission? You mean *your* mission, don't you?" Celeste said. She stood and walked to the stasis table, looking down at Alan lying there.

"Oh, come on, Celeste, finding something like this— I'll admit, not exactly this way, but indisputable proof that other life than our own exists—has been a goal of yours all your life, hasn't it? I mean, why become a xenobiologist in the first place? It's not to study the microbes on Mars or grow spore colonies off Jupiter, it's to find the big one, to be the first one to discover the proof that other intelligent life exists in the galaxy, right? Tell me I'm wrong."

Celeste heard Jackson's words, but she was focused on Alan's enlarged gold eyes.

"Help me . . ."

"Touch me . . . please . . ."

Alan's voice. That's Alan's voice, she thought.

She looked up at Jackson, who was standing up now, on the other side of the table.

"Yes, it's true, but not at this price," she told him.

With that Celeste hit the button that turned off the stasis field and placed her hand on the alien's bone-white cheek.

*　　*　　*

The room around Celeste shrank to nothingness, the walls, ceilings, Alan, and Jackson, everything vanished into a pinhole of golden-white light. A wave of sensory images flooded through every synapse of her brain, impacting her consciousness with the force of a thousand sledgehammers.

. . . Floating, rising above the planet, soaring above the Solar System, past the stars in our arm of the Milky Way . . . flying faster, ever faster, traveling millions of light-years, until the Sun was just a white speck, a star among millions of other stars.

*. . . Returning, moving back faster and faster, shooting
forward until she could see the universe expanding, the
Big Bang, spraying cosmic matter into space, trillions of
stars, billions of galaxies, tens of millions of planets being
formed, waste matter being pulled into orbits by the inexorable gravity of stars across our spiral galaxy, throughout
each arm.*

*. . . Flying closer and closer to the arm that she some-
how knew contained our solar system, seeing it approach
and our Sun burning ever brighter in her vision. Like the
universe, it was expanding, growing, forming, a cluster of
heavenly bodies, eight planets rotating around a yellow
star. Eight planets . . .*

*. . . A shadow crossed her sight, and Celeste saw a huge
craft passing between herself and the Sun, swallowing all
the available light, cloaking her in darkness . . .*

The vision began fragmenting before her eyes. *Other-
worldly intelligence . . . a ship the size of a moon, oblong,
a gigantic dirt-colored egg . . . slender, pale aliens scurrying about . . . the sudden flare of a collision . . . debris
splintering off the ship . . . explosion . . . powerless
hulk . . . drifting in space . . .*

Ghosts . . .

*A spark of power . . . radiating down . . . toward
the core . . .*

"Celeste? Are you all right?" Jackson asked.

Celeste opened her eyes and looked at him, then looked
down at her arm in his hand. "What did you do?"

"Saw you put your hand on that thing and convulse.
I got over here as fast as I could. What the hell
happened?"

Power. "We have to get out of here, right now," Celeste said. "The things that took Alan are going to come
back here."

No sooner were the words out of her mouth than the
lights flashed off, replaced a second later by the red
emergency lights. Both Celeste and Jackson knew what
that klaxon meant. They ran for their suits, struggling
into them.

Her suit half on, Celeste waddled back over to Alan, trying to read the unfathomable expression on his face. His bulging, golden eyes met hers.

"Leave me . . ."

Celeste nodded, bending down and kissing her ex's forehead. Once again the tingle of unearthly awareness. . . . *Bone-white forms, swimming/scuttling through slushy tunnels carved in the planet's surface. One of them came to a section of ceramsteel and flowed right through it, melding with the wall as though it wasn't even there. Entering the base . . .*

"Celeste, that's the general evac alarm! Come on!" Jackson yelled from the doorway.

She slipped her arms into the sleeves and activated the electromagnetic closures to seal her suit, hearing the welcome hiss of pressure as her internal environment stabilized. She turned and headed for the door.

"What about him?" Jackson asked. "He's the find of the last two thousand years."

"He'd never survive," Celeste said. "And we don't have the time to secure him. We have to go now!"

Once outside the medlab, Celeste hit the keypad, sliding the door shut. She took one last look at Alan, who was sitting up, his taloned hand raised in a farewell gesture.

Celeste just had time to return the wave before Jackson was pulling her down the hallway.

"Clay, what's happening? Is there a shield leak?" she asked into the comm, panting as they ran.

"We just got the command room systems on-line when sensors detected a major shift in the methane plate the base rests on. The disturbance is emanating from underneath the shield, and indicates increasing seismic activity, although I don't know why it's happening. Julian and Tony said they hadn't found any more bodies. Rather than risk anyone else, we're getting the hell out of here."

"Good that's just what we need to do," Celeste replied.

"What? How do you know that?" Clayton asked.

"You wouldn't . . . believe me . . . if I told you," she said, panting. "I'll tell you all about it back on the ship." *If we get back to the ship,* she added to herself.

Just then Celeste and Jackson were almost knocked off their feet by a massive tremor. Jackson maintained his footing, but Celeste was sent skidding into a wall, hitting it with an audible crack.

Jackson was by her side instantly, helping her up. "We've gotta move!" Celeste didn't reply, but pulled him with her down the corridor.

The pair ran down the hallway back to the T-intersection, where they met up with Clay, Gorman, Tony, and Julian.

"The ship is ready to go. Rydell and Maggie are already on board," Gorman said. "The sooner we get the hell off this iceball, the better I'll feel."

They ran down the hallway as fast as the bulky suits would allow. But halfway down the corridor, Jackson held up his hand.

"Listen."

For a moment, there was just the sound of everyone's noisy breathing. Then their audio pickups registered a noise . . . a whispery brushing of something on metal.

"Company's here, so we shouldn't be." He resumed the run, with the rest of the team falling in behind him. Everyone tried to focus on the doors at the end of the hallway, ignoring the shushing sound that seemed to be growing louder, coming from all around them.

"Almost there, come on, we can make it," Celeste said.

"Rydell, open the hangar doors, we're twenty meters away and closing!" Clayton said. The massive doors began to slide apart, revealing the blackness of the hangar, now split by the landing lights of the *Rhiannon.*

"Damn, she never looked so good," Gorman said.

"Amen," said a voice Celeste thought was Julian's.

"Everyone aboard, we're fast-burning out of here," Gorman said, standing at the door and making sure the others got out safely.

Celeste was passing through the doorway when another shock wave hit, causing the corridor to twist and
buckle like a plastic straw in the hands of a giant. There
was a thunderous noise, and it felt to Celeste like the
floor had just dropped out from under her.

"The antigrav generators must be off-line! This place
is going to go under in a few minutes," Gorman yelled.

They followed the rest of the team into the ship, Gorman cursing as he struggled past them and into the cockpit. The *Rhiannon* was listing to port, slightly at first,
then the tilt becoming more pronounced as the base continued to sink.

"Everyone strap in and hang on!" Gorman shouted
over the intercom. Celeste hurried to buckle herself in
as the roar of the ship's engines drowned out everything
else. Still, she could feel the vibration of the base shaking itself apart around them.

The *Rhiannon* lurched to one side as it lifted off,
throwing everyone hard against their harnesses. The engines screamed, and the ship vaulted straight up, out of
the collapsing hangar and into the violent atmosphere.

The dropship was tossed like a leaf in the storm, and
Celeste's stomach, mind, and throat all seemed to switch
places. The repulsor field hummed like a swarm of angry
bees, repelling the clouds of supersonic particles that
slammed into the field. The ship continued to buck and
spin, helpless in the thousand-kilometer winds that threw
it around.

"Gorman . . . why . . . isn't the gravity tether on?"
She dimly heard Clayton shout into the comm.

"The . . . wave . . . is . . . on," he shouted back.
"We'd . . . all be . . . dead if it wasn't. The gravity . . . of
the planet . . . is fluctuating . . . for some reason."

Just then the ship righted itself and leveled off.

"All right, we're out of the storm and heading into
the upper atmosphere," Gorman said. "Is everyone all
right?"

Clayton made sure he got nods from everyone.

"Clay," Gorman continued, "as soon as we're out of the

atmosphere, radio the *Epona* and have them prepare to leave orbit. As soon as we're aboard, they have to move to a minimum safe distance of five billion kilometers."

"Why? And where did those ground tremors come from?" Maggie said as much to herself as to her crewmates. "Neptune doesn't have any seismic activity. The wind systems are caused by the movement of the frozen chemicals on the surface."

"You wouldn't believe me if I told you," Celeste whispered.

"Something seismic is happening down there, there's no way it could be anything else," Clayton said. "Given the intensity of the activity we felt, something huge is going to happen. Whether's it large enough to warrant moving the *Epona* out of orbit . . ."

"Clayton, it is," Celeste said firmly. "When you see what's going to happen, you'll understand, but if we stay where we are, then we're all dead."

"All right, Celeste." His expression told her he wanted an explanation—as soon as possible. "Gorman, send the message to prepare to leave orbit. "What's our ETA?"

"I'm going to try and use the winds to slingshot us out of the atmosphere, then we can full burn out to the ship. Should be about forty-five minutes."

I just hope that's enough, Celeste thought.

* * *

Other than a few turbulent moments leaving the atmosphere, the rest of the journey went off without incident. An hour later, the team was safely back on the *Epona,* which was cruising toward a point billions of miles away from Neptune.

Since Celeste had actually made contact with an alien organism, she was hustled off the *Rhiannon* into immediate quarantine. Sealed behind a repulsor wall, she looked up to see Jackson and Clayton both walk into the med quarters.

"How you doing?" Jackson asked, a tentative smile on his lips.

"I'll be okay, as soon as they stop trying to debride me. I don't think I have many more layers of skin left."

"They're just doing their job, you know that," Clayton said. "Since you were the one who figured it out, I thought you might want to see this. *Epona* launched a weather satellite into orbit just before we left. It's transmitting back now."

A flatscreen monitor winked to life on the far wall, showing a picture of Neptune. As Celeste watched, the brilliant blue cloud hung there in space for a few seconds, then started to change before her eyes.

The gas giant began to flatten on one hemisphere, as if a powerful vacuum had suddenly developed and was sucking in all the gas in that area. Celeste watched, transfixed, as the sapphire cloud began shrinking, faster than she would have believed possible.

"But this can't be happening," she heard Clay say. She didn't dare look away, transfixed by what her eyes were showing her.

"You think that can't happen, just watch what's coming up," Celeste said under her breath.

The two men didn't hear her, they were so engrossed by the spectacle unfolding before them. The cloud was rapidly disappearing now, revealing the pale surface of Neptune. Even from fifty thousand kilometers away, the roiling, heaving surface of the planet was plain to see. Jagged continent-sized plates of frozen methane smashed into each other, sending plumes of ice crystals hundreds of kilometers into the atmosphere.

Now the cloud covered less than half the planet, collapsing in on itself, drawn toward the core, revealing Neptune in all its furious power. Celeste watched, half-expectant, half-fearful of what she would see next.

With what she imagined was a huge rumble, as there was no sound transmitted, the sheets of methane began flaking off, peeling from the planet like layers of an onion, spinning and colliding and sailing into space in all directions. Just before the satellite was destroyed, Celeste caught a glimpse of something even she found hard to believe.

The hot core of Neptune emerged from the fragmented remains of its crystalline prison and began cooling off. As the three watched, huge cracks appeared in its surface as the crust froze, then also began to break up. Like an icy phoenix emerging from a crystal egg, a secondary core, perhaps a tenth the size of the former mass that had made up the planet's center, emerged from the fragmented rubble and began moving. Not in a random direction, not spinning aimlessly through space, but deliberately, on what had to be a plotted course. Just before the satellite camera went dark, she saw it begin to change direction, avoiding a massive chunk of solidified methane that was already shattering apart. Then the camera went dead, and the monitor switched off.

Celeste walked back to the clear repulsor wall and stared at the two men on the other side. "Dear God, tell me you got that recorded," she said.

Clay spoke first. "Of course we did. But I don't know if anyone will believe it."

"Oh they'll believe it when Neptune doesn't show up in their telescopes. Jesus, we just lost one of our planets, for God's sake," Jackson said.

"Neptune wasn't a planet at all. It was a huge . . . spacecraft," Celeste said, as if thinking out loud. "Thousands, maybe hundreds of thousands of years old. The craft was . . . damaged, maybe a collision of some kind. The crew put themselves in hibernation, waiting for the right time to awaken."

"So when a source of power became available, one that could jump-start their engines—or whatever they used to propel something that massive, they were woken up and came to investigate."

"And we came along and provided just the thing," Celeste said. "That's where the power drain was. For months, the entire output of Poseidon's reactor had been feeding their ship. They must have had some kind of self-renewing power source that needed the energy to start. I don't know, maybe their technology amplifies gathered power in ways we haven't dreamed of yet. Who knows? But we gave them the key."

"And that's why they left Alan," Celeste said, almost to herself.

"That was going to be my next question," Jackson said. "But please, don't let me interrupt you."

"He was put there as . . . a warning, perhaps, that's the best way I can put it. I don't think the aliens really cared too much about what happened to us, but they wanted to send us a message, keep us distracted while they . . . topped off, so to speak."

"Which was?" Clayton asked.

"I think . . . they were quoting Shakespeare," Celeste said.

"What?" This from both men in unison.

"A quote from *Hamlet*, act one, scene four; "There are more things in heaven and earth, Horatio, then are dreamt of in your philosophy," Celeste said, grinning. "Maybe they were letting us know we're the little kids on the block."

"But what about the rest of the base crew?" Jackson asked. "What happened to the rest of them, the ones who weren't in the command center?"

"I don't know, but it's possible they were taken like Alan. Maybe they're on that ship we saw," Celeste said.

"And the command crew," Clayton mused aloud. "Maybe they guessed what was happening and tried to barricade the entrance to the hangar and the command room, then purge the base's atmosphere, hoping it would kill the extraterrestrials. When their air ran out, they tranquilized themselves into unconsciousness and froze to death."

"But we'll never really know," Jackson said. "Unless someone manages to get something from the data we retrieved from the base computers."

Clayton shook his head in disbelief of everything. "Celeste, get some rest, and we'll go over the whole thing in the morning. Coming, Jackson?"

"In a minute." Jackson watched as Clayton walked

out. When the door slid closed, he turned back to Celeste, a grin pulling up one corner of his mouth. "You know more than you're telling, don't you?"

Celeste shrugged.

"You know NARA's going to want to talk to all of us for a very long time. With all this evidence and eyewitness accounts, who knows how long they'll detain us."

She shrugged again.

"God, I wish I knew what he . . . Alan . . . told you," Jackson said.

She just stared at him.

"Right. Well, if you . . . want to talk or something when you get out of quarantine, you know where to find me."

"Yes, I do," she said.

Jackson nodded, turned on his heel, leaving Celeste alone.

Yes, you're right, there was plenty more that Alan told me, she thought. *The ship, carrying hundreds of thousands of aliens . . . the impact of the meteor, killing thousands and crippling the ship . . . the repairs, but with no power for their main engines, they were stuck in orbit around this yellow star . . . helpless . . . how they set up a reaction to freeze their population until somehow an energy source came along . . . and how we gave them the means to escape their frozen prison . . . and let them continue traveling on their way. How they did take the rest of our crew . . . transforming them into hybrids like Alan, to learn about us . . . learn from us . . . and how they will learn from these beings as well . . . Alan couldn't take it . . . he gave up, wanted to die, not realizing the opportunity he had been given. Still, could I be that cavalier, if it had happened to me?*

And the message they left, the last thing Alan said to me . . . The real reason he was there . . . because he knew I was coming . . . and only he could contact my mind . . . having been so close to me before . . .

"When the time is right, we will return . . ."

Celeste walked to the sliver of window and looked out at the vastness of space stretching before her. *God, please let that be in my lifetime.*

MOMENTS

by Kristine Kathryn Rusch

Kristine Kathryn Rusch writes novels in five genres under several pen names. She has just sold a cross-genre sf/mystery series. The books will appear later this year. Her most recent science fiction publication is a collection of her short stories, Stories for an Enchanted Afternoon.

1

"We have to be prepared," Hoa Nguyen said as she strapped on her laser pistol. She also carried a stun stick. She had attached an emergency aid patch to the inside of her left wrist. Her black hair was pulled back, and she wore a medium level environmental suit. With a soft voice command, the suit would seal around her ankles and wrists, raise a hood that would cover her entire face, and protect her against a hostile environment. She hoped she wouldn't have to use it. "Everything could change in an instant."

The two members of her security team watched as if they had never seen her before. JaVon Daschle and Nils Svenson were men used to routine; they'd never encountered a situation like this one before.

She hadn't either, but she had encountered other things. And the only control she had was in her preparation.

They stood in the prep room near the docking ring. Behind her was an interlinked series of locking doors, all of which would shut in case of a structural breach or damage to the environmental systems.

The prep room was small, and only the security teams had access to it. Inside were the environmental suits, weapons, and other gear specially designed for trouble on the docking ring.

"Traffic Control tells me the landing was rough. The compensations we sent for the new docking ring were not used, and no one answered when we tried direct contact. The ship stabilized, depressurized, and went through standard procedure, but no one has disembarked in the hour since landing."

JaVon strapped on his own laser pistol. He was large, muscular, barely within the physical requirements for security on the space station. "Has the ship been decontaminated?"

"Decontamination can't proceed until the crew is evacuated," Hoa said, letting her annoyance show. Her security team should know procedure.

"Then I'm not going in," Nils said, his pale skin flushed. He had never defied her before.

"Fine," Hoa said. "You don't go in, and you're fired."

Anger flashed through his blue eyes, but he said nothing. The termination of any member's position on the space station meant that the person had to return to Earth at his own expense. The return trip would be taken on the first Earth-bound ship leaving the space station, and there was never time for review.

In Hoa's fifteen years here, only five employees had been terminated, and all five were off the station within twenty-four hours. The journey was long since the space station, called ISS3 because it was the third International Space Station in a series of five, floated in geosynchronous orbit above Mars.

"I don't like this," Nils said, his tone sullen. It was an acquiescence, but a reluctant one. They both knew she would write him up when this day was done.

"You don't have to." She slipped on her gloves. The

thin material was cool against her skin. "I have no idea
what we will encounter inside. This ship came from Europa, one of Jupiter's moons. We've been checking the
nets and our other information, but so far, we've heard
no whisper of trouble there. Other ships, including those
that work for the same company, Pribox, have made the
trip with no difficulty."

She was doing her best to reassure both men, although
she resented them for it. They had signed onto security
understanding that the job had risks. Quelling disturbances outside the restaurant in the main section, settling disputes among the locals over personal items,
investigating petty thefts and assaults did not count as
risk.

Approaching a ship that had landed under strange circumstances did.

"I'll go first," she said. "You will follow my lead and
take instructions from me. Any deviation from standard
procedure will result in black marks. Is that clear?"

She didn't wait for their responses. Instead, she
palmed the door latch, letting them into the docking
ring.

The open doors created a brightly lit tunnel that ran
to the ship. The tunnel's silence was eerie; usually fresh
docked ships were full of noise—the laughter of crew
members, happy to be somewhere new; the clangs of
equipment being moved; or the voice of a commander
shouting orders.

In all her years, she had never approached a silent
ship.

Her stomach clenched, and she felt a whisper of
nerves which she wasn't about to let her team see. She
stepped inside the tunnel, resisting the urge to activate
the environmental controls on her suit. Nils' worries had
infected her, more deadly than any microbe that had
somehow escaped all the filtration systems in the docking ring and on the still-functioning ship.

Her boots clanged on the metal floor. She moved forward slowly, straining to hear anything beyond her own
breathing. The men were close behind her, their boots

clanging against the surface. She glanced over her shoulder. Even JaVon looked nervous now, his tall powerful body bent to accommodate the tunnel's low ceiling.

As she got closer to the ship's entrance, she saw that the regular lighting was on. The ship appeared to be functioning normally. She caught the faint whiff of something fetid, but told herself that was her imagination. Strong smells were filtered like everything else; the air, even in this small a space, should have had a clinically pure, almost metallic odor if it had any odor at all.

But the closer she got to the ship, the more she was certain she was smelling something new, something she didn't like.

"Skimmer 4," she said as she reached the last of the ring's doors. "This is space station security. Is everything all right?"

Her warning was standard, something any ship's crew, no matter how inexperienced, should recognize. All pilots were trained in the standard response. Any deviation was to serve as a warning of danger ahead.

But she had been trained to expect a verbal deviation, not silence. And silence was what greeted her.

Sweat ran down her spine, pooling against the small of her back. The tunnel was perfectly cool; it was her nerves that were creating her discomfort.

"Skimmer 4," she repeated as she reached the ship's open door. "This is space station security. Is everything all right?"

The fetid odor was stronger now, as if the stench were so overpowering that the ship's standard systems couldn't compensate. The hair on the back of her neck rose, and she resisted the urge to look at her team. Something told her that if they saw her face, they might run.

Even though the ship had had a difficult landing, the seals were all intact. The doors met perfectly, giving her a view of the ship's main corridor—if she could call it that.

She'd never seen a ship so small. Normally the main corridor split and circled the ship. This corridor seemed to go straight. It ended in a small area that served as

MOMENTS   129

the main recreational center. The ceilings were so low
that she felt uncomfortable—and her slight frame was
perfect for the close quarters found so often in space-
going vessels.

Hoa climbed down two shallow steps into the ship.
Her discomfort grew. The air had an almost oily feel to
it, as if it had been recycled one too many times. It was
too late to put on her environmental suit—she'd have
to go to decontamination when this was all over.

The men behind her wouldn't feel the strange air.
Both of them had put on their full suits before stepping
into the tunnel. She was going this part alone.

The ship's systems seemed to be fine. Full lighting,
normal temperatures. The equipment, including the nearby
computer controls, seemed to be functioning. The door
to the cockpit was closed, just as it should have been for
landing, securing the pilot and copilot inside.

Cockpit doors had special locks and seals which activated automatically when landing or docking sequences
started. She wouldn't be able to enter, but she knocked.
The pilot should have shut off the automatic system
when the docking was successful.

No one answered. Even though she had expected that,
her unease grew. Where was everyone?

She glanced over her shoulder. Her team had moved
in different directions, just like they were supposed to.
She could see the back end of JaVon's suit, but saw
nothing of Nils. She could hear him, though, his boots
shushing on the plastic flooring. His steps were hesitant,
as if he was afraid of what he would find.

She was growing afraid, too, and it pissed her off. One
of the reasons she went into security was so that she
would never feel afraid again. She got training, learned
how to be brave in any situation. Her slight stature was
a benefit, not a liability. She was strong. She had to be.

As she recited her mantra, she walked past through
the recreation area into the galley. The kitchen was
tiny—barely large enough for a person of her size. Prepared food rotted on an open tray and a digital display
informed her that the galley's stove had been shut down

by computer. The gravity had never been off, or the food would have splattered all over the galley.

Her mouth was dry, and her fingers itched. She almost opened her communication line, then decided to wait. She had proof something was wrong, but she didn't know what it was yet. No sense bringing in extra security when there was no obvious threat.

She slipped through the galley into the mess. The fetid stench seemed stronger here, and she realized she hadn't smelled it at all in the tiny galley. Obviously the rotting food hadn't been the source of the odor.

Hoa reached for her stun stick, keeping the pistol attached to her side. She was so nervous that she might strike the trigger accidentally, hitting her own men.

The mess was L-shaped, with no portals open to space as was customary in most vessels. The table and chairs before her were bolted into position, their surfaces empty.

She felt as if she were being watched. She whirled, looked into the bottom part of the L, and froze.

They were all there, all five crew members. Four were clearly dead, sprawled across tables, under chairs, arms extended and blood everywhere.

The fifth, a bald man of indeterminate age, sat in the center of the carnage, his pale eyes watching her every move.

"Did you come to take me home?" he asked.

2

Darren Alnot stepped out of the med center, hands shaking. He hadn't seen anything like this in twenty years of detective work. Four people killed by a swift and savage attack, then left to decompose in the ship's mess. The virtual med lab was able to reconstruct the bodies as they must have looked when they were newly slaughtered—the expressions lax, the hands open in supplication or protection, the wounds gaping and clear.

Most of the blood spattered across the tables and chairs had been arterial. That suggested the wounds to the jugular came first, followed by the narrow slashes to the hands—defensive wounds found in the pilot and co-pilot (who were probably killed last and figured out, in those brief seconds between life and death, what was happening to them).

The deep puncture wounds to the chests and backs had been the final insult. Most of the blood had come from the knife, mixing the various types. By the time the puncture wounds were inflicted, the hearts had stopped pumping and blood no longer flowed through the bodies.

It flowed out of them.

Alnot clenched his fists, willing his hands to stop shaking. Most of the cases he investigated in Ares, Mars' main domed colony, were domestic abuse. He'd only covered a handful of homicides, and those had generally been the product of too much drink, or a beating that had gotten a bit too violent.

He'd never seen anything like this before.

He wasn't qualified to be here. He'd only been assigned to this case because he was the closest investigator with the most years on the job. There were other investigators with more experience in homicide, but they were on the Moon. The Moon's older, more established colonies had gradually developed the vices of Earth. Most of those hadn't hit Ares yet.

And, of course, there were no investigators on ISS3. None of the space stations had a real police force. Security was supposed to handle the complaints—separate the brawling drunks and investigate petty thefts—sending any notes they needed for potential trials to investigators at nearby colonies.

Alnot had received hundreds of reports over the years from ISS3, all of them minor. They had never requested his presence on the station before.

He wished they hadn't requested it this time. The ship had been hard enough to take, with the blood dried brown on the surfaces, the rotting food on the floor, mixing with the dried fluids left by deceased bodies.

Hoa Nguyen told him that the stench had left with

the victims, but Alnot didn't believe it. He had still been able to smell it, faint and ever present, as he stood in the center of all that carnage.

Nguyen was competent, one of the best he'd ever seen in station security. She'd made sure the evidence was left intact. She'd taped the scene before the bodies were removed using three different cameras—a video camera, a holoprojector, and a VR vid which allowed him to walk through the scene as she had found it.

He didn't have the nerve to do that just yet. He barely survived the Med Center.

But he had all he needed to know. The physical evidence from the bodies alone confirmed the obvious; Gil Houk, the only surviving member of the *Skimmer 4*, had slaughtered his crewmates. The attack had been swift and vicious, completed with a great deal of force. The weapon was a sharpened steak knife of a type banned from all government and most commercial vessels. It had been found next to Houk and had only his fingerprints on it.

Alnot knew the who and the how, but those were only the beginning. He needed to make a case, an example of Houk, so this sort of thing never happened again. The case needed to be airtight because news of the attack had leaked in the three days it took to get transport to ISS3.

He'd only been on the station a day, but he'd already heard rumors of a space-borne parasite that caused men to go mad, and other rumors of a disease so subtle that it affected the primitive response areas of the brain. He knew, because he'd seen the charts, that Houk had been tested for such things and the tests had come up negative.

No. Houk had done this of his own volition.

Alnot hugged that information to himself. People in the far reaches of space believed that such behavior couldn't happen. Anyone who lived on a space station or routinely flew in spacecraft had to suffer through a thousand psychological batteries, testing everything from ability to handle stress to reactions to extreme solitude.

No one wanted to believe that someone who had failed those tests had been allowed on a vessel. Alnot didn't want to believe it either, but he had to start somewhere.

And he needed help. All sorts of expert help, so that this case was conducted by the book—or at least, by his book. The ship was registered in Moon Colony Armstrong, and that colony's laws would apply. Houk would send for assistance from there—which would take some considerable time to arrive here—and, in the meantime, he would work the case according to Ares law.

He had no other choice.

3

"We have a problem," Eden Frazier said. She stood in front of Hugh McCaron's desk, wishing she could sit down. She was over six feet, and Hugh McCaron, Prosecutor for the Colony of Armstrong, had short man's disease He hated to be reminded of his lack of stature—in anything.

Instead of focusing on his face, Frazier stared at the domed Colony of Armstrong through McCaron's floor-to-ceiling windows. When Armstrong had been founded almost a century ago, the dome had been five times larger than the city built beneath it. Now the colonial government was going through the International Tribunal to find ways to buy outlying land and expand the dome.

"I don't like problems," McCaron said, leaning back in the leather chair he'd ordered directly from Earth.

That chair, more than any thing else about McCaron, made Frazier nervous. They were both public servants, and his salary, while double hers, was still only three steps above subsistence. That chair probably cost one year's pay.

"I know that, sir, but you have to hear this." Frazier threaded her hands together. She knew McCaron would dislike this next part of what she had to say even more than her opening. "It's about the Houk case."

"Houk?" He stared at her blankly. She had expected that. The murders had occurred only the week before. She had received the assignment because the reports were already coming in, but the prisoner and the evidence in the form of *Skimmer 4* wouldn't be here for more than a year.

"The crew murders on the Pribox ship," she said, to clarify. Anyone who lived on the Moon knew the name Pribox. It was the biggest employer in all three domes, and had even built a private dome for its employees who couldn't travel back to a colony during the work week.

McCaron pursed his lips. "I knew the moment we got this case, it would be trouble. The timeline and the publicity both are enough to taint the jury pool. Add to that an off-Moon investigation, and we've got more problems than I want to consider."

Frazier remained silent. She'd already heard that speech from him. It had ended with the reasons he wanted her on the case—all flattery and emptiness. They both knew the only reason she got the Pribox murders were because she was the newest member of the prosecutor's staff. Her five-year contract guaranteed she'd be in the offices long enough to handle this case from start to finish.

"What's the new wrinkle?" he asked as he pushed a button. One of the chairs that had been leaning against the wall unfolded itself and zoomed along a planned path on the carpeted floor. The chair stopped near her. The first time she'd seen McCaron's moving chairs, they'd startled her—more Earth gadgetry—but after a year in the office, she was used to them.

"The psychological reports," she said. "Two are in so far, but I have a hunch the others are going to be the same."

McCaron squinted at her. "If this guy was legally insane, how the hell did he get on board that vessel?"

She shook her head. "It's a little more complicated than that. How's your space history?"

"Weaker than it should be." McCaron folded his

hands over his flat stomach. He kept himself in shape by walking all over the colony.

Frazier sighed. She had been afraid of that. McCaron was current on the politics of Armstrong, the way that the criminal laws worked, and the skeletons in every closet of every lawyer he'd ever come across. With that much information rattling around his brain, he had little room for anything else.

"In the latter half of the twentieth century," she said, "only two Earth countries had viable space programs."

"The United States and whatever Russia had been under the Communists. I know that," McCaron said. He sounded annoyed.

Frazier continued as if McCaron hadn't spoken. "In the course of their independent work, they discovered the same thing. Long-term missions were dangerous."

"No kidding," Frazier said. "The equipment alone—"

"I wasn't talking about the equipment, sir," Frazier said, struggling to keep her tone level." "I was talking about the psychological health of the space traveler."

McCaron's eyebrows narrowed, creating a slight crease in his forehead. Finally, Frazier had his full attention.

"Remember, these early space travelers were incredible individuals. They were strong, resourceful, and balanced. They managed to survive confinement in spaceships smaller than this office."

"But?" McCaron said, that momentary interest already fleeing.

"But they shared an experience, no matter what their personality type. On missions that lasted months, their emotional stability weakened. After thirty days, they developed an intense dislike for each other and a strong desire to go home."

"I take it this applies to the Pribox case?"

Frazier nodded. "The early space travelers dealt with the emotional deterioration as best they could, and nothing happened. But the various space agencies studied this problem and realized that most of the effects could be alleviated by making certain that ship's crew had enough personal space that they could spend time alone. They also needed entertainment and windows—lots of windows—even if those windows only showed the vastness of space."

McCaron closed his eyes. "I'm not going to like what you're going to say next, am I?"

He was quick. She would give him that. That was how he'd held onto his position for this long.

"Pribox designed their own cargo ships for the run from the Moon to Europa. Those ships can carry more cargo than any other ship that currently exists."

McCaron rubbed his nose with his thumb and forefinger. "At the expense of crew quarters."

"No, sir." Frazier waited until he opened his eyes to continue. "At the expense of all areas designed for human use only. *Skimmer 4* has one-tenth the crew space of any ship her size."

"One-tenth?" McCaron's voice shook.

"There was only one recreational area which was large enough to allow for some exercise equipment, but not nearly as much as the regulated minimum on government ships. The entertainment programming was limited, net access only went to the pilot and copilot, and the only windows on the entire ship were in the cockpit, which was restricted."

"How'd Pribox manage that?" McCaron asked.

"The vessel is private. So long as it met safety specs, it could fly."

"Aren't these safety specs?"

Frazier shook her head. "They're recommendations for private vessels, laws for public ships."

"Wonderful," McCaron said.

"It gets worse," Frazier said. "The only law that Pribox had to abide by was crew size. Five members are mandatory for a vessel of that class."

McCaron scratched his chin, then leaned back in his chair. Frazier recognized the look. He was already building a case, trying it in his mind, testing the angles and searching for an out.

"How do we know all this had an effect on Houk?"

"It doesn't matter whether it did or not," Frazier said.

"It matters," McCaron said, as if she were a first-year law student. "No matter how it seems, the defense still has to show a causal link."

"They have it," Frazier said. "Houk's first words to the ISS3's security team."

"Which were?"

" 'Did you come to take me home?' "

"Jesus," McCaron said, "the most stupid defense attorney on the Moon could get him off."

"No kidding," Frazier said, dryly repeating the words he had used earlier.

McCaron stood and shoved his hands in his pockets. "We got psychological testing history on this guy?"

"No," Frazier said. "Pribox isn't releasing it."

"Isn't . . . ?" McCaron turned, then cursed. "They didn't do any."

"Or if they did, it's not up to standard."

McCaron shook his head. "I don't have the money or the resources for this case. If it were Earth, maybe. But Pribox is our largest employer."

Frazier waited. She'd already gone through these arguments in her own mind.

"I need airtight for Criminally Negligent Homicide. Hell," he said, "I need perfect for Murder."

Frazier's heart was pounding. He was already using the word "I." That was what she wanted to hear. She didn't have the skill to go after Pribox. He did.

"We might be able to manage airtight," she said.

He snorted. "I can already tell you how they'll argue this. Flawed design. Ship company's fault. The company'll blame the designer, and the designer'll spend the rest of his life appealing either extradition or execution."

Frazier nodded. She was already wise to the ways of Moon law. At first, she'd thought the colonies would be a second chance, a place to make new rules, to throw out the old. But she'd learned the mistakes in thinking that during her second week on the job. *You want a*

place where the rules don't apply, you go to Europa,
McCaron had said to her. *Armstrong's been here for a
century. It's too late for us.*

"So what are you going to do?" she asked.

"I'll need some time on this one." McCaron walked
to the window. "Got any suggestions?"

Frazier stood and joined him at the window. For the
first time, she didn't mind towering over him. "As a
matter of fact," she said, "I do."

4

"Scare tactics," said Brian Pagoda. "They're just trying to see if we'll give in."

Nadia Shelmet glared at him. Pagoda was a heavyset
man whose thinning hair revealed a flaky scalp. She suffered Pagoda's presence in this meeting because he was
the project manager for Pribox's Europa Division, and
she needed his expertise. But his expertise didn't cover
legal matters, particularly those that had to do with the
conglomerate.

Those were her problems, just like this damn ship was
her problem. She'd been on notice since word came in
from ISS3, sending Legal out to discover their liabilities,
and to try to anticipate all the negatives this particular
crisis would cause.

She, Pagoda, the Chief Financial Officer, and all the
important people from Legal sat around a real oak table
in the conference room. The room was the largest in
Pribox's original building in the very center of Armstrong's downtown. From the windows, she could see the
courthouse, its whitewashed spire reflecting the sunlight
that filtered through the dome.

Ten scientists from various divisions waited in the
lobby outside. She'd already spoken to them, and hadn't
liked what she heard.

"I think McCaron's office has a point." Nadia's voice
carried. It didn't have to. Everyone in the room was
trained to listen closely to anything the CEO had to say.
"Those scientists out there tell me if we continue to run

the Europa operation like this, we can expect incidents like this one almost annually. Imagine what that publicity will do for us."

Pagoda frowned. "Do you know the capital outlay we've put into this?"

Nadia frowned. She'd had enough. "You're excused, Mr. Pagoda."

"What?"

"Excused. Welcome to leave. We have other things to discuss here."

"But I'm the one who knows the Europa operation. I'm the one . . ." His voice trailed off. His cheeks flushed as he understood his new role. "You can't blame me for this. I never heard of this guy Houk before he went nuts. I—"

"There's plenty of blame to go around." Nadia glanced at Legal. They were watching the exchange with interest. "I'm sure any press releases we issue will make certain the blame is well distributed."

"You're going to give in?"

"Scuttle the ships, promise better psych training for the crews, admit some blame without legal liability, and with minimal loss. Donations to specified charities, and some sort of nod to preventing future disasters. Of course I'm taking the deal. It's win-win for all of us."

"Win-win?" Pagoda shook his head. "This'll put Europa back five years. We may strand some of our people there. Not to mention the cost to the operation—"

"We've already gone over the costs," Nadia said. "It's an acceptable risk. All of it. Now, Mr. Pagoda, leave us to complete this meeting."

He stood, shaking, although she couldn't tell if it was with anger or terror. He wasn't bright enough to realize that he would keep his job—the last thing she needed was him out of work and blabbing to the net reporters. She'd keep him under control, in much the same way that Houk would be controlled.

So easy, really. It had been McCaron's suggestion, and it had come to her privately while the overall offer had been making its formal path through Legal.

Assign your best criminal lawyer to Houk, McCaron

had told her when they'd passed at the designated place on the street. *Make sure he's declared incompetent, unable to handle his own case. We'll take guilty by insanity, lock him up for life.*

Confine him? She'd asked, mostly because she couldn't resist. *Wasn't that the problem in the first place?*

McCaron had shaken his head and said no more. The retainer she paid him, laundered through more accounts than she cared to think about, had worked to her advantage again.

This incident would be a blip, a little notation in the history of private space travel, a cautionary tale for smaller companies who believed they could cut costs by trapping humans on long voyages in spaces too small for comfort.

"Let McCaron know," she said to the nameless lawyers, "that we're prepared to take his deal."

Both deals—the one that had come through channels and the one that hadn't. She handle the fallout, even out the blame, find the funds to compensate the victims' families so that they didn't sue.

She'd also set aside funds for future victims, because she was convinced that Pribox wouldn't just strand their people on Europa. Pribox would abandon them.

Her stomach fluttered—a momentary unease which she quelled with a ruthlessness she'd learned when she was ten, on that private shuttle her family had taken to their new home on the Moon.

Halfway there, everything had changed. Life support failed, only a handful of oxygen masks and even fewer environmental suits for more than a hundred crew and passengers. In her dreams, sometimes, she still saw the haze in the cabin, her mother's worried face, her father's fearful one, and the single yellow mask dropping down between them.

She'd reached for it, her tiny hand straining, and they'd let her. They let her take it because she was the most vulnerable, a child, the only one with a future. They probably thought that everyone on board would die anyway. But she'd been too young to know that, to think in such logical terms. Instead, she had pressed the mask to her face, and huddled in her seat, watching as people suffocated around her.

Nadia shook off the memory.

"We've done all we can here," she said, and made herself believe it.

5

Just like that, they shut him down. Darren Alnot stared out the portal in his leased room. The *Skimmer 4* listed slightly, the effects of its difficult docking just beginning to show.

The ship was off-limits now, the evidence he'd accumulated already bundled up and tucked inside. All of his files had been downloaded and encoded, sent to the prosecuting attorney's office on Armstrong.

Something had happened, something he didn't completely understand. One moment, he was trying to figure out the order of events from the splatter patterns, and the next he was forced out of the ship, told that Houk had been pleaded guilty by reason of insanity and the case was closed.

Other fingers had reached into this pie and contaminated it. If this had been an Ares case, Alnot might have fought it. But he didn't know the powerful on the Moon. He didn't even know the name of the prosecuting attorney. He had no resources, and no time.

Alnot had gotten rid of his files, but he would never forget the case, never forget the emptiness of Houk's face as he stared at the four walls of ISS3's brig.

"Home," he'd say if anyone spoke to him. "Just send me home."

Alnot was going home, too, to a world where he understood everything, where he knew exactly what was going on.

He would go home without a complaint, and once he was there, he'd finish the last task connected to, but not a part of, this investigation—a task he knew no one else would complete, not for months, or a year.

Or maybe even not at all.

6

The house's system was beeping—not the standard you-have-an-important-message beep, but the loud, obnoxious beep of an emergency. Darlene stood on the remains of her lawn, brown in the heat of a West Texas summer, and stared at the horizon.

She knew. She'd known for more than a month, when the news had trickled back to Earth about the Pribox shuttle that had been the scene of all that carnage.

Teresa would have contacted her somehow. As the news broke, even if she'd been in space, she'd have found a way to get a message home.

There hadn't been a message. Just silence.

Teresa had never been silent. From the moment she was born, Teresa had been a squalling, active bundle of energy.

"Momma," she said after they sent her to pilot school, when she'd come for what they both knew would be her last visit to Texas. "I'm probably gonna die out there, long before you do. Just remember, I'm doing something I love. I'll go happy."

But she hadn't gone happy. The news accounts said the unnamed pilot had died defending herself. She'd known what was about to come.

Just like Darlene did now.

The sunlight was golden on the abandoned oil fields. Darlene took one last look, then went inside, telling the house's computer to play a message she didn't want to hear, a message that had been routed, and rerouted through the silence of space. A message, the computer told her, from a man named Alnot, a message that would lance through her like a knife through the skin.

She had had both a moment and a lifetime to prepare—and somehow neither of them had been enough.

'ROID

by Jeff Crook

Jeff Crook is a novelist, game designer, and technical writer who lives and works in Memphis. His novels include The Thieves' Guild, The Rose and the Skull, *and* Conundrum. *He has written material for the* AD&D *and* Sovereign Stone *games, and he is currently building an online role-playing game called* Qigung *for Skotos Tech (www.skotos.net). Unfortunately, he can't have fun all the time and the baby still needs diapers, so he works as a technical writer for the U.S. Postal Service.*

TUBO starts awake in his gravi-chair, Earth impact alarm screeching. He has fallen asleep. Yawning, he aborts the autocorrect three seconds before burn initiation. He then fingers the controls, feels the *Walter Scott* awaken and move beneath him, the deep volcanic throbbing, a dragon stirring under the floor. The timer starts, and he targets a trajectory in the naviscreen that will bring the asteroid back to an orbital approach.

He also keeps a close eye on stress indicators in the docking piles, for they weren't built to withstand the repeated strain of these corrective burns. *Walter Scott*'s engines are among the most powerful machines ever built, powerful enough to rip the *Walter Scott* apart should a single docking pile fail. Each pile is sunk five hundred meters into the stony heart of the 'roid and

143

fixed directly to the structural frame of the ship. If one
pile were to break, the engines could rip the other pile
out of the ship before Tubo could even react, leaving it
embedded in the 'roid with the ship's guts still attached
and dangling, like a bee stinger ripped out of the bee.
Tubo remembers being stung by a bee; he has not been
on Earth in thirty-seven years.

Three seconds have passed. He lifts his finger off the
trigger. The engines power down and the ship shifts
slowly back onto its support coils, gradually settling in
the .1G pull of the 'roid's gravity. He checks fuel re-
serves, mentally calculates how much that one cost him,
then glances at the naviscreen.

In the screen, Mars is a left parentheses in 12-point
font, a bloody fingernail clipping, the old warrior god
with his back turned. Earth hides behind Sol, that bright
point of light to the left and a little lower than Mars.
Below this, a long irregular gray tongue of carbonaceous
chondrite stretches out into the uniform blackness of
intrasolar space. Already, it has drifted .01 points back
toward an impact trajectory.

At the bottom of the naviscreen, a small fossil is visible poking up out of the pockmarked meteoric stone. It
looks like the flare of a hipbone. Other shadows suggest
a skull, legs, possibly an arm, and part of a tail. Tubo
has been looking at the fossil long enough that the surprise has worn off. Now it is merely puzzling, and a little
frightening. He noticed the bone as he swung around
the back side of Jupiter and turned toward Sol. Only
then did the shadows cast by the rising sun gradually
resolve into these suggestive features.

Tug captain Tubo Prohng shifts his weight in the
gravi-chair. His 'roid is the size of Manhattan, a fat haul,
but it is displaying some unusual gravitational potentials.
Every hour or so, wakened by the Earth impact alarm,
he makes small adjustments to its trajectory, but even
these require the expenditure of vast amounts of fuel.
And this eats away at his profit margin. Every three-
second burn of the momentum engines of the Planetary
Hauler *Walter Scott* consumes 314,159 units of fuel. At

current market price, that's close to a million EUs. He
keeps a close eye on the Belgrade fuel markets through
a DeepSat node, but it usually depresses him beyond
words. This one is going to cost him, but it is too late
to withdraw. He could radio for help, but that would
cost even more. It is his 'roid. He captured it and steered
it into Earth orbital approach.

Seventy-three years ago, amateur astronomer Maxwell
Franck cataloged this unremarkable piece of rock and
named it Delilah. Mr. Franck never explained what was
behind the name. According to modern science, which
hasn't changed much in the last hundred years, Delilah
had been in a regular orbit within the Asteroid Belt near
the Trojans Resonance for nearly ten billion years, until
Tubo Prongh drove the docking piles of the *Walter Scott*
into its stony heart, fired up his ungodly engines, and
nudged her into a slingshot trajectory around Jupiter,
some three hundred and thirty-seven days ago.

Between the hourly burns, Tubo Prongh has time to
study and meditate and form his own inexact theories
about the history of the solar system. But he has no time
for sleep, nothing beyond these brief naps. He has not
slept longer than an hour in seven hundred and forty-
four hours, and he cannot, not if he doesn't want the
Walter Scott's navigational computers to initiate their
own indelicate corrective burn and ruin his fortunes. The
strange gravitational potentials working on Delilah have
him puzzled, but he doesn't care to think of them. If he
wants to make a profit, there is nothing he can do except
to keep firing up *Walter Scott*'s engines for brief nudging
burns. He is not ashamed to admit that he is not the
equal of gravity.

But this bone, this curious arc of hip shadow thrown
across the bottom edge of his naviscreen, almost like an
afterthought, an oh-by-the-way, is a wrinkle in the rug
over which he trips. There was life here once, even here
where no life should be, life so long ago that it could
lay down its bones and turn them to stone. Such
thoughts people the 3 degrees Kelvin shadows outside
his ship with very real ghosts. Tubo Prongh has never

been to Mars and seen its phantoms, though he has passed it seven times, and is approaching his eighth.

His grandfather could never have imagined such voyages. He was a gentle old white-whiskered man whose three great loves were pigs, children, and wives, in that order. He cared little for the world beyond the rice fields of his village. Tubo Prongh often thinks of his grandfather on these voyages to the Asteroid Belt, for he is fast approaching the age at which his grandfather died. But at eighty, his grandfather had been a beaming toothless monkey with one foot on the funeral pyre, while Tubo at seventy-six is still in the genetically-manipulated prime of his manhood. He has a boy at home, two years old, and a wife of twenty-three (the law still only allows him one of each). Tubo is wealthy and still considered handsome; he has all his original teeth. He has a two-thousand-square-meter geodwelling inside a rock in space above the dying Earth. He has a New Antilles bank account filled with digits.

Yet he cannot bear the clamoring of home life, the shrieking demands of wife and child. He prefers the dark empty spaces of his thoughts and his studies and meditations. He prefers the humming muscle of the *Walter Scott*, the Zen simplicity of its stark interiors juxtaposed with the extravagance of Io off his starboard bow passing into the shadow of Jupiter. He loves running the Kirkwood Gaps in search of asteroids of suitable mass and composition to sell to the military and habitat developers back in Earth orbit, like the whalers and ivory hunters of olden days. He likes his mercenary selfhood. Only he is alone, bleakly alone, with a 'roid that won't behave.

He leans forward in his seat and stares at the left edge of the screen. There is a boulder visible on the 'roid's horizon. He hasn't noticed it before. It concerns him, because it might indicate the 'roid is actually a conglomerate bound together by weak gravitational forces. This might explain the gravitational potentials he's been fighting. But his initial geological survey indicated solidity with only minor faulting near an impact crater on the opposite side. He is sure the boulder wasn't there before.

It casts a rather long shadow across the surface, reaching almost to the ship. Tubo drags a navigational marker line across the screen so he can note any movement or change in either the object or its shadow after he performs the next correction. Then he calls up the Lisbon fuel markets on a comm screen.

*   *   *

Tubo starts awake, Earth impact alarm screeching. It seems only a minute has passed. He reaches for the auto-correct abort button, but his hand pauses twenty centimeters above the board. The seconds continue to click down to burn initiation. Tubo stares at the naviscreen. The boulder has moved. Its shadow has reached the ship. It isn't a boulder. It is a man-shape, bipedal, with thick brachiated arms and a large, round head. Tubo blinks. His hand drops with .31 seconds to go.

Still watching it, he fingers forward the controls, the engines wake. Out on the 'roid, the man-thing staggers, pauses, then starts to walk again, slowly, with the exaggerated movements of someone wearing gravitational boots. It is pulling something behind it on a type of travois. Its face is hidden in shadow. Tubo powers down the *Walter Scott*. He turns to the communications screen, pulls up a broadband comm channel, initiates a scan.

A sound crackles low in the FM band range. The computer pauses to examine it, tunes, filters. A voice emerges into the empty air, speaking English ". . . inside the ship. Hello inside the ship. Are you reading me?"

Tubo waits a moment before touching the comm. He takes a deep breath, lets it out slowly. He looks at his tongue in the reflection of a dark screen, grimacing. It occurs to him that he might be hallucinating, or insane, or asleep. He feels fine, just a little tired. He touches the comm, but still he doesn't speak. He lifts his finger without making a sound, unsure what to say.

"I heard that. Who are you? What's that ship?" the voice says, a little out of breath. It is a male voice, English accent.

Tubo leans forward, trying to see closer into the navigational screen, to see a face. The head turns slightly as the figure stumbles. A glint of gold flashes where the face should be. Tubo touches the comm switch and says softly, blankly, "This is the Planetary Hauler *Walter Scott.*" He lifts his finger.

"Bloody wog. You sound like a bloody wog. Where are you from, woggy?"

Tubo touches the comm, calmly, "Identify yourself."

"Identify *your* fucking self."

Tubo touches the comm, repeats, "Please identify yourself."

Grover Nuttbaum, you wog bastard."

Tubo laughs, fingers the comm, "Please identify yourself."

"My name is Grover Nuttbaum. Doctor Grover Nuttbaum. Look it up, wog." He never pauses in his progress toward the ship. He is close enough now for Tubo to see what he is dragging on the travois—two small metallic canisters, flat, like old satellite battery casings. He wears an old-fashioned environment suit, once white but now dirty gray, patched, bulky, late twentieth-century NASA vintage, with a gold-visored helmet.

Tubo pulls up an archive search on the communications screen, enters NUTTBALM >ALT NUTTBAUM, GROVER, DR. It takes a few seconds for the information to arrive via the old NASA Deep Space Network. He reads it.

He reads it again.

Tubo touches the comm. "Dr. Nuttbaum, it has been some time."

"Not long enough, wog," the figure responds as it disappears at the bottom of the naviscreen.

"I'm afraid there isn't any way for you to get inside this ship, Dr. Nuttbaum," Tubo says. "Not from where . . ." He pauses, his finger still on the comm. It is impossible. Impossible for a man to survive this long alone on an asteroid in an environment suit. "How?" he stammers, his finger slipping off the comm.

". . . survive?" the voice asks, laughing. It grunts, and

he hears the gurgling of the environment suit through
the comm. "How did I survive? You'd like to know,
wouldn't you? Make yourself a fortune back on Earth
with my technologies, wouldn't you? Fountain of youth,
all that rot. To hell with you, capitalist pig."

"How did you get all the way out here, Dr. Nuttbaum? We weren't sending anything but robots out this
far when you disappeared."

Laughter over the comm. There is a strange quality to
the doctor's laughter, even over the comm. Tubo cannot
identify it. He touches the comm, his lips hang open,
breathing the stale recycled air through his teeth. It is
air that has been off Earth longer than he has. He has
breathed it so many times now, it feels like a part of
him. A part of him that fills the entire ship, a part of
him running like blood through the ducts to the recycling
plant deep in the *Walter Scott*'s bowels. Suddenly, he
feels something is wrong, an imbalance in his extended
chi, a blockage of fiery yang.

An anchoring pile indicator flashes yellow. He re-
moves his finger from the open comm, and panting
laughter again fills the small speaker. He punches up a
ship diagnostic, initiates it, leans into the chair and—
without relaxing the sudden tensing of his back—waits,
his brows furrowing over his dark eyes. While he waits,
the anchoring pile indicator switches to red. The diagnostic returns with a volcanic stress reading deep in the
pile's bore chamber. Impossible. It is impossible. He re-
minds himself of this. He runs the diagnostic again. The
'roid has been cold for ten billion years.

"You'd better pull out, or you'll lose it," the doctor
says over the comm.

The indicator light winks red once more, then stays lit.

"What are you doing?" Tubo demands now. A warning appears on the naviscreen. "You couldn't cut through
that pile, not even if you had a plasma saw."

"Do you know how the pyramids were built?"

"The pyramids? What do the pyramids have to do
with anything, you crazy fucker?" Tubo barks without
touching the comm. His fingers dance across the boards

in front of him, pulling up stress projections, running simulations, calculating trajectories, fuel and engine readings. A geological window opens on his screen.

A shudder passes through the ship, rattling the little plastic container of dietary supplements sitting next to the naviscreen. "What was that?" Tubo asks no one. The geological window scrolls off a seismic recording of the event, showing epicenter and magnitude.

"I'll bet you are wondering what the pyramids have to do with anything."

Tubo slams the comm with his fist. "Whatever it is you're doing, you had better stop. If you damage that pile, do you realize what will happen?"

But the doctor ignores him. "The pyramids have everything to do with everything. I'll bet you think I'm suffering from paranoid delusions. Space madness, we used to call it."

Another 'roidquake shakes the *Walter Scott,* almost tossing Tubo from his gravi-chair. The geological window dutifully records the event. Meanwhile, stress indicators on the damaged pile reach critical, while the secondary pile is now showing nonfatal damage. A metallic groan echoes up through the ship. Tubo runs a repair schedule, inserts the mean estimate into his navigational calculations.

He sits slowly back in his chair, his eyes rising to the navigational screen—.5 outside safe orbital trajectory, and increasing. "Do you know what you've done?" he whispers. His fingers fumble along the buttons on the arm panel of his gravitational chair, thumbing through various monitoring cameras affixed to the ship's hull. One shows him the intrasolar commdish hanging from a bent bracket. He clicks through several more images, finds the orbital antenna array. It looks operational, but its range is limited to .1 light-minutes. Not powerful enough to call for help.

He leans forward and presses the comm. "Do you know what you've done?" he asks softly.

"Do you know, no one has solved the mystery of how the pyramids were built. Oh, they think they know, simply because they know a way to do it, a difficult, inelegant way to do it. But there are always other ways, better ways."

Tubo continues flipping through the monitoring cameras. He finds the port docking pile camera. A grainy gray image appears, showing the doctor in his suit sitting on a rock beside his travois. The two battery casings lie beside him. The pile is sheared almost in half, its guts spitting magnesium sparks. A spiderweb of fracture faults spread several dozen meters across the ground in all directions.

"Just because you have a solution that works doesn't mean the mystery is solved."

"Do you know what you've done!" Tubo screams.

"Of course I know what I've done, you stupid wog. If you light up those beautiful momentum engines of yours without uncoupling from this rock, you'll tear your ship apart. So unhook and leave. I haven't compromised your safety unless you do something stupid. This is my home. You've no right to steal it."

"This rock is headed into an impact trajectory with Earth!" Tubo cries shrilly.

"So how can we expect to solve the mysteries of space if we don't even know how the pyramids were built?"

"Shut up about the pyramids, okay?" Tubo shouts. He keeps his finger on the button. "Just shut up. The pyramids aren't important. I need to contact Earth and get help, or else this rock is going to destroy everything down there. Do you have radio equipment able to contact Earth?"

"Yes."

"Great," Tubo sighs. "Excellent, perfect. You've ruined me." He punches up the undocking procedures and initiates them.

The doctor says, "I've been monitoring Earth broadcasts since I arrived here. I hear all about you bloody capitalists from your bloody capitalist media, twenty-four bloody hours a day. I don't know how you stand it. When the BBC went private, I knew it was time to leave Earth. I had more money than I knew what to do with from selling back nuclear waste to the various space programs. The funny thing is, my family became wealthy leasing storage space for nuclear waste in the first place."

With the remaining docking pile withdrawn, the *Walter Scott* rides lightly back on its support coils. A brief burst from two steering rockets is enough to lift it free of the .1G pull of the asteroid. The pocked surface of Delilah begins to draw away.

"Then, when I invented the momentum engine," the doctor continues, "I intentionally used nuclear waste as its fuel. Thought it would make for a good way to get rid of the stuff, don't you know, quit poisoning the Earth. Instead, I created a market. Nuclear plants built everywhere just to produce waste, not even making electricity. I wanted to become a hermit. But there weren't any mountains left that didn't have an advertisement painted on their slopes with genetically altered trees. So I came out here in a ship I financed myself, the first man to visit the Asteroid Belt, and I didn't even get a write-up in *Science & Nature*."

As the *Walter Scott* continues to rise, Tubo switches through several cameras until he finds one pointed directly down. The doctor still sits in his environment suit beside the severed docking pile. He is already tiny, insignificant.

"You know, if early rockets had used fossil fuels instead of hydrogen and oxygen, we'd already be living among the stars. You might have been born under a different sun, wog. But capitalists can't make money selling what can be had for the trouble of dipping your hand in the nearest ocean. That was the beauty of burning nuclear waste. It was a finite resource made suddenly valuable, and mostly in the possession of poor countries that had agreed to accept it for the sake of a little cash injected into their outmoded and uncompetitive economies. But the poor countries I wanted to help turned out to be just as heartless and greedy as the imperialists whose missionaries and journalists they used to murder. However, there wasn't enough nuclear waste to meet consumption demands, and now they're destroying the Earth, making it uninhabitable, just to make more waste, so bastards like you can come out here and drag back asteroids for rich capitalists to build houses on, safe and high above the clouds spewing from your reactors. You bastards have even used up your nuclear weapons making waste to burn. Now, militaries keep arsenals of asteroids ready to de-orbit and drop on whoever isn't playing the game according to the rules. We've gone back to throwing stones at one another."

Tubo thumbs the comm. "How long will it take you to reach your communication equipment?" he asks.

"I can't contact Earth," the doctor answers.

"What do you mean? You said you have the equipment . . ." Tubo's voice trails off.

"I do. I use it to melt water ice."

Tubo sits stunned for a moment, his finger prodding at the comm.

"I'm not going to call someone in to help you steal my home to make weapons for your imperialist capitalist military."

"You've destroyed the Earth," Tubo whispers. "You've done a million times worse than all the militaries in the world."

"No, I haven't."

"Yes, you have," Tubo whispers. He thinks of the green fields of this grandfather's farms, the pigs in the mud, the women young and supple and old and hoary, and a naked child standing in the doorway of the house. He is the child that he sees, a silvery streak running from his nostrils to his lip. He has been crying, wakened from a nap by a dream. This dream.

"No, I haven't," the doctor taunts.

"Yes, you have," Tubo insists.

"So what if I have? What possible difference could it make?"

"Everyone will die. By the time I reach comm range, it will be too late to divert it. A dozen planetary haulers couldn't divert it."

"Do you know how the pyramids were built?"

"Shut up about the pyramids! Shut up about the pyramids. I don't want to hear about no damn pyramids! All life on Earth will be destroyed."

"When has all life on Earth ever been destroyed? You think you can destroy it with one asteroid, and still you take it upon yourself to control the destiny of an entire planet, all for a little profit?"

"It's perfectly safe. It's been done hundreds of times," Tubo says.

"No, it isn't. Look at the situation you are in now."

"You aren't supposed to be here!" Tubo screams. He grasps the control, fires a steering series to turn the *Walter Scott* around and slow the ship.

"Yet here I am. I could just as easily be a flu virus, or a faulty processor board, or a weak docking seal, and the same space rock would be hurtling along the same collision path and all life on Earth would be destroyed, according to you. Capitalists like you take for your own uses without consideration for the people who can't get out of the way. The Earth deserves destroying if it allows capitalists like you to exist."

"I'm just a small businessman, trying to make a living. I'm not a statecorp," Tubo says. He punches up a trajectory projection, then begins running simulations. "You've no right to judge me, Doctor Nuttbaum. You don't know me at all."

"I've every right to judge you, wog. You tried to steal my home."

"I didn't know you were there." He watches the simulations play out, with Earth impact the inevitable result each time.

"You think that just because somebody's name isn't on it, you can take it? How does that make it yours?"

"Standard salvage law, Doctor. You know that." He looks up at the naviscreen as the last simulation plays itself to an inevitable conclusion. The screen then snaps back to forward view, showing him the bloody fingernail paring of Mars. A thought occurs to him. He enters adjustments, then initiates a new series of simulations.

"The law of the jungle, you mean. The law of the scavenger. Finders keepers, losers weepers, you mean."

"Is that any less noble than intentionally steering a Manhattan-sized asteroid into an Earth impact?" Tubo asks, a grim smile spreading across his face as he watches the simulations play out.

"I haven't done that, wog."

"Yes, you have, Doctor."

"No, I haven't."

"Yes, you have," Tubo says. He compares the results of the projections produced by the simulations to his available fuel supply. He then pulls up the stress specs of the *Walter Scott*'s spaceframe and hull.

"No, I haven't."

"Look, Doctor Nuttbaum, I don't have time to argue with you," Tubo says. There is only one thing to be done. It isn't to ram the 'roid. That was his first idea, but the *Walter Scott* doesn't have enough mass to counteract the 'roid's odd gravitational potentials. He grasps the controls and fires a steering sequence which takes him slowly across the Delilahian sky. In his screen, he sees the doctor stand up and watch him pass overhead.

"What are you doing, wog?" There is a note of concern in his voice.

"I'm going to push this rock into a Mars impact trajectory," Tubo says calmly, victoriously.

There is a pause, then the doctor says gently, "What's your name, Captain?"

"Tubo Prongh."

"You don't have to do this, Tubo," the doctor says. "How old are you? Are you married?"

Tubo ignores him. "The force of the engines will probably crush the hull of this ship. But at least it can be done. There's only a few small research communities on Mars. The chances of an impact near one are negligible. It's a chance I'm willing to take. To save Earth."

Tubo steers the *Walter Scott* nose-first into a soft descent, aiming for a point that is three meters in diameter directly over the 'roid's adjusted estimated center of gravity. The push must be a direct push with the nose

of the ship, as the remaining docking pile isn't strong
enough to withstand the force needed to move the 'roid
into Mars impact.

"Have you had your child yet?" the doctor asks. Tubo
can no longer see him in his monitors. The doctor is
beyond the 'roid's horizon, almost on the opposite side.

The blunt nose of the *Walter Scott* nuzzles up against
Delilah with a scraping noise that echoes through the
ship. She looks so close in his screens, Tubo feels like
he could almost reach out and touch her.

"You don't have to do this, Tubo," the doctor says.
He is running now, almost, if you could call running a
prolonged forward fall. Tubo cannot see him. But he can
hear his voice in the comm and knows that he is running.

"Why not? Will it ruin your fun? You won't get to
die knowing you destroyed the world that you hate?"
Tubo asks as he powers up the engines. The structural
frame of the ship groans as the engines begin their inexorable push.

"Power back your engines, Tubo. Listen to me. This
asteroid isn't going to impact Earth unless you keep trying to steer it into an Earth orbit."

"It's too late. I don't believe you," Tubo says. "How
can you possibly affect this 'roid's trajectory? Your old
momentum engines weren't powerful enough."

"Do you know how the pyramids were built?" the
doctor asks. He is huffing into the comm speaker of
his helmet.

"I'm not listening to you anymore, Doctor. In a moment it will all be over, and you'll be on your way to
Mars," Tubo says.

"You saw the fossil, didn't you, Tubo? You saw it. It
was right there."

Tubo pauses. The ship shudders throughout its frame,
rattling. He hears bulkheads buckling. The air suddenly
grows oven hot. "Yes," he says.

"Haven't you ever noticed the relatively low amount
of crater density visible on most asteroids? You've been
to the Belt a few times, I take it. Have you ever noticed
it?" He is still running.

"Yes." The ship lurches to starboard, and Tubo fights to keep the ship upright, its forces aligned in a vector which will guide the 'roid into Mars impact.

"Planetary geology says that this is a result of an impact breaking the planetoid-body into smaller asteroid bodies, exposing surfaces to cratering relatively recently. But my analysis indicates a low amount of impact fracturing in this 'roid's crystalline substructures, while surface samples show that the surface of the 'roid has only been exposed to sunlight for some two hundred thousand years. If you search planetary geology databases, you'll find that most asteroid theory was formed and set in concrete a hundred years before the first visit by a craft capable of making a detailed analysis of an asteroid within the Belt."

"So," Tubo says, his teeth grinding. He is nearly blind from cryogases bursting from environmental systems. The nose of the ship is crushed, and his board is glowing with hull stress warnings. He blinks away the film to check the naviscreen and finds that the 'roid is almost within a Mars impact trajectory.

"Listen to me!" the doctor is shouting. He stops, gasping, bent over with his hands on his knees. "Power down and listen for one moment! The two-hundred-thousand-year-old event, coinciding as it does with catastrophic changes in the Martian atmosphere and the emergence of modern Homo sapiens on Earth can only mean one thing. There was a fifth inner planet, and something had happened to it. Maybe it was some kind of catastrophic event, the planet exploding, but that really isn't the way things happen. Likely it was something less spectacular if not less violent, a simple sheering of tidal forces as it passed through the Roche Limit of some large wandering body. There isn't enough mass in the Asteroid Belt to form a planet because most of it was pulled away by whatever destroyed it."

"Almost there," Tubo hisses.

"The residents of that planet sent their children in escape pods to Earth, but those children arrived without their parents' culture to guide them. They adopted the most advanced technology available on Earth—stone tools. But not all their knowledge was lost. Some relearned it and passed it down to their children and their children's children. They built the pyramids, Tubo, using the same theories that allowed me to use the weak solar energy all the way out here to outmuscle your momentum engines."

He pauses, listening, but there is only static in the comm now.

"Tubo, listen to me. I want you to run a new simulation. I'm giving you the data. With this data, you'll be a rich man, the richest man on Earth if the nuclear waste industry doesn't assassinate you for ruining their business. Get ready to receive."

As quickly as his bulky gloves allow, the doctor punches up a series of numbers on the keypad attached to the right forearm of his environment suit. "Sending," he says as he touches the last button.

He waits, listening to the static. There is no response. He waits.

Then, through the noise, ". . . blind. I can't see. What . . ."

"It's the solution to everything, Tubo," the doctor says excitely. "How the pyramids were built and why they are all located in the tropics, that fossil bone you saw and what happened to this planet, the gravitational potentials you were trying to counteract, not knowing that your corrections were keeping the asteroid headed into an Earth impact trajectory. I discovered writings here on this asteroid, Tubo, ancient writings carved in stone that explain . . ."

In one racking scream of metal, the *Walter Scott*'s three momentum engines tear through the ship's superstructure in less than a microsecond and gouge their way sixty meters into Delilah before exploding. The now-hollow hull of the *Walter Scott* and a two-hundred-meter diameter of rock are blown free of the asteroid's gravity. The pieces spray out into space, mingling, twinkling like fairy dust. Doctor Nuttbaum watches a glittering arc of debris appear above the 'roid's horizon, spreading and dissipating, a colorless rainbow, even as the shock wave passes beneath his feet, tossing him like chaff a dozen meters high. His gravity boots float him back down to a surface jumbled and broken.

And Delilah gradually returns to its original trajectory, a trajectory that will bring it looping past Earth and back into its original place in the Trojans Resonance, twelve-point-three Earth years from now.

THE DEMONS OF JUPITER'S MOONS

by Mike Resnick and Mark M. Stafford

Mike Resnick is the author of forty science fiction novels, ten collections, and one hundred and thirty stories. He has also edited more than twenty anthologies. He has been nominated for nineteen Hugos (seventeen as a writer, two as an editor) and won four. His work has been translated into twenty-two different languages.

Mark M. Stafford graduated from the 1996 Odyssey and 1999 Clarion writing workshops. His story "Power Tools" appeared in The Tale Spinner *magazine in 1996, and he won the University of Alaska/ Anchorage Daily News Writing Award for 1999. He is currently writing a fantasy novel and works as a flight-test engineer on the F-16 Fighting Falcon.*

THE demons watched the frost crunch beneath Lucine's boots as she trudged across ruddy orange ice. The sun hung in the azure sky like a spotlight, painfully bright to look at, yet leaving the landscape in shadow.

Despite Europa's tenuous gravity, her shoulders slumped under the weight of her protective suit. She wanted to lie down and never get up, and yet she forced her leaden legs to carry on. Only the knowledge that the demons were waiting for her to quit made her continue walking.

"You won't stop me!" she grated to the demons, who grinned wordlessly at her. "The Lord is my shepherd!"

*   *   *

The gutted mining station of New Matewan was ugly by any definition of the word. Huge pipes stuck out in all directions, and most of the superstructure lay exposed. Only the living quarters and desalinization plant remained intact, while landing pads of various sizes ringed the complex.

Lucine went to the dull gray cubicle that passed for her private quarters, stuffed her protective suit in a bag, and donned a pair of jeans and a faded T-shirt.

She entered the mess hall and veered around the small cluster of people to the refreshment table. The only one she knew was Jack, one of New Matewan's transport pilots.

She put her bag down next to the meager spread— soft drinks, a few canisters of beer, a bottle of tequila, a container of dried apricots, and a bowl filled with punch. She poured herself a lemonade.

"Glad to see you made it!" said Jack, crossing the room to greet her.

"Yeah," she replied. "I had to move around some pressing social engagements."

Jack chuckled and held up his drink. "Come on, you want something stronger than lemonade to celebrate! We're standing on the brink of history. We're about to usher in the age of terraforming."

"No, thanks," said Lucine. "Got to keep my wits about me."

"At least have some apricots. You're getting too thin."

She looked at the apricots. A small demon squatted next to them, leering at her. Another pretended to urinate in the punch bowl. She knew better than to mention it. It was obvious that no one else saw them, and she didn't plan to spend her final night on Europa confined and sedated.

"I'm fine," she said at last.

Jack seemed about to argue the point when the PA system blared and drowned him out: "Okay, folks, let's do this one last time! Ship on approach. Hop to it!"

The room began to clear. Jack set his beer down. "I gotta go."

"Why?" asked Lucine. "Pilots don't pump water."

"We're a skeleton crew," answered Jack. "Today we *all* pump water."

So she pumped, too, and tried not to notice the demons.

* * *

Lucine opened her eyes. The demons were perched at the foot of her bed.

"I'm too tired to pray or fight right now," she muttered. "Come back later. I'll sic Christ on you then."

We'll take him in straight falls, said a demon.

We'll murder the bum, said another.

"Why are you tormenting me?" she demanded. "Why don't you pick on someone else?"

You know why, said the demons. *You're the Boss Lady. You did the calculations. You're the one we want.*

"You can't stop the project."

Oh, yes, we can, said the demons. One of them worked a huge imaginary scissors. *We're a bunch of Samsons, and we're going to give Delilah a crewcut.*

Another pretended to be wielding a barber's razor. *Gonna shave her bald,* he giggled.

* * *

Lucine had barely fallen asleep when the intercom woke her.

"This is Admiral Kearns. Are there going to be any further severe icequakes? We're behind schedule because we had to send our engineers out to inspect for damage." She was too groggy to answer, and after he waited an appropriate time, he continued: "You can understand our concern. This stop for water is our last stop before we leave the solar system forever. We can't afford to set out in a damaged generations ship, and I have no intention of scrapping this mission."

"There's nothing to worry about, sir," Lucine intoned as the demons laughed uproariously.

"I'd better not be getting the runaround here!" snapped the Admiral. "I'm going to ask one more time: should I, or should I not, be worried about my ship being damaged by any more icequakes?"

"Probably not," answered Lucine.

"*Probably* not?"

"I can't say for sure. They're unpredictable, like earthquakes. They are more likely at the apogee of Europa's orbit, which we're at now. During apogee, Jupiter pulls on Europa's crust just as the Moon pulls on Earth's oceans. The same type of force that creates high tide on Earth caused that icequake."

"So it's just a coincidence that the day you're abandoning New Matewan it has the most severe icequake ever?"

"Absolutely."

"Bullshit!" snapped the Admiral. "I'm not blind! I know you're moving an asteroid into Europa's orbit! You people tried to do something like this with Mars and it didn't work. Now suppose you tell me exactly what the hell is going on."

"Delilah," said Lucine.

"Who is Delilah?"

"Delilah is the asteroid you spotted."

"Explain."

Lucine sighed deeply. "The Mars team used asteroids to try to adjust Mars' orbit for terraforming. Planets aren't moved that easily; it didn't work. But we learned from experience. We're not trying to change Europa's orbit. Delilah will simply increase the strength of the tidal force here."

"And why do you want to do that?"

"It should be obvious, sir," continued Lucine. "Friction from the pushing and pulling of Jupiter's tidal force generates the heat that keeps Europa's ice-covered ocean liquid. Delilah will generate enough extra heat to melt that ice and turn Europa into a water world. We'll pay a one-time cost for the nuclear charges to move the asteroid and put it into orbit, and then it's there forever. The generations ships won't have to pay to load water from Earth for their centuries-long voyages. They can pick it up here for a tenth of the price, because the desalinization cost will be cut by a few levels of magnitude if we don't have to melt the ice first."

"Why wasn't I informed?" demanded the Admiral. "Right now, my ship is sitting at ground zero of your company's profit-making scheme."

"You'll be safely away before Delilah becomes a danger."

"The damned thing's already a danger!"

"Not so, sir. It's moving smoothly into orbit even as we speak."

"The hell it is," said the Admiral. "It's hurtling hell for leather toward Europa."

"A visual illusion, sir."

"Tell that to my computer!"

He broke the connection.

He's right, you know, said the demons.

"He's wrong," answered Lucine. "This was all checked and rechecked and triple-checked to the very last decimal place."

What do we care about decimal places?

"This is science," she said, wondering why she was even responding to them. "And science is never wrong."

We are a power older and stronger than science, said the demons. *You have come unbidden to our world, and have planned to change its makeup. We will never allow it.*

"Why?" demanded Lucine. "What do you care?"

If we invaded your body, you would call it rape. You are invading the body of our world. What do you think we should call it?

"It's not the same thing."

No, it's not. You would survive being raped. You

*would still be Lucine. Europa would not survive. It would
not be Europa any longer.*

"And you'd sooner crash Delilah into it?"

Death before dishonor, said the nearest demon.

She was so annoyed that she knew she would never get
back to sleep, so she dressed and walked to the control room.

"Hi," she said to the crew when they had noticed her.
"What's going on?"

"I don't know," said Jack. "The generations ship's
away safely, but we're getting some funny readings."

"Funny ha-ha or funny strange?" she asked.

"Funny serious," he said, frowning. "Delilah's coming
awfully fast."

"An illusion," she said uneasily.

"Well, if it is, it's not *my* illusion." He pointed to a
computer screen. "Take a look," he said, nodding toward
the readout.

She stared at the screen, which displayed Delilah hurtling across the void at them. "This can't be," she said.
"The computer has checked those figures every hour
for months!"

"Can we get away in time?" asked one of the staff.

Lucine nodded. "Even if that readout's right, you've
got hours left."

"But there isn't going to be much left of Europa,"
said Jack grimly. "I hope to hell there weren't any undiscovered life-forms here."

I wouldn't call them life-forms, thought Lucine wryly.
Aloud she said, "I think we'd better prepare to evacuate
New Matewan right now."

"You're the boss," said Jack.

"And you're the pilot," she replied. "It's up to you
to decide how much equipment we can take once you
load everyone aboard."

Jack nodded. "We'll go to the base on Ganymede,"
he announced. "That will require the least amount of
fuel and allow us to take the heaviest load."

"Take care of it," said Lucine. "That's your business.
Mine is finding some way to divert Delilah."

"Can you?" he asked dubiously.

"I doubt it like all hell—but I've got to try."

She stared at the screen again. How could it have happened? It couldn't be human error; all the humans did was load the programs and make sure they were running. Computer error? Not a chance, not when the life-support and communications systems and everything else that ran off the same computer were working perfectly. A faulty program? No way; they'd checked it too many times.

But there was Delilah, filling the screen, racing head-long on a collision course with Europa.

She had to find some way to divert it. She had the computer determine which still-untapped nuclear charges would jolt Delilah off its current trajectory, what it would take to put the asteroid into the required orbit around the tiny moon.

A few minutes later Jack signaled her that the ship was ready to go, that all the members of the New Matewan station except her were aboard it, and that it would be nice if she'd get her ass in gear. She tried to ignore the sense of panic she felt as she went over the figures one more time. The computer gave her only a one in five chance of success.

Finally, when she felt she couldn't wait an instant longer, she ordered the computer to blow the charges that would make Delilah's orbital adjustments.

The computer waited to receive the new readings, then began blinking the word MANEUVER SUCCESSFUL over and over again.

"I did it!" she said. "I've beaten you."

I wouldn't bet on that, said demons.

"It's done," said Lucine. "Even *you* can't change an asteroid's orbit."

That's true, agreed the grinning demons.

"Then I've won."

We can't change an asteroid's orbit, continued the demons, *but we can change the way it looks on your computer.*

"What are you talking about?" she asked, a sudden tightness in the pit of her stomach.

Her screen showed Delilah racing for Europa. *This is*

what you saw, they said. The screen changed to show Delilah settling into orbit. *And this is what was.*

She blinked at the screen, trying to comprehend.

And thanks to you, they said as Delilah once again raced toward Europa's unprotected surface, *this is what is now.* They grinned like gargoyles. *We're reconsidering what we said about science. It can be a useful tool after all.*

"God forgive me," she whispered.

God's not a forgiving type, said the demons. *But we know a good cheap shyster.*

Lucine uttered a scream of rage and lunged toward the demons. Her body passed through them and crashed heavily into the wall.

*   *   *

A hand touched her shoulder. She tried to turn away. The hand shook it.

"Wake up," said a voice.

"Go away," she said.

"She's awake," said the voice.

"Good," said Jack's voice. "I was getting worried."

"Leave me alone," muttered Lucine.

"Lucine, listen to me," said a female voice. "I am Doctor Beatrice Chamanga. You are in the infirmary of the Ganymede Station. Don't try to sit up or make any sudden moves. You're tied in to a number of IV tubes and monitoring devices."

Lucine finally opened her eyes. Jack stood at the foot of her bed. A woman wearing medical insignia was bending over her, checking the various tubes.

"What happened?" asked Lucine.

"You've been unconscious for almost forty Standard hours," replied Doctor Chamanga. "You seem to have taken a serious fall back at New Matewan."

"It must have happened during one of the icequakes," added Jack. "They got pretty bad just before we took off. When you didn't show up at the ship, I had two of the men go looking for you. They found you lying crumpled in a heap on the floor."

"What happened to Europa?" she asked, trying to sit up.

"It's gone. You did your best." Jack sighed. "They'll be years trying to figure out how the computer fucked up. Maybe decades, since there's no longer any computer to check."

She closed her eyes and lay back down.

"Will she be all right?" asked Jack.

"No problem," answered Doctor Chamanga. "Let's let her get some sleep now."

But she didn't sleep. She considered what had happened, then went over it again and again in her mind. Finally she sensed another presence and opened her eyes again.

Hi, Lucine, said the demons. *You proved the sword is mightier than the pen. You destroyed an entire world. Aren't you proud of yourself?*

"It wasn't my fault," she replied calmly. "I bear no blame." She stared at them. "Why are you here? I thought you lived on Europa."

There isn't any Europa, not anymore, they said. *So now we'll live on Ganymede, until you destroy it, and then we'll move to Io, and when that's gone, why, we'll find someplace else.*

"I didn't destroy anything," she said. "You did."

The first caveman who rubbed two sticks together and created fire did, said the demons. *No fire, no technology. No technology, no explosives. No explosives, and Europa still exists.*

"Why are you still here?" she demanded softly. "What do you want of me?"

We'll think of something.

"Have you always lived on Jupiter's moons?" asked Lucine.

Always.

"You know," she said softly, "I could get to where I like destroying moons."

The demons looked at her curiously.

"You say your power is older than science? Fine. My power is hatred, and it's stronger than science, too. Your power used science to destroy Europa? My hatred will use it to destroy Ganymede." Suddenly her voice became stronger. "How many moons has Jupiter got—including the tiny ones? What's going to happen to you when I blow up the last of them?"

And for the first time since she'd known them, perhaps the first time ever, the demons of Jupiter's moons looked very, very frightened.

RINGFLOW

by Tom Dupree

Tom Dupree has been a newsman, adman, critic, and editor. His work has been featured in a number of science fiction, fantasy, and horror anthologies, including DAW Books' Historical Hauntings. He lives in New York City with his wife, Linda.

*I*T FLOWS.

Jensen almost whirled around at the words, but he kept staring out the port window. Because it was true.

He had *known* it, but now he *felt* it.

Ever since he was a kid, tearing through as many science fiction novels and comic books as he could afford, this had been the symbol of the future—of human progress, of the promise of space exploration, of the surprisingly close relationship between the profound and the mundane. It represented triumphs as grand as the machine that had brought him here, now, face-to-face with the spoils of technological achievement. And comforts as numbing and ill-noticed as the microchips that were built into everyone's toasters back home.

Through most of the dark, cold journey of the U.N.S. *Zelazny,* there had been little to look at. Black expanse studded by the dotted light stream of millennia, a first-hand lesson in the sameness of distance and vacuum. But as Jensen approached the magnificent orb that had seemed to grow so slowly, as if atom by atom, from the tiny speck he had first plotted at liftoff, he could feel the blood racing through his body. For now he could see the flow.

That icon of things to come, the mammoth ringed planet, reflected light back at him from the star that marked the length of his voyage. A deceiver it was: it dwarfed everything in the solar system save giant Jupiter, but it appeared more substantive than reality would allow. Jensen would never set down on the planet. No one would. It was a gargantuan pale-gold sphere made mostly of hydrogen and helium, a towering wisp with a surface gravity lighter than water's. But even the great splendor of the mighty gasball dominating the port view could not tear Jensen's eyes away from the miracle encircling it.

The rivers of rings.

The circular rivers that flowed around Saturn.

From the great distance across which he had always beheld Saturn, when the plane of the rings was tilted toward the Earth just so, a telescope showed thin, bright concentric layers banded by divisions of nothingness. Whenever Jensen had come across an old long-playing record and held it close to study its grooves and divisions of silence, somehow he had always thought of Saturn and its own cosmic music. But now that he was close enough to see the outer ring for what it really was, the enormity of its composition struck him like a blow.

It flows.

Jensen stared like an awed child, mouth agape. He wasn't looking at a solid sheet like his old phonograph platter. Whirling below him—or was it above him?—was a flat white river that only appeared solid in the aggregate, for it was actually made of billions of particles, each tumbling in its own orbit around the giant planet. He knew most of it was water ice, with some pieces perhaps enveloping a mineral core in an eternal cocoon. Some of the teeming crystals were as small as dust motes, others were frozen behemoths that would have dwarfed the *Zelazny* had it come much closer.

As the roiling pieces approached and affected each

other's magnetic fields, they joined, collided, broke, and shot off in unison toward others. A motion in one direction caused more and more particles to join in, rolling like an ocean wave. A single soft undulation headed off until it reached a responsive wave aimed toward it; the two crested against each other and the glistening Brownian motion began again. Random movement was all over the glittering edge of the ring, the reflected light softly twinkling everywhere. Jensen thought of ants scurrying over their hill, or flocks of birds changing direction on some invisible signal.

It was all happening against the inexorable flow of the vast white sheet that girdled the planet. Jensen's craft precisely matched the circular orbit of the outer F-ring, so the independent eddies and swirls of the ring's components were even more vividly pronounced. It was a dance, a procession, a liquid march across the infinite. The resemblance to water motion was so acute that Jensen imagined a sound, the sweet gurgle of a forest brook.

Take a look at this.

He turned this time, but of course he was alone in the forward capsule. Of course. He was more utterly alone than he had thought it possible to imagine.

It had been more than two years since Jensen had set foot on anything but metal and plastic. That was the price an astronaut paid, and he had paid it gladly, eagerly. He had never wanted to be anything else, not since the first time he saw the great rings through a telescope. He announced the news to his parents at five years of age. They smiled and nodded with exaggerated encouragement, as if he'd said he wanted to be a cowboy. But Jensen's was a rare ambition. Unlike nearly everyone else with a childhood dream, he never changed his mind.

For many kids of his generation, school was a rite, a gentle hazing ritual to be endured on the way to the stolid security of the courtroom or the trading floor. But Jensen luxuriated in learning. His friends were surprised, and sometimes a little dismayed, at his fixation. He excelled, particularly in science and math, simply because he devoted his life to it. Not for honors or ego, but to prepare for what he was certain was his destiny. He threw himself into athletics and fitness with the same ferocity, and willed his body into strength and gracefulness—not because of talent, but determination. Winning was irrelevant; Jensen preferred situations where scores weren't even kept. The point was to push and strain and test his body. Physical weakness was unacceptable, a clamp that kept people on Earth.

His most remarkable achievement in self-improvement came early in his military training as a pilot. During a routine MRI examination, Jensen was suddenly gripped with panic as the imaging machine moved over his chest and covered his head. He gasped and sucked for air. The scanner was moving so slowly that it seemed to have stopped. Had it really? He stifled the urge to thrash and scream. Panting, he tried to think of something, anything else. He began going through the list of prime numbers in his head. Absurdly, the immutable order of these digits gave him the room he needed to quash the suffocating terror, or at least set it aside until the machine finished its work.

The anxiety was a total surprise to Jensen. He'd been fine in cramped cockpits, even in simulators that lent the illusion of being in midair. There he could see the outside—or fool himself into thinking he could—and register the fact that he was part of a wide open space. Now, he had just found out that his particular debilitating fear was of being closed up, shut off, left aside. He shuddered as he thought of a prisoner shackled in a medieval dungeon, of a premature burial, of an avalanche of earth careening into the musty Roman catacombs.

He knew instantly what that episode might mean for his future. It was a hulking beast that stood between him and his destiny. He revealed his weakness to no one. And starting that afternoon, Jensen fought the fear the only way he knew how: by sheer force of will. He sat for hours in tiny closets. He toured caves and submarines, and stayed inside all of them as long as he possibly could. He forced himself to learn to scuba dive—that had actually been kind of fun—and then signed on excursions to dive at night, to explore caves and crannies inside sunken ships that he knew would place him in tight dark spots and test him in the only way that produced real answers.

Jensen faced a demon, and conquered it by essentially boring it to death. By the time he was finally selected for deep-space training—a day when he was so thrilled he could hardly swallow—the regimen had long since become second nature to him. He never quite joined most of his colleagues in the strange, solitary land of the claustrophile, but the panic and suffocation were gone forever. He excelled because he had prepared.

You're ready. You're always ready.

With a great effort, he tore himself away from the port view and left the jeweled river. It took some practiced contortions to turn himself around in the tiny capsule, but in a moment he was able to vault over the copilot's station and reach the seal to the life-stage. This simple maneuver was the tiniest bit more difficult than it had been for the duration of the journey; Jensen sensed the slight tug of the gas giant's gravitational field, the same force that kept the white flowing circles from spilling into space.

Was Saturn pulling against him? He wanted to scratch his head as he pondered, but he had already put on his helmet and it kept his hand away.

He coded the seal open and kicked against the headrest he had just left. He floated into the *Zelazny*'s lifestage. Into the great hall that had celebrated victory over monotony.

Here there was room enough even for the most whimpering 'phobe. The massive cylinder was built to whirl with enough centrifugal force to offer its passengers a semblance of Earthbound existence. High above one's head was someone else's floor, like an M. C. Escher print, but with plenty of room between. And enough faux gravity, separation of top and bottom, to let the crew walk, maintain muscle tone, make love, anything idle minds could conceive over the frigid black months.

But that had been long ago, when the life-stage was still bustling with activity. Now it was idle and motionless. No feeble semblance of a planet's pull had any effect on Jensen's silent flight. There was nothing to change his course as he glided past the detritus of the mission, suspended in space.

Like an exploded down pillow, the *Zelazny*'s accessories spun wildly, ridiculously, all over the life-stage. It was hard to focus on any one item; it was a blizzard made of recognizable objects. A magnetic chessboard tumbled forward as slowly as a flower petal might open, the pieces waiting forever for an opponent's next move. A guitar collided against a rest chamber but made no sound. A long, urgent, white stream—brother to the rings?—issued from the waste-paper maker, still recycling matter at a snail-like pace. A metal skillet hung in the ether, a pancake attached by its gooey bottom, all of it frozen solid. A ring binder banged into the skillet and sent it careening off, then silently unfolded, its individual thermal sheets splaying out like peacock feathers.

Jensen reached out for the binder and brought it close enough to read.

EVA Procedure.

For the first time since he could remember, Jensen laughed.

He buckled his suit onto a safety tether, and swam through the sea of banality to the jagged hole that had sucked the atmosphere out of the life-stage. Still holding the binder, he leaned outside to look.

A fading but still quite visible line of Earthly paraphernalia trailed the *Zelazny,* piece by piece, each as its own place in the crazy random motion had escorted it out of the life-stage. The self-jettisoned parade began far behind them. It would be a permanent memorial to the mission. Graph paper, macrame, wrenches, compact discs, Cheerios, bras, heads of hydroponic lettuce, laptops, a collection of items that would defy even the greatest sociological minds of any alien civilization unlucky enough to wander upon them.

Jensen had no idea of the size of the object that had

burst through the hull to cause this damage. He only knew that it had happened while he was up front, that the atmosphere had been compromised to such a degree that the outrush widened the breach further—he actually heard the groan of metal as it tore itself outward amid something that sounded like a hurricane—and that the other five were instantly depressurized, suffocated, and flash-frozen. Cause of death? Take your pick.

It had happened quickly, but Jensen had heard at least one scream as he flicked on the comm. Two of them were already gone before he was able to suit up to investigate. He wrapped the other ripped, burst bodies in government-issue blankets and pushed them out into the bizarre shipwreck parade as if they belonged there. He had always counted on the airy life-stage to remove any residual jitters he felt after a stint in the command module. From now on, it was just as cold and cloying.

Thus ended the scientific portion of the first manned Saturn mission. And thus, the stream of data returning to Earth: the transmission towers were among the first things to go as the outrushing torrent began. Jensen's colleagues back home would be left to continue wondering if water ice could actually be harvested to wet the parched tongues of off-world colonists escaping the overpopulated, overheated Earth. Or if the great ringed ball harbored even rarer elements than the ones already detected. Or if some of the prodigious number of moons whose gravity helped their host keep the rings in place might be hospitable to the inexorable spread of human life. All that now was over.

Remaining were only Jensen, the shell of the *Zelazny*, and Saturn.

He leaned out and gently laid the EVA binder in space, sending it on its own extravehicular activity. It floated there, motionless, just outside the ripped hull. Jensen pushed against it, and the binder slowly began to move away, like a ghost fading into the distance with giant Saturn as a backdrop. He watched it go for a very long time. Then he bumped into a microscope. He grabbed it and jettisoned it as hard as he could. He lost his mind for a moment and began to grasp wildly for anything near, slinging other things out of the life-stage, sending each of them on a random trip into infinity. He worked faster and faster, whirling furiously and panting with the exertion, but couldn't make a recognizable dent in the cloud of commonality that swarmed all around him. Then he realized he was holding a barbell, a ratty old thing he had used since flight training. He did a few quick curls, lifting it to his helmet with two fingers. Just like Superman, that strange visitor from another planet. The absurdity made him laugh and brought him to his senses. It was no big deal. This had happened before.

It's time.

He shoved the barbell on its way around Saturn and headed back through the floating mess for the only atmosphere left on the *Zelazny:* the capsule.

The breach had come almost exactly amidships, so life support and power, housed in the stern, were still functioning—the life-stage just couldn't hold a fill. There was recycled synthfood, both protein and carbohydrates, that was easy to reach. Jensen was fairly sure that more substantial food had also survived below, but he had no way to heat or even thaw it. There was propulsion enough to affect attitude; he had pretty well matched the ring's orbit by sight. But the damage made a complete return impossible, and without telemetry from Earth, fraught with potential catastrophe even if there had been enough fuel for the trip.

He was alone, and he was marooned.

But he had made it to Saturn.

There was just nobody he could tell about it.

He coded the seal shut and felt the rush of atmosphere as the inner door opened into the command module. He wormed his way back into the seat and wrenched off his helmet. The closeness didn't bother him much anymore; it was far preferable to the madhouse beyond the seal. His breathtaking view was still there, just out the port window. The console blinked green and gold numbers and shapes, as if in time with the mesmerizing ringflow.

Jensen sat up suddenly. A tiny black speck was headed

for the plane of the ring. He could just barely see it. Maybe the barbell, or the binder, or something else flung toward the flow during his latest fit. Then it hit. Or something did. Because a perfect circular wave had formed, and the particulate collisions were spreading outward in beautiful harmony. As Jensen watched, the waves made it to the edges of the band and returned the way they had come, accompanied by dozens of other swirls and eddies that danced across the ring. Gorgeous.

Jensen shuddered with insight and purpose. Of course. It was clear to him now.

He straightened up. Adrenaline pumped through his body, and he felt his most alert in months. He hit the starboard thruster, a short burp that moved Saturn horizontally in the window. He took a deep breath and waited for the *Zelazny* to revolve.

Soon the sun peeked into his field of view, and before the clear field of stars was dominated by its golden light, he tried to make out some of the inner planets. Towering Jupiter was easy. Was that Earth beyond, or just a pathetic wish? Call it Earth for now; what could it possibly matter?

It would be a crapshoot, a message in a bottle, but he was going to take the chance. He waited for the star to center and fired the thruster full. He was shoved back in his seat by the momentum but managed to keep firing for several minutes, his eyes never leaving the fuel readout. Finally he shut off.

That decision was now irrevocable. The *Zelazny* was headed sunward. Assuming it prevailed through the Asteroid Belt—without telemetry, completely a function of chance—it still might miss the inhabited bodies altogether; who knew where they might be in their orbits when the ship reached them? But some telescope or computer might pick up a crazily jumbled craft, and if—*when*—it did, they would finally know what happened to the Saturn mission. Maybe.

At least it beat sitting and waiting for nothing to happen.

Jensen tensed and readied himself.

He paused over the handle. Waggled his fingers. Grasped it tightly. And pulled.

The command module uncoupled from the rest of the *Zelazny*.

Jensen popped another short burst, and the capsule moved below the ship. A decisive retrofire, and the capsule was again under the gravitational influence of Saturn as the burst hull of the *Zelazny* moved overhead, trailing more garbage in its wake, and headed beyond on its long voyage to the inner system. It was gone in an amazingly short time. But he watched and watched and watched.

Jensen rotated the capsule to face the F-ring again, still awestruck. Now the closeness actually felt comforting, like a nest. It had been worth it. Sweet, sweet Saturn hadn't disappointed. Unlike the *Zelazny,* he knew exactly where he was headed. He was close enough to see house-sized boulders now, swimming in the great river. He punched in the code to open the seal and paused before the last number.

As his orbit decayed, he wondered what patterns he would make.

MARTIAN KNIGHTS

by Stephen D. Sullivan

The distant sun arced slowly toward the horizon, painting the twilit sky pastel shades of pink and blue. A dust devil danced across the red dunes, stirring up food for the giant, baglike floaters. The translucent creatures hovered around the funnel's outer edges, straining their microscopic nutrients from the clouds of sand kicked up in the tornado's wake. Nearby, the hab's recyclers hissed quietly, as if whispering the secrets of this cold, dry planet. The author looked away from the window and back to the empty tablet in front of him. How long had he contemplated Mars? Seven years, at least, though he'd never told a story about the place before.

Up to now, Stephen Sullivan had written about youthful detectives, giant bugs, mutant ninja turtles, speedy race car drivers, talking ducks, and even a superhero named after the sun. And samurai, of course—many samurai, acting out their age-old feuds in a fantasy world based on a long-dead culture. Where would his flights of fancy take him next? Back to ancient Japan? To The Twilight Empire™ once more? To some far-off world he could hardly guess? Or perhaps to Mars again? Mars. The thin air sang against the hab's window, making the glass shiver. Overhead, the stars began to open their sleepy eyes. The tablet remained empty. The author decided to down an oxi-pill

*and go for a walk. For more information on Stephen
D. Sullivan, visit www.alliterates.com.*

"PERCIVAL'S bones! It looks like you've got half
of the Hellas Planitia in here, Morris! I've never
seen so much damn sand." Sigourney Saxon crinkled her
nose and glowered at the old scrounger. She thrust one
gloved hand into the turbine of the hover-car, pulled out
a fistful of grainy red dust, and cast it away from the
dune where she was working. A summer breeze caught
the powder and swirled it into the thin Martian air.

Morris shrugged and rubbed the graying stubble on
his chin. "I don't know how it coulda happened, Sy,"
he said.

"I know how it happened, Morris," Wolfgang McDonald said, the edges of his black mustache drooping with
annoyance. "You forgot to put the dust shield on last
night." Wolf adjusted his grip on the open-topped car,
and the servos in his power armor whirred. With very
little effort, he held the vehicle at chest-level so Sigourney could crawl around and work underneath it. The car
swayed slightly, and red sand poured out of a hole in the
grille and settled around Wolf's feet. "Are you gonna be
much longer, Sy? This armor's made for combat, not
lifting."

Sy stuck a wrench into the car's innards. "Just a couple of minutes, Hawkeye," she said.

Morris tugged on the collar of the parka he was wearing over his battered P-suit. "You're the best mektek in
the south colonies, Sy. I always said that."

"We'll see if you think so after you get my bill," she
replied. "You're damn lucky you broke down near our
squat."

The old scrounger dug his toe into the red dust. "You
were on my way—to this job, I mean," he said. "This is
a good car, though. Quality stuff. Shaftco—prewar."

"It doesn't matter who made it if you leave the dust
shield off at night," Sy said. She stopped working for a
moment and regarded the older man.

Morris' eyes were watery and bloodshot. He wore a

parka over the top of his fraying P-suit, suggesting that the garment's enviro-system wasn't working properly. The suit's dome was conspicuously absent; the chilly afternoon breeze tousled Morris' sparse gray hair. Sigourney wondered if her friend was "going native."

"You can put the car down now, Wolf," she said.

Wolf grunted slightly, the servos in his armor whirred and clicked, and he set the car onto the sand. He was a handsome devil, Wolfgang McDonald: tall and dark-haired with a rugged face and a long black moustache.

Feeling suddenly warm, Sy adjusted the trim of her skinsuit and turned down the environmental controls at her belt. She brushed the dust off her legs, her arms, and her chest, and pulled her gloves tight once more. The Martian breeze tugged gently at her bobbed ebony hair, and prickled some color into her smooth cheeks. She winked slyly at Wolf, and he winked back.

Sy walked around the car, leaned over the door, and made a few final adjustments near the steering column. "Well, Morris," she said, "your main E-cells are almost shot, and your turbines need an overhaul. Your MPS is working, but your scanner's blown—so don't count on any weather warnings. Plus, your com system is down to audio only, and . . ." She reached into the back of the car, and pulled out a battered P-suit helmet. "Your dome's cracked."

"You can say that again," Wolf quipped.

Sigourney tossed the dome to Morris. He caught it and put it back in the car.

"You'll get that fixed before you go out, right?" she asked. "Oxi-pills are good for a short stint like this, but . . ."

"Um, I'm short on hydrocredits right now," the old scrounger said, forcing a smile onto his leathery face.

"Great," Wolf grumbled. "How's he gonna pay *us,* then?"

Morris flushed all the way to the top of his balding head. "I'll have plenty of creds soon," he said. "Gared Jacob commissioned this trip. When I get back, I'll be square with him *and* be able to pay you, too. Gared's got more money than God."

Wolf and Sigourney glanced at each other and frowned. "You hang out with Jacob long enough, Morris, and you'll get yourself killed," Sy said. "Especially if you don't take better care of your equipment."

"What's this *job* Jacob has you doing?" Wolf asked.

"Some deal with Pig Town," Morris said. "Jacob needs some old tek for barter."

"Old tek?" Wolf asked, arching an eyebrow.

"Cybotek," Sy said, frowning as she leaned into the car's open cockpit again. "That explains the illegal chip sensor patched into your panel here."

Morris ran around the car to where Sy was standing. "You got no business fiddling about in there!"

"Just making sure you don't end up stranded out in the dunes somewhere," Sy said, poking around the interior some more.

The scrounger's face grew bright with anger. "Look," he said, "I called you buttinskis to do a job—not to run my life." He climbed into the hover-car's cockpit without looking at his friends. "Send your bill to my flop, and I'll pay it when I get back." He punched the starter and the car's turbines whirred to life. The battered vehicle lifted off of the red ocean of sand.

Sy and Wolf stepped away from the backwash as Morris skimmed away, his car quickly gaining altitude in the thin Martian air. The pair glanced apprehensively at each other.

Wolf shrugged. "Well," he said, "it's *his* funeral."

Sy frowned. "I hope not. I kinda like the old coot."

* * *

Abel Morris scowled and cursed himself for being such a hothead. He punched the master course into the car's control panel and a tiny nav map came up on the windscreen. He pulled the hood of his parka up tight around his face, to stave off the chill, and adjusted his wind goggles. He wished the terraforming of Mars had been completed before the *Collapse* on Earth. Even at the height of summer, Mars was still damn cold.

He flipped the scanner switch once, twice, three times, and then banged on the box with his fist. Sure enough, it was fried. Why did Sy always have to be right?

Morris cursed again and checked the heads-up map display. The old battlefield shone with a big green *X*. Morris had marked the spot on the navicomp last night, just before forgetting to clip the front dust cover onto the car. The location was in the middle of the desert; no settlements anywhere near. The closest things to the site were an abandoned Martian archaeological dig, and—many kliks beyond that—a decommissioned power plant.

The battlefield had been picked over since the Cybowar, of course. Most of those searching, though, were amateurs; Morris was a pro. Plus, he had an advantage that previous scavengers didn't—the illegal chip sensor he'd gotten from Gared Jacob. The sensor could spot most cybotek from a klik away. The old scrounger chuckled to himself: an illegal sensor to find illegal chips.

Cybotek was even more illegal than the sensor, but what did Morris care? He was working for Gared Jacob, and Jacob made his own rules. Gared was descended from the founder of Jacob's Well, and he kept the settlement under his thumb just as easily as his forefathers had. If the cityboss wanted cybotek, he'd get it—whether or not Morris helped him or not. Morris figured he might as well cash in on the deal.

The battle of Podkayne's Dune had been one of the last gasps of the Cybowar. The conflict capped the colonial civil war, involving nearly every settler on Mars. Shaftco and its corporate allies pitted their cybernetically enhanced warriors against the combined armies of the Martian city states. Each side fought for planet-wide domination and the right to control mankind's destiny. Cybo generals and their war-machines strode across the sands like monstrous spiders. Brave handfuls of men and women in power armor rose up to meet them, like knights pitting themselves against metal dragons. In the end, the human forces triumphed—barely—and cybotek was outlawed. The remaining cybos were hunted down and destroyed.

On Podkayne's Dune, the Colonial Power Cavalry had finally crushed the troops of the cybo General Toth. The cost in CPC lives and material had been great, though. The wreckage of machines, cybos, and humans littered the field until the sands reclaimed it. Even now, nine years later, people avoided the place. The native Martians said it was haunted, but Morris didn't believe in ghosts; he believed in hydrocredits.

He turned the wheel until the car's course angled straight for the *X* on the map. Then he leaned back in the seat and admired the landscape. Rusty dunes stretched away in every direction, wind rippling their surfaces and filling the air with tawny dust. To the northwest, the distant crags of the *Hellisponte Montes* loomed out of the afternoon haze. Closer by, a pod of floaters drifted lazily through the air, the breeze tugging on their huge, baglike bodies. The enormous translucent creatures waved their long tendrils, siphoning their invisible food from the atmosphere.

The creatures were beautiful with the pale, distant sun shining through their purplish membranes. The afternoon sunlight caught the edges of the floaters' bodies and their outlines shone like silver. Despite himself, Morris watched the graceful, shimmering herd for the better part of an hour as his car angled toward Podkayne's Dune.

He had just begun to doze off when a noise disturbed his reverie: a howling whine, similar to the hover-car's turbine engines, but much louder. The old scrounger blinked twice and wiped the dust off his goggles.

Ahead, a monstrous twister cut through the dunes like the finger of Ares himself. Red dust billowed up around the towering cyclone and blotted out the landscape below. The intense winds sucked the placid floaters into the funnel of the storm. The creatures collapsed into umbrellalike shapes to ride out the tempest; they'd survive, little the worse for wear. Morris knew he wouldn't be that lucky.

Cursing his broken scanner, he twisted the steering column and banked away from the huge tornado. Out the corner of his eye, he saw the buried shapes of the ancient Martian town less than a klik away. He aimed the nose of the hover-car for that small pile of rubble, knowing he'd never make it. The twister reached out one dusty arm and swept Morris and his car up into the whirlwind.

The roaring in his ears reminded the aging scrounger of waking up in a turbomill after a three-day bender. The wind threatened to rip him out of his restraining belts. The air around him swirled, thick with rusty sand and ocher dust. Morris clamped his mouth tight in an effort to keep the biting grains from smothering him.

A shudder ran though him as something large hit the hover-car. Morris caught a glimpse of flailing tentacles and a huge, bulbous body. A floater; he'd hit a floater. The engines suddenly died, and the car nosed down into the maelstrom. Morris pulled on the steering column to no avail. The wind ripped a terrified scream from his parched and blasted lips.

The hover-car spun in a dizzying circle, the wind tossing it like a child's toy. The tornado buffeted Morris, bruising his body and straining nearly all his muscles. Something bumped, and then thumped, and then the car spun and the autocushions deployed. Morris' world went black.

*   *   *

He awoke coughing sand from his lungs. The deflated autocushions covered his lap like a giant plastic balloon with all the air run out. He noticed a smear of red on one, reached up to his weathered scalp, and quickly discovered the source of the blood. It was a nasty scratch, but not too deep.

"You're one lucky S.O.B.," Morris said aloud to himself. He threw the switch to deflate the autocushions, and the soiled bags crept slowly back into their deployment hatches. They jammed about three-quarters of the way in. Morris cursed. He reached around, undid his restraining belts, and hopped out of the car.

The nose of the hover-car was almost completely buried in sand and rubble. Dust from the storm's passing still saturated the air. The old scrounger coughed and tried vainly to wave the grit away from his face. Peering into the gloom, Morris saw that he'd not only crashed into a sand dune, he'd also hit a wall of the half-buried Martian ruins.

A big block of stone sat squarely on the car's hood, making a nice dent in the battered steel. The sleek metal of the hover-car's nose was crumpled like an accordion. At the back, one of the turbofans hung by a few scarred wires.

Morris swore again. No way he'd be driving away from this. He walked around the half-buried car and kicked the side panels. Then he hopped back in and pulled out the radiophone. He brushed the dust off the handset and punched up Sigourney Saxon's number.

Her machine answered, and Morris left a message—hoping that she and Wolf would extend his credit far enough to tow him back to Jacob's Well. Images of winged hydrocredits flying out of his moneybelt danced through Morris' groggy brain. Then something else caught his attention: a light blinking near his control panel.

The chip sensor!

The chip sensor was registering a cybochip somewhere nearby. Morris peered into the dusty darkness. The Martian ruins rose around him like tombstones in the twilight. Right in front of the car, between two of the ancient buildings, he noticed a gap in one of the monolithic Martian walls—a gap the same size as the rock on his hood.

He pulled the chip sensor from its harness and swept the area. Sure enough, the signal emanated most strongly from the hole. He dropped the sensor and let it dangle on its long, springy cord. He'd have to leave it behind; it needed the car's E-cells for power.

He stepped into the sand once more, his head swirling with possibilities. This buried Martian town had been well-picked over before the Cybowar—stripped of any-

thing valuable the natives had left behind. He doubted
that many people had visited the ruins since the war
ended.

Something hidden since that time might still remain
undiscovered. Morris licked his rough, parched lips.
Hardly daring to hope, he walked forward. He pulled
the glowlight from the belt of his battered P-suit and
shone it into the hole, illuminating a wide chamber on
the other side of the broken wall.

Cautiously, Morris stepped through. The room beyond
the hole was as wide as three heavy hover-tanks, and
twice that deep. A dusting of red sand covered the
stone-paved floor. There was a doorway on the far side
of the chamber, but something shiny and black obstructed his view.

Two light cybotanks, their spidery legs splayed around
them as if they might strike at any moment, stood
blocking the far passage. Sweat beaded on Morris' balding pate. He stood stock still, fear gripping his aching
muscles. Only after several long minutes did he realize
that the tanks were dead—out of energy. Perhaps their
organic brains had perished long ago. Why had they
come here, though? And why had they sealed themselves within this rocky tomb?

Suddenly, a strong desire to see what lay beyond the
cybotanks seized Morris. He ran across the room, carefully avoiding the tanks' sharp spines, and stepped into
the crumbling corridor beyond. Inside lay a body.

Morris had never seen a cybo like this before. It was
dead, there could be no doubt about that. From its chest
down, it was mostly a skeleton. But the right side of the
body from the waist up, the arms, the spinal cord, the
clawed feet, and nearly all of the head were entirely
mechanical.

The old scrounger frowned and let out a long whistle.
Most cybos had just a few body parts replaced; legs,
perhaps for speed, or arms for combat, or a cybo implant
in the head to enhance neurological functions. This thing
seemed to be nearly half machine. The thought of it
made Morris shudder, but the workmanship was exqui-

site: Vintage Shaftco, probably manufactured just before the company's destruction at the end of the war.

Morris grinned. These cybos were a treasure almost beyond price! With them, he could pay off all his debts to Gared Jacob and still have enough left to live like a prince for the rest of his life.

The only trick was figuring out how to get his prizes back to Jacob's Well. For a moment, he regretted having called Wolf and Sy. Now he'd have to think of a way to keep the discovery from them. It would be dark soon, and that might help.

He could pull the smaller cybo out of the ruins and hide it in the trunk of his car. He'd have to conceal the cybotanks where they were. Using the tarp from his trunk, he could block off the hole in the wall. If he covered the tarp with sand and a few rocks for camouflage, Sy and Wolf *might* miss the hole in the darkness. Yes. It could work.

Morris pulled back the hood of his parka, and wiped the sweat from his brow. He stepped up to the cybo's body and kicked the dusty bones away from the machineworks. Then he knelt down and picked up the gleaming metal skeleton. Long, wirelike strands of servos connected the thing's spine to its clawed "boots."

He put one of the cold arms over his shoulder and hefted the weight of the machine onto his back. It dangled down behind him like a cape, its feet scraping against the stone floor. "Just like carrying wounded during the war," Morris muttered.

The thing jangled like coins as he walked. Visions of swimming pools and showers filled the scrounger's mind. And women—bevies of beautiful women, lounging on the patio by his pool. And shade palms blocking out the distant sun.

Lost in his reverie, Morris hardly noticed the clacking of the metal as he pushed past the dead tanks with his precious burden. He never felt the spinal cord of the dead cybo brushing up against his P-suit's belt power pack.

Suddenly, a red haze of pain flooded the old scrounger's senses. Morris gasped and staggered forward, falling to his knees—almost losing his grip on his burden. Why did his back hurt so? Why was it hard to think?

He glanced over his shoulder into the glaring green eyes of the cybo. The eyes blinked away the dust covering them. Morris tried to scream, but the blood bubbling out of his mouth smothered the cry.

*   *   *

The morning sunlight reflected through the high windows and caught the water as it fell, turning the precious liquid the color of gold.

Artificial rain cascaded down from the arched ceiling and over Sigourney Saxon's smooth, well-muscled body. The warmth and wetness made her skin tingle. She scrubbed herself carefully, lingering over every wonderful sensation, then washed her hair.

The smell of soap and shampoo thrilled her. And the water . . . the fresh, mineral tang of the liquid! It was almost too much to bear. She let the spray run into her mouth, over her teeth and tongue, then squirted the water out between her lips.

Warm light filtered through the fronds of the plants growing at the chamber's edges and dappled the rainroom in shades of living green. Everything seemed so wonderful in this place, so alive. How thrilling this opulent liquid; how fleeting the luxurious sensations. Sy wanted to stay here forever.

"Sy . . ."

Far away, someone called her name, but she couldn't place the voice.

"Sy, wake up."

Wolf. The voice belonged to Wolfgang McDonald. Was he hiding in the foliage? Sy smiled at the thought.

With a soft sigh, she opened her eyes.

The gentle thrum of the turbine generators filled the caravan. The hiss of the recyclers as they turned waste back into potable water and dry fertilizer tickled her ears.

"I was dreaming," she said sleepily.

"What about?" Wolf asked.

"Rain."

Standing next to their air mattress, he sighed.

Sigourney Saxon sighed as well. No rain. Never any rain here. All rain on Mars was an illusion. Only the rich could afford rain, and then only in their private habs. She chided herself for desiring such a thing.

"Do you miss the life you had before the war?" Wolf asked. "Do you regret giving up the wealth and power to come live with an old cavalryman?"

She shook her head. "Never," she said. She took a deep breath of the filtered air. "Sometimes, though, I wish for rain."

He nodded, and sat down on the bed beside her.

"What about you," she asked. "Do you miss the cavalry, the camaraderie, the excitement of battle?"

"The cramped quarters, the smell of machine lube, the sound of gunfire. . . ?" he added with a laugh.

She smiled and sat up. "Why'd you wake me? I thought this was a rest day."

"Our autorob took a call from Morris last evening," Wolf said. "He's crashed out in the old ruins, near Podkayne's Dune."

Sy rubbed the sleep from her eyes. "Shit. What time is it? Is Morris okay?"

"He sounded fine on the recording," Wolf said.

"Shit. We shouldn't have had the machine on. We should have gone out when he called."

Wolf shook his head and smiled sympathetically at her. "With the storm, we couldn't have gone out last night anyway. Besides, even Morris can't expect two service calls in one day."

Sigourney stood and pulled on the top of her skinsuit. "Well, let's get dressed and rescue Morris' sorry ass. You fire up the mini: I'll take the sled. He and I can ride back together while you tow that heap he calls a hover-car. Assuming he needs a tow."

"After what I saw of his car yesterday, I wouldn't doubt it," Wolf said. "But I'll pack your toolbox, just in case it's something *small* this time."

*   *   *

Sigourney Saxon throttled back and skimmed the hover-sled low over the sand, angling for the half-buried Martian ruins. Wolfgang MacDonald swooped in behind her, showing off the driving skills that had done him proud during his stint in the Colonial Power Cavalry. Sy smiled, despite her worries about Morris. Seeing Wolf at work always thrilled her. He spent too much of his time assisting her on repair missions; riding free over the dunes in his power armor was where he really belonged. No matter what he said, he was still a soldier at heart.

"See any sign of him, Wolf?"

"Nope. His emergency transponder's gone dead, too."

"That's odd."

"Yeah," Wolf said. "But the message he sent had an MPS reading attached. He should be just behind that native building ahead."

"Roger," Sy replied, adjusting her heading appropriately.

She coasted to a stop on the ridge of a dune near the MPS coordinates. Wolf brought the mini-transport down to rest gently beside her. He checked the sensor readout in his suit. "Looks like he might be in that building," Wolf said, pointing.

Sy nodded and started to hike down the dune toward the ruined Martian plaza. As she took the first step, though, a huge, flabby tentacle rose up to meet her.

The lithe mechanic sprang to one side, hit the sand in a roll, and landed in a crouch, her left hand instinctively reaching for the lectro-blade strapped inside her boot. Wolf's autogun leaped into his hand, his reflexes automatically tracking the menace.

"Hold it!" Sy said. "It's just a grounded floater—one of the filter feeders. Not carnivorous. No danger to us."

Wolf's brown eyes studied the creature for a moment. "What's it doing here?" he asked.

Sy skidded down the dune beside the huge, flabby beast. "It's wounded," she said. "Looks like a hover-car hit it."

"Morris," said Wolf.

"Probably," she replied. "I think I see his beater up ahead. "C'mon. Nothing we can do for the floater. It'll either get airborne again, or become food for something else." She headed for the ruins.

"Too bad," said Wolf, admiring the floater's translucent body. "Let's hope that Morris fared better." He shambled down the hill behind her, leaving the huge wounded animal flapping on the side of the dune. The couple soon found their friend's car at the edge of the ruins.

Inside her domed helmet, Sy frowned. "What the hell happened here?" she said, her gray eyes flashing over the wreckage of the hover-car.

"No floater did this, that's for sure," Wolf added.

Sy nodded, suppressing a shiver that ran up her spine. She leaned over the side of the car and inspected the damage. "Last night's storm didn't do this either," she said. "The car's been stripped. The E-cells are gone, along with most of the electronic equipment. That explains why his emergency transponder's not working."

"Why would Morris strip his own car?" Wolf asked. Then he paused a moment and nodded grimly and said, "Oh. He probably didn't."

"That's what worries me," Sy said. "Any reports of bandits or dune pirates in this area?"

Wolf punched up a display inside his helmet. "Nothing within twenty-five kliks for the last thirty Sols or more," he said.

Sy shrugged. "That doesn't rule them out, of course," she said, but . . . what's this?" She turned from the car toward the broken wall nearby. The two of them walked toward the ragged opening. "Maybe Morris took shelter inside."

"Let's hope," Wolf replied. They ducked through the hole and into the broad stone chamber beyond.

Sigourney gasped and clenched her teeth tight to fight a wave of nausea. "I think we found Morris," she said.

"What's left of him," Wolf added.

Blood stained the rough flagstones of the wide room, leading a gory trail from the middle of the chamber to

near the opening where they stood. Strewn along the
way were an assortment of body parts: fingers, toes, two
arms, and part of the old scrounger's head.

" 'Cudas, you think? Or a dune shrike?" Wolf asked.

Sy shook her head. " 'Cudas wouldn't leave so much
behind. Neither would a shrike. Besides, that big floater
outside hasn't been eaten. Martian animals would never
pass up a floater for stringy meat like Morris."

"What then?"

Sy shook her head. "I don't know. What worries me,
though, is . . . where's the *rest* of him?"

Wolfgang and Sigourney glanced warily at each other.
"Check the far side of the chamber," she said. "I'm
going to look out near the speeder, in case we missed
something."

He nodded. "Roger."

When she returned to the big room, Wolf was waiting
for her by the opening.

"I didn't find anything," he said. "There's a passage
at the far end, but it's collapsed just a couple of feet
beyond the entrance. Some scratches on the stone floor,
but that's it. The only tracks I got on IR belonged to
Morris. The strange thing is, they look like they leave
the building."

"I think Morris *did* leave the building," Sy said. "At
least, *part* of him did."

"What do you mean?" Wolf asked, worry playing
across his handsome face.

"I found some tracks by the car," she said. "I didn't
notice them before, because it never occurred to me to
look. I'm guessing that what made those tracks is probably
the same spidery limbs that made the scratches you saw."

Wolf blanched. "Shit! Not . . ."

Sy nodded. "Cybos."

"Percival's bones," Wolf whispered. "I thought we'd
gotten them all in the war."

Sigourney laughed ironically. "You know better than
that, Wolf—even if that's what Gared Jacob and the
other citybosses want everyone to think. There are still
a few dangerous ones lurking around."

"Podkayne's Dune isn't far from here," Wolf said. "It was one of the last Cybowar battlefields. Maybe that's where Jacob was sending Morris to scrounge. If you want cybo parts, that'd be a good place to start."

"Makes sense," she replied. "With that illegal chip sensor, Morris might have found some cybo pieces that others missed."

"Pieces, yes. But—after all these years—how could he have found something that murdered him?"

"We won't know that until we find his killer," Sy said. "C'mon. I spotted the chip sensor unit hanging by its cord in Morris' car. The thing that dusted Morris must not have known what it was. We can hook the unit into the mini and find the bastard."

Wolf nodded. "I'll break out the heavy weapons."

*   *   *

Sigourney's sled and Wolf's mini-transport rose into the dusty air. The dunes and the ruined Martian town rapidly fell away below them. The afternoon sun arced high in the pale pinkish-blue sky. In the distance, a dust devil danced across the rippling sands.

It hadn't taken Sy long to adapt Morris' sensor chip into the mini-transport's console; she'd even beefed up the range a bit. They'd have to follow the cybo's tracks as best they could until they got within the scanner's range, though. Fortunately, the sand storm that grounded them last night would have kept the cybo in the ruins as well. It was on foot and couldn't have that much of a lead on them.

"Don't worry," Wolf said, "I've followed colder trails in my day. Don't know how I missed the tracks in the first place. What do you think—a light cybotank?"

Sy pulled her hover-sled into the mini's slipstream to conserve power. "I figure," she said. "We'll do a quick recon and then, if we're right, call Gared Jacob. His security team can mop up this mess. He and the city can afford the cleaning bill."

"Think Gared will go for it?"

She shrugged, knowing Wolf would see her in the mini's rearview scanner. "He wanted cybotek," she said. "Looks like he's got it—in spades."

"I'm not too keen on Jacob getting his hands on whatever this thing turns out to be," Wolf said.

"Me, neither," she replied. "But I figure he'll have to pound it to hell to kill it. Probably won't be able to salvage much—if anything—after it's dead."

In the open cockpit of the mini, Wolf nodded. "Hang on," he said. "The chip sensor's picking up something. Okay, I've got a lock. Stay close, we're going in." He kicked the throttle of the mini, and it shot forward; she sped after him.

Minutes later, they spotted a small black dot atop a far dune. "Can your helmet binocs make that out?" Sy called over the vox.

"Just a mass of metal legs from here, I . . . wait a minute . . . Shit! I think there's more than one."

Sy cursed. "That'd make sense. Walking in each other's tracks is standard cybo procedure."

"Makes it worse for us, though," Wolf said.

"Not if it's Gared Jacob's problem," she replied. "We'll get close enough to verify the formation, then call in the big boy's private army."

"Roger," he replied.

As they approached the small shapes, Sy pulled her sled alongside the mini-transport, to get a better look at the creatures they were pursuing. Ahead of them, two light cybotanks crawled purposefully over the dunes, their spidery metal legs churning up the ocher dust.

"Where do you think they're headed?' Wolf asked.

"Probably carrying out whatever mission they had before they deactivated," Sy said. She did some quick calculations in her head. "Isn't the old power plant in this direction?"

"Yeah," Wolf replied. "But it was decommissioned ages ago."

"But these cybos don't know that," she said. "They're still fighting the battle of Podkayne's Dune. Shit! Look out!"

One of the cybotanks suddenly swung its main gun in

their direction and fired. The energy pulse seared the thin atmosphere between the two vehicles as Sy and Wolf peeled off in opposite directions. As they maneuvered, the air filled with small arms fire.

"What the hell is this?" Wolf called. "We should be out of their tracking range."

"Apparently not," Sy called back. "Keep your head down and let's get out of here." As she said it, though, a blast from the second tank's gun seared the rear turbine on her sled. "Shit! I'm hit!"

"How bad?"

"Just the car's turbine," she replied. "But I can't stay airborne."

"I'll cover you and follow you down," Wolf said. He pulled out his autogun and fired it over the mini's windscreen at the cybos. The dunes near the tanks erupted into a cloud of dust.

Sigourney twisted the controls of the sled, trying to keep its flight path steady. The ground rushed up to meet her, the nose of the sled burying itself in the rough sand. The hover-sled's autocushions deployed, protecting Sy from most of the impact.

She unbuckled her harness and pulled herself off the damaged vehicle, quickly taking cover behind a larger dune. Moments later, Wolf landed beside her. "Are you okay?" he called.

"I've been better," she said, brushing the dust from her skinsuit. "Are they coming for us?"

Wolf checked the scanner in his helmet. "No, thank God. They're still on their mission to frag the power plant. I put out some decoy smoke before landing. They probably think we're fragged."

"Either that, or they think we're no threat," she said.

"Then they'd be dead wrong," Wolf replied. A grim smile played across his face.

"Don't be so sure," Sy said. "I spotted something as I was going down. One of those tanks has a rider."

"What?"

"Yeah," she continued, "I saw him melded into the thing's cockpit. I think it was General Toth."

"Toth? Are you sure?"

"I'm pretty familiar with Shaftco and their more infamous creations," she said.

He nodded. "But isn't Toth dead? I thought he'd been killed at Podkayne's Dune."

"Some cybos are harder to kill than others," Sy replied, frowning. "I heard a rumor that Toth had his human memories burned into cybochips. If that's true, he—or some element of him—might have survived the death of his human parts during the war."

"Shit. And he's used Morris for raw materials to rebuild himself."

Sigourney nodded. "Looks that way. Morris' body and the E-cells and parts from his hover-car."

"Well, like you said earlier, this is Jacob's problem now. I'll get him on the box." He went back to the mini and worked the radiophone for a few minutes before returning.

"Jacob's not buying it," Wolf said, turning up his palms in disbelief.

"You told him they'd killed Morris? You told him they're heading for the old power plant?"

Wolf nodded. "I told him, or rather, *her*. Kali White, his security chief, intercepted the call. She wouldn't let me speak to Jacob directly."

"Did you mention that Toth will go looking for fresh targets when he finds out the power plant is dead? Did you tell her that he'll probably come for Jacob's Well next? It's the closest place for replacement parts—and fresh meat."

"I mentioned all that. Kali thinks this is some kind of stunt—a trick to get her to expend valuable resources."

"The arrogant bitch," Sy hissed. "I'd spit if I didn't have this dome on."

Wolf laughed. "So, what do we do? Tow the sled back for rep s and let Jacob stew in his own juices when the cyb come calling?"

A momentary grin tugged at the corners of Sy's mouth, then turned into a frown. "Shit. We can't do that, no matter how much I'd like to. I wouldn't mind

Toth killing White and Jacob, but a lot of innocent people will get hurt with these cybos on the loose."

"I guess we'll just have to kick his metal ass, then," Wolf said. "Just like my old days in the Colonial Power Cavalry. We'll need a plan, though. I've only got a half-dozen or so guns in the mini. Those tanks will cut us into fillets if we face them out in the open."

"I've got an idea," Sy said. "Let's see if any of my weapons got damaged in the crash. We'll have to come back for the sled later. Otherwise, Toth'll beat us to our objective."

"Which is . . . ?"

Sy smiled. "The old power station."

*   *   *

The wreckage of the old power station loomed out of the red sand like broken teeth. Most of the workings and metal had been taken for salvage long ago, but the hulking Marscrete walls still remained, bleached pale by the passage of time.

Sigourney Saxon sat atop one of the old turbomill generator towers and scanned the horizon. A fully-loaded autogun rested on the roof at her side, and she'd activated the wrist- and ankle-units that turned her skinsuit into custom, ultralite power armor. The hum of the armor made her skin tingle. She called up her helmet's binocs and trained them on a dust cloud to the northwest.

"Wolf," she said into her vox, "I see them. Are you all set up?"

"Yeah. They're registering on my scanner, too."

"We'd better fire a few volleys at them before they get too close," Sy said. "Make them think that this is still a working installation."

"Roger," Wolf said. "I'll move to the front of the complex and take some potshots, just to keep them interested."

Sy watched as Wolf sprinted over the dunes. With his power armor active, he bounded lightly across the red

sand like a huge Martian hopper. Wolf positioned himself behind a large drift hill and scrambled up the side.
He used the periscope on his armor to target the cybos
and then popped over the top of the hill and fired.

The slugs screamed across the dunes, impacting the
metal shells of the cybo machines, but doing little damage. Wolf ducked down and moved to another hillock
as the cybos returned fire.

"That's got them going," he said over the vox.

"So long as they don't get you," Sy said.

"Don't worry," he said. "I'll lure them into our ambush just as pretty as you please." He popped up over
another dune and fired again, retreating before the sand
exploded with deadly cybo counterfire.

"They're buying it," Sy said. "The tanks are splitting
up to blanket your side of the complex. Toth's dis-
mounted and is coming in on his own. Make sure he
doesn't catch you napping; it looks like he's armed to
the teeth."

"Those would be Morris' teeth," Wolf's voice said
over the vox.

Sy's mouth drew into a thin line. "Yeah," she said.

The dune where Wolf had been shattered under the
cybos' next volley, but he had already moved on. The
cybotanks fanned out on either side of him, trying to pin
Wolf down. Toth ignored the former cavalryman, striding toward the complex on his half-human legs, deadly
purpose shining in his metallic green eyes.

Wolf ducked under the fire of the advancing machines.
"Think they've figured out there's only one of me yet?"

"I doubt it," she said. "They're firing slugs, saving the
plasma cannons for taking out the complex's power
generators."

"If they're relying on the E-cells from Morris' hover-
car to power those cannons, they may not have much
energy," Wolf said.

"Let's hope," she replied. "I don't know how long we
could stand up under that kind of barrage."

Suddenly, Toth spotted Wolf moving through the dunes.
At the cybo general's silent command, the machines swiv-

eled their guns toward him. Sigourney felt, more than heard, the tanks' main guns charging for a lethal blast.

"Wolf, they've seen you!" she yelled. "Get out of there!" As she spoke, she punched a button on her wristband. At her signal, two pre-placed gunchers swung on their tripods and fired grenades at the cybotanks.

Sigourney cheered as the explosives hit home. The tanks rocked and reeled for a moment, and Wolf leaped out of their target lock. The cybos shook off the effects of the grenades and began to track the former power soldier once more.

"Thanks, darlin'," Wolf called to Sy. Two servo-assisted leaps took him behind the battered Marscrete walls of the power complex. White-hot tracers cut a swath through the late afternoon air as Toth fired at Wolf. Wolf dodged the last few slugs and then sprinted into the city, moving toward a defensible position they'd scouted earlier.

As Toth fired at Wolf, Sy ripped another volley at the cybotanks. The machines sputtered and hissed. Small pieces of metal flew off their armored carapaces, but they still didn't fall. Acting as one, they trained their guns on Sy's automated emplacements and blasted the gunchers to smithereens.

"Ouch," Sy said. "That's a few hydrocredits up in smoke."

Wolf laughed, then stopped suddenly. "Hold on," he said. "Those tanks are entering the complex. Gotta run. Take care of Toth for me, will you?"

"Roger, Hawkeye," Sy said. She watched as Wolf bounded through the complex, heading to intercept the nearest cybo. With luck, he could draw it into the trap they'd planned. Her heart fluttered for a moment at the thought of her bond-mate fighting the hellish monsters alone. Then she steeled herself for the job at hand. Raising her autogun, she clicked it into guncher mode and trained it on Toth as he approached the power plant's main entrance.

The binocs in her helmet gave her a good view of the cybo general's half-human face. Her jaw tightened as she saw the stubble of Morris' beard peeking out between the general's metal "enhancements."

She only hesitated a moment, but it was enough. Toth spotted the laser sight on her gun, and he leaped to one side just as she squeezed the trigger. Her grenade exploded five meters from Toth as he landed. Dust and rocks showered down on the cybo, but Sy knew she hadn't come close to killing him. She cursed and fired again.

Toth dived out of the way once more, sheltering behind a crumbling wall. A small cannon sprouted from his arm when he reappeared. He fired a plasma blast toward Sigourney's position.

The burst hit Sy's tower and shattered the weathered Marscrete. The steel reinforcements within the structure groaned, and then bent, as the tower toppled toward the ground. Sy leaped. Her gloved fingers found purchase on the rough surface of the next tower. Her body hit hard, and the air rushed out of her lungs. The strap holding the autogun around her shoulders snapped and the gun clattered to the rubble-strewn ground below. She clung to the wall for a moment, like a human fly, and caught her breath.

"Sy! Are you all right?" Wolf's voice blared over the vox.

"Too busy to talk right now," she said. As she spoke, Toth shattered her new perch with another plasma round. She jumped again, this time angling for an old catwalk support. The ultralite's servos kicked in, propelling her easily across the vast space. The catwalk itself was gone, salvaged long ago, but she landed lightly atop the pylon, grabbed hold, and quickly shimmied toward the ground.

Toth bellowed with rage.

"You run like a Cavalry trooper, little bug!" he called in a voice eerily like Morris'.

As she hit the sand, Sy pressed the speaker button on her skinsuit. "And you fight like a rusty machine!" she called back.

Wolf's voice came over the vox. "Sy, don't talk to him; kill him!"

"What do you think I'm *trying* to do?" she snapped. "Just keep those tanks off my ass!"

"Roger. Will do. Love you."

"Love you, too." Sweat beaded on her forehead and ran down to her lips. She pulled the small stinger from her hip and switched off the safety. With her other hand, she found the sole grenade hanging at her belt. She darted behind the wall and checked her helmet's tactical display.

Toth carefully picked his way through the decommissioned power plant; only a half-dozen pylons and a few meters of Marscrete separated him from her. She checked his coordinates one last time, stepped out, and lobbed her grenade in Toth's direction.

The general fired at Sigourney as she appeared. His tracers hummed past her, the polarity of her armor turning grazing shots into near misses. Not everything missed, though. A blast caught her left shoulder, burning in one side and out the other. Sy gasped with pain. Her grenade exploded a few meters short of the general.

Too late, Toth realized her plan. The detonation ripped through the pylons in front of him, sending them toppling on the surprised general. Toth's automated weaponry swung up, firing a deadly barrage at the tons of Marscrete falling toward him.

Precious oxygen hissed out of Sy's ruptured skinsuit armor. She knew she could survive in the thin Martian air for a time, but there was no way she'd be able to fight. Popping her helmet open, she pulled an oxi-pill from her wrist medikit and dropped it into her mouth. Ignoring the pain in her arm, she aimed her stinger to where she'd last seen Toth.

The displays in her helmet told her he was still there, amid the smoke and rubble. She couldn't tell whether he was alive. A moment later, though, the cybo warrior charged out of the dust cloud toward her.

Toth's cybo armor was battered, and many of his

weapons had been destroyed. The sharp spines on his carapace still made him a formidable opponent, though. Sy knew he could crush her easily within his metal arms. "Bitch!" he hissed. "You'll die for that."

Sy fired a full stinger burst into the human part of Toth's face, hoping the drugged needles would slow him down. She jumped, the servos in her suit and Mars' low gravity allowing her to clear twenty meters.

Toth spun toward her and followed, the drug didn't seem to faze him at all. Sy was lucky, though; even with Toth's cybo enhancements, Morris' old P-suit was no match for her ultralite armor. Darting between the columns of the crumbling power plant, she easily kept ahead of her foe.

"Out of ammo so soon, soldier-borg?" she called back. "I'd have thought the great General Toth would be better equipped."

"No need to waste energy on one such as you," he replied. "I can kill you just as easily with my own hands!" He caromed off a wall unexpectedly and bounded right into Sy's path.

Toth thrust a spiny arm at Sy's head, but she ducked under the blow. She hammered her right fist into his human gut, putting all her strength behind the punch. She felt something pop within Abel Morris' old flesh.

The cybo spun through the dusty air and landed hard against a broken wall. A gun emerged from the general's metal forearm, and he fired at her. She dodged the first few shots, but the last got through her suit's deflection field and traced a long scrape down her thigh.

Blood leaked from the wound, and her leg felt as though it were on fire, but she ignored it. "Changed your mind about shooting me, Toth, or are you running out of options?" she asked.

As she landed, he pointed the gun at her again, but this time the chamber clicked empty.

"Too bad Morris didn't bring you any ammo," Sy said, a wry smile washing over her sweaty face.

"Do I know you, meat?" Toth's metallic voice hissed.

His cybernetic eyes burned green in the gathering twilight.

"I doubt it," she replied. "You've been dead for most of my life. Unless you're remembering the memories of the man whose flesh you've stolen."

"Meat is meat," Toth replied. He sprang, razor-sharp spines bristling. She leaped backward, somersaulting into the air. As he passed beneath her, she dropped her stinger and drew the lectro-blade strapped inside her boot. She pressed the blade's power switch with her thumb.

Sigourney landed catlike behind him, and in one swift move plunged the blade into the metal joint at the base of Toth's skull. The servos of her skinsuit whirred as she bore down, driving the electrified metal in as deeply as she could.

The cybo general shrieked as electricity arced through his armored frame. Toth wheeled, yanking the blade from Sy's hands. He turned on her, his mechanical eyes blazing. Sigourney took a step back, tripped, and landed hard on her tailbone. Fire sprang up in her wounded leg and arm, and spots danced before her eyes.

Toth staggered forward, his spines sparking, his mouth sputtering incoherent obscenities. Groping blindly, Sy found a medium-sized rock, the only weapon at hand. She tried to get enough traction to stand, but her legs merely kicked the sand out from under her.

The cybo general closed in. Sy threw the rock, but it bounced harmlessly off his metal skull plates. Morris' tongue lolled out of Toth's mouth, like a snake looking for a victim. Toth took one step toward her. Then another. His green eyes burned with hatred of all things human. His claws stabbed toward the dome of her helmet. His fingers fell short and he collapsed in a heap at her feet. A great cloud of ochre dust welled up where Toth's huge frame hit the sand. The cybo's metal limbs twitched briefly, then he died for a second time.

Sigourney Saxon let out a long breath. Slowly, she forced her aching body to stand. Then she remembered.

"Wolf!" she called into her vox. "Wolf, Toth is dead. Where are you? Are you all right?"

In reply, a huge explosion shook the crumbling power plant. She looked up and saw the flash and dust, but no sign of Wolf.

Panic welled up in her guts. Pausing only long enough to retrieve her blade, she bounded through the Mars-crete ruins toward the site of the explosion. When she got there, she found Wolf standing proudly between two burning cybotanks. Seeing her, he smiled.

"Our plan worked," he said. "I got them to fire on each other. Some cybos never learn. Thanks for keeping Toth distracted. I'd never have gotten them if he'd been directing the battle."

Sy pounded her fist onto his armored chest. "Take that helmet off, idiot," she said, doffing her own bubble.

He did the same and they kissed until his air ran out. He put his helmet back on. Then his face fell. "Uh-oh," Wolf said. "My scanner is showing incoming vehicles."

"God, not more cybos!"

His frown turned to a smile. "No," he said. "Jacob's private security force, I think, judging by the signals. Looks like they believed us after all."

"How long until they get here?" she asked.

"Ten, fifteen minutes. Why?"

"I need to make sure they don't find anything useful on General Toth."

"Better bandage that arm first," he said. "If Kali White catches you bleeding, it'll ruin your rep."

Sy forced a grin and glanced at her wounded shoulder.

*   *   *

Kali White wasn't pleased to find them there—but then, she was seldom pleased about anything. Jacob's security chief lectured the couple for a while, but in the end merely ran them off before scouring the old power station for pieces of the cybos that her boss could use.

Sy and Wolf retrieved their mini-transport from where they'd hidden it in the dunes southwest of the plant. Then they drove back and picked up Sy's wrecked sled. By the time they reached home, the sky was dark and

Phobos and Deimos were arcing high overhead. The moons shed their pale light on the red dunes outside the caravan.

Sigourney Saxon stripped off her skinsuit and collapsed onto the air mattress. The weight of the hab's grav plates tugged at her tired bones; so much weight after hopping around outside all day.

Wolf collapsed into a chair near the caravan's kitchen and slowly removed his armor, one piece at a time. "You think there's anything else buried out in those ruins where Morris dug up Toth?" he asked.

"I don't know," Sy said. She closed her eyes and listened to the soft hum of the recyclers. "If we move our caravan there, though, no one else will have a chance to make trouble. We could keep other squatters away, as well as nosy tourists. And that big chamber in the ruins would make a fine garage, once it's cleaned up." She opened her eyes and gazed at him. "Our repair business could use a more permanent home. Plus, you could dig around the ruins a bit—indulge your archaeological bent. It'd give you something to do while I work."

"Are you saying you don't want my help anymore?"

"Of course not. But I know you get bored with mektek sometimes. Admit it. You'd be happier poking around the ruins than lifting cars all day."

He smiled, "Okay, I'll cop to that. But Jacob probably won't like us moving into the ruins. His family owns title to most of this sector."

"Screw him. Besides, he owes us one here—even if he won't admit it. We took some heavy losses protecting his ass today. And those cybo parts we left for him will get him the supplies he needs from Pig Town."

She sat up, reached into her skinsuit's belt pouch, and pulled out a handful of cybo chips she'd salvaged from the evil general.

"What are you going to do with those?" Wolf asked.

She turned the tiny wafers over in her right hand. "Melt 'em down tomorrow, probably," she said. "Unless I can salvage something."

He nodded. "How's your arm?"

Sy peeled back the burned skin and inspected the damage. Clear lubricant leaked out of the wound and dripped down past her elbow. Inside the ragged hole, sparks arched between the exposed microwires. Toth's bullet had torn up the mechanisms pretty badly. Nano-circuits hummed, futilely trying to repair the injury. The servos of the arm's steel muscles whirred as she flexed the fingers of her left hand. She winced against the pain and said, "Nothing I can't fix." Sighing, she lay back on the bed once more. "Tomorrow."

"Let me tend to your human parts, then," Wolf said, rising and fetching a roll of bandages from the caravan's medikit. "You know, Sy," he said, mopping the red blood from her leg and winding the clean white gauze around her thigh, "you are without a doubt the nicest cybo I've ever met."

"You're just saying that because I'm the only cybo you know who's never tried to kill you." Reaching up, Sigourney Saxon extinguished the overhead glowlights, and Martian night descended inside the caravan.

OMEGA TIME

by Russell Davis

Russell Davis lives in Maine with his wife, the children, and a psychotic cat. His short fiction has appeared in numerous anthologies including Merlin, Single White Vampire Seeks Same, *and* Civil War Fantastic. *He coedited the anthology* Mardi Gras Madness *and the forthcoming DAW anthology,* Apprentice Fantastic, *both with Martin Greenberg. He is currently at work on his novel,* The Crown of Sands, *and numerous other writing and editing projects.*

1

AUTO Launch, 25 Minutes.
   " 'All that matters is that we're together. *Together.* The where, the how, even the why of it is unimportant. All that matters is that we can see and touch each other, love each other, *be* together. That's all that matters.' "

I can remember her saying this to me late one night in bed, just after we were married. It's been too many years, and I can't recall what prompted this statement, nor even the discussion that followed—and I'm sure there was one. Just as I'm sure that we made love that night; the passionate breathtaking kind that happens early in marriage and goes on for hours and hours where more of your time is spent kissing and giggling than is ever spent in doing the actual deed. That time when you are discovering each other, exploring the lost continents of the body, finding yourself in the other. It was a long time ago.

It was long before what the scientists have dubbed Omega Time—the end of all things. I know a lot about it—I'm one of the scientists, as was she. Now, though, she is gone, out there among the stars, and I am here, for better or for worse, and watching Omega Time take its inevitable toll on planet Earth. The last ship, my ship, will auto launch in just under a half hour. About two, maybe three hours after that, the Sun will finish its rapid growth into a red giant star, and the Earth will be ashes on the solar winds.

I don't think I'll miss it all that much.

2

Auto Launch, 15 Minutes

I miss her. The smell of her skin, lilacs; the way her eyes sparked like angry blue stars when she laughed; the way she whispered, just before sleep, that she loved me, would always be with me. She didn't lie, of course; she just didn't know.

And that sums up Omega Time so well—nobody knew. After all the calculations had been done, what it really amounted to was nothing more than a simple mathematical error, the kind they made back when humans were using desktop computers and handheld calculators, back before the invention of true cybernetics. Hell, I'd had advanced geocalculus and quantum mechanics program chips installed way back in high school.

But then again, even the best program chips can have flaws. So, the calculation-prediction on when the Sun would go red giant had been off by a little, just five thousand years or so. The human race has advanced so far, changed so much, but we are still babes compared to the stars—not prescient beings of light, but animals made of blood and bone and fear.

Who would think that such frailties could lead to Omega Time?

By the time we'd caught the error, it was almost too late. A mass exodus from the planet ensued, and my wife, my joy, was among the first to leave—they needed a geneticist with them—and though we promised to meet at the rendezvous station set up safely beyond the hot zone, it was not to be. She never made it to the rendezvous station in orbit around Saturn's moon, Triton—a cold place of barren, icy landforms and liquid hydrocarbon seas, but with a nitrogen rich atmosphere much like Earth. It had been hoped that with the change in the Sun, and some advanced terraforming, Triton might become a permanent way station to the stars.

But her ship had a major oxygen malfunction only thirty-eight minutes after take off and had exploded into a gigantic ball of fire that quickly went out in the cold vacuum of space. No one lived, of course. No one lived.

Now she's out there, among the stars she loved to look at, but knew so little about, returned to the cosmos, her promises to be with me always so much ash.

But I lived. I had to. I had to go on living and helping, trying to save as many as we could. And most of them, those who hadn't gone into hiding somewhere here on Earth, and those whose hastily constructed ships—like my wife's—hadn't blown up in route to the station—had made it to safety.

3

Auto Launch, 10 Minutes

My ship is the last one. I am the only one on board, and I am more than qualified to fly it with the help of the computer—my time as both an astronaut and an astrophysicist has seen to that. The final data streams from our growing Sun are already set to transmit to the station. But I'm not going to the station. I'm going to the stars, returning myself to the cosmos to keep our mutual promises.

She would have wanted me to do it this way, I think.

To have stayed long enough to help as many people as I could, and then to join her.

I remember our wedding night, and—like an old man in physical stasis, whose body has failed but whose mind continues to remain annoyingly sharp—I've gotten sentimental about it. I still celebrate our anniversary, still set out the dishes and the wine goblets that were kept all these years, still drink a toast in our honor. Then, when it's time, I go into our room and lie down upon our empty bed. I ache for her presence, the soft touch of her hand on my cheek, her breath tickling the hairs on the nape of my neck—but these things are like wraiths in my mind. I remember them, but they slip away before I can touch them. I lay there remembering how she looked, her skin alabaster in the moonlight from the windows, her eyes flashing. It makes me smile to remember these things.

The last time we made love, the night before she launched into the infinite sky to find not freedom but death, she drew me into our bedroom, pulled me down onto the synth-silk comforter. She didn't want to go, but had to go, much as I had to stay. That night she was fiercely passionate, sometimes crying, sometimes laughing, reminding me of all the reasons that I loved her.

Now on our anniversary I lie in bed and wonder if some part of her, deep in her womb, knew she was already dying. I didn't, only knew that I wanted to be with her, a part of her, that she could take a part of me with her. But technology and love are mutually exclusive—at near-light speed, a flickering heartbeat, a hand raised in desperate farewell, is invisible.

I think of this launch as my arms reaching for her, a supreme gesture of fire and desperate wanting as I head toward the stars where she rests.

4

Auto Launch, 5 Minutes

The ship is ready to go. Strapped in, I can already

imagine seeing her again. The flight path is programmed for the heart of the Sun, the heart of my life. The journey, awaited for so long, will be short—a few minutes as fast as this ship will travel. We will be reunited among the stars and the heat, and perhaps in some other form I can't even begin to grasp, we will speak our vows again. She is out there, waiting for me, our promises to be fulfilled.

5

Auto Launch, 1 Minute

Over the roar of the igniting engines I can hear her laughter, her voice calling to me. I close my eyes and bring her form into focus. She is smiling. She is stretching out her arms to me, wanting to hold me again, sorry we have been apart for so very long. The ship is very fast. I love her, and there is no other for me in this universe of possibility. I will be with her soon.

I remember a colleague once telling me that women were like stars: the tricky, bright, and seemingly everywhere at once. I don't know about other women, but he was right when it comes to her. She is here somehow, with me again, already by my side in the cockpit, yet I know that she is Out There, too.

I unbuckle my shoulder straps so that I can kneel at her feet. I have missed her so much that to be this close and not touch her is unbearable. Her hands stroke my hair.

6

Auto Launch

We are together again, the rocking of the ship as it blasts through the atmosphere, making its way toward another place, the gentle rumble of a spring thunder. Her kisses are moist with her tears. She is crying and telling me silently that she has missed me, too. She is sorry. She didn't want to break her promise to be with me always.

7

Post Auto Launch

I shush her, caress her hair, forgive her as I wrap myself in her warmth. She meets me halfway, and we hold each other like twin stars caught in a gravity well. I can feel her smiling against my shoulder as though being with me is a joy for her.

We move together with the ship. Her arms cling to my back, a hug that stretches on like the cosmos. The Sun is blinding and hot, and the pillow of her hair is damp with sweat and tears. It's hard to breathe, she's squeezing me so tight, and she looks infused with joy—almost burning with an inner light and heat. Vaguely, I wonder how long we have before the Sun takes us, then dismiss all, focusing on her.

It is almost finished now. The heat in the ship is unbearable and sweat rolls off our bodies and pools on the metal deck of the floor only to evaporate in a hiss of steam. Our sounds—crying, laughing, whispering—mingle with the sounds of the ship, the sounds of the hull creaking under the strain as the Sun's gravity takes us.

We're going faster now, the Sun is burning through the metal plates that protect the ship and in the cabin; it's so bright I have to close my eyes. It doesn't matter—I can still see her. The heat reaches an apex, a moment when it passes beyond anything imaginable, and then, all at once, I am cool. A chill passes between us.

We are there, and time slows itself to the film reel of memory. She cries out my name, and I tell her that I love her. That I was wrong—technology and love are not mutually exclusive. This ship has brought me back to her. It is quiet, and I can hear the ship burning. I can hear her breath, feel it on the nape of my neck. Her hand, like a wraith, touches my cheek.

We are children in the Sun, our shadows stretching across the burning cosmos, our lives and memories

ash, our time passing into the infinite span of sparking stars.

Then, I know four things almost at once.

The ship is at the end of its flight path.

I can smell lilacs on her skin.

We are together.

I love her, even in death, even in Omega Time.

SON OF A BELTER EARL

by Roland Green

Roland Green is a persistent writer of fantasy, science fiction, book reviews, etc. His most recent book is Voyage to Eneh. *He lives in Chicago with his wife Frieda Murray and daughter Violette Green. None of them has auburn hair or freckles. "Son of a Belter Earl" takes place in the 2080s, in the Starworld Federation timeline, best known as the setting for the* Starcruiser Shenandoah *series.*

NOW I have a problem with dry air.

I also have a problem with a dry throat right now, so if you are thinking of offering me a drink, I won't say no. But nothing stronger than punch, if you don't mind. The reputation of the Irish for drinking will be upheld too much without my help, and when they patched up my skull, they did not do such a perfect job that I can hold my liquor.

It's not wonderful to have a problem with dry air if your family came originally from Limerick in Ireland, which I hear is about the wettest place on an island where nobody has yet found a desert, or even a place where the sun shines for a week at a time. In Limerick, wholesome greenery turns to slime and mold, and if your lungs and throat aren't resisting the damp, you will have the tuberculosis much faster than you want.

But the Touhy lungs were strong—

You say that Touhy is not a true Limerick name? Well, I would not say that it was a Limerick name at all, for the first of my ancestors who lived in Limerick lived there nearly two centuries ago. He couldn't afford to be truthful, if the tales about what they sought him for in Armagh were true even in part.

You look ready to ask why I am out here in the asteroids, where the air doesn't run to humidity except in certain places at certain times which may be discussed in more detail later if I can finish this story. Yes, I am probably making it longer than it needs to be, but did you ever know an Irishman who did not take ten words to do the work of five?

I won't say why that first recorded ancestor came to Limerick, and I won't say why my great-grandfather came to New Orleans, except that it was probably for something else also done in Armagh. He left after the Troubles, and I do not think he learned everything he knew about explosives in chemistry class at the Christian Brothers'. But he soon knew that the skill of his hands would suffer from lack of practice, and no one on this side of the water would pay him to practice, nor was there anyone he was really willing to blow up for free!

Work for the militias like the McVeigh's Avengers and that breed? Don't insult his memory with that idea! Have you forgotten, or did you never learn, that they were mostly red-hot Protestants who'd likely enough bought ammunition for the UDL to *shoot* at my great grand-da or anybody else who smelled like a Catholic?

But he went to work on the Gulf oil rigs for long enough to bring up my grand-da properly, which was not that hard in New Orleans. It had plenty of Irishmen going all the way back to the time of the Civil War, and a fine lot of humidity to keep Touhy lungs in order. New Orleans has no dry spells either, although it did have a dusty spell for about ten years when the Army Engineers were digging like madmen, to lock up the Mississippi in its old channel so that it wouldn't leave the city high and dry.

You say you're from Chicago, and there's a North

Side street named after a Touhy who was an Irish immi-
grant big in real estate? Not my kin, if they settled in
Chicago. Too cold and dry in a winter that seems to last
forever, from what my father said about the one year
he worked there.

So grand-da grew up and started my father, and the
Gulf of Mexico drillers went deeper to find more oil,
putting remote-controlled rigs a mile (or even two kilometers) down on the bottom, and the oil companies
went deeper into their pockets to find the money to pay
for the rigs that had begun to cost as much as an aircraft
carrier. Some of the money ended up in Touhy pockets
honestly, some through high-stakes poker games, which
may also have been as honest as my father had it in him
to be.

But after a while the mass-energy converters knocked
the bottom out of fuel-oil prices, and what the world
needed to make lubricants, chemicals, and nutrient cul-
tures, the Chinese could supply more cheaply. (They
worked in shallow water, certainly—the tales about their
being careless over leaks are a possibility.)

I had learned just about everything the two men and
my apprenticeship could teach me by the time jobs on
Gulf rigs became scarcer than shrimp—

You say they've come back—the shrimp, that is?
Good if they have—but find a nice out-system sea-
quarium, if you take my advice, or at least persuade the
whales not to come back and develop a taste for salt-
water gumbo.

So I borrowed a bit from grand-da and a bigger bit
from da, ate flavored kelp for two years, and ten years
ago signed on with Serious Rockheads Ltd. They were
a Canadian firm, which is why they were "Limited" instead of "Incorporated"—if they'd been Brit, I might
not have taken even their damned fine offer. You can
still find them, incidentally, if you look under the "Divisions" of Shanghai-Singapore Fraternal Cooperation and
Coordination, which is *not* a Triad organization. Mostly.

I was a fair all-around rockhopper, a better than fair
mechanic, and—if I do say so myself—a fine hand with

a liquid-bearing drill in most any kind of rock. Bear with
me if I don't use the technical terms for all the different
kinds of—well, stuff—you find in an asteroid. On my
end of a stealth drill, you class rock more by how it feels
when you're drilling into it, and by what you're paid for
what comes out when you've drilled, than by what the
geologists call it.

Ah, thank you for the punch. Now let me wet my
whistle, before I tell you of a couple of Brits and a
damned fine offer I did accept from them.

No, "my whistle" is a bloody *figure of speech*. If I
tried to really whistle—well, I'm told there are earplugs
on sale at the bar.

                    *   *   *

And it came to pass, that—

Well, no, Caesar Augustus didn't have anything to do
with it. It was pure market pressure—needing metal for
building the great driveships, some not much smaller
than an asteroid themselves. The less of a gravity well
the metal ores came through on their way to the orbital
shipyards, the better. Or the cheaper, which is to say the
same thing in different words.

Where's the best combination of light gravity and
heavy metal? No, not a nostalgia bar in orbit! The asteroids, of course. The Jovials might point out their satellites, likewise the Saturnines. But most of the smaller
satellites of the gas giants are kidnapped or aspiring asteroids anyway.

So the big and little hoppers swarmed out from Mars
orbit and in from Jupiter orbit and started popping up
wherever there was supposed to be an asteroid whose
spectrogram said it might be pay dirt. It was even better
to pop up in the middle of a self-contained cluster.

What's a cluster? I can see some of you looking dis-
gusted at how few wits a person must have to ask that
question, when they're already out here ready to board
a driveship for the stars. But some of you are also looking blank, so there's reason to give a brief explanation.

A cluster is any gaggle of asteroids where you'll mine profitable ores and also extract oxygen for breathing, hydrogen for fuel, and—if you're lucky—ice to melt down for water. If you're *very* lucky, enough ice so that you can breathe, bathe, and fuel your in-cluster transport without breaking down hydrocarbon deposits. That takes energy, which is not so easy to come by in the Belts, which are a good ways off from the Sun.

And of course there's the kind of luck that comes with finding a nice ice-loaded piece that turns out to be the head of a comet on a long-period orbit. Do you try to peel it while it's a ways out and not out-gassing layer after layer of your money besides trying to blow you off into space, as Sol warms it? Or do you try to shift its orbit by turning some of the ice into fuel and brewing up a modest propulsion system?

If you do that, by very careful even today. We were even more careful then, because the Sky Watch was in full cry after the Big Graze. At one point they had *Yamato, Victory, Enterprise,* and *Borodino*—the mighty names that were supposed to make for mightier ships— all crewed and supplied to drive out to the Belts and arrest people suspected of leading asteroids into sinful lives or near-Earth trajectories.

And they have confiscated and been compensated for any stray asteroids they had to "arrest," for good measure. They do not call it "prize money," the money that the United Space Forces pick up that way, and to do the spacers justice, I would not say they often neglect other duties to pick up a profitable rock. But their profits have long rankled with us rockhoppers who don't and never will have service base pay.

By the time I wrote about it, I was long-gone from Serious Rockheads, who were seriously under the Shanghai-Singapore umbrella. I was working for a small outfit that had its roots and some of its financing with Eurochem, the one big outfit still working the North Sea oil fields. There's still oil down there, and accessible with the cheap rigs that hardly anybody except the Brits and the Chinese know how to build anymore. And the British build with a deal of Irish help—Harland & Wolff in Belfast still bends metal with the best of them and ahead of the rest of them.

Now this small outfit, which shall have no name, was not dealing with once and future comets, or anything else where you had to raise up a great beacon, signaling to the whole universe that it's wide open for business. But if you're caught stealth-drilling on any asteroid that crosses the orbit of Mars, the law still says things that make it prudent to be wonderfully quiet with every form of emission that can carry through vacuum so that you won't have to listen to them!

Well, yes, that does include some of the emissions that you seem to be thinking about. They do disperse rapidly, by the laws of physics governing the behavior of gases in vacuum. We also recycled rather more than the average, thanks to a new model enviro system that Eurochem gave us for free as long as we'd report on the results. (This gave a whole new meaning to the idea of being deep in it over an unfavorable report, but the beast worked splendidly.) And nobody dumps big solid pieces, even in junk space where it might be hard for the survivors of a collision to tell what hit them, man-made or natural.

You *can* pollute space.

So we were working this cluster, with nothing farther apart than, say, twice the distance from the Earth to the Moon. This meant the cheaper sort of in-cluster shuttles, because they could make a tour of all five sites with maybe half the fuel load needed for one leg around the Dickson Cluster, which I hear is making a lot of Titanians richer.

Never call them Titanics, by the way. It is not forgotten out here where we have nothing between us and the stars that we are coming and going and building *ships,* and that many of the laws governing ships of sea, sky, and space are the same and best obeyed to the letter, unless you want some one to make a famous holo about you with a wee romance thrown in to keep people's attention. So no use of bad-luck words, please—and one "please" is all you're allowed.

To be sure, this is no barrier to letting Harland & Wolff build us those ships. They did good work even the time you're thinking about. It was the handling of her that made the difference. We try to do better.

Now, all five sites in our cluster had first been reached out and touched by robots, dropped in a bus by one of the big Eurochem driveships on her way out to the Jump point.

How do you think they're paying for the in-system wear and tear on a ship's hull? The odd lemonade stand with a view of Saturn's rings? And is the fact that some of you aren't laughing is proof that my joke isn't funny, or that some strange fellow is actually doing that? If it's the second, I'm not so unhappy as I might be otherwise to be leaving Sol and her children behind.

So the assayers and the workshops and the fuel plant all went in several years before any of us organic types and did their work. Once it had dropped them, the bus shut down and waited to be turned into one of the shuttles, when we arrived in the second, towing the living quarters behind us.

This was a more automated plant than usual, so we were a small crew of live bodies in a quarters module (Home, we called it) designed for a rather larger one.

It sometimes seems that space is either too big or not big enough.

So we were six people, three of each—if you count the two who were either, neither, or both depending on how you looked at them. I looked at them with neither distaste nor fervor—just at the jobs they did, and both Nell and Khalal did as good work in their ways as I did in mine. Belters can afford eccentrics—Mary pray for us, they—*we*—are eccentrics—but they can't afford anybody who cannot work their twelve hours regularly and twice that when it's called for. Eccentrics have lived long in the Belt or on the giants' satellites. Lazy folk, never.

So there we were, me, Stephen, and Nell, coming in

with Shuttle One after the grand tour. Nell flew and handled everything shipboard, I did everything with the on-site equipment, and Stephen relieved the two of us when the payload wasn't a full-time job and even some-times when it was. This trip he'd been a busy lad—not only did we have nine bundles of nickel-alloy and one of carbon for structural work, we had two insulated bun-dles of ice to prime the enviro system. And one of the communications arrays on the ice site needed more than we could give it on-site, so we pulled it, replaced it with our embarked spare, and loaded One with the down-checked beast.

Back Home, you see, we had more spare parts, a bigger computer for simulations, a centrifuge anchored solidly to good rock for anything that might need more than micro-gravity, and even a modest workshop inside the pressure zone so that you need not keep one eye on your work and one on the monitors of your suit. Of course, it had its own insulation, ventilation, and con-trolled access—which made it the most private place in the quarters, if you hung out the MAINTENANCE IN PROGRESS sign.

Let me have another glass of punch, and I can tell what happened when Shuttle One came home, and afterward.

*   *   *

A crew of three in one of the shuttles really needs for one of them to be a thark—you haven't read Edgar Rice Burroughs, so I'll just say that they were nine feet tall, had four arms and green skin, and ran around Mars with all of that skin showing. Of course, no one nine feet tall can go to space in anything but a driveship and even then there are problems, so we might be casting out one devil and getting back seven, so that our last state would have less room than the first.

By the time we were on our final approach, Nell was picking up another shuttle also approaching Home. We knew that Eurochem's *Simonides* was doing a close pass and likely to drop off a disposable resupply pod—a big reinforced plastic can with minimal propulsion and maximum storage capacity. But this was a standard personnel-transfer pod, on a faster trajectory, and we hadn't been warned about that before Shuttle One left.

"There's one sweet-handed pilot in that pod," Nell said. "I think they're going to try docking under power."

We normally greeted pods with a tether-towing robot, or if somebody wanted to fatten their EVA time record for the month, that somebody in question in an EVA suit. This poddie came right in and did it with only three tries.

I wondered how many new faces were going to surprise us when we finally docked, which was likely to be a while since we now had three vehicles needing docks and only two collars for docking, both of them occupied. Oh, maybe we could have designed the module for three, but then we'd have had the people pod and the cargo pod come at the same time. Murphy works overtime in space, so that rockhoppers say, "Anything that doesn't kill me makes me laugh."

Blessings on friend Khalal, however, in whatever sort of Paradise he's found. He undocked Shuttle Two by remote, leaving its collar free for us. Nell brought us in—that was *two* sweet-handed pilots roaming around our little cube of space today—and we floated across the threshold almost as soon as the hatch opened—

—to be confronted with a youngish but not girlish female person peeling down for her time in the after bath bag. (Oh, we had luxury with only six people in a module designed to support twenty. Even unto *two* baths—and sometimes water to let us use both of them at once!)

She had everything off above the waist, and was undoing the band of her pants with one hand while holding a strap with the other. I could see that she was no stranger to Zero-G— and I could see other things, that I am still too much of a gentleman to describe in detail.

In due time, we all saw more, which made Nell's nostrils flare. She always opened a conversation by flaring her nostrils, which were well-shaped like the rest of her nose and indeed like the rest of her. Stephen nodded politely, which is the mid-course answer to the situation of seeing a workmate as nature made him/her. It's rude to grab, but it also never goes over terribly well, saying or doing anything to imply that you'd rather flee screaming from the sight.

"Welcome aboard *Eurochem Epsilon Six*," I said. "I'm driller and general toolpusher Martin Touhy."

"I'm Charlene Haverford," she said. A nice controlto then, and I trust now. By the time the rest of the crew introduced themselves, Haverford was inside the bath, after stuffing her dirty clothes into a standard utility bag racked beside the water exchanger. Beside the air exchanger, a standard wear-or-tow web harness held another clutch of her bags, like so many blue-and-yellow dragon's eggs. Some of them bulged; none of them showed the outline of hard objects within. Charlene seemed to know the rule that had followed us from the sea to space, which is "no sharp corners," and if you don't think that rule is often broken, ask the baggage room of your next ship. Or don't ask, if you're one of the violators.

By then Khalal had also come down from the control panel to welcome us back and arrange the turns on the baths, which we all needed. The shuttles are a bit short of that kind of convenience, although not of the public kind. (In truth, there's nothing that *isn't* public aboard all but the largest Belt shuttle, which has more room than one of the old Apollos only because it needs more for the extra equipment.)

I was the last to leave. I think I wanted to see if anyone else came out of the pod, although I was morally certain that if Charlene was the right sort, she'd have let her passengers bathe first. I am pretty sure I had some hope of another look at her in the time between her coming out of the bath and pulling on those clean clothes. I was curious about the number of freckles in certain places. I risked being distracted in the line of duty by the "certain places" where the freckles grew, but a careful worker is always ready to make sacrifices in the pursuit of accurate data, without which all engineering is impossible!

However, the "stealth peek" is not much more tolerated in space than the sharp corner, and besides, I had the feeling that Charlene had her own even more demanding set of rules about that sort of thing. While wanting to have the possible pleasure of finding out what they were, I thought it best for now to take myself off in case I met the certain pain of being clouted in the teeth.

The Haverford had long fingers, of the kind which can make a fine fist if they're clenched right, and the height, the muscle, and the bone to propel that fist to any destination she wished.

*   *   *

Now I spare you many details, and not only because I am a gentleman. Some of them, even including the details of our excitement, are simply *too bloody dull!*

And the excitement is—?

An old Limerick word, for what happens when a man and a woman (or these days, some other combination of which I have no personal experience, for better or worse) decide that it's time to count each other's freckles.

Now, Charlene had come on short notice, which bent rules, and had flown her pod in alone, which broke them into so many pieces that we thought *Simonides* might be trying to track them down. That we had a fugitive on our hands was not a pleasant thought.

When asked, she explained that she'd been supposed to bring a metallurgist along with her, on a temporary assignment to tour the Belt rigs and measure stresses on heavily-used equipment. Metallurgists being scientists in this Our Belter Realm of the engineer, we welcomed this news a little more warmly than we'd have welcomed a case of tuberculosis.

We hoped the man (she did call him "he") wasn't the sort to miss his ride. If he was, we would not miss him. We hoped harder, if more quietly, that it hadn't been a "personality clash." This can mean anything from disliking somebody's taste in lipgloss on up to whatever the limit is when you're already far *beyond* the sky. I've known cases where murder was not beyond the limit, although I thought an objective case could be made that Haverford was not the sort to push a coworker overboard, even with good cause, and then bubble and romp through a full day's very good work.

Because she was good. First-class as a pilot, which gave us three primary pilots and three backups for three vehicles, and a quick study at everything except Zero-G cooking. We quickly stopped losing sleep over having an inert payload aboard.

When the resupply pod came in, we had a busy day unloading it. It carried more processed fuel (high BTU than homebrew, by orders of magnitude) and overdue replacements for several pieces of on-site equipment. With the new fuel, Haverford's pod had enough range to reach the two nearest. Two-crewed, we could service two sites at once. That left Home down to three, which was the regulation minimum and not always the prudent one, but we had to strike a balance, so we launched a double flight.

Now, I hadn't been ignoring it, the way the Haverford was giving me the kind of eye that says a woman likes what she sees in principle but may not do anything about it in practice. There can be so much looking back that a woman thinks the man is either begging or taking it for granted that she will do something, and with a woman like the Haverford what she will usually do is something the man won't like.

Nell was more optimistic. When she heard Haverford and I were outward bound, she punched me in the ribs, then clapped her hands to her mouth in horror.

"Oh, I'd better be careful to leave some of you for Herself. And she'd better leave enough of you for work after you get back."

I contrived to look boyishly modest and forthrightly proud at the same time. "I expect to be able to serve all purposes when I return."

"Even mine? Even Khalal's?"

"That's two unfathomable purposes, which is far too many for me. If it comes about as it might with the Haverford, at least she's been honest about everything so far."

"Except her metallurgist."

"Oh, sod her metallurgist."

"Better you than me. And better her than you," she concluded, planting a foot on my rump to push me down the tunnel toward the docking bay.

*   *   *

Oh, Haverford and I had our share of *the* excitement, not so much of the everyday kind. Just as well. Micrometeorite punctures, for example, mean full clothing if not EVA gear and your mind elsewhere than a gentleman has it when a lady like the Haverford has her arms around you.

We think that like a couple of good Belters, we were careful. Not in all ways, or so it seems, but enough that we were both alive and with a good count of one another's skin features by the time we returned. Also, she'd rigged a humidifier in the ventilation system, so that I never had to say, "Not now, Charlene, I've got a headache."

The problem was that we returned only hours before the metallurgist arrived, after transshipping to the inbound Eurochem *Montesquieu* and riding out to us in a drone pod.

The metallurgist's name was Peter Ogden, a lean, quiet Brit with the indefinable air of being ex-military. Someone whose regimental ancestors probably shot at your biological ones is apt to bring out the paranoia that is the birthright of any Irishman dealing with the English. You can forget all the words to "Roddy McCauley" and not forget the snippets of news and the slabs of rumor, about the two countries trying to put one over on each other even in the Great Peace since the Union.

It was also even plainer than Ogden that there'd been something between Charlene and Ogden, and that one of them (likely enough, him) had put a foot in by way of breaking it up. However, it was soon plain that whatever had been, could be again, and if Ogden had anything to say about it, would be.

If I owed him anything, however, he'd have to ask. And if he couldn't find the breath to ask—well, no Touhy in a long while has died without some sort of heir!

Where he'd end up in relation to Haverford was a mystery for a while. He was fit enough, but both shorter and slighter than her, and not even a giant would have tried the caveman bit on the lady, not without two or three impeccably loyal assistants. Once the bruises on my vanity had begun to heal, I could contemplate Ogden's trying to shape a trajectory for a new rendezvous and docking with Charlene Haverford with amusement more than anything else. I had not the kind of claim on her that would have come from wanting to marry her, and I suspected that Ogden did.

What she wanted, or whom, a prudent man would let her decide.

It helped rather more than somewhat that I found myself liking Ogden more the less time I spent with Charlene. What he didn't know about metallurgy was probably not knowable by mortal men, and while he was not a polished mechanic or the best hand at EVA, he could make computers sit up and sing "The Risin' of the Moon." Also, he slipped out of that Oxbridge accent into something neutral so quickly that a man had to wonder what his natural speech might be.

So altogether, the jokes and winks weren't what I had feared, when Ogden, Haverford, and I went out in a pod for one of Ogden's tests. What there were, Ogden and I ignored, and Haverford did most of the glaring. I made ready to guard her back, but of that the lady needed little.

Until then, Ogden had been finding his own "excitement" with the experimental testing equipment he was trying out. He more or less annexed the workshop, and Haverford twice had to all but drill through the hatch and bodily push him into a bath to have time alone with him. That fretted me more than jealousy—if Ogden was to have eyes only for the task in front of him when he also needed the ones in the back of his head—we would see.

Three days out from Home, we saw.

We were at Site Two, and I was drilling hard and fast, to let Ogden test his machine's ability to read the dynamic stresses of a stealth drill at work. We were neither of us watching the rock scan as closely as we might have, or probably should have—although pockets of gas in deep-space rock can lay a better ambush than many a guerrilla.

Drill heat passed through the rock to the chemical pocket, turning it into gas.

Compressed in the rock, the gas continued to heat until it blew.

The first I knew was the rock under my boots vibrating. Then I felt it shifting, and a slab of the asteroid's surface bigger than a football pitch tilted up, my end flinging me toward the stars.

"Evade!" I shouted to Ogden, and "Mayday!" for the benefit of Haverford, who was keeping a safe distance in the pod.

Then I locked myself onto the drill and cut us both loose from the slab as it came completely apart, some of the bits hitting escape velocity. Whether the drill and I did the same, I wanted us to be one object on a single trajectory, not two objects on different trajectories that might bring us together in a hurtful way.

Once I knew we'd flipped clear of the asteroid's microgravity, I started worrying about Ogden, about objects other than the drill hitting us, and about Haverford and the pod evading junk and finding us. My hopes for her survival had nothing to do with the happiness of either Ogden or myself—right then, I'd have prayed for the safety of an augmented chimpanzee or even a serial murderer, if their hands held open the road Home.

Perhaps I wasn't exactly praying. Going to Mass has not been one of my strongest habits for a while. But I did say enough "Hail Marys" and "Our Fathers" that I may have impressed Someone with my intensity if not my faith. Presently the rocks thinned out, and I started picking two beacons out of all the other odd bits. One was Ogden, the other the pod.

Our metallugist was unconscious when I made rendezvous, but he'd locked himself to his equipment as I had to mine. I'd used most of my suit's maneuvering fuel to make the first rendezvous, so I hoped that Haverford would bring the pod to us rather than us having to go to her.

By the time Ogden woke up, I was beginning on a nasty feeling that wasn't going to happen. So I broke radio silence to ask what the devil was not going on.

The answer wasn't what I'd expected, or liked when I heard it. Lost fuel, lost oxygen, the main computer and radio both down and probably not getting back up again, and some of the thrusters disabled even if we had the fuel for them.

So I strapped Ogden and his equipment to one side of the drill and myself to the other. A liquid-bath drill can be rigged to vent the pressurized lubricant directionally enough to generate a bit of thrust. It's not something every drill man can do equally well, and even the cunning hands at it (like me) can do without meeting an occasion for this trick. Nor is that trick one that lets you be in a hurry to get anywhere.

But we'd met the occasion, and its name was Death. Or it would be for me and Peter Ogden if we didn't puff our way back to the pod. Which we did, with the extra luck that Ogden passed out again an hour along our trajectory, and used rather less oxygen than he would have done if awake, so that with an umbilical rigged to my supply we both kept breathing all the way back to the pod.

There we ended the first stage of our troubles, and began the next.

The pod might as well have been a grouse in the path of a shotgun blast, when the erupting gas pocket blew out a great chunk of the asteroid's surface. Not to be

boring with the details, we could not hope to get home
before we ran out of either power or air unless we called
for help and it came, and the radio for that calling was
as dead as Michael Collins. We had more fuel than Haverford had thought at first, but too much damage to the
thrusters to allow the necessary maneuvering to put us
on to the right trajectory, even with a working computer
to calculate what that would be.

By this time, Ogden was waking up, although if he
didn't have a concussion and fractures, he had enough
aches and pains above and below to make one wonder.
He'd been muttering as he woke up, though, and some
of those mutterings made Haverford turn pale. For the
first time in a while, I held her while she told me why.

"I think he wants to do an Oates."

That made me wonder out loud what horses had to
do with our situation. She bit my ear in a not-so-friendly
way and explained about Scott's daft expedition to the
South Pole and Captain Oates stepping outside to reduce the burden on his friends.

I swallowed and put on as much of a brogue as I could.
"Sure, and it's you and the Ogden who ought to be goin'
on breathin', and this Irish rockhopper who gives—"

"Like bloody hell you will," Ogden said. "And if you
two can untangle, I have an idea."

"It's more than one idea we'll be needin', to get ourselves—" I began.

"My dear chap," Ogden said, in ripe Oxbridge tones.
"If you will drop the brogue, I will *not* talk like this as
long as there is air for me to talk."

I gave him something between a wave and a salute
and nodded. "I'm listening."

So, for a wonder, was Haverford. Maybe her look at
the air-supply readings had something to do with it.

It would take all three of us together to give any one
of us a chance of surviving. Haverford piloting, Ogden
using his tester's computer in place of the disabled main
pod machine, and me installing at least one drill as an
improvised maneuvering thruster.

"If we can run a fuel line with a valve to it, we might

even cut enough time off the return trip to give us a margin for air," he concluded. "Not, I may add, for *error*. But fortunately we should be able to get back into radio or even visual range in time."

"Does your little improvised tinker's thinker have proper graphics for at least a rough visual?" I asked. That's admitting I'm of the generation who's lost their visual imagination to cheap graphics, but I would sit still for worse insults than that to have a better chance of seeing Home again.

"Yes."

I unstrapped, and reached for the hatch to the EVA bay.

"Wait," Haverford said.

"Charlene, is this the time—?" Ogden asked.

"After he's dead is far too late!" she snapped. Ogden sighed, winced, and relaxed.

"I'm a Lieutenant Commander in the Royal Naval Reserve," Haverford said. "Air-Sea Rescue speciality. Once—betrothed, to use the old word—to Mr. Ogden, and I believe now again."

"I've told you three times," Ogden said. "I hope that makes it true."

I raised eyebrows. That explained the sweet-handed piloting. "And Mr. Ogden?"

"The Earl of Westridge, at your service," Ogden said. He actually managed a sitting-down bow that wasn't a parody.

The revelation jerked a "Holy Mary!" out of me.

Haverford laughed. "Surely you're not the first Irishman to amuse himself at the expense of the English peerage, Martin?" she asked. Ogden made a noise like a drill hitting dense rock. "Well, all right," she went on. "It's not quite that amusing to me either. In fact, I may ask for a refund on my implant."

The last word conjured up a precise and not at all appealing vision. "Christ," I said. "No, that was an Immaculate Conception. This, I take it—"

"Was not," Haverford finished for me. "Nor an Emasculate Conception either. You both work fine," she concluded.

Ogden grunted. I had the feeling that he and I agreed about Charlene's low taste in humor.

Haverford went on. "But the calendar isn't going to tell us who's the father. We'd need a DNA test for that, and it would cause talk. Talk that might reach the wrong ears."

Applying my memory of rumors to what I was hearing made me nod. "Chinese ears. Their British sympathizers. And PolarStar. All the people who don't want the European out-system colonies to have an independent base of key skills. Like piloting, metallurgy—"

"And asteroid mining," Ogden added. "Another reason for not stepping outside, unless you want us to drag you back by the ears.'

"Always looking for a chance to beat on an Irishman—" I began.

"Seriously," Haverford said. "This little—zygote, for now—can have two legal fathers. Will each of you stand by the other, and by me?"

Ogden muttered something. I thought it was along the lines of, "Better that, than certain people hearing about our little fight aboard *Simonides*." Then I recognized poetry—Kipling, to be exact.

"Cook's son, Duke's son, son of a belted Earl—"

"I used to wield a formidable hot plate, at school," Haverford said. "I'm sure there's at least one Duke in each family tree. And make that a *Belter* Earl."

"Also, remember that it might be a girl," His Lordship said. "Not that she won't inherit, if there's anything *to* inherit—"

I would have taken off a cap if I'd been wearing one, but I did draw the line at touching my forehead. Mostly because I think that would have started us all laughing hard enough to use up time and air we didn't have.

Instead, I nodded. "Well enough. Now, my lord, if you can start running the pretty pictures and my lady, if you can put your lovely hands on the control yokes to steer us home, I will go out and turn a drill into a thruster."

*   *   *

Everything worked out in the end, although we were a bit short of breath by the time the alarm Khalal had put on the telescope went off. I was the shortest, the dry air having given me a blistering sinus infection that needed antibiotics and a moisturized breather mask to drive out.

Khalah burned fuel with abandon, however, and made rendezvous in time to take off the three and a fraction of us fit to recover in days rather than weeks. The pod is still out there, on its way to the saints-know-where, but a big and slow-moving target easy to see with its radar reflector deployed. I think the statute of limitations has run out on that particular violation, as well as on everything else I've told you tonight.

It was seven years ago, after all. The boy has just started school on Aphrodite, and from what they tell me, they still haven't done the DNA scan. Which means that I have to think seriously about heading for Aphrodite from Charlemagne, to help raise that son of a Belter Earl.

They never offered me money, not a penny. They knew that would be an unforgivable insult, but also that even if the boy was disguised as a well-born Sassenach by the name of Ogden, he'd be the next Touhy heir, and I would come.

AN ACCEPTABLE RISK

by Ed Gibson

Ed Gibson is an aspiring novelist and writer who previously focused on game material. He has penned award-winning fantasy, horror, and science fiction adventures for the RPGA Network. West End Games published several of his adventures in the Paranormal supplement. His "Web Wanderings" column on utilizing the internet in home gaming campaigns is in its fourth year in Dungeon/Polyhedron magazine. Ed resides in Beavercreek, Ohio, where he is working as a software engineer at Reynolds and Reynolds until he wins the lottery. Ed shares his home with a 1991 Chevrolet Corvette ZR1 and plans to take her racing in order to determine if life really begins at 180 MPH.

"SEVENTY-NINE," he whispered.

The computer monitor displayed the number, bright white against an ash-gray screen. So placid and peaceful Venus looked, that viewing it as a harbinger of imminent death was hard to imagine. But that seventy-nine was his percentage chance of successfully completing the current mission.

The other twenty-one percent represented a quick and merciful death by impacting on the surface of the planet—or a slow and agonizing death if the spaceship ran out of fuel due to a miscalculation of engine usage.

Without engines, he would die of thirst or starvation, provided his oxygen lasted that long.

"Seventy-nine," he repeated, a twinge of hope in his voice.

After sixty days in space, Colonel Jim Kelmmer was so accustomed to the display that it only attracted his intention when it beeped to indicate the change of odds. His chances had worsened during the trip, starting out at eighty-four percent, but emergency maneuvering to avoid debris had cut into his safety margin. The display was his idea—he didn't want to be on this mission to begin with, and he wanted to do everything possible to make it home on time for his stepdaughter's upcoming wedding. If the percentage became too low, he was going to abort.

Colonel Klemmer reflected back upon the events of the past three months and what brought him to this point. He had retired after a long and distinguished career with NASA and looked forward to spending time with his second wife and her daughter. The fun and wonder of being an astronaut had become stifled anyway—as repeated budget cuts hit NASA, and the bureaucrats in charge diverted funds to the space station project. There was little money anymore for astronaut training or exploratory space flights, and it was only a matter of time until another disaster occurred. So he had decided to take his pension and work in his garden, and savor memories from a time when NASA was thriving and work was exciting.

He was pruning his prized Queen Elizabeth roses when NASA Director Bill Powell stopped by two weeks after the retirement party. Powell couched it as a friendly visit, but it quickly became obvious there was more on the director's mind.

*   *   *

"Hello, Jim. It's good to see you," Powell started. "How've you been? Enjoying your retirement?"

A nod. "I'm having a great time. Gardening's relaxing.

Ed Gibson

And I've been helping my stepdaughter plan her wedding. She's getting married in six months. I helped her pick out the dress. It's going to be quite the event." Klemmer paused and studied his old friend. "What brings you out this way? What *really* brings you out here?"

Powell ground his heel into the lawn and stuffed his hands in his pockets. It was a gesture that told Klemmer something was definitely up. "Okay, Jim," he said after a few moments had passed. "I'm not going to beat around that proverbial bush. We've been friends too long for me to do that. The space station is complete, and the politicians in Washington are talking about cutting NASA's budget again. We need a big success to get the public involved in the space program and increase our funding. It's been fifty years since Neil Armstrong walked on the moon, and the program needs another hero."

Klemmer raised an eyebrow.

"I want you to be that hero, Jim."

Klemmer gave a clipped laugh, then drew his lips into a thin line. "Thanks. But I'm not in the program anymore. I retired, remember? You threw the bash and handed me a watch."

"Jim . . ."

"What can you possibly be planning? And why can't one of the active people do it?"

"There are advances in rocket technology which dramatically reduce the time required for space flight. We've run computer simulations for the proposed mission to determine who has the best chance to succeed. They ran the tests for all the active astronauts and some of the recent retirees—including you. The computer says you have an eighty-four percent chance of success."

"Eighty-four. I've seen better odds."

"That's an acceptable risk," Powell shot back.

"Acceptable?"

"The best result for any of the other contenders is sixty-eight."

"You're kidding, right? An old man like me with a

better chance than your kids." Klemmer made an exaggerated tsk-tsking sound.

Powell shrugged. "You know why, Jim. Budget cuts and resulting lack of flight time means that because of your experience you have a better chance of responding correctly if any problems arise during the flight. You'd be looking at a two-month trip in each direction. We want you to be the first man on Venus."

Klemmer let out a low whistle as he looked on in disbelief. "You want me to come out of retirement to make a trip to Venus? And you're willing to accept an eight-four percent chance of success? That's not the NASA I remember. You used to aim for one hundred. What about Tom Bridges? He did an excellent job as my copilot."

"Times have changed, Jim. If we don't do something dramatic to catch public attention, there won't be a NASA in a few years. I don't like those odds either, but I'm playing the hand I was dealt. Tom Bridges scored the second highest in the computer simulations. He was the sixty-eight. And that's not good enough," Powell continued.

"Well, sixty-eight is what you're going to get. I'm retired. I'm going to stay home with my wife and stepdaughter. I should have some grandchildren to spoil in a couple of years. Tell Bridges that I'll say some prayers for him."

"He already said no."

"Smart man."

"Which would leave Melody Anderson. She's jumping at the chance, says it would be appropriate to have the first person on Venus be a woman."

"Now I know you're joking. Melody Anderson's barely more than a rookie. She doesn't have nearly enough experience for this type of mission. She really has no chance of completing it," Klemmer said, his voice rising in anger.

"No chance? The computer gives her a twenty-seven."

"Twenty-seven. Ha! And if she doesn't make it, I bet your marketing research people have it already figured out. The loss of a young, attractive female during this mission would create a mandate for increased NASA funding. You'd be showing the government you really *do* need the cash for training. Melody can do more for the program dead than she ever will alive. You bastard."

Powell offered another shrug. "Your choice. It's Melody if you won't sign on. Don't take too long thinking about it," Powell called over his shoulder as he headed for his car.

Colonel Klemmer talked it over with his wife later that day. The discussion grew heated at times, but eventually his sense of duty won out and won her over. He knew deep down that if someone unqualified was sent on the mission and died, it would be tough to live with himself. Besides, there was something intriguing about being the first man to land on Venus. He felt a touch of giddiness as he called Director Powell later that day. "All right," he said. "It's an acceptable risk."

Klemmer asked for a video monitor which would display the current chance of his successfully completing the mission, interfaced with the ship's computer system and updated continuously. The director didn't want to install the equipment, as he was concerned about the time to perform the work and make the programming changes—as well as the added weight. But Klemmer prevailed and the equipment was installed. The necessary preparations were made, and he left on his journey to Venus.

The screen read eighty-four percent shortly after liftoff.

* * *

The swirling cloud cover of Venus gradually came into view as Klemmer's ship neared the end of its thirty-nine-million-kilometer journey. The most dangerous part of the mission was approaching.

The beautiful clouds were composed of fine droplets of sulfuric acid, attractive but deadly. If a single drop were to penetrate into the engine or navigation controls, Klemmer could plunge helplessly to the surface.

"Seventy-nine percent," Klemmer mumbled. "Why am I doing this?"

Even if he managed to navigate the clouds and swirling winds to land safely on the surface of Venus, the risk factor was still high. The surface temperature of Venus was recorded as a searing four hundred and eighty-two degrees Celsius—a heat that he was certain promised to eventually ruin one of the millions of delicate circuits, wires, and other components on which his life depended.

A single failed connection could doom him to slowly baking alive, as the rest of the ship's systems failed one by one. Previous unmanned craft had landed on Venus and operated for more than an hour—more than two in one case. However, none of them had attempted anything as complex as a takeoff; they merely sat and took pictures of the surface until their cameras or communications failed and the housings melted.

Klemmer put the ship into orbit. When it reached the apex, he would descend to the surface in a landing module. The module had two small tracked drones he could dispatch—on autopilot they would gather samples and transmit video back to the ship in orbit and then on to Earth.

Klemmer knew he was allowed just fifty minutes on the surface. It was a painfully short time after his long journey, but the risks of equipment damage from the heat rose exponentially after that point. He had his wife and his stepdaughter to consider.

If everything went according to plan, he would then take off, leaving the husk of the landing module on the surface and rendezvousing with the ship in orbit. The entire operation was simple enough, but there were thousands of things which could go wrong.

An acceptable risk, he thought.

He took the controls and nudged the ship into the proper orbit. "Perfect," he said. But a mechanical beep and a bright glowing seventy-seven informed him the computer did not share his opinion.

"Seventy-damn-seven percent," Klemmer hissed.

He completed preparations to detach the module from his ship and land on Venus, before he lay down and slept fitfully, his dreams filled with beeping computers and bright numbers that were as white as his stepdaughter's wedding dress.

When he woke, he was feeling refreshed, telling himself he was ready to face the challenges of the coming day. However, his forced optimism wavered when he discovered his success chance had fallen to seventy-five. Then seventy-three.

He shook his head and contacted mission control, exchanging pleasantries and asking if there were any last minute alterations in the mission. A quick check of the computer determined that there was no obvious cause for the latest downgrade in his percentages.

He could abort; he could tell them he had a bad feeling. He could. He didn't want to be here, he told himself. But there something about being in space, there was an excitement stirring in him that he couldn't put down. "First man on Venus," he whispered. He could abort, but . . .

"Colonel Klemmer, this is mission control. We have your wife and stepdaughter here. They want to wish you good luck on your landing." The words came out of the control panel speaker, just as the screen flashed seventy-two.

"Jim, I love you and want you to know that I'm very proud of you. I'm expecting you back in time for Sarah's wedding. She'll be very disappointed if you're late."

A second voice chimed in. "Dad, I love you. I really want you to walk me down the aisle. So you be careful. Understand? If there's some snag, I'm gonna postpone the wedding. The caterer'll pitch a fit, though, and probably bump up his bill. So don't be late."

Klemmer wiped at a tear. "I love you both, too. I'm proud of my little girl and wouldn't miss the wedding for anything."

The computer said, "Beep." And the display read sixty-eight.

Klemmer swallowed hard. "But if something were to happen to me, I want you both to be strong and make me proud of you."

"Dad, don't talk that way. I want you home so . . ."

A crackle of static cut her off. "Colonel, this is mission control, you have five minutes to start the landing process. Otherwise, you'll have to wait three hours for the next orbit."

"Beep," said the computer. The screen blinked sixty-six.

*   *   *

Klemmer sat at the controls and made his final preparations. As the landing module separated from the orbiting vessel and began its descent to Venus, the mechanical beep and sixty-three displayed left no doubt that the optimum entry had been missed by a fraction.

The acid clouds and swirling winds tore at the module, scouring its exterior. Klemmer fought to keep the craft under control and was successful, although he was physically and mentally exhausted by the ordeal. The instruments didn't show any problems, but the computer slowly clicked down to fifty-seven, tallying unseen damage. Finally, he passed through the clouds and began to set up his approach for landing.

His landing spot had been carefully chosen—it was located near one of the arachnoids, a geological structure found nowhere else in Sol's system. This particular structure was about forty kilometers across, circular and showing the spiderweblike ring of fractures in the soil which led to its name. Adjacent was an expanse of parallel lines that cut through the rocky surface, each spaced about a kilometer apart, and each appearing as regular as if it had been drawn on graph paper. NASA scientists contended that taking surface samples and making close observations of this area could provide important information on how the crust of Venus was reworked half a million years earlier. If the drones functioned according to plan, they would be able to gather samples and return them to the landing module for retrieval. Then they could continue traveling across the rocky terrain, recording and transmitting more images even after the landing craft had taken off.

The computer beeped and dropped to fifty-five percent, but Klemmer was too absorbed in watching the terrain below to notice. If one of the legs in the landing module were to catch in a crevice, it could bend or break, making a takeoff impossible. Too, setting down with one leg on any of the large rock slabs could unbalance the craft, which could be equally deadly. His eyes focused on the controls, his fingers making minute adjustments in response as the rock-strewn brown surface loomed ever closer. Within moments, the target arachnoid came into view.

"Amazing," Klemmer breathed.

The formation was at least forty kilometers of rock jutting up from the surface, with concentric rings of circular fractures surrounded by intricate spiderweb fracture lines. He muttered a silent prayer that the spectacular pictures were making their way back to earth, as he guided the craft toward the edge of the arachnoid. The parallel lines were discernible now, spaced a kilometer apart and running as far as he could see, almost like the claw marks of some immense beast.

He guided the module to the spot he and NASA had chosen and carefully approached for a landing. "Easy, easy, Ah, hell." The craft hit with a sickening crunch.

It vibrated momentarily, then settled down at a slight angle. The computer beeped and the display dropped to fifty percent, but the instruments indicated that nothing vital had been broken. Examining the camera display of the craft's exterior, it was easy to see that one leg had been twisted in the landing and the entire platform was listing a little bit.

Colonel Klemmer's words were captured for posterity, "Fifty-damn-fifty! Today we have taken another giant leap for mankind. I'd like to thank all the hardworking people at NASA who made this day possible. This is Colonel Klemmer live from the surface of the planet Venus."

He sat still for a moment, then he turned his attention to dispatching the drones. The first one slowly drove out onto the dusty brown soil and moved about a dozen meters away before a small panel opened and an arm emerged and began to dredge up a sample of soil and stones. The drone quickly returned to Kellemmer's module, where the samples were transferred before it headed off again, this time for the distant parallel lines.

The second drone crawled across the rocky surface, gleaning samples as it reached the fractures. Details began to appear as the construct's camera peered into the depression. At first glace, the fractures seemed smooth because of erosion—centuries of being battered by rushing wind. But Klemmer studied the data coming in. The fractures were still too regular to have occurred naturally. A close examination of a relatively sheltered portion revealed tool marks, slightly eroded by the wind, but still quite noticeable.

"Nothing natural about that," he said to himself. "Let's have a closer look-see."

The second drone returned to the ship to drop off its samples before it continued to record more images of the arachnoid's fractures to determine if other portions were artificially created.

This activity consumed twenty of the fifty-five minutes Klemmer had allocated for the surface. As the minutes ticked down, the computer beeped several times and made its way down to forty-four percent.

The first drone had now reached the parallel lines. Knowing what to look for, Klemmer was easily able to pick up the telltale signs of tool marks. The drone began the journey to the next parallel line, and the next, and the results were the same. The furrows were definitely artificial. Man-made or something-made. Someone or something had gone to the trouble of digging up hundreds of kilometers in the rocky ground to create an image. But who and why? The video display for the first drone went blank as it succumbed to the intense heat of the surface. The second drone was still functioning.

More time passed, and the computer beeped again.

The display changed to thirty-eight percent. Klemmer hadn't noticed the warning, he was so caught up in his discoveries.

The remaining drone made its way back to the arachnoid and was continuing to examine the furrows. Once again, a careful look revealed signs that the fractures were hand- or claw- or tentacle-made.

"Definitely not natural," Klemmer stated.

The effort required to carve thousands of kilometers of furrows into Venus, if all the arachnoids were artificial, must have been considerable. It would have required years and thousands of workers, an effort of similar proportions to building the pyramids of Egypt.

"Klemmer," the word echoed inside the tight cabin. "Klemmer, this is mission control. You have five more minutes before you need to leave the surface. Initiate preparations for take-off."

The computer beeped and displayed thirty-three.

Klemmer cursed as the steering of the second drone became erratic, the metal deteriorating in the heat. It tumbled into a large pit and fell three meters onto the rocks below. There, it continued to record, but it didn't budge. Its autopilot controls were jammed, and Klemmer was going to have to take over its entire operation, as if the thing was a radio-controlled car. He nudged the levers and coaxed it to trundle forward.

One minute passed. Two.

"Yes!"

The drone recorded something truly amazing—there had been life on Venus. Intelligent and purposeful life. Klemmer's heart hammered in his chest. The pit the drone traveled in was lined with murals, images painted on the rock walls in delicate patterns.

The first mural showed an alien race, shorter and darker than humans, but bipedal and of a similar external physiology. The beings held out their hands to enormous spider creatures, which gave them tools and grain. The background suggested a lush landscape with unfamiliar trees and grasses.

"Colonel Klemmer, initiate take-off procedures immediately," came the voice from mission control.

The computer chimed in with another beep and flashed the number fifteen. Klemmer continued to absorb the drone's readings and continued to remotely pilot it.

The second mural showed the same people, but this time the background was not as lush. The sun was quite prominent and totally out of proportion to the first scene.

"Damn it, Klemmer! Take off now, do you hear me? That's an order." Powell's words rang out loudly. The computer beeped and flashed ten.

The background in the third mural looked parched and dark. The grass was mostly dead, and the few remaining trees were stunted and thin. The sun showed still more prominent than in the prior murals. Armies of people were digging patterns in the dirt-fashioning circles and lines, and creating large spider images—the arachnoids. A few people were rendered as simply staring off into space.

"Honey." This time the voice Klemmer heard was feminine. His wife. "Why aren't you taking off? Why don't you . . ."

Klemmer considered his reply, as he directed the drone to move again and thumbed one control after the next—sending all the data back to the ship in orbit and from there on its way to earth. His computer acknowledged the successful transmission with a musical burst of static.

Powell continued: "Klemmer, your time is up. You've been there over an hour. The systems on the landing module are going to fail at any minute in the heat. If you don't leave now, you'll die."

The drone reached the fourth mural, still continuing to send, still being urged along by Klemmer.

"An acceptable risk," Klemmer said finally. "An acceptable cost for this information. The drone can't move without me. Acceptable . . ."

"Klemmer," Powell persisted. "What are you doing?"

The drone moved along the depression, revealing that the fourth mural was unfinished.

The computer beeped and read zero.

PATIENCE

by Donald J. Bingle

Donald J. Bingle is a well-respected, but somewhat eccentric, corporate attorney, working on mergers, acquisitions, securities offerings, and the like. His writing career has moved from RPGA sanctioned role-playing tournaments to gaming material (including Ruins of Undermountain II: The Deep Levels), *movie reviews, screenplays, and short stories. He is also the top-ranked player of classic role-playing tournaments and part-owner of two game companies: 54-40' Orphyte (owner of the* Timemaster *role-playing game) and Rio Grande Games (producer of English versions of Europe's finest cafe games). He is firmly convinced that enough time spent contemplating the mysteries of the universe in the hot tub could result in a unified field theory, but prefers spending his time with his wife, Linda, and playing with their puppies, Smoosh, Makai, and Mauka. He can be contacted through www.orphyte.com.*

CLIFFORD Hurling used more dental floss than anyone else on the moon.

Flipping open the plastic lid on the Johnson & Johnson waxed variety, he grabbed the loose end of the string and spooled off precisely fourteen inches, using the metal tab to cut it and hold the end for the next night. Wrapping an end several times lightly around one finger, he looped the middle part of the floss around the spout of his tube of BriteWhite toothpaste, at the lower edge of the cap, where a residue of the paste always squeezed out a bit when he closed it. A thin film of congealing paste clung to the floss as he drew the string tight.

Dropping the tube back onto the metal sink, he crossed over to the bookshelf and pulled down a post-card his sister had sent him years ago from home. A small packet of white sand, labeled "Genuine Sand from Cocoa Beach, Florida," was taped to the card. He gazed at the picture of the sun rising behind the gantries of the launch pads at Kennedy Space Center on Cape Canaveral as he efficiently loosed the open end of the plastic packet from the tape, opened it, and dropped the center of the loop of floss into the white sand. He smiled as he remembered, for the thousandth time, that his dentist always told him that his extra-whitening toothpaste was too abrasive on his teeth. He pulled the floss out and carefully closed the packet and reaffixed the tape.

Finally, he looped both ends of the floss more tightly around his index fingers. Folded pieces of cardboard from a paperback novel cover kept the floss from cutting into his fingers. Then he set to work. Not too fast. He had plenty of time. He would be at this for hours. Rhythmic and methodical, he started to work the floss back and forth.

*   *   *

The phone rang shrilly in the dark room. Swenson slapped at the alarm clock twice before the sound fully registered, then woke up, swearing vociferously. It didn't matter. No one shared his bed to be disturbed or offended. Finally he found the light, and—after being assaulted by its brightness—found the offending phone and snatched it from its cradle.

"Do you know what time it is?" he growled by way of greeting. He didn't care if his voice had an edge to it.

"Seventeen hundred Lunar Standard Time," responded

the smooth, slightly effeminate voice at the other end. Swenson did not recognize the caller's voice as it continued. "Let's see, in Tallahassee it would be . . . oh, dear . . . that would be four . . ." The voice faltered and seemed flustered for a moment, then it regained its composure and confidence. "My apologies. This can wait until later."

"Look, buddy-boy. If you got the balls to call me at this hour, it better not be able to wait until morning. I'm up now, so spit it out. What's the emergency?"

"No emergency, Detective Swenson. The file jacket indicates that you are to be notified immediately in the event of any unusual development. I was just following the instructions."

"What file? What development? Maybe you'd better start from the beginning. Who is this, anyway?"

"I'm Corporal Pancek at the Lunar Correctional Facility. It seems that your prisoner, Clifford Hurling, has escaped."

A loud "clank" reverberated through thousands of miles of optic cable and satellite wave transmissions to assault Pancek's ears as Swenson's phone hit the wall. The line remained open, however, and Pancek listened to Swenson's swearing receding as the detective threw on some clothes and headed into the office.

Pancek disconnected the lunar end of the call. He didn't understand the problem. The prisoner's file said he was incarcerated for something to do with substandard electronic components—hardly the type of thing that should have gotten him a stint in the moon's finest prison facility. Usually only the hard cases came up here. Besides, where could Hurling go?

*   *   *

Swenson was waiting for the captain when he arrived at the station house at 6:30 A.M. He pounced before the man could pour himself a cup of coffee.

"I have to go to the moon."

"Excuse me?" replied the captain, unimpressed that Swenson was on the premises a good three hours ahead of his normal schedule.

"Hurling's escaped. There's no telling what he might do."

"Hurling, hmmm . . . Hurling . . . Oh, the fraud case that you were following so closely when I first got transferred here. I don't see why the Bureau of Prison's incompetence should entitle you to a joyride to the moon. Just because some fools in the legislature want to waste the taxpayers' money by putting a prison facility up there, doesn't mean I have to waste any more money sending you up because a minor-league crook wandered out of the facility."

"He's not a minor-league crook, Captain. He's a stone-cold killer."

The captain's eyes narrowed in thought and minor consternation. "I thought it was some procurement scam or something with NASA . . ."

"They plea-bargained it to that. They didn't want any publicity."

The captain waited silently for Swenson to continue the explanation. Finally, he did.

"Actually, he was the guy behind the Nassau incident."

"Jesus . . ." exhaled the Captain.

Everybody knew about the Nassau incident. It was the worst public-relations disaster for NASA since the *Challenger* explosion, not to mention the thousands of dead in the Bahamas when a NASA booster rocket went haywire and crashed into the outskirts of the town, leveling buildings and setting up the closest thing to a firestorm since Dresden, Tokyo, Hiroshima, and Nagasaki.

"No wonder they sent him to the lunar jail. If word ever got out that his faulty components caused the Nassau incident, a mob would storm the prison and lynch him for sure."

"It's worse than that, boss. It wasn't a faulty component. Almost nobody knows this—and NASA will have both our butts if this gets out—but . . ." Swenson's voice hardened to steel. "Hurling planned the whole thing. The damn chip was programmed to direct the rocket exactly where it landed. The guy's a cold-blooded killer—a thousand times over."

"Sure, and he's behind the Kennedy assassination, too. C'mon, Swenson, get a grip. Those chips and components in the space program go through hundreds, thousands, of tests. You just can't slip something in at the last second that sends a rocket careening off course."

"That's the thing, Captain. The guy's patient. He designed the component years beforehand, set it up so that it would pass the tests and only change its behavior when it was in actual flight—altered the telemetry coordinates or gimbals or some such rocket science. I gotta go to the moon and catch him. They don't know what they're dealing with."

"I don't know. I think you're overreacting. I mean, the place is isolated from even the other moon outposts. There's nowhere to go. Check in with the warden and keep track, but I need you here. We have a few unsolved murders to take care of, you know."

"A few . . ." Swenson shook his head wearily in exasperation. "You just don't get it. This guy is in jail for fraud, but he's one of the biggest mass murderers ever. Heck, if it wasn't for those terrorists that released sarin at the Pro-Bowl in 2012, this guy would probably have the record. And he wants it. I questioned him. You can tell . . . Kept asking for the final 'collateral damage' count all through questioning."

"You're being paranoid, Swenson. Check in with the moon and keep me informed, but don't spend too much time on it."

*   *   *

"I assure you, Detective Swenson, that no one has ever successfully escaped from the Lunar Correctional Facility and that Clifford Hurling will be caught momentarily." The warden was irritated. Swenson wasn't sure if it was from his phone call or the fact that the warden's monotonous, but well-paid job with a nice view had been interrupted by something so mundane as a prison break.

"How'd he get out anyhow? Living in a vacuum, you'd think you guys would be careful about closing the door." He hated bureaucrats. They never volunteered anything. They always made you seem like a hard case just for asking for the basic facts.

"He cut through the bars."

The street-wise detective whistled softly between his teeth. "You guys in the habit of leaving hacksaws lying around up there?"

"No . . . it appears . . . it appears he used dental floss."

"Criminy! He cut through steel bars with dental floss?"

"He seems to have accelerated the abrasion with a mixture of toothpaste and silica."

"Sand? You guys have a beach in that jail?"

"I don't really see how this is constructive, Detective. He had a small packet of beach sand among his personal effects. Nobody thought it could do any harm."

"How many bars did he cut through?"

"Three—well three and a half. He appears to have started the project in another cell before he was moved. We found the other bar on a closer inspection after the breakout."

"Are you housing those guys in chicken wire cages or something? How long does something like that take?"

"Well, our bars are somewhat more lightweight than standard fare in a state facility," the warden sniffed haughtily. "No need to boost extra weight all the way to the moon, you know."

"You're avoiding the question. How long has this been in the works?"

"He was transferred from the old cell five and a half years ago. Our records show he first put in a toiletries request for dental floss and abrasive toothpaste three weeks after his arrival—almost seven years ago."

Swenson paused at the sheer audacity of it. Seven years of meticulous, but monotonous work, abrading the bars without being noticed, then covering his work so as to keep it secret. "You have to get this guy, fast, do you understand, Warden? You cannot take any chances. If there is any risk of him getting away, you have to shoot to kill." His voice involuntarily became more shrill than he intended. "Shoot to kill, you hear me?"

"I don't think that is in any way . . ."

"Shoot to kill, I said!"

There was a brief moment of silence before the warden responded, condescendingly. "Those of us living in pressurized environments amidst a vacuum generally avoid the use, even the availability, of projectile weaponry. You see, Detective, explosive decompression can result from any puncture . . ."

But Swenson wasn't listening anymore. He didn't care if it took his life savings. He had to get to the moon.

*   *   *

Thirty-six hours and $187,000 later, plus tips, Swenson demonstrated his own version of explosive decompression in the warden's office.

"What do you mean, you think he stole a rocket?" Swenson might have weighed one-sixth as much on the moon, but his voice boomed even heavier in the close confines of the pressurized and compartmentalized facility.

"An ore freighter, actually. Used to carry ore from the Asteroid Belt to the moon for construction. Heavy metals mostly. Much cheaper and more plentiful than bringing things up from Earth. They can move a great deal of mass, not quickly, but inexpensively."

"Thanks for the economics lesson, Warden, but what happens when this guy plows that craft into Mexico City from high orbit?"

"Ohh . . ." whimpered the warden. "perhaps we ought to call in NASA-Lunar HQ."

*   *   *

Jason Petterlie, the resident rocket scientist at NASA-Lunar, was unimpressed with Swenson's concerns.

"You just don't understand. First off, it's a deep-space

craft—not designed to land where there's an atmosphere. It's not even streamlined. All, or at least everything but the reactor, would burn off in the atmosphere. The reactors are designed to avoid irradiating the countryside if they accidentally reenter the Earth's atmosphere. Shaped shielding, automatic ejection of the core so it burns up at high altitude, that kind of thing. Someone could have the minor remains of the thing fall through their roof, I suppose—a few hundred pounds at the most—but the odds are . . ." he looked at the two concerned officials smugly, ". . . astronomical."

Swenson was unimpressed. "What about if it's full of cargo?"

The technician brushed away his concern. "It's not. It's empty. Supplies for six crewman for several months, but no ore. Even if it did have cargo, ore is loose rock— it would behave just like any other small particulate matter once the hull ablated away. Good meteor shower—no damage."

Swenson's mind raced. "The lunar colony, then, or one of the other near space outposts."

"In theory, I suppose. But he's not headed in that direction. If he was, we'd send up a laser mining ship and shoot him down."

"You mean you know where he is! Shoot the bastard down, then."

"This isn't Buck Rogers, Detective. We don't have fighters patrolling the solar system looking for alien ships to blast. It could be done, but it would be expensive. Besides, it is completely unnecessary. He's boosted to a moderate rate of speed. It is inefficient for him to change course, and we'd see it coming if he did. Besides, Detective, he's headed out of the solar system."

"What about the mining colonies in the Asteroid Belt? Won't he have to go by them?"

"Well," the technician paused to tap out a few commands in the air on his virtual data-pad. A three-dimensional hologram of the solar system popped up on the tabletop with outposts and trajectories highlighted. "The orbital dynamics don't put him near anything at all on the way out. The portion of the Asteroid Belt he'll near in a couple months is not populated. He might skim by a few rocks when he gets to the Oort Cloud, but that's about it."

The tech turned off the projection, the science lesson over. "Look, he probably just got stir crazy and headed away from the moon without any thought to where he was going."

"Thank you, Dr. Petterlie," interrupted the warden, once more confident. "We will worry no more about it."

Swenson wished that were true, but the mealy-mouthed warden didn't speak for him.

* * *

The ore ship was not elegant, but compared to the cramped facilities in prison, it was roomy. Equipped for six, Clifford had plenty of food, air, and water—the hydroponics room even had a few scrawny tomato plants. His only company was the crew vid-cube collection (mostly action movies and porn) and a couple of cockroaches. He preferred the cockroaches to the porn, but he did not have much time for either.

He had things to do.

Fortunately, the nav-computer was first rate. And once he was up to speed, he didn't need to expend fuel until he wanted to stop or change vectors. He could coast while he finished his calculations.

* * *

As the months went by, the guys at the station house grew bolder and bolder about teasing Swenson for blowing his retirement money on a "working" trip to the moon. He hadn't even taken in the sights in Lunar City or visited the low-grav brothel in the port district. They laughed at him, and "mooned" him in the locker room. Even the captain, initially sympathetic, found an excuse to pass him over on the next round of promotions.

Still, every week Swenson checked in with Petterlie, the confident technician at NASA-Lunar.

"No, Detective. There's no change at all. For all we know, he's not even alive. His course is unchanged. There is no answer to our periodic hails. We can tell his computer and life-support systems are operating, but that's about it. He probably committed suicide or is gibbering away while he looks out at the vast reaches of space. I really do have better things to do with my time than chat with you, Detective."

"Just tell me, right away, if anything happens."

Petterlie tapped at his virtual data-pad again. "We'll lose him for a few weeks about the time he arrives at the Oort Cloud—it's on the other side of the sun from us at that point."

"Isn't that dangerous? Could we set up a relay station to monitor him from another vector?"

"Detective! He's hundreds of millions of miles away on a ship that takes a week to even stop. Don't you have criminals down there on Earth to catch?"

*   *   *

Hurling finished the computer work with months to spare, but there was some detail to adjust as he got closer. The rest of his time he spent in a painstaking effort to train the cockroaches, but to no avail.

"Too stupid to learn, yet smart enough to survive. That's evolution."

A week out of the core of the loosely-defined and scattered Oort Cloud, he started the burn to stop. Hurling turned his attention to locating the right real estate.

*   *   *

"I told you he was alive. He's up to something." If the detective gripped the phone any tighter, the plastic would be sure to break.

"I didn't say he was dead. I said he could be dead."

"So, what does this burn mean?"

"He's probably just going to settle the ship down on the biggest chunk of rock he can find and declare it his

own personal planet or something. Or maybe he put the
ship on scouting auto-pilot and it has located a potential
ore body. He could still be dead for all we know."

"You've got to send someone to shoot him down . . ."

"You police and your guns . . ."

And the line went dead.

*   *   *

Petterlie ducked Swenson's calls for the next month.
If he'd had the money, Swenson would have gone back
to the moon just to strangle the scrawny tech's neck.

Then finally, Petterlie called him. "There's been a development, Detective."

"I told you . . ."

"Well, yes. Right as his position on the other side of
the sun became visible to our instruments, they indicated
that he was in the midst of another burn. We don't know
when it started and an asteroid was partially blocking
our view. We probably wouldn't have seen the end of
the burn, but the solar flares have died down unexpectedly early, possibly giving credence to the Wyzinski theory as to their source of periodicity . . ."

"Yeah, yeah. Whatever." The guy was a geek, a geek
that couldn't stay on the subject; at least not on Swenson's subject. "You're avoiding something. What else is
there?"

"We received a long-range signal this morning."

"You waiting to engrave it on a Hallmark Card and
mail it to me?" Why couldn't some people ever get to
the point?

"It reads: 'In a game with a real pro, the cockroaches
win.' " The technician cleared his throat. "I told you he
was probably gibbering to himself."

A vise gripped Swenson's chest. It suddenly made
sense. The damn rocket scientist was going for the record. He didn't want those terrorist psychos from the
Pro-Bowl to best his numbers. And though he was no
scientist, Swenson knew how Hurling was gong to do it.

"Sweet Jesus, Petterlie. The bastard's pushing a rock."

The technician felt suddenly light-headed, even for lunar gravity. An asteroid six or seven miles across falling toward the Earth was the type of calamity that had befallen the dinosaurs at the end of the Cretaceous, not to mention the similar event exterminating the trilobites and the gorgons before that, ending the Paleozoic Era. Impacts like that typically were believed to have caused the extinction of seventy to ninety percent of all species. It was the type of event that could wipe out humanity completely . . . efficiently.

Petterlie started analyzing the data even before the surly detective asked him to.

*   *   *

Properly motivated and with more than a year's notice, even much-maligned NASA managed to track and destroy the ten-mile wide asteroid nudged onto a collision path with Earth. There were much congratulations and backslapping and bottles of champagne (from Oregon these days).

Swenson finally got his promotion.

Petterlie was similarly slated for rapid advancement.

The warden, on the other hand, was quietly cashiered.

After sending the rock on its way, the ore ship drifted in space. Computer-enhanced analysis of the end of its burn suggested that it had run out of fuel, rather than ending the burn with a fuel shutoff.

Most of the world did not even know of the danger it had faced, but even those who did stopped worrying. Except for Swenson. He awoke one night with a start and called Petterlie.

"How much fuel did it take to send that rock?"

A day later, he received the reply. "About twenty percent of what Hurling had left when he got to the Oort cloud."

There was a long pause. "Damn it. Don't you see, Petterlie? He sent more than one. I know it. Deep down in my bones, I know it. There are more rocks headed for us."

The tech contemplated a moment. He had to admit it was a possibility. "It could be," he said evenly.

"How many?" pressed the detective. "How many could he have sent?"

"Two, maybe four, depending on how far apart they were, how big they are, and how much juice it took to nudge their orbits."

"Good God, four . . ." muttered Swenson in awe.

"But we've scanned the area," continued the scientist. "Nothing else is headed directly for us—well, directly in the sense of an intersecting elliptical orbit now moving toward our orbital path, that is."

"He's a rocket scientist, Petterlie, just like you. What would you do?"

Petterlie bristled at the "just like you" remark, but thought quietly for almost a minute. Swenson showed unusual patience and left the line open without uttering any rude comments.

"I'd send something on an elliptical orbit away from us, to arrive later, when we weren't looking."

"Bingo. The bastard's still after the record. He wants to be the biggest mass murderer of all time."

"But he's failed, Swenson. Don't you see? You've caught him. We're onto his game. We know what he's done. We'll watch the skies. We've been warned. Whether it's next year or five years from now, you have my word. I'll make sure we're watching."

"Don't you understand, Petterlie? The man cut through three steel bars with dental floss and sand. He's patient. It won't be next year or the year after. These rocks are coming decades, centuries, millennia from now."

Tears welled in Detective Swenson's eyes as he continued—tears his squadmates had never seen. "Who's going to remember your warning two thousand years from now? You're clever, Petterlie, but you're not Nostradamus. What about fifty thousand or a million years from now?" The tears stopped as his anger took over again. "He's right, you know. He's got the record. Cockroaches will be the only survivors and there's not a damn thing we can do about it."

Petterlie strained against the logic of it, but somehow
he knew the detective was right. "I guess," he said quietly, "we'll just have to wait and see."

*   *   *

Hurling reviewed the nav-computer logs one last time.
Everything was in motion, just as it should be. One or
two of his "projects" might miss or be detected, but
almost certainly not all of them. One would hit—it was
just a matter of time and sophisticated orbital mechanics.
He would die knowing he had the record, a record that
could never be broken.

He had thought of bleeding the air from the ship to
commit suicide, but that wouldn't have been fair to the
cockroaches. He wondered how long the insects could
live on the remaining provisions (which he took care to
conveniently open) and, of course, his body. As the future rulers of Earth, the species deserved some respect,
he believed.

Instead of suicide by decompression, he had raided
the medical supplies and cooked up something suffi-
ciently lethal to take. It wasn't really that hard.

It wasn't rocket science.

A COIN FOR CHARON

by Janet Pack

Author, singer, composer, actress—Janet Pack has no dull moments. She lives in a sightly haunted farmhouse in Williams Bay, Wisconsin, with cats Tabirika Onyx, Syrannis Moonstone, and Baron Figaro di Shannivere, surrounded by rocks, music, and dusty books. Her published works include twenty-eight short stories in science fiction, fantasy, horror, and mystery anthologies. Her musical compositions have been published in Weis and Hickman's Death Gate Cycle and in the DragonLance sourcebooks. Janet works as the manger's assistant at Shadowlawn Stoneware Pottery in Delavan, Wisconsin, and writes feature articles for The Beacon newspaper in Williams Bay and Lake Geneva's At the Lake magazine. She acts in amateur outdoor theater with the Pace Players from the George Williams Campus of Aurora University in Williams Bay, appearing as Starkey the Pirate in Peter Pan, and Gollum in The Hobbit. An avid people-watcher, Janet also invents tasty recipes, enjoys good wine, reads, listens to music, watches good movies, exercises, plays with her companions, observes local wildlife, and excels in her role as the neighborhood's most atypical resident.

DR. Velerie Heyer didn't look up as Dr. Konrad Gregorius stormed into the control room of the tiny

Pluto International Research Station. The fact she didn't
immediately acknowledge his anger made him seethe
more—Velerie could tell by the way the pudgy scientist's
short breaths became even shorter as he whistled harshly
through his nose.

"How dare you send a message about our project to
Mars without my knowledge!" Konrad grated between
clenched teeth. His gray eyes were as hard as the frost on
the planet's surface. "You've shattered our agreement!
I won't stand for this!"

Velerie closed the tightband pulse channel before she
swung around in her chair and allowed her dark blue
eyes to rest on her colleague's homely face. Behind his
bristling salt-and-pepper beard, his face glowed like a
small red sun.

"Hello, Konrad," she said evenly. She knew her vocal
control had always infuriated him. "I expected you."

But she truly hadn't expected him. How did he know
she'd be here sending a message?

"And you can't claim that you haven't sent similar
messages at least twice in the past dozen cycles," Velerie
continued. "I just didn't take the time to catch you at it
in person." She pointed to the textured button marked
"Security" on the console, nodding a head that was
capped with short whiskey-colored hair. "The digital records are right there. I've seen them. All of them. I
know what you're doing."

Purple veins popped into sight on his temples and on
his fleshy nose. "How did you get the code to those?"
Konrad growled. "That's a security breach. They're private, for the use of the Tessavalle Company only."

Her smile was slight, barely lifting the corners of her
shapely mouth. "And Korum International, too, which
is who I work for. Or Naganta Worldwide, since that's
who Torumi works for. This is still an international research station, it doesn't belong only to your company."

She cocked her head. "I figured out the code in my
spare time. Despite what you think of me I'm not a
vapid female. Nor am I a research slave." Velerie inhaled a deep breath of the station's thoroughly condi-

tioned, slightly oil- and musk-tainted air. "I'm as resourceful as you are, possibly more so. I have to be, considering some of the company I'm forced to keep while I'm here. Your company, in particular. But that won't be for too much longer. My stay is up for renewal in fifteen standard cycles, just about when the next supply ship arrives. And I'm not renewing my contract no matter how much my company begs me." Her eyes held his. "Survival of the fittest, Konrad. You're doing the same thing, but in your own irritating way. And you *have* to stay here."

Konrad straightened, his face flushing even darker with outrage. "How dare you accuse *me*—"

"Oh, come on." Velerie's patience with Konrad's constant superiority snapped. "Don't you ever tire of these stupid games? I know I do. Let's cut the crap and acknowledge things as they are: you're watching me, and I'm watching you. We're both sending preliminary reports back to our companies before the final data is in. We have to do that to keep each other relatively honest so we can share the incredible discovery of simultaneously finding Pluto's new magnetic metal. I'm not going to let you squeeze me out of an amazing credit like that." *Bad enough that I'll have to share it,* she added to herself.

She glanced out the viewport at the tiny frozen ball of rock and methane-ethane-nitrogen-carbon-monoxide frost that would provide her and Konrad the means of becoming famous, wealthy, and finally getting at least a planet's distance away from each other. Proximity to crusty, pompous Konrad was just too close in the Pluto International Research Station, or PIRS as the residents called it—a place which was only the size of six ancient Mir space stations.

Her company adviser at Korum International hadn't told her that PIRS was the outpost where brilliant scientists who couldn't work with anyone else—but who still had valuable ongoing research—were sent as a last resort. Velerie wished she'd done more to investigate the personalities she'd be involved with here before making the journey to research Pluto's, Charon's, and asteroidal ores in the Kuiper Disk. She'd been too excited about the prospect of seeing the solar system's farthest planet and its satellite close up to care back then. After she'd arrived on PIRS and came to know Dr. Konrad Gregorius, Velerie had more than once regretted not following up more thoroughly.

Konrad was definitely the most irritating of the eight people living on the tiny station, a grandstanding *primo don* of the worst sort.

Astronomer-physicist Dr. Ahmad ibn Hassam, seemed only interested in his research, and hence kept himself glued to his computer-telescope and notes for his book— except for meals and required exercise periods. He was pleasant enough in a distant, monosyllabic way.

Dr. Torumi Naganta was studying Neptune and its moons during Pluto's closest pass to the larger planet. She was a plump older scientist on her last foray into space. Despite occasional moodiness which made her snappish, Torumi owned a sly sense of humor, and she was occasionally willing to loan a shoulder to cry on. Of all the station's inhabitants, she was Velerie's favorite.

The rest of the staff included three research assistants: Tobias Wellett, a pasty-complected man with cottony hair who possessed a somewhat morose but dependable nature; Birgit Struve, a strawberry blonde with a mind as bright as her hair; and Suramayam Charanduhar, the polite, gregarious East Indian who loved telling jokes— badly. The assistants were supposed to rotate between the doctors who were collecting data about various projects. Because Ahmad kept to himself most of the time, the other three had claimed one assistant each.

The last crewmember Velerie and the others knew simply as Gonzales. A muscular man with shrewd dark eyes and a ready smile, he was secretive as well as kept busy by duties that didn't correspond with their own, including those of pilot, maintenance man, and supply officer.

Velerie pulled away from her wandering thoughts. She interrupted Konrad's latest splutter, returning her rock-steady gaze from the port to her associate. "In the meantime, we hang here in blackness about as close to the end of the solar system as one can get, waiting for our research to back up one another's findings. By the way, my latest hypothesis should be ready to add to the data within two hours."

She rose from the padded chair, a lithe movement she'd worked on especially to make Konrad feel clumsy. Velerie looked trim even in her official merlot-colored Korum International coverall. "We're stalemated until the last group of probe samples is finished running through the analyzer, Konrad." For some reason she felt generous at the moment, and decided to offer one last olive branch. "What say we make the best of a bad situation and call a truce until then? It'll make things more pleasant for everybody on the station."

"What do you mean, a truce? You've just proved by sending out that report that we can't achieve a truce. Agreement is impossible. You have no social consciousness at all—"

"Oh, right. *You* haven't done anything wrong." Velerie felt despair—how could such a good scientist go through life without realizing the messes he made in other people's lives? His anger battered against hers again, draining away her energy and will to resist. Konrad's arguments always worked this way. Stiffening her defenses, Velerie captured enough energy to make an impressive exit and get herself back to her office. She couldn't stop the next spate of words as they formed and jetted from her mouth. Not that she wanted to.

"I don't think you of all people should be discussing social consciousness," she said tartly, "considering your reputation for empirical and theoretical data theft."

Konrad's face sagged, turned gray, then bright red again. "You damned little hussy!" he hissed. "How dare you accuse me of that heinous crime!" He took a threatening step, his fist raised, putting himself momentarily off balance. It was obvious he intended to box her in against the communications panel with his greater girth.

Velerie ducked and whipped past his shoulder before he could completely block her path. Opening the door to the station's main hallway, she aimed a space-cold smile over her shoulder as he turned to keep her in sight. "All right. The gloves are off, Konrad. Now you'll find out just how good I am at your own games. That metal will be named heyerite, after me." She slammed the door and bounced her hand against the corridor control panel, jamming the old electronics pad and trapping the irate scientist inside. She knew it wouldn't take long for Gonzales to learn of the problem, pull the keypad from its housing, clear the conflicting signals, and reenter the code to open it and let Konrad out.

Konrad began battering at the inside of the door and yelling. The muffled sounds followed her down the narrow hall.

"Sorry, Gonzales," she muttered as she trotted through slightly below-Earth gravity toward her office. Velerie regretted making more work for the man. "I had to do that." Her sudden grin, an expression as rare as sunlight in this part of the solar system, helped rocket her spirits upward. "And it felt really good!"

Her office was tiny, complete with her name on the door and floor to ceiling soundproof walls. No one could get to her here unless she allowed them in through the coded security door. Slipping inside and fingering the door code to "Private," Velerie relaxed into her chair, enjoying the motion of the warm turgid gel beneath the velvetlike fabric as it conformed to her body.

She let two more thoughts about Konrad intrude, knowing she wouldn't work well with them still spinning in her mind. She'd been grateful when the eminent scientist had taken her under his wing shortly after she'd arrived on the station. But Velerie had been smart enough to listen to Torumi's veiled warnings about the man, as well as wide-eyed enough herself to realize when she was being forced into a subservient position as Konrad's research slave. He had an assistant for that, but seemed to want her instead. When Konrad had tried to force sexual attentions on her, she'd knocked him senseless with a well-placed kick to the crotch and another to his jaw. The two scientists had been openly antagonistic ever since.

Velerie put her hands over her eyes. That antagonism made trying to share credit for one of the most remarkable scientific finds in the past twenty years very difficult. Her most recent hypothesis proposed that the new magnetic metal was at least part of the reason why Pluto and Charon were in such perfectly synchronous orbits— there was enough of it on the planet to react to either a similar deposit or something equally magnetic on Charon. The computer had churned through the last set of joint entries she and Konrad had made. It had spit out the confirmation shortly after that battle. Ever since, Konrad had tried to discredit her and claim the new magnetic metal as entirely his own discovery. Korum International had stood by her proof, although they couldn't give much more than lip service from their Mars-based headquarters until the supply ship arrived with a company investigator.

"There. Konrad's out of my mind," she muttered to herself. "Time to go to work." Velerie tapped the intercom button that connected on Tobias Wellett's desk in the Assistants' Lab he shared with Birgit and Suram. "Tobias, are my latest test figures done?" she asked.

His surprisingly deep baritone answered immediately. "Another fifteen minutes I think, Velerie."

"Is our fast probe ready?"

"Yes."

A noncommittal answer. Good, since Birgit or Suram might be listening. The East Indian had shown no preferences toward one doctor over another: he served Torumi or whoever needed him with the same dedication and bizarre good humor. Birgit, however, had early been cowed by Konrad, and she'd tell him what she overheard if he bullied her. Velerie was nearly certain that Tobias' sympathies leaned toward her. At last the pallid man had never given her reason to think the opposite.

"Is anyone else preparing a probe launch?"

"Konrad has one coming out of stores, but it will take at least two hours to program it."

"Good. Launch the probe. Konrad is, umm, busy for the moment." Velerie hunched forward on her elbows, eagerly counting seconds.

"Probe launched. Impact in three hours."

"Thank you, Tobias. Put the data through to me here when it starts coming in." *Good,* she gloated. For once things were going in her direction. Suram had come up with the idea—the PIRS staff offering the mythological boatman Pluto's moon was named for a coin each time one of them started a new project or wanted data to work out right. Perhaps she should give Charon a coin just for good luck. Shrugging at her silliness, she pretended to toss a half dollar from her father's extensive antiquities collection in the direction of the partially-visible moon.

"Uh, Velerie?"

Her assistant's conspiratorial tone made her almost-relaxed insides clench. "Yes, Tobias?"

"I just thought you ought to know that I saw Konrad trying to do something to the computer system earlier today. It looked fairly complicated, especially for him, and I'm pretty sure it didn't work. He got very angry at it, then shut the program down and moved to do something else when he heard me passing by. In fact, he yelled: "What do you think you're doing here? Move on!' at me, as if I had no right to be walking in the passage."

"What did the program look like?"

"I caught only a glimpse of it. Some sort of override maybe."

Velerie was mystified. "For what, I wonder?"

"May I make a guess?" Tobias sounded a little perturbed.

"Sure, go ahead."

"I think—I think the override has to do with something you need, but whether it relates to your research or the personal side, I couldn't tell."

"He wants to hit where it really hurts, so it will be

my research," Velerie sighed. "Probably a randomness program that will garble incoming information about the magnetic metal. I'd better check all the inputs and make certain there are no cysts on them." A cyst was a nasty little program that could be attached to activate at a verbalized word or phrase, leaving a path open to randomize a file or files associated with that word or phrase.

"And Velerie," Tobias began, then stopped, almost as if he was afraid of his next words.

"What?" she encouraged.

"Check all your tightband messages back to the company, and resend anything that looks peculiar. He may have gotten to those, too. I don't know how since they've usually got a very specific code associated with the individual who sends them, but he might have stumbled on something he could use, or picked up one of your security words while overhearing a conversation. You know how he is."

"Yes, he's always looking for a tool he can use against someone. Thank you, Tobias."

"Uh, if you want, I can help. I don't have all that much to do right now. Just waiting for that next set of proofs to work through the computer."

The scientist smiled. "Thanks very much. I'd appreciate that. Velerie out." She set up an override on her computer that would allow the data from Pluto's surface to interrupt her checking all her files and data feeds for Konrad's tampering.

"Maybe I should offer the ferryman Charon another coin," she said to herself, smiling a little. "Perhaps a half dollar wasn't enough."

Shaking her head at the strong temptation to imagine another coin floating toward Charon, Velerie banished the thought and settled down to work.

* * *

Two hours and some minutes later, a soft buzz alerted her to an incoming message. She hit the switch. "Velerie here."

"It's Torumi." The small Asian scientist's soft voice
was modulated even more than usual, sounding as if she
leaned close to the pickup to whisper her news. "Konrad
has just finished a full complaint about you to both the
International Space Commission and the International
Science Research Board. He cited you for scientific espi-
onage and theft of his theories. This is serious, Velerie.
You must defend yourself immediately! Don't let him
get away with this—he's out to ruin your career."

Velerie looked at the featureless plastic ceiling. "Thanks,
Torumi. I was afraid he'd do something drastic after our
last little scene."

"What scene?"

"The one a little more than two hours ago, where he
tried to trap me against the main console. He threatened
me with a fist, as well as words."

Torumi inhaled in shock. "I didn't think he'd go that
far. You do have your own protections in place?"

"Yes. They've been ready for some time. All I have
to do is alert a few people that Konrad's on the ram-
page. My company knows about the situation. I've sent
my supervisor reports regularly, so there's a backfile
about Konrad's conduct almost from the beginning. I
just checked them all, and everything got to the company
without being hit by a randomness program. Just between you and me, Korum International is sending an
investigator in on the next supply shuttle."

"Ooh, I hope he or she is short, and has a good sense
of humor. That investigator's not going to be in a good
mood—those supply shuttles aren't built to accommodate more than the two pilots and anything larger than
a medium-sized dog." She dropped her attempt at levity.
"It's good your company is taking your complaints seriously." Torumi paused and sighed before going on. "I
hate to see this happen. Konrad is a brilliant scientist,
but his ego gets in the way. And he never seems to
notice that it affects his work. He also insists on misusing
his influence, and diverts the energies he should pour
into research into vendettas. If something goes wrong,
it's never his fault. If it can be proven to be his fault,

he retaliates vindictively because he won't admit failure. It takes someone strong like you to write a detailed report about his actions."

"I'm going to make sure he gets slapped this time." Velerie's tone was stony with determination. "I've made certain that the details are going into his permanent records. If Konrad ever gets back to Mars or Earth, it isn't likely he'll be welcome in many research projects. The entire scientific community will know about him."

Torumi's voice quavered with reaction. "You went to the division supervisor, Dr. Mardiat?" she asked softly.

"Better than that. I have a good relationship with Dr. Mardiat," returned Valerie. "She read all my reports about Konrad, decided the case was serious, and took everything to Dr. Fronal, including the verifications from you and Tobias. Fronal's on the international board of directors. He'll make the final decision about Konrad's future." She smiled at the voice pickup. "Or nonfuture."

"Good girl! I had no idea you'd been so busy."

"It helps to have Mardiat as division supervisor—she was once a teacher at my university, and was impressed with my work. Now if I can just get the preliminary report that brings all the previous communications I've sent to the company reconciled and compiled before the probe findings come in, everything will be in place."

"I'll let you get back to it," Torumi said. "Keep me posted."

"I will, thanks. Velerie out."

She touched the button, severing the comm link. No doubt about it this time, she felt *very* good about the way things were shaping up. With all her protections in place and all the reports she'd written to the company, Velerie felt assured of at the very least co-credit for the magnetic metal's discovery. There were certainly worse things than sharing that credit with a slime like Konrad.

* * *

The computer chime indicating new incoming data and the blow on Velerie's door happened at the same time. The startled scientist sat bolt upright, causing the warm gel in her chair to adjust to her new position. She stroked a few keys, allowing the information to swarm onto the flat screen hovering at eye level, and read it hungrily. Whatever had bashed at her door could wait while she digested her probe's latest findings about Pluto's magnetic metal.

Her eyes swept across the data. There, there, and there—her hypothesis, the one she'd sent to Korum International on Mars just before her encounter with Konrad earlier today, was proving out. Her theories were sound. Excitement flooded her body.

"Wonderful!" Velerie said. "Perfect! All that careful background work is paying off." She began adding the new information to the file she'd been preparing for Korum International, which was already coded for a tightband signal to their Martian headquarters.

Her door groaned. Why was it making that peculiar noise? It had never done that before. Velerie read faster, unwilling to take her eyes off the fascinating information scrolling onscreen.

The door groaned again. She spared a glance toward it, noticing this time that there was a two-inch gap between the jamb and the edge of the steel-core plastic of the door itself. The faint light from the corridor beyond shone through. Sudden alarm bells in her mind almost buried her concentration, but the scientist called up the discipline of many early years spent in noisy school study areas and kept reading.

After its third lament, the door opened enough to let a rotund body pass. Konrad Gregorious squeezed himself into Velerie's sanctum, his breath coming heavy in triumph and effort.

"Go away, Konrad. I'm busy," she said shortly.

"You won't get rid of me that easily," the male scientist sneered. "Not now. I know what you're doing."

"And you're going to stop me, right?" Velerie snorted derisively and shook her head. Her eyes were still glued to the monitor, but she could see part of Konrad's repellent reflection darkening one side of the figures.

How the hell had he gotten in? She'd never given out her security door code to anyone. And she'd never opened the door when there was another PIRS staff member within view of her keypad. Had someone hacked her security measures, just as she'd hacked into the station's tapes to spy on Konrad?

"I expect to stop you, yes. And so will your company when they hear my well-founded complaints about the way you've manipulated the data of this discovery, as well as tried to keep all the credit for yourself."

"We've been over all that earlier. I don't want to waste time rehashing the whole thing." She sat back from the screen a little, her concentration finally broken. But she'd seen what she needed to see.

The findings were better than she'd expected. The new metal was very magnetic, and would prove an excellent mining opportunity for both Korum International and Tessavalle. It was worth a fortune.

"Look, Konrad," Velerie said evenly, tapping the monitor, and refusing to look at him. "There's plenty of wealth and fame here for both of us. Why don't we just agree to share it, and let things go from there?" *With my name listed first on the credits,* she told herself.

"Impossible," he grated. "It was my discovery, and I will have all the credit. I will stop your devious little game." His arm was raised.

Catching an abnormal glint in the monitor, Velerie whirled her chair around. Konrad held a small surgical knife in his right fist, the kind kept in the station's emergency medical kits.

The door rattled, an odd spectral sound. Velerie glanced at it, but didn't dare take her eyes off Konrad for long. She felt a tiny rivulet of cold sweat slip down the back of her neck. She wasn't really afraid of Konrad; after all, she'd dealt with him before, and more than once. The door rattled again. Was someone else there?

She shivered as a peculiar specter appeared in her mind. Charon, that faceless ferryman, was suddenly haunting her. Panic nearly claimed Velerie as a half-dozen disturbing thoughts slammed together into one huge warning: there must be someone else involved in her and Konrad's argument.

"After reading your final statement, which you conveniently left in the comm for someone to find, the world will believe you're that kind of person," gloated Konrad. "I wrote it for you. It's a masterpiece."

"Konrad, look behind the door." Slowly, very slowly, as if trying not to spook a dog with bared teeth, Velerie stood up.

"I won't let you distract me again with such nonsense," the male scientist declared. "Don't ask me about the door again. It's just settling. And don't hit the alarm button that wails in the Assistants' Lab. There is no help for you. Your statement reveals your unbalanced mind, which a few of us here on PIRS were aware of almost from your arrival. What a pity. Such promise."

"You're using the royal plural now, Konrad. Your claims are drivel, and you know it. No one will fall for your cinematic narrative, nor the strange manner of my death. Now will you please look behind the door?" She tried to force her way past him to reach the panel that was now jigging in its track.

Konrad reached out his other arm and swept her back to lean against her desk, her white-knuckled hands gripping the rounded plastic edge on either side of her body. "We're going to end this," he whispered loudly, his eyes wide and round with madness. "Here and now."

Something in the corridor hit the door with a solid *thunk,* then everything grew silent again. Where was Torumi, her little feet padding down the hall at odd times? Where was Suram with his bad jokes when she needed assistance?

"Look behind the door," she demanded, her voice trembling for once in her life. "Konrad, please! Someone's there!"

Before Konrad could react, there was a final thunk, and a figure flew through the opening behind them. A body hit Konrad hard from behind, causing an *ooof!* of air to rush through his lips. Konrad slammed into Velerie, his sudden weight pushing her down on her desk. Disbelieving it was happening, she felt the chill blade of the scalpel scrape high against a rib on her left side and penetrate her lung. She gasped with shock, and from some part in her mind she registered surprise that there was little pain.

Konrad couldn't recover his balance before a hand tangled in his hair and snapped his head back. Another hand holding a large knife reached across his throat and drew the sharp blade across it. Velerie's nose filled with the iron scent as the rival scientist's blood splashed across her face and coverall. The hand dropped the head, which fell on her stomach, the weight of Konrad's beefy torso holding her prisoner against the desk.

She couldn't take her eyes off the knife that killed Konrad. It was familiar. It was hers—her father, a prominent collector of antiquities, had treasured it, and had left to Velerie in his will. It and the coins were the only personal luxuries she'd brought with her to PIRS. She'd kept the knife in security box near her bed. Not having checked on it while the excitement of discovering Pluto's new metal had escalated, she didn't even know it had been stolen.

Her eyes raised. She gasped at the face now hovering above her.

"Yes, it's me," a familiar, surprisingly deep baritone sneered. Tobias Wellett smiled at her, but in a way Velerie had never seen before during her almost two-year stay on the research station—it was smug, excited, and gloating all at once. A very ugly expression, she decided. "Thank you both for making this so easy."

"What so easy?" Velerie asked, sucking in her first painful breath after her stabbing. She was certain she didn't want to hear the rest.

"The new metal," the research assistant replied. "I'll own the credit for its discover in a few hours. It was me all the time: you started the fight with Konrad, but I kept it going. All those little details I fed you both, and you never saw through the lies." He smiled. "Both of you were so blind, so easily led."

"I doubt you'll get discovery credit," she wheezed. "We documented absolutely everything—" Velerie tried to wriggle out from beneath Konrad, but remained pinned.

"And I redocumented it," Tobias replied. "Every report, every data sheet, every computer notation now has my name on it. I discovered welletite. It's mine."

"The security cameras—"

"Will see exactly what I tell them to see." Tobias's smile widened a fraction. "I played with them, too."

"But . . . but why?"

Tobias laughed. "Now I can get away from this damned frozen hell of rock and darkness, and back to civilization. I don't have to be a research assistant forever, not now. The performance I'll put on after I reveal that you and Konrad have just killed each other will be really good. Your fights kept everyone's attention. No one noticed a thing I did."

Velerie struggled harder despite the jagged pain from the blade. "I won't let you do this!"

"You haven't got a choice, my dear Doctor Heyer," Tobias said softly, reaching forward.

She noticed for the first time his hand was encased in an almost invisible protective glove. No fingerprints.

So she hadn't paid Charon enough. Or perhaps Tobias had paid the ferryman more. She was going to die, and all her careful research would belong to another. The thought hit her harder than had Konrad's hateful words.

Tobias laid her father's knife next to her right hand, then hit the scalpel's handle. Velerie tried to scream, but couldn't. She felt the sharp little blade reach upward into her body and slide deep into the bottom of her heart. The organ shuddered, managed three more arrhythmic beats, and stilled. She sagged, then collapsed backward, jostling the floating screen where new data from Pluto continued scrolling.

"And see, I brought each of you a coin to pay

Charon," Tobias whispered, pulling off the glove, folding the few drops of Konrad's blood inside, and producing two metal bits from his pocket. "I can't thank you both enough. You've just made my career very, very successful."

A slight noise from down the hallway caused Tobias to alter his expression to one of horror. Quickly he hid the glove and the coins in his coverall pocket. As Torumi peeked around the corner, the research assistant turned slowly, tears streaming down his face.

"Look," he said brokenly, pointing back into the room. "Velerie and Konrad. They've killed each other!"

THE GRAND TOUR

by Brian M. Thomsen

Brian M. Thomsen has been nominated for a Hugo, has served as a World Fantasy Award judge, and is the author of two novels, Once Around the Realms *and* The Mage in the Iron Mask, *and more than thirty short stories. His most recent publications as an editor include several anthologies in collaboration with Marty Greenberg for DAW Books, including* The Reel Stuff, Mob Magic, Oceans of Space, *and* Oceans of Magic, *and as a coauthor with Julius Schwartz on his memoirs entitled* Man of Two Worlds—My Life in Science Fiction and Comics. *He lives in Brooklyn with his lovely wife Donna and two talented cats by the names of Sparky and Minx.*

I was the official mission poet.

Poet, you say? What is a poet doing on an interplanetary mission of discovery?

The answer is simple—it's required.

All major government projects are required to have one assigned ever since the NEA was reestablished after the first and only Republican-controlled joint congressional and executive administration succeeded in abolishing it as part of its Coalition for America program. That was during its eight-year reign of terror (which mercifully ended with the outlawing of the Republican party and the establishment of the Democratic Coalition, which has governed for close to a hundred years since).

As a result, the NEA is intrinsically involved as the artistic chronicler of the so-called American saga—and, as a result has to assign an artist to all major capital expenditures beyond ten million dollars.

And thus I, Newton (after the politician, not the scientist) Stradivarius (no relation to the fiddle guy), who flunked pre-calculus, physics, engineering—and all those other courses that were considered the prerequisites for all positions in the space program—found myself as a charter crew member of the *DC Phineas Ffogg,* the first inner-system cruiser to journey from the fiery orbit of Mercury to the frigid reaches of Pluto as official mission poet.

It wasn't because I was a great poet (the jury was still out on that one, and my income was low enough to prove it) or that I had garnered national acclaim (a few nice reviews in the right places, but no fellowships or laurels), or that I had even requested this gig—even a poet isn't that crazy. It was something much simpler than that . . . unpaid student loans.

*   *   *

"So, I see you finally got your sorry ass out of bed."

"A good night's rest is the best remedy for a coldsleep hangover," I replied, adding, "even an astrophysicist knows that."

"Unfortunately, astrophysicists aren't allowed to keep poet's hours. We're actually expected to do some work."

"Oh, big man," I chided, "has to launch some probes, observe some readings, do some calculations."

"Yeah," Santiago replied, "all in a cycle's work. Inferior planets all done, and halfway through the superiors."

"And what do you have to report, oh-hard-working-numbers-cruncher?"

Santiago punched a key on his handcom and reported officiously: "All figures confirmed with exceptions as follows: Inferior—Mercury, deviation of .008 days in actual

observation of period of revolution from initial calculation for an actual revolution period of 87.98 days rather
than 87.97 as calculated. Superior—Jupiter, deviation of
.0007 days in actual observation of period of revolution,
no resultant effect on revolution period as previously
calculated when rounded off to two decimal places for
a confirmed period of revolution of 4332.71 days . . . and
that's *Doctor* hard-working-numbers-cruncher to you."

"I stand corrected," I replied, adding a perfunctory
salute, which my best friend returned with his personal
middle digit variation as a flourish. "So basically nothing
new so far?"

"Well, at least not in my department," he replied. "In
a way, it's rather heartening the idea that Newton, Gali-
leo, and Keplar and everyone who came after them basically got it right . . ."

". . . or at least close enough for horseshoes' sake . . ."

". . . or at least close enough for horseshoes' sake—
without ever having the luxury of leaving Earth, I
might add."

"Ah, the power of mathematics," I extolled with mock
reverence, "and to think of all the money we could
have saved."

Santiago frowned.

"Don't say that," he chided. "Confirmation is as
important as discovery as far as the mission objectives
are concerned."

"Once again, the all-important mission objectives. To
boldly go where no man has gone before, to seek out
planets, make sure they are doing everything we think
they're doing, and make our notes from real close up.
Not that it will yield any real discoveries, just so that
we, as a planetary race, can say—been there, done that,
bought the official T-shirt for the Grand Tour. Aren't
we special?"

I didn't christen our mission the Grand Tour. The
media did. The powers that be were closing down the
space program for the foreseeable future . . . but not
before one last mission of discovery—a final double-
check of our data before turning in the final report.

Our ship, the *P. Ffogg* after the Verne circumnavigator, was a retrofitted generation ship, redesigned to allow a coldsleep crew nine wake-up periods to coincide with the ship's planet passings so the hand-picked crew of experts could have a chance to discern and confirm planetary data from up close. Not withstanding the Mars missions (the good and the bad), man had relied on predominantly long-range probe data and observational calculation to define the other planets in our solar system, and so our space swan song was the chance to see if we got it right.

I guess I had to be encouraged by the confirmation of our Earth originated numbers. After all, the guys, or at least their spiritual descendants, who had initially made the calculations were the same guys who did the math that was involved in assuring our safety on this mission. Everything had been worked out to the .0000005 degree of error. X amount of oxygen, water, and supplies for Y amount of hours of consciousness for a crew of Q, coupled with a preprogrammed course with the precise amount of fuel and resistance (space friction, etc.) That would take us by all nine planets from Mercury to Pluto and most importantly return us back home safe and sound.

Everything to .0000005 degree of error. Sounded good enough for me. Take that, you Cold Equations!

"How's your part going?" Santiago asked.

"I'm one planet behind. It's hard to be creative when you spend most of your time in coldsleep."

"But I thought that poets loved to sleep. You know, to sleep, perchance to dream . . ."

"Shakespeare never spent a night in a coldsleep tube, let alone nine to the nth planetary cycles."

"Oh, how the hard sleeping poet has to suffer."

"That's the official *P. Ffogg* mission hard sleeping poet to you."

"I stand corrected," he replied with his signature salute, and off he went back to work.

I returned to my yellow pad and the draft at hand with an eye and ear toward finishing Jupiter and Saturn

before the next hibernation period . . . and if worst came
to worst I would just take some notes and finish it all
on the ride home.

*   *   *

If the mission had a slogan, I guess it had to be "you
had to be there!"

Somehow "just double-checking our data" didn't seem
to have the right ring to it.

As NEA's artist on the spot, my job was to capture
the essence of our mission in art (a painter or other
visual artist was ruled out due to spacial concerns involving their equipment; ditto for musicians, though I really
didn't see where slightly overweight me was better than
some thin guy with a harmonica) for the alleged future
appreciation of posterity.

It's a funny thing, though. In all of my experience and
studies, I've yet to come across a publicly funded (or
more precisely state funded) work of art that was worth
the reputation of the artist who composed it.

This is not to say that the work was inferior or
flawed—it just lacked heart, spark, magic, or whatever
that little doodad that separates the competent from
the inspired.

Maybe this was why I really wasn't that upset about
being a planet behind.

I hadn't chosen this assignment.

They were going to get what they paid for.

No more. No less.

And when it was over, no one would care. Who remembered the epic poem of five thousand rhyming cou-
plets on the history of American Law on the occasion
of the dedication of the Supreme Court Video monitor
or the saxophone symphony that commemorated the opening of the William Jefferson Clinton Law Institute? No
one except their families and friends, I can assure you.

And when it was all over, I would go back to some
teaching position where I would single-handedly try to

revive the Beat Generation or some other equally dubious academic pursuit of a poetic nature.

*   *   *

One coldsleep cycle later . . .

Santiago was excited.

"I've got the perfect title for your mission poem," he insisted.

I knew he had to have been waiting since before the last sleep cycle to share his genius with me. Maybe he was just one of those guys who thought that every twilight inspiration was a gem. (You know the guys who keep a memo pad by their bunks so they wouldn't forget last night's inspiration in tomorrow morning's haze.)

"Oh, enlighten me," I offered, trying not to be too sarcastic. He as the closest thing I had to a friend after all.

"You should call it 'The Capstone,' since it is the metaphoric capstone of man's exploration of space."

"Not bad," I said insincerely. "But I was leaning toward 'The Grand Tour.' "

"Why?"

"Well, our mission is sort of the classic grand tour of the solar system after all. The ultimate scientific travelogue."

Santiago's disappointment showed on his face.

"I guess you're right," he replied. "That is the mission . . . but I always thought that poets preferred high falootin' metaphors and such. For us it's all numbers and confirmations, but isn't it supposed to be more than that for you? You know, the end of man's search for new horizons, infinity's end, that sort of thing."

"Sometimes a broken statue in the sand is just a broken statue in the sand," I mused, surprised at my own profundity.

"What?"

" 'Ozymandias.' It's a poem about the fleeting nature of fame and the whims of history. It's also about a broken statue in the sand. As far as I'm concerned, paying off my student loans is worth the price of a poem about a broken statue—or, more correctly, a voiceover for a travelogue. If they wanted profundity or some higher meaning, they picked the wrong guy. Metaphors cost more, and I just so happen to be fresh out of them anyway. Case closed. Here's to 'The Grand Tour.' So let it be written, so let it be done."

Santiago seemed about to argue, when we were fortuitously interrupted by yet another data guy who didn't mind conversing with the resident nonscientist.

"Did you guys get off your last message home?" Jensen the spectrologist asked. "If not, time's awastin', and the lines are long."

"Explain it to me again," I queried, playing the dullard. "If I actually had someone to talk to back on terra firma, why can't I call them next cycle?"

"Let me try to explain," Santiago interrupted. "Remember your last call home?"

"Yup."

"Remember the delay between exchanges?"

"Nope."

Santiago fought back a puzzled look, and asked, "When did you make the call?"

"When I dropped out of NYU," I replied. "They disowned me on the spot, and I haven't talked to them since."

"So you've made no calls since the start of the mission?"

"Two. One to my bookie, the other to my agent," I answered. "Both had the same answer. 'Give me a call when you get back in town. We'll do lunch.' "

Jensen tried to bring closure to my nonsense.

"The farther out we get, the longer it takes for messages between us and Earth to travel back and forth," the spectrologist explained. "With me so far?"

"By your side to the end of the universe," I replied.

"Okay. Now given the parameters of our wake cycles for the next two planets," he continued, slowing down as if that would make things simple enough for even a nonscience guy like me to understand, "it will be impossible for us to receive a response to a transmission in the same cycle in which it was sent. Understand?"

"Sure," I countered. "It's like when a guy says he can have your computer repaired and back to you in three business days, but since it is Thursday, you still won't see it until the following week."

Jensen and Santiago just looked at each other dumbfounded.

"I understand," I assured them, "and since I don't have anyone back home waiting for a message, it really doesn't concern me, does it?"

* * *

Before freezing down for the next sleep cycle, I reviewed my work so far. It was more reminiscent of Koffiev's "Ode to a Tractor" than Ginsberg's "Kaddish," but at least I was back on schedule.

Two more planets to go, and home again, home again (dancing a jig).

* * *

Now, you are not supposed to dream during coldsleep, but I just couldn't seem to blank out my mind.

Lines from the greats—Shakespeare. "Oh, Brave New World!" Whitman: "I hear America singing," and others "the rag and bone shop of the heart," "the answer is blowing in the wind," "not with a bang but a whimper," and "my heart lies bleeding in the vacuum of infinite space."

I was haunted with the voices of poets who had something to say.

What they created was original. It was their own.

What their work was to literature, mine was to Monarch notes . . .

. . . and for the first time it began to bother me.

* * *

Normally I had a good twenty-four to thirty-six hours to myself at the beginning of each wake cycle, but as we started our final wake period, my solitary and antisocial routine was interrupted by an announcement summoning all hands to a meeting immediately. And despite my personal inclination toward considering myself sort of separate from everyone else, I realized that I probably had to attend.

The meeting was held in the largest of the storage bays, and it was the first time since the liftoff press conference that we were all together in one place at one time.

(Schedules had been planned and implemented to allow the maximum productivity of every second of the wake cycle and as a result most folks simply got up and did what they had to do. Fraternization was held to a minimum, and little slack was allowed in any of the data cruncher's schedules. The fact that the almighty schedule was being interrupted for a meeting more than gave credence to the importance of the matter to be discussed.)

Captain John J. Grubbin, chief data cruncher and mission overseer, had a troubled look on his face, and as soon as the tabulo sensors indicated all present, he clapped his hands together for attention and began the meeting.

"As you recall," he began, "our mission goal was clear and specific—confirm all available data on the planets in our solar system. One last double-check of the math before we close the book and devote our studies to other matters at hand."

He steepled his fingers. "Everything has been carefully planned to allow us the maximum amount of time to complete this mission, with just enough of a margin of supplies and assets to assure our safe accomplishment of that task and our safe return back home. No more. No less. As scientists, we understood our task at hand and the responsibilities it entailed, or at least we thought we did at the time."

"At the time?" someone whispered.

"As you know, as captain and mission overseer, my wake cycle begins forty-eight hours earlier than the rest of the crew so that the systems at hand can brief me on any situations that might be coming up and that might necessarily influence the mission goals for the upcoming wake cycle. And I can learn of any other pertinent matters deemed noteworthy by the AI."

The AI, I thought. The real mission overseer.

"As a result, I have learned of situation that can directly influence the successful completion of our mission."

Grubbin took a breath and hit a button on the holo-control, which triggered a three-dimensional model of the solar system to be projected over our heads.

"Our mission was to confirm the data at hand, to double-check our work . . . but that only works if we knew in advance everything that we were going to have to check. Unfortunately, we didn't."

I raised an eyebrow.

"Many of you have heard of the myth of Planet X. Well, it seems it isn't a myth."

*　　*　　*

As a result of the problematic revelation, the current wake cycle was extended for an additional three days to allow time to study and evaluate possible solutions to the proverbial matters at hand.

As always, my routine was more or less oblivious to the situation . . . though it did free up more time for Santiago and Jensen to "pal around" with me.

"So, there's a planet beyond Pluto," I baited. "How did you science types miss it?"

"Well," Jensen replied in his academically relaxed manner that was more akin to a PBS panel than an informal conversation. "Really only every other generation has missed it. The debates on the existence of Planet X began roughly around the time that we concluded that there was no Planet Vulcan."

"Planet Vulcan?"

Santiago jumped in quickly while trying not to interrupt Jensen's scholastic momentum. "Vulcan was a planet believed to exist between Sol and Mercury, but that theory was discounted back in 1915."

". . . and confirmed by the findings of our very own

mission," Jensen joined in, once again picking up where he had left off. "But Planet X as a theory has fallen in and out of acceptance pretty much every other generation. Depending on who was doing the theorizing, the existence of a planet beyond Pluto was always considered either theoretically possible or impossible."

Not satisfied with the scientific perspective smoke screen, I concluded bluntly, ". . . and you guys, and by 'you guys' I mean your generation of data crunchers and scientists, got it wrong."

"Correct," Jensen said, without a trace of acceptance of blame or guilt.

"But at least we can update the data at hand," Santiago offered.

"How so?" I had to admit I was curious.

"Since the safety parameters of the mission would be jeopardized by extending our route to include Planet X, the captain is talking about launching a long-range probe—the type that initially gathered the data before our mission—to transmit pertinent data back to us during our next wake cycle. Of course, it's not as good as being there, but since this is man's last space mission, the matter is moot anyway. Unfortunately, your 'Grand Tour,' will be that much poorer. To my knowledge, long-range probes aren't set to pick up poetic inspiration."

"Or satisfaction of scientific curiosity either," I parried. "Doesn't it seem a shame that it has to end this way? I always thought that scientists were always ready to explore strange new worlds, seek out . . ."

". . . yadda, yadda, yadda . . ." Grubbin interjected. I hadn't heard him walk over. "Nope. That only applied to Canadian TV actors. Most of us just want to work with the right numbers and prefer to do it from our own homes. At this stage in mankind's development, there are a lot more pragmatic things for us to be curious about. Another planet geographically undesirable. It just doesn't make the cut."

*   *   *

It really bothered me.

It was bad enough that I was a poet without passion . . . but scientists without the conviction of their curiosity?

And, worse off, it was my job to politically correctly commemorate this great moment of Earth's greatest minds putting their heads in the sand for possibly all eternity in deference to more pressing and pragmatic matters at hand.

*   *   *

The captain furrowed his brow.

"Now, let me get this straight—you want to accompany the probe to Planet X?"

I nodded. "And beyond, sir," I affirmed. "As mission poet, it is the only way I can fulfill the complete obligation of my part of the mission."

"But it would be a one-way trip," he countered. There was quiver in his voice. "There is no way we can bring you back."

"But the poem would be complete, and my obligation to the mission and indeed to the state . . . nay, to the people of Earth would be met. My words could be transmitted back to Earth with the data from your probe."

"You would give your life for the sake of a stanza?"

I smiled. "If that's the way you want to phrase it, sir. The answer is yes."

He shook my hand and assured me that he would make it so, laced his remarks with numerous platitudes that he probably didn't believe nor did I deserve.

I was okayed for a one-way trip to Planet X and beyond . . . but not for the reason I gave.

*   *   *

There was no time for any festivities or bon voyage affairs. The probe was refitted into a lifeboat shuttle that was reprogrammed outbound to intersect with the orbit of Planet X in the manner that we had done with what are now referred to as the Known Nine.

In recognition of my needs as a poet, as well as a human being, life support was configured to allow me at least seventy-two hours more than I would need, with a gradual decrease in oxygen content that would make my passing as minimally unpleasant as possible.

My last official action would be to data dump the probe's findings and my poetic creation into a single bit transmission that would be forwarded back to the *P. Ffogg*, and simultaneously back to Earth.

The launch was successful, and I was on my way.

*   *   *

Poets and scientists are supposed to be mankind's big thinkers.

Scientists are supposed to discover new questions to be answered, while poets are supposed to raise questions that can never be answered.

That is why I disabled the probe's data findings once I had read them. Nonthermal radiation readings, atmospheric constituency, rotation periods, mass, gravity, and density data could never paint the whole picture of what Planet X really was.

Planet X was an invitation, a harbinger that maybe man's mission to space shouldn't come to an end.

It inspired me.

P. Ffogg's mission was a failure. Their data was incomplete. They would have to settle for their nine known planets or try again.

And what about the last stanza of the Grand Tour?

I've just sent that as the transmission:

There once was a P. Ffogg poet
Whose mission was to lyrically show it
Of Planet X there were readings
Data, facts, intellectual seedings
But you'll have to come out here to know it.

True, it's not great poetry, but then again the education I received from my student loans wasn't so hot either.

Maybe man's exploration of space isn't worth the bother.

But making sure that he doesn't delude himself with a false sense of security on all the facts available to him was.

See you in infinity.

Newton Stradivarius,

Signing off.

LEAST OF MY BRETHREN

by Michael A. Stackpole

Michael A. Stackpole is a writer/game designer whose writing career started at six years old when his mother submitted a poem he'd written to a magazine. The first piece of mail Mike ever had addressed to him, then, was a rejection slip. He's spent the rest of his life trying to prove the publishing industry was wrong about him. This story is the third one in his Purgatory Station *universe, and was written while he was still working on* Fortress Draconis, *a fantasy novel and sequel to* The Dark Glory War.

FATHER Dennis Flynn glanced away from the spacescape projected on the walls of the system-ship's saloon and over at his traveling companion. "Say that again, please, Meresin. I'm not sure I'm believing what I heard you say."

The Mephist priest, with black thornlike horns stabbing up from his skull through long black hair, smiled carefully, exposing black teeth. "I *did* enjoy touring Terra's cathedrals, my friend." Meresin's tall slender form, aided and abetted by his scarlet flesh, bright red eyes, and sharply handsome features, did make him appear quite diabolical—though the gaily-colored tropical shirt did weaken the image a little. The humanoid alien looked as Satan might, were he beachcombing Oahu.

Flynn sipped some Scotch and held it in his mouth,

letting the vapors work up into his sinuses, then swallowed. "I was under the impression, my friend, that Mephist dogma portrayed our cathedrals as monuments to heresy."

"Oh, it does, but dogma is composed by scholars who have an investment in solidifying tradition and defending it against all assaults." The Unvorite hooked a black talon over the edge of the small bowl of peanuts on the table between them and dragged it toward him. "Our dogma is very clear. Before there was any light, there was the Void. One emerges from the Void to experience the chaos of life, then, upon death, returns to the Void to enjoy its complete peace. Your faith, which preaches resurrection, denies the reality of the Universe, so, of course, you are heretics and evil."

"But you enjoyed our cathedrals?"

Meresin popped a peanut into his mouth and crunched it with enthusiasm. "Perhaps not as much as these legumes. Are you sure we can get them shipped out to Purgatory Station?"

The white-haired priest nodded. "They'll be expensive."

"Life's pleasures often are." The Unvorite sipped some of his Scotch. "While the dogmatists of my faith would look at your cathedrals as stone paeans to a false god—seeking to placate him so he would offer the people resurrection—I saw something different. Mephisti preaches pleasure above all, and in the hard work and artistry in your cathedrals, I could see the sheer joy, even ecstasy, workers must have felt. Watching people come to worship, I saw the reverential awe the buildings inspire. They are beautiful, and no dogmatic squabble can take that away. So, I enjoyed them, yes."

Flynn smiled and snagged a small handful of peanuts. "Well, I'm thinking it was good you had something to enjoy. I should have been better company."

The Mephist priest shrugged. "You traveled thousands of light-years to visit a sick friend. You could not have known she would die after your arrival. You must bear in mind that this Agnes Kelloch got to see you before

296 Michael A. Stackpole

she died. That made her happy. And, though a funeral is not a pleasant experience, the solemnity of it is what opened me to the insights I gleaned when traveling."

"I'm glad of that, but you give me too much credit." Flynn sighed. "She was fair far gone when I arrived. I don't think she recognized me."

"The nun at the convalescent home said Mrs. Kelloch mistook you for her son."

"She did. He died a long time ago."

"You knew him?"

"Yes, and her. Grew up in Dublin together, got into trouble. I learned from it and became a priest. He didn't and died. We'd lost touch, but the Catholic grapevine let me know she was dying."

The Mephist nodded. "You got here in time to see her and even give her the Last Rites. Your eulogy was beautiful. I praise the Void knowing she and her son are now united once again."

"I'm sure they will be—unlike you Mephists, we wait for the return of our Lord before we go to heaven and are reunited with loved ones." Flynn gave him a wink. "Of course, you'll be saying that's just our denial of reality, but we cling to it."

Before Meresin could reply, a ship's steward appeared at the cleric's table. "Father Flynn, the captain sends her regards and would like you to meet her in the communications center. Mephist-ka Meresin, I was to relay the same message to you."

The two priests rose and followed the steward through the ship. While the Qian had given Terrans the secret of hyperspace drives when it accepted them into the Commonwealth, system-ships like the *TSS Achilles* took care of all transport within the solar system. Multiple pods were joined to a drive core, allowing the ship to change its configuration from luxury liner to packet-boat as load factors required. The traffic to the spaceport at the end of the solar system could be heavy at times, but since Terra was not a full member of the Commonwealth, ships with interstellar drive components were restricted to the area outside Pluto's orbit.

Their journey took them in toward the *Achilles'* central core, through layers of pods that had been grafted together. They reached the communications center quickly and met the ship's captain there. An older woman, with steel-gray hair pulled back into a bun, she nodded to Flynn and acknowledged Meresin with a flick of her brown eyes. At the open throat of her maroon service tunic Flynn caught the glint of a gold cross, which explained her not letting her eyes linger too long on the Unvorite.

"Thank you for coming." Captain Geary pointed to a viewscreen on a console. It displayed a young woman with auburn hair and blue eyes, looking somewhat impatient. She wore a white wimple identical to the ones worn by the nuns at the home where Mrs. Kelloch had been cared for. "This is Sister Ellen LaSalle. She runs the infirmary on one of the small asteroids out here in the Belt. There's been a mine accident and they need a priest. She wanted us to relay a message back to Terra— their communications array is temporarily blocked by the asteroid Patrocius. Her message is already going, but will take over thirty-seven minutes to get the transmission to Earth and at least that long for a message back."

Flynn nodded. "And it's taken us a week to get here, so they couldn't have a priest out here for at least a week."

The captain nodded. "I can let a lifeboat shuttle you down there. The *Horatio* is three days behind us in the circuit. Every three days or so you can pick up a ship heading back out to the star-station, if you want to go help them out."

Flynn's head came up. "You thought there would be a question of my going? You could have told me all this by relay in the lifeboat. Of course I will go."

Meresin nodded. "I will join you."

Geary frowned. "The mines are Catholic, Mephist-ka."

The Unvorite smiled. "But Catholics have no monopoly on compassion, Captain. I would support my friend and offer help where I could."

The Catholic priest looked at the nun on the screen.

Anxiety flooded her expression. "Tell Sister Ellen we're on our way."

*   *   *

The only detour the clerics made on their way to a lifeboat was to their cabins. Flynn grabbed the supplies he'd need for anointing the sick, as well as the things he'd need for saying Mass and offering Communion. He thrust them into a bag, included his toiletries kit and some clean underclothes. When he met Meresin in the passageway, he found the Unvorite clutching a bag roughly the size of his own.

Meresin had also changed out of his flashy shirt, and into a black one that complimented his dark slacks. "I felt this would be more appropriate."

Flynn nodded. "If there's been an accident, it could be very messy."

"Well, blood wouldn't have been noticed on the other shirt." Meresin smiled. "Dark is more soothing, and that is what we will need to be. You realize, of course, I will attempt no conversions nor intrude on what you are doing."

"You didn't need to be saying that, my friend, but thank you." Flynn clapped him on the shoulder as the Unvorite ducked his head through the lifeboat hatchway. The Catholic priest joined him and strapped into the small, cylindrical ship. They brought the control systems up, and Captain Geary's face appeared on the main screen. "We're ready, Captain."

"Good. Course downloading now. Docking codes and piloting sequences have been squirted to M4311. Sister LaSalle and Dick Heller, the facility manager, will meet you at the docking station. Good luck, God speed, and bless you, Father."

"Thank you, Captain. God grant you a smooth flight."

A little jolt shook the lifeboat as it blasted away from the *Achilles.* Acceleration pressed Flynn back into his seat before the inertial compensators came online. Meresin had a good hold on the arms of his chair and his fleshtone had grayed a little.

The tiny lifeboat moved through the asteroids and debris with a high degree of maneuverability. As they entered the Asteroid Belt, the *Achilles* sent them some data packets, but interference ruined the transmission of several. What they did get was a briefing on the nature of M4311, which was a metallic asteroid roughly seven kilometers in diameter.

A series of companies had owned it, the latest being Alloy Metals LTD. Many of the crew on the asteroid had actually been there through multiple ownership changes. The basic facility had been built a quarter century earlier by the first owner that had actually sent personnel to the rock. The next owner decided to work with muscle power alone, and the next brought machines in. The remaining crew had survived downsizing and, it appeared to Flynn, as if the operation's profit margin had likewise been downsized.

Flynn smiled as the lifeboat swooped down between two asteroids. "Bit more fun, flying this way, than lumbering along in that behemoth, I'm thinking."

"I can understand your thrilling at this sort of a ride, though I must admit I miss the amenities offered back on the *Achilles*." The Unvorite had opened a small metal storage unit built beneath his seat and pulled out a packet of supplies. "Food pastes and pills to flavor water? These might allow people to survive, but they would also rob them of the will to live."

"Sooner into the Void, then."

"Subsist on this for long and the Void might spit you back out."

Flynn raised an eyebrow. "The Void might give someone another shot at life? Heresy, Meresin?"

The Mephist priest sighed. "Apocrypha, the existence of which afflicts Christianity, too. Legends tell of creatures so evil that the Void refused to shrive them of their life experience. They exist much as do your ghosts, to perpetuate their evil."

"Odd how goodness often dies with the person who performed it, but evil has a way of lingering." The Catholic priest suppressed a shudder, then nodded to the forward screens. "There it is."

The ship shook as the station's tractor beams reached out and caught it, drawing it into the illuminated cavern near the middle. M4311 had an oval shape to it, though the narrow end had been gouged deeply by a glancing contact with another asteroid. To Flynn it looked a lot like a potato that a rabbit had nibbled.

The lifeboat landed with only a minor bump. Flynn and Meresin freed themselves of their restraining straps before the air lock had fastened onto the side of the ship. While the Unvorite worked the hatch open, Flynn pulled his liturgical stole from his bag and stowed it in his pocket. He also pulled out a small jar containing blessed olive oil. The oil of the sick was vital for offering anyone Last Rites.

Meresin exited first. A dockworker took their bags and pointed them at the two people waiting for them. Sister Ellen LaSalle surprised Flynn only in that she looked smaller than he'd anticipated. The petite woman wore a white jumpsuit which, while hardly a nun's habit, seemed quite practical for her job in the infirmary. Her blue eyes brightened as Flynn stepped out of the Unvorite's shadow.

The man beside her stood a bit taller than Meresin, and had the white pallor of someone who had not been kissed by the sun's rays in a long while. Bald, save for a fringe of white hair, and slender to the point of being gawky, the man wore a sour expression spiced with serious disgust. Flynn wondered briefly if the man were a neo-Puritan who had taken to working on such a distant station as a way to free himself from temptation.

"Father Flynn, I'm Dick Heller, station manager and work foreman. This is Sister LaSalle, our medical practitioner."

Taking Heller's proffered hand, Flynn found the man's grip to be firm, and his palm dry, but that did little to dispel the sense of unease just looking at the man caused. "Pleased to meet you. This is Mephist-ka Meresin. He's a friend, not a zealot, and is here to help however he can."

Meresin pressed his hands together at his waist and bowed a greeting. "Some of my training does include the medical arts, though xenobiology is not a specialty."

His latter comment surprised Flynn. He'd known Meresin for years and had come to think of him as very human. *Sapient, not human.* The priest knew very well that they were entirely different under the skin, but he still felt a kinship with his friend. That kinship seemed to outweigh biological and theological differences.

Sister Ellen shook Flynn's hand. "The *Achilles'* captain said she sent you a briefing of our situation here."

"We reviewed some files on the way in. I'm thinking we know what we're up against." Flynn nodded. "The infirmary is where we start, yes?"

"This way, yes."

The quartet moved through the station quickly. The few people they saw—mostly humans, but a few aliens included—sprang out of their way. A couple crossed themselves as Flynn moved past, and one gasped when the Mephist came into view. A conveyor provided them with hand- and footholds, then lifted them up two levels to where the infirmary had been built. They passed through a pair of automatic doors and into the empty waiting area.

Large rectangular windows with rounded corners gave them clear views of both the empty lab off to the left and, straight away, the ward. Only two patients occupied beds, leaving six others open. One, a grizzled man hitched up to a couple of IV tubes, rested comfortably. Flynn did notice that his right leg appeared to end below the knee, at least judging by the lumps beneath the sheets.

Dick Heller tapped the glass. "That's Jake Blanchard. When shaft 38 collapsed, he lost his leg."

Meresin frowned. "And the other man?"

Heller hissed. "Do we all look the same to you?"

The Unvorite lifted a dark eyebrow. "I beg your pardon."

"That's not a man, it's a deman." Pure contempt poured through Heller's voice. "It's a waste of resources."

Flynn took out his liturgical stole, kissed it at the center, then looped the purple strip of cloth over his shoulders. He entered the ward and did his best not to be distracted by the sound of the respirator keeping the deman alive. He approached Blanchard's bed and smiled carefully.

"Mr. Blanchard?"

The miner's eyes popped open. "Good, Father, you've come. Thank God." Blanchard quickly crossed himself and pressed his hands together in an attitude of prayer. "I've been praying you'd get here in time."

Flynn frowned. "If you don't mind me saying so, Mr. Blanchard, you seem very alert and in better shape than I would have thought. I can perform for you the Sacrament of Extreme Unction, if you wish, but I'm not thinking you need it."

The man shook his head. "No, Father, it's not the Last Rites I want for me." He jerked his thumb at the deman two beds over. "For Chris, you have to do it for Chris."

The priest's jaw dropped open for a moment, then he snapped it shut. "Mr. Blanchard, Chris is a deman. I can't . . ."

"You have to, Father. Chris is going to die." The miner grabbed his wrist in an iron grip. "You have to give him Last Rites. He's one of us."

"One of us?"

"Yes, Father." Blanchard's brown eyes blazed. "When we were down there, in that hole, I baptized him. I did all *I* could for him, now he needs you to do the rest."

*   *   *

Flynn emerged from the ward ashen-faced. "He wants me to give Chris the Last Rites."

Sister Ellen looked closely at him as the door to the ward closed behind him. "That was in the briefing we sent along. That was the core of the message the *Achilles* sent to Terra for us. I thought you knew that and came here to explain to Jake why the deman couldn't be given Last Rites."

"No, no, we didn't know. Not all of the files the *Achilles* tried to send us got through. I thought, because of the accident, someone needed the sacrament." Flynn rubbed a hand against his forehead. "Sister, you tried to explain it to him, yes?"

She sighed. "Yes, and Jake just smiled at me. He said, 'Sister, you're fine at doctoring, but this is theology we're talking about, so I'd not be expecting you to know it. I baptized Chris, used water, said the words, so it's done. He needs a priest, and there's no shutting that machine off until he's been sent off proper.' "

"No chance he will recover?"

Heller snapped an answer to Flynn's question. "None. He's a waste of resources, Father. You need to go in there and tell Blanchard there's nothing you can do, then we shut things down."

Meresin raised an eyebrow. "A waste of resources?"

The company man nodded. "We're a small mining station. All we do is make rocks. We can keep ourselves in oxygen, and generate our own electricity, but beyond that things are shipped in. We have enough to feed the two of you while you're here, but I've already sent a request for more supplies to cover what you will use up. Chances are we'll get it from Mars, but maybe it won't come for a week or more from Terra."

Flynn frowned. "Can't you get food from Io or some other place closer?"

Sister Ellen shivered. "Trust me, better to go hungry tan to eat what those folks think of as food."

The priest nodded, then looked up at Heller. "With all due respect, Mr. Heller, I'll not be eating while considering what to do, so I'll not be a resource drain."

"What is to consider, Father?" Heller jabbed a finger toward the ward. "Chris is a deman. The thing was a relic from an early crew here. Blanchard adopted it as a pet, and it kept morale up, so we kept it on. That's all it was, though, a pet. It's all but dead, and would be were that machine not breathing for it."

The nun nodded in agreement. "Chris suffered a blow on the head, crushed a portion of his skull. He kept going for a little while, but by the time Blanchard baptized him, he was dead."

"*It* was dead, Sister, *it*." Heller snorted angrily. "It was a foul-mouthed beast that parroted every curse the miners taught it."

Meresin held a finger up. "Please, clear up my confusion. I take it from the way you pronounce the word, 'deman' is not the same as 'demon.' "

"It might as well have been a demon." Heller's brown eyes narrowed. "Whenever I saw it, it would grimace and snap and snarl and tear off a string of invective. Never made any sense, but the men howled. It would have fits."

Flynn ignored Heller's outburst. "Deman is shorthand for demi-human. When the Qian invited Terra to become a Commonwealth ward-world, we only had two things to export: cultural exotica and creatures, including humans. The influx of Qian technology also started a research renaissance on Terra. Someone got the idea that crossbreeding humans and their nearest, great ape cousins would produce a creature of limited intelligence and great strength that would be very useful.

"It had be known, for over two centuries, that such a hybrid was possible. Tales had persisted of experiments in the old Asian Communist Hegemony. I'm thinking that was likely propaganda. After the Qian arrived, it became reality and demi-humans were created."

The Mephist nodded solemnly. "And the churches declared them to be animals?"

Flynn shook his head. "Would be convenient if that were true. Animal Rightists coopted demi-humans and declared them to be animals. They pushed the idea that something that was so like us should have had all the rights we did. They thought the logic of inalienable rights for *all* nonhuman creatures would follow."

Heller sneered. "It was a stupid idea."

Flynn ran a hand over his jaw. "What they got was a backlash, since it made folks think that maybe the Qian would view humans as cute animals. Humans hated that idea, so the production of demans was outlawed. The surviving stock of frozen embryos was destroyed or moved to the colony worlds. Some companies produced them to staff hazardous operations like this place. That's how Chris came to be here, isn't it, Mr. Heller?"

"We inherited it, yes. It's the last one here." The station manager folded his arms across his chest. "I wanted to be rid of it long before this, but Blanchard insisted it remain. I will say that Chris was strong, but since most of the heavy work was done by machines, it was an anachronism."

The Mephist priest half-closed his fiery eyes. "And in your theology, an animal is barred from funerary rites."

Flynn nodded, then glanced at the creature lying in the hospital bed. "The church never said whether or not demen were human. I don't know how to proceed."

Heller let a look of disgust pour over his face. "Come now, Father, it's clear the thing is a beast."

Flynn's head came back around. "How would you be determining that, Mr. Heller? On genetics? Half the DNA in Chris is human, half isn't. And if he's not human, what would be the outcome of his mating with a human? Would the resulting offspring be human, since they would be seventy-five percent human—all the while bearing in mind that the difference in the DNA that separated the chimp and the human that created Chris is infinitesimally small?"

"No, not human, not human at all." The gaunt man shook his head. "It's got to be genetically human, one hundred percent."

"Does it?" Flynn's blue eyes tightened. "You know, Mr. Heller, there were once children who had a genetic problem known as Down's Syndrome. They had too much human DNA. They had the minds of children as their bodies grew into those of adults. We could baptize them."

"That's different, Father, they could function as human beings."

"So they could, Mr. Heller, and were treated as human beings by the Church. On the other hand, a microcephalic child, or a child born with some other spontaneous mutation that would stop it from functioning any way as a human, is someone I can baptize. It is even my calling, mandated by the Church, to baptize an aborted child, even if it shows no signs of life. Few would recognize them as human, but the Church does."

"Well, Father, there would be no recognizing that thing as human if you'd seen it cursing and carrying on."

Flynn said nothing, but felt like cursing at Heller himself.

A video screen built into the wall of the receiving area flicked to life. A tech in a headset appeared there. "Mr. Heller, we have the reply to the messages sent to Earth."

"Play it."

"Begging your pardon, sir, but the message is for Father Flynn."

Flynn looked at the administrator. "Do you have a facility where I can take the message?"

Heller nodded sourly. "Sister, they'll be in 3-47."

Sister Ellen nodded. "Follow me."

Heller grabbed Flynn's arm as the priest moved past. "Mark my words, Father, we're going to be turning off life support on that thing no matter what you decide."

"I understand that, Mr. Heller." Flynn's voice got very cold. "Your resources are balanced against his possible salvation. I understand very clearly indeed."

* * *

Sister Ellen conduct them past what served the station as a chapel and down a low corridor. She stopped at a hatchway numbered 3-47, which opened when she punched the room number into the keypad. The hatch revealed a room small enough to cause a claustrophobic to twitch, but it seemed large in comparison to the cabin Flynn occupied on the *Achilles*. The chamber had been roughly hacked out of solid stone, but a coat of beige paint over gray rock stopped it from being depressingly dark.

Meresin pirouetted in the center of the room, taking it all in, then sat on the edge of the bunk onto which had been set his bag. "I've been in worse places."

The nun stepped over to the small communications unit built into a cabinet. She flicked it on and punched up the communications center. The tech appeared on the screen. "Stand by, Phillips."

She turned to Flynn. "Do you want us to leave?"

The priest shook his head. "Put the message through, Mr. Phillips."

The tech's image dissolved mid-nod, to be replaced by the coat of arms of the Cardinal for the immediate, extra-Terran Dioceses. When the Cardinal appeared, the image surprised Flynn. He'd expected to see a doughy-faced older woman, but dimly remembered that Cardinal Margaret Kendall had been replaced. *Have I been away from Terra that long?*

The new Cardinal had a dark-eyed gaze only slightly sharper than his features. "Greetings, Father Flynn. May the Peace of Christ be with you. I am Arnold Winters."

Flynn felt a chill run down his spine. Even out at Purgatory Station, at the far edge of the Qian Commonwealth, Flynn had heard of the ambitious cleric. He had joined the College of Cardinals fairly young, and had performed services for the Pope that resulted in his present office. His influence, and his ideas especially regarding the relationship between the Church and native non-human religions, was filtering slowly throughout the Qian Commonwealth.

"I deeply regret that the distance from the Mother Church precludes a dialogue on this most troubling of subjects. Fortunately for us, the Church's teaching in this area is very clear. Genesis 2:7 tells us that only man was created in God's image. Only man has a soul. And as Genesis further elaborates, only man knew a fall from grace. Jesus Christ came to redeem mankind. Animals were saved from the fall, which is their blessing. Their curse is that they have no souls, so redemption is not for them.

"You, Father Flynn, have had contact with many alien species. Please do not let that cloud your vision here. They are sentient and sapient. This deman was, at best, sequacious. You cannot grant it the sacrament of Extreme Unction."

The small man's face composed itself in a mask of contemplative peace. "I expect to hear back from you within two hours of this message's receipt. I await your report of the situation's resolution with interest. Thank you for attending to this so quickly, Father. What you do here shall not be forgotten."

The screen went blank, leaving Flynn staring at a dark, distorted reflection of himself. He shivered again, then shook his head. "I've been given my orders."

Sister Ellen nodded slowly and rested a hand on his left shoulder. "That's not the message I had hoped we'd get back from Earth. I'd sent the message to the diocesan office for the outer planets, but Bishop Angleton hasn't much of a spine. I'm not surprised he kicked the decision up to the Cardinal."

"You did what you thought best, Sister." Flynn brought his right hand over and patted her fingers.

"I know Blanchard. If you want, I can tell him what the Cardinal said."

Flynn shook his head. "No, not your burden to bear. If you wish, you can go tell him that we've heard from Terra regarding Chris. I'll deliver the message. I just need some time to pray on it, to figure out how to tell him."

"I'll do that. I'll be in the infirmary if I can help at all." She gave him a quick smile. "God be with you, Father."

"Thank you." Flynn took a deep breath, then slowly exhaled as she left. When the door closed behind her, he shook his head violently. "I heard those words. I understand the thinking. I just don't think it is right."

Meresin smiled. "That's because it isn't."

"No?"

The Mephist shook his head. "As we are taught, all life comes from the Void and returns to it. Does water change to wine just by being transferred from one vessel to another?"

"There is a difference, my friend, between man and animal."

"Semantics, Flynn. I know your Bible. Your God breathed life into man, that is how it reads. It's the same life as in the beasts. You see, this is the problem with your religion. You seek to separate yourselves from the beasts because you try so hard to separate yourself from what you see as bestial. Normal, biological urgings like lust or gluttony are seen as evil because these are things you so want to give into. A beast in rut is not sinful. A scavenger glutting himself on a carcass is not evil, so why would you be?"

Flynn smiled, appreciating Mersesin's baiting tone. "There is the difference. Being as how I'm a conscious thinking creature—a consciousness that I get by virtue of having a soul—I get to choose what it is I do. Sinful actions distance me from God. Virtuous actions, they bring me closer to God. An animal, through training, or instinct, or a desire to please a master, may ape good social behavior. We might label what they do as good, or as loving, and it sure feels like that, but they're not making a conscious choice to move toward God."

The Catholic priest thrust a finger at the darkened communications screen. "And I'm not saying I'm liking the idea that animals are barred from heaven. When I was growing up, we had dogs. I loved them something fierce, and they loved me. A loving God wouldn't keep them out of heaven, but His Church will tell me they're barred from salvation. So is Chris."

Meresin frowned. "You make it all too complicated, Flynn. With us it is simple. Life is life. We would accept him regardless, animal or human."

"Perhaps it's time for me to convert."

The Unvorite laughed once, sharply. "You never would, Flynn."

"You're right, I wouldn't." Flynn sighed. "Dogmatists, like the Cardinal, as you noted earlier, need to protect tradition. You know, God being infinite and unknowable, makes Him incomprehensible. Dogmatists, they attempt to define paths to Him, so He's not so scary."

"But there is the paradox, is it not, Flynn?" Meresin gave him a wry smile. "You and I are rational individuals, yet we have *faith*. Faith is belief despite the total absence of proof. It is not reasonable in any way. Dogmatists attempt to create a logic of rules, so dogma is almost antithetical to faith."

"Except where dogma serves to warn the unknowing or unthinking away from heresies that will carry them further from God." Flynn shook his head. "So the difficulty I face is that a man's interpretation of what God wants is running nose up into my sense of what God would prefer. Still, if Chris were a dog, I'd see the logic in what Cardinal Winters says. A deman, though . . ."

The priest scrubbed his hands over his face, then looked at his friend. "Out there, on Purgatory Station, I've given the Last Rites to creatures that were so alien that I couldn't breathe what they breathed and my flesh would burn if I touched them. And yet, here, a creature whose blood could run in my veins, whose heart could beat in my chest, that creature is one I can't be offering the solace of the sacraments. It doesn't feel right."

Meresin rose from his bunk and gave Flynn a solemn nod. "Trust yourself, my friend. I know you need time to think about this. You need to determine what you will do, and to figure out how to tell Blanchard what it is the Church teaches on this subject. I shall go and talk to Sister Ellen. Despite what Blanchard said, I'm sure her insights into this situation will prove interesting."

"Thanks, Meresin." Flynn gave the Unvorite a wan smile. "If either of you can spare some prayers, I'd appreciate the help."

Flynn wandered to the station's chapel, but found it a place of little solace. Some giant machine had bored it out of solid rock and, for a moment, it looked as if it would have been a suitable substitute for the Holy Sepulcher. Flynn found, however, that such an image was far from granting him strength. The chamber would have as easily housed Chris as it would have a body of human proportions.

Flynn didn't let himself flirt with seductive heresies. While Meresin's statement that a vintage didn't change because of the vessel it had been poured into was inviting, Church teachings were clear. The soul was not separate from the body, but a vital part of it, a part that could live forever. It was an inborn aspect of being human. If Chris had it, he was human; if he didn't . . . *And the Cardinal was clear. He did not.*

The priest knew he had two deadlines. The first he prayed through, not sending a report out on time. When his report failed to reach the Cardinal, the clock would start on the other deadline. Thirty-seven minutes after the Cardinal decided to give up waiting, very specific orders would come to Flynn from Earth. The Cardinal had spoken, and would speak again. For Flynn to defy him would result in dire consequences, up to and including excommunication.

With not much time left on his second deadline, and with all his prayer having failed to bridge the gap between dogma and his sense of what felt right, Flynn made his way to the infirmary. He held a hand up to forestall any comments by Meresin or Sister Ellen, both of whom waited in the small lab.

Flynn walked over to Blanchard and smiled. "How are you doing, Mr. Blanchard?"

"Call me Jake, Father." The miner's eyes softened. "I'm doing better now that you're here. Aren't I?"

"Jake, Sister Ellen told you that the Cardinal sent a message. A message concerning Chris."

"Good, Father, good, because that rat bastard Heller is going to shut the machines off." Blanchard looked over at the deman and sighed slowly. "I'm not an idiot, Father. I know he's dying, that the machines is what is keeping him alive. I knew it then, down in the hole, which is why I baptized him. Used some water, said the words. I ain't been a good Church-goer, Father, I know that, but the words, they'd take, right?"

"Jake . . ."

"Father, they have to take." Tears began to well in the miner's brown eyes, and trickled out through the crow's feet at the corners. "When we was down there and things busted loose, bang, I was down hard and fast. Didn't know what hit me, you know. Big support beam was down, part of it had whipped across my leg severing it clean. Just pulverized everything, including arteries or I'da bled to death.

"Everyone was yelling and running, getting out, like you're supposed to do, Father. Them's the rules. Get out, see who is where, get the equipment, come back to save folks. They was all running. All of them, save Chris. He was standing there, Father, I could see the dent in his skull, blood running down his face. I yelled at him, I did . . . I told him to run. Yelled at him to run, and he started too, Father, started to run."

Blanchard slapped his hands over his eyes, smearing tears on his cheeks. "Then he stopped, Father, he stopped clean and came back for me. He knew it would cost him, Father, I could see it in his eyes. But he bent that piece of metal back—he was always powerful strong, Chris was, Father, he was. And he took hold of me and dragged me out of there. He got me to safety. He smiled, then his eyes, they just rolled up in his head and he went down. And that was why, Father, I had to say the words over him, baptize him like my momma said we could when I was a kid. I had to do it and I did, for what he did, Father. I had to."

Flynn nodded solemnly. "Yes, Jake, I understand."

"So you see why you got to do the other for him, the Last Rites."

The priest laid his left hand on the man's forehead. "I see what I have to do, yes."

Flynn turned from Blanchard and walked over to the deman's bed. The creature had never attained full human height, and Flynn reflected that the small chamber he'd been given as a home would have perfectly suited the deman. Chris's legs were of shorter proportions than a man's, his arms longer, and his body a bit broader through the chest.

The priest studied his face, from shallow brow and big ears, to a long nose that ended above a slightly jutting muzzle. He wished the deman's eyes were open, just so he could get a chance to see in them what Blanchard had seen. He took one of the creature's hands in his and felt how easily they meshed, how warm his skin was, and how rough and leathery years of hard work had made his palm.

"I don't know, Chris, what you thought you were, or if that ever concerned you, but I think I know what you were. 'Greater love hath no man than this, that a man lay down his life for his friends.' " Flynn smiled slowly. "Jake says you knew the risk and did what you had to do. Well, I know the risk I'm taking."

Before Flynn could settle his stole around his neck, Sister Ellen entered the ward. "Father, there's a message from the Cardinal."

"I don't care."

"I think you should listen to it."

"No, Sister." Flynn's nostrils flared. "The Cardinal would not dream of interrupting a priest administering a sacrament. I'm not thinking you want to be doing that either. Now you can stay here and pray, or get out, but I'm giving Chris here the Last Rites."

The nun joined Flynn at the bedside and prayed wordlessly as he anointed the deman and intoned the ritual words. "Through this holy anointing and His most loving mercy, may the Lord assist you by the grace of the Holy Spirit so that, when you have been freed from your sins, He may save you and in His goodness raise you up."

Flynn closed his eyes, and offered a silent prayer for Chris's salvation, then opened them again and nodded to Sister Ellen. "Well, shall we see what trouble I've caused?"

He preceded her from the ward and found Meresin

standing beside by the communications monitor. Flynn nodded to him, then looked at the screen. "Mr. Phillips, was it? Let's have the message."

Cardinal Winters appeared centered in the screen. The impassive mask he had worn previously seemed a bit frayed, but Flynn only got that from his eyes—otherwise the man looked perfect. His voice, however, contained a trace of strain that matched the flickerings of his eyes.

"Father Flynn, in light of the supplementary evidence supplied by the medical staff at M4311, you are authorized to provide the Sacrament of Extreme Unction to the patient. I will pray for you and for him, and especially pray that you are more diligent in your service to our Lord that you were in communicating with me."

Flynn blinked as the screen blanked. "Did he say . . . ?"

Meresin smiled broadly. "He did, indeed. Sister Ellen and I took the opportunity to communicate with the Cardinal on your behalf, providing some more information about the situation."

The nun nodded. "It was Meresin's idea, really. He asked about Chris' outbursts of profanity. He noted that when the Mephisti had first come in contact with humans, there was an affliction among humans that they had mistaken for ritualistic behavior among some Mephisti sects. He had me look up and test Chris' DNA for the markers for the disease, and we found it."

"What disease is that?"

"Tourette's Syndrome. It's characterized by facial ticks, twitching, and spontaneous outbursts of profanity, especially at times of stress." Sister Ellen smiled. "Mr. Heller certainly provided Chris with plenty of stress."

The Unvorite laced his fingers together. "While the syndrome is largely unknown on Terra now, because of gene therapies, it has not been wholly removed from the human population and, apparently, was present in some of the people used to create demans. Tourette's, as it turns out, is still classified as a *human* disease. We communicated this fact to the Cardinal and he changed his mind."

The nun shot Meresin a sidelong glance. "It did not

hurt that he had me include a note that based on the evidence, he would be more than willing to accept Chris as human and induct him into the Mephist faith were he repudiated by the Church.''

Flynn threw his head back and laughed. "Oh, very well done. You trapped a dogmatist on the horns of a dilemma.'' The priest sighed. "I'll be paying for that one for a long while, I have no doubt, but it'll be worth it.''

A light flickered on the ward console, catching Sister Ellen's attention. "Jake needs something. Excuse me for a moment.''

Flynn nodded, then waited for the door to close behind her before he turned to his friend. "Why did you do that? You told me earlier that you didn't differentiate between animals and sapient creatures. You let Sister Ellen report you would accept Chris as human, forcing the Cardinal's hand. Why? If you hadn't, Chris would have been yours.''

The Unvorite shrugged slowly, then walked toward the ward viewport and waved Flynn over. "The dogmatist in me would tell you that Chris will be mine no matter what. But, you see there, Jake called her in to do something for Chris. Jake's faith, just like your cathedrals, is a thing of beauty. The joy he feels now, because he's done the right thing, because he's paid a debt to Chris he could not otherwise pay, this I would not deny him. You didn't, and the risk to you was far greater than any risk I incurred.''

Meresin rested a hand on his friend's shoulder. "Why did you do it?''

Flynn hesitated for a moment, then nodded. "There are a lot of people who were born with souls, but they never live up to the obligations having one comes with. Even though they never show it, we know they have one. With Chris, what he did in saving Jake left no doubt he had a soul. His sacrifice earned him his salvation. Dogma be damned, it wasn't for me to stand between him and his creator. Being able to speed him on his way, well, I'm thinking, it was the only truly human thing to do.''

JULIE E. CZERNEDA

"One of the fastest-rising stars of the new millennium"—Robert J. Sawyer

Web Shifters

☐ **BEHOLDER'S EYE (Book #1)**   0-88677-818-2—$6.99

☐ **CHANGING VISION (Book #2)**   0-88677-815-8—$6.99
It had been over fifty years since Esen-alit-Quar had revealed herself to the human Paul Ragem. In that time they had built a new life together out on the Fringe. But a simple vacation trip will plunge them into the heart of a diplomatic nightmare—and threaten to expose both Es and Paul to the hunters who had never been convinced of their destruction.

The Trade Pact Universe

☐ **A THOUSAND WORDS FOR STRANGER (Book #1)**
                                        0-88677-769-0—$6.99

☐ **TIES OF POWER (Book #2)**   0-88677-850-6—$6.99

C.J. CHERRYH

Classic Series in New Omnibus Editions!

☐ THE DREAMING TREE
Journey to a transitional time in the world, as the dawn of mortal man brings about the downfall of elven magic. But there remains one final place untouched by human hands—the small forest of Ealdwood, in which dwells Arafel the Sidhe. *Contains the complete duology* The Dreamstone *and* The Tree of Swords and Jewels.
0-888677-782-8 $6.99

☐ THE FADED SUN TRILOGY
They were the mri—tall, secretive mercenary soldiers of almost un-imaginable ability. But now, in the aftermath of war, the mri face extinc-tion. It will be up to three individuals to retrace their galaxy-wide path back through the millennia to reclaim the ancient world that gave them life . . . *Contains the complete novels* Kesrith, Shon'jir, *and* Kutath.
0-88677-836-0 $6.99

☐ THE MORGAINE SAGA
Scattered through the galaxy are the time/space Gates of a vanished alien race. They must be found and destroyed in order to preserve the integrity of the universe. This is the task of the mysterious traveler Morgaine . . . but will she have the power to follow her quest to its conclusion—to the Ultimate Gate or the end of time itself? *Contains the complete* Gate of Ivrel, Well of Shiuan, *and* Fires of Azeroth.
0-88677-877-8 $6.99

Kate Elliott

The Novels of the Jaran:

C.S. Friedman

☐ **THIS ALIEN SHORE** UE2799—$6.99

It is the second age of human space exploration. The first age ended in disaster when it was discovered that the primitive FTL drive caused catastrophic genetic damage—leading to the rise of new mutated human races on the now-abandoned colonies. But now one of the first colonies has given rise to a mutation which allows the members of the Gueran Outspace Guild to safely conduct humans through the stars. To break the Guild's monopoly could bring almost incalculable riches, and to some, it would be worth any risk—even launching a destructive computer virus into the all-important interstellar Net. And when, in this universe full of corporate intrigue, a young woman called Jamisia narrowly escapes an attack on the corporate satellite that has been her home for her entire life, she must discover why the attackers were looking for *her*. . . .

☐ **IN CONQUEST BORN** UE2198—$6.99
☐ **THE MADNESS SEASON** UE2444—$6.99

THE COLDFIRE TRILOGY

Centuries after being stranded on the planet Erna, humans have achieved an uneasy stalemate with the *fae*, a terrifying natural force with the power to prey upon people's minds. Damien Vryce, the warrior priest, and Gerald Tarrant, the undead sorcerer must join together in an uneasy alliance confront a power that threatens the very essence of the human spirit, in a battle which could cost them not only their lives, but the soul of all mankind.

☐ **BLACK SUN RISING (Book 1)** UE2527—$6.99
☐ **WHEN TRUE NIGHT FALLS (Book 2)** UE2615—$6.99
☐ **CROWN OF SHADOWS (Book 3)** UE2717—$6.99

Prices slightly higher in Canada **DAW:140**